A Simple Gift

KARYN WITMER

A Simple Gift

A DELL BOOK

A SIMPLE GIFT
A Dell Book

Published by
Bantam Dell
A Division of Random House, Inc.
New York, New York

Book design by Karin Batten

ISBN 0-7394-6049-8

Printed in the United States of America

For
Meg Ruley

✳

Because you're wise and because you're savvy.

Because you're thrilled when the news is good
and kind when the news is bad.

Because you've always believed in the work I do,
and encouraged me to do my best.
(Even when you wished I did it a little faster.)

Thanks.

A successful marriage requires falling
in love many times,
always with the same person.

—*Mignon McLaughlin,*
THE SECOND NEUROTIC'S NOTEBOOK, 1966

Avery Parrish
Fourth Grade – Mrs. Hoffman
Language Arts
December 10, 1965

"My Family's Christmas Tradition"
by Avery Parrish

My family's Christmas tradition isn't like anyone else's. It isn't making Christmas cookies. It isn't going down to Klein's department store and having your picture taken with Santa. It isn't decorating the tree on Christmas Eve.

Our Christmas tradition is different. It is a Christmas cactus that has been passed down in my family for over a hundred years. It's a big plant with these flat, lumpy branches. It has long pinky-red flowers that hang down like bells, or like the skirts that fairies wear. It is really pretty when it blooms. I guess that's why we've kept it all these years.

My great-grandmother Letty got it as a special gift from my great-grandfather Gill before he went away to war. Great-Grandmother Letty gave my grandma Ada a pot with a piece of the special Christmas cactus in it when she said she'd marry Grandpa Tom. My grandma gave my mother a plant grown from the Christmas cactus the very same night she met my papa.

Someday I'll get a piece of my family's Christmas cactus. I'll water it and give it plant food, and repot it when it gets too big. I'll take good care of it, so when my daughter is grown, I can give her a Christmas cactus, too.

Chapter 1

A very Montgomery's life changed in the checkout line at the Food-4-Less, right between the Bounty paper towels and the Heifitz hamburger dills.

"You got coupons, Avery, honey?" the checker asked.

Avery flashed the woman a smile and dug into the side pocket of her purse. She'd gone to high school with Loretta McGee; Loretta Polk she'd been then. They were awarded their diplomas at Larkin High two students apart—Parrish, Pettigrew, Pignoli, Polk. Loretta had been so pregnant that afternoon not even her graduation gown had been able to camouflage her condition, and she'd been married to Sam McGee before most of the senior class had recovered from their graduation-party hangovers.

Avery handed Loretta a fistful of coupons and glanced past the woman's care-weathered features to the people lined up at the next checkout. A burly man in a red plaid shirt jammed change into the pocket of his jeans and grabbed up the twelve-pack of Budweiser like he wanted to get home to his TV for the second-half kickoff.

As he turned toward the door, Avery caught sight of the

checker at the next register. She was new to the Food-4-
Less, sharp-featured and bony in the way kids consider
provocative these days. With her bird's nest of raspberry-
purple hair and the silver studs inching up the curve of her
ear like a metallic centipede, she wasn't the type of girl Gill
Matheson usually hired.

Then, as the new checker turned to greet her next customer, her gaze caught—and held—Avery's own.

In that instant, a shock of recognition thundered through
Avery. The air in her lungs went vaporous and thin. Cold
doused her. A maelstrom howled in Avery's head, as years of
cherished memories swirled past her eyes.

Instinctively she reached back, seeking her husband's
hand. Mike was there, just like always, clasping her fingers
in his own, pressing his thorny thumb into the hollow of
her palm. Holding her together.

"It's—it's her!" Avery whispered.

Mike squeezed in confirmation.

It was their daughter Fiona—Fee who'd run off eighteen
months before to tour with Jared Hightower's rock band.

Deep inside, the fragile vessel where Avery had stored up
every dram of her anguish and fear for her daughter
abruptly burst. Thick, sweet relief spilled through her chest
and belly.

Fiona was here.

Fiona was safe.

Fiona was home.

Then, Fee shifted her gaze to her next customer. Without
the intensity of that contact, Avery wavered, then felt her
husband steady her.

Every morning since her daughter ran away, Avery had
risen from sleep with a hot, nameless dread squirming in

her chest. For an instant she couldn't remember why that was, then she'd see Fee's photograph on her nightstand, and it gave that dread a name. It gave it substance and form and urgency. It stirred up grief that lay like a burden on her heart, a weight she carried around with her no matter what she did or where she went.

Avery had spent every day since Fiona left, listening for the phone to ring, waiting for one of her daughter's infrequent e-mails to arrive. Every night she'd scurry back to the house where she and Mike and Fee had lived together, open the door hoping—then stand staggered by the emptiness. Not once in all those months had Avery closed her eyes at night without wondering where Fiona was and if she was well and safe.

It's going to be all right now, Avery told herself. Now that Fee was back in Larkin, Avery would find a way to make it right.

She drew herself up tall and fought to find her balance. She needed to go to her daughter, clasp her hands around those bony shoulders, and smooth that haystack hair. She needed to kiss her daughter's cheek and seek the child she'd lost in the body of this stranger.

Avery stepped forward, meaning to greet Fee, to hold her safe in her arms, but Mike tightened his grip on her hand. "You don't mean to confront her here, do you?" he asked in an undertone. "Not with half the town watching to see what happens."

Before Avery could think, he turned to Loretta. "I'll be back to get the groceries later."

Loretta glanced first at Avery, then at Fee. "I'll have someone put them in the cooler out back."

"Thanks," Mike said and shifted his grip to Avery's

elbow. He steered her down the checkout lane, propelled her past the row of teenage baggers, and through a clot of abandoned shopping carts.

Fiona didn't so much as glance their way, concentrating instead on the queue of Sunday afternoon customers backed up at her register.

The door into the parking lot *whoosh*ed open before them. The toes of Mike's work boots nudged the heels of Avery's pumps as he urged her through. He bustled her down the ramp and across the blacktop to where his mid-night- blue Silverado was parked.

Any other time, Avery would have resisted, but she was too shaken by seeing her daughter and too unsure of what she should say to her to pull out of Mike's grasp. Over the years she'd trusted Mike to do what he thought was best for her, to do what he thought was best for all of them. So she let him hand her into the cab of the truck. She waited for him to stride around to the driver's side.

He had barely slammed the door behind him, when she burst out, "That *was* Fiona, wasn't it?"

She was almost afraid to believe what she'd seen, to believe that the terrible months of anxiety were over.

"Yes," Mike confirmed.

"After all this time," she wanted to know, "how could she just turn up here? Right in the middle of the grocery store?"

"I don't know, sweetheart."

Avery looked up in to her husband's angular, sun-browned face and tried to gauge his reaction to unexpect-edly encountering their daughter.

"Where do you suppose she's been all these months?" Her voice wavered a little. "And why did she decide to come back to Larkin now?"

Mike reached out and took her hand.

"She has to have been in town for at least a little while," Avery went on, reasoning aloud. "Prime jobs like checking at the Food-4-Less get filled the minute the kids come back to college."

"I suppose."

Mike's deep, sure voice steadied her, just the way it always did. She stared past him out the window and tried to think. "Where do you think she's been staying?"

"With Casey?" he guessed.

Casey DeCristo had been Fiona's best friend ever since the day her daughter had been summarily promoted from second to fourth grade. She'd arrived in Mrs. Lapp's classroom a scrawny, fierce-eyed seven-year-old. Fee had already figured out that being smarter than everyone else made you a freak and wanted her classmates to know she wasn't going to let them bully her.

But that first day at recess, Casey, who was a pretty, popular, self-possessed ten, had gone out of her way to befriend the younger girl. That simple kindness had forged a friendship that was going to last all their lives.

Since then, the two girls had ridden bikes together, tried out for school plays together, "eewed" through dissections in biology class together. They'd had sleepovers at each other's houses, baked countless pans of butterscotch brownies, and gone off to band camp arm in arm.

Fee and Casey had shared clothes and worries and girlish secrets. Then, in the middle of their junior year of high school, Casey had met and fallen in love with Dan DeCristo. From that day on, she and Fee had set about making very different lives for themselves—but their friendship had never wavered.

Avery nodded in agreement with her husband. "If Fee is back in Larkin, she'd be staying in that tiny little house of Casey and Dan's."

The tiny little house mere blocks from where Fee had grown up, from where she and Mike were living now.

"Oh, Mike!" Knowing how close her daughter had been put that quaver back in Avery's voice. "Why wouldn't Fee come home to us instead? Why didn't she even let us know she was back in Larkin?"

Her husband slid an arm around her shoulders and pulled her toward him across the seat. He wrapped her against him, drawing her close. She nestled into the hard breadth of that workingman's body, breathed the tang of freshly sawed wood that was so much a part of who he was, and closed her eyes against the sting of tears.

He stroked his hand the length of her ruddy-brown braid, feathered kisses against the faint crease that had formed between her brows. He hugged her close, and Avery indulged herself in the comfort she'd always found in her husband's strength.

"Fee's always insisted on having things her own way," he murmured.

As if that explained why Fiona had kept her return to Larkin a secret, as if *he* could accept the pain not knowing caused. But even as mildly as he'd spoken, Avery heard the edge in his voice. Because Fee had always been her daddy's girl, Mike had been angry and deeply hurt by the way she left.

"If she wanted us to know she was back," he went on, "she didn't have to guess about where to find us."

After all these months of silence, Avery didn't care what Fiona wanted. She didn't care that Mike was advocating caution in approaching her. Right now Avery knew exactly where her daughter was, and she meant to have a word with Fee before she slipped away again.

Avery lifted her head from her husband's shoulder and looked up into his deep-blue eyes. Her gaze skimmed the angle of his long jaw, touched the sprinkling of gray in his dark hair.

"Thank you," she whispered. She eased out of his arms and reached for the door handle.

"What are you doing?" Mike demanded and caught her arm.

"I'm going to talk to Fiona."

"You're going in there and will make a scene"—he notched his chin in the direction of the grocery store— "that will set the whole town talking!"

Avery turned and looked back at him. "If people know Fiona's back in Larkin," she pointed out, "they're talking already. As fast as word usually gets around, I'm surprised no one's seen fit to tell one or the other of us that Fee's returned."

If Avery hadn't been looking at Mike directly, if she hadn't known his face as well as she knew her own, she might have missed the faint shift in his expression. She might not have seen the nearly imperceptible tightening at one corner of his mouth, the shadow that crept into his eyes.

In that instant, Avery felt the weight of certainty settle over her. "My God!" she said on a shaky breath. "You knew Fiona was back in Larkin, didn't you?"

✳

Sometimes, for a smart girl, she was just too stupid to live.

Fiona eased her purple Neon into the parking space

behind Dan and Casey DeCristo's tiny brick house and killed the engine.

"Damn it!" she shouted, pounding her palms on the steering wheel. "Damn it, damn it! You knew if you came back to live in Larkin you were bound to run into your parents!"

On the drive from California to Kansas, Fiona had brooded over that first meeting for miles on end. What she *ought* to do, she'd told herself, was drive directly to her parents' house and announce that she'd come home to Larkin in disgrace. But she hadn't been brave enough to do that.

Fee thought about stopping at the Holding Company on her way into town, the stuffed-animal business her mother had founded when Fee went into kindergarten. Once the women who'd been doting on Fee since she was five years old had welcomed her back, what choice would her mother have except to greet her with open arms?

Since she hadn't had the courage to do that, either, Fee had been considering asking Casey to invite Avery over for coffee. That way, at least, she would have been able to confront her mother for the first time in private.

Fiona hadn't *dared* to think what it might be like to confront her father.

She wrapped her hands around the steering wheel and shook it hard. Since she'd made this mess, she should have taken responsibility for arranging the first meeting with her parents. It might not have been comfortable, but at least it would have been on her own terms.

Instead she'd glanced up from her register at the Food-4-Less and found them staring at her from the next checkout. Her heart had leaped so hard against her breastbone Fee thought it might pop the snaps down the front of her scum-green smock.

Fee raised her fist to her chest and tried to rub away that lingering tightness.

Since her parents almost always shopped at the Food-4-Less in town, she thought she'd be safe taking a job at the store out by the highway. Yet there they'd been, right in the middle of the Sunday afternoon rush: her mother, whey-faced and swaying on her feet, and her father, glaring as if he intended to incinerate her on the spot.

In that instant, Fee had been shocked not just at the sight of them, but by the new creases that stood out around her mother's eyes like wrinkles in a bedsheet. The open hostility in her father's face had forced her back a step, and she wondered if he was more angry with her for what she'd done, or how it had affected her mother.

It's all my fault, Fee conceded, her conscience jabbing her. She'd deliberately snatched up the chance to get away, chosen love and adventure over what she realized *even then* was the wiser choice. Knowing the things she and her parents had said to one another that last night and remembering the way she'd left, Fee hadn't wanted all that much contact. So she'd fallen silent, making her mother worry and her father...

God only knows what her father thought.

Fiona huffed out a shaky breath and scrubbed at her eyes. She climbed out of the car and darted across the backyard to the DeCristo's side door. As Fee jerked it open, Casey appeared on the landing trailed by her sturdy two-year-old son. Casey had on a frilly lavender sundress in deference to the lingering mid-September heat and had curled her hair.

Guilt prodded Fee hard. She'd forgotten she promised to baby-sit for Casey and Dan tonight. Now she was late and had wasted their precious time together.

"I'm sorry," she apologized hastily. "I didn't mean to hold you and Dan up."

"Not a problem," Casey assured her and gathered Derek up in her arms.

Fee followed Casey and her toddler into the hall, then headed directly for the bedroom at the back of the house. It was barely large enough to accommodate the low toddler's bed and the battered maple crib set up in the corner. Still, the creamy yellow walls and bright strip of Winnie the Pooh wallpaper that banded the waist of the room gave the place a bright, whimsical feeling.

Fee crossed to the crib and looked down at the baby asleep inside. The pink-and white-perfection of those tiny features caught her by surprise, just like the flood of tenderness did.

"So how are you, kid?" she whispered as she smoothed a fluff of strawberry-blonde hair back from the child's flushed face. She bent nearer, breathing deep of the milk-and-baby-powder scent, and was overwhelmed by possessiveness.

This was her daughter, her love, her delight—and her most terrifying responsibility. If Fiona had any second thoughts about coming back to Larkin, watching her daughter sleep silenced them.

Casey spoke from the doorway. "I just put Samantha down for her nap. Shall I pour us some coffee?"

"You're dressed to go out," Fiona hedged, not sure she wanted to talk to anyone right now.

"Dan's still in the shower," Casey answered and turned to go.

Fiona heard Casey's sandals clatter down the uncarpeted hall as she headed for the kitchen, but Fee stayed where she was, hovering over Samantha's crib a few minutes longer.

When she heard the plumbing in the upstairs bathroom yowl, signaling that Dan had turned off the water, Fiona straightened. If she was going to talk to anyone about seeing her parents, Casey was the only one who'd understand.

Her coffee was poured and perfectly doctored with sugar and cream when Fee took her usual chair at the brightly painted kitchen table. She fortified herself with a good long swallow of coffee, then made her announcement.

"My parents showed up at the Food-4-Less."

"I guessed that," Casey answered, glancing at Fee across the rim of her cup. "What happened?"

"I was working checkout." Fiona's belly fluttered with the memory. "When I glanced up, my mom and dad were standing at the next register."

Casey bent to where Derek was building with blocks and settled one with red roosters on the top of the tower. "What did they do when they saw you?"

"We stared at one another for about a week and a half," she answered. The moment spooled out before her eyes: her mother's pallor, the set of her father's jaw, the way Loretta McGee had turned and looked at her. "Then my father took Mom's arm and bustled her out of the store as if he were afraid she'd be contaminated by breathing the same air as me."

"So your mother didn't speak to you?"

"Not a word." Fee shook her head. "She was with my *father*." As if that explained everything.

"Did your dad say anything?"

Fee's laugh was bitter. "My dad wouldn't give me the time of day if he were Big Ben."

"Well," Casey inclined her head. "That explains why your mom's called here four times in the last hour and a half."

"She what?" Fee's mouth went dry as the Sahara.

"I was bathing Samantha the first time she called, and since then I've let the machine pick up."

The thought of having to actually talk to her mother made Fee go cold and queasy. What in God's name could she say to her? How could she explain everything that had happened since she left Larkin or apologize for all the months of silence?

Fee sagged back into her chair and swiped at her mouth. "Maybe coming back to Larkin was a mistake. Maybe I should have tried harder to make things work in L.A. I really did love Jared...."

"And Jared loved you," Casey assured her. "But, Fee, sometimes even people who love each other aren't meant to be together. Sometimes they find each other in the wrong place or at the wrong time."

Fee had done everything she could think of to try and find a way to stay with Jared before she left L.A.

"You did your best to make things work," Casey said gently, leaning forward to lay a hand on Fee's arm. "You tried and Jared tried. But in the end, you did what you had to do. You came home for Samantha's sake."

Fee hated admitting how much she needed reassurance. How could Casey be so certain that what Fee was doing was right? Did that kind of confidence come from being three years older, from being mature and settled, from having already taken on the responsibilities of a husband and child?

Or maybe that kind of certainty came from not having screwed up your life before your twenty-first birthday.

Casey gave Fee's arm a final pat, then bent to lift Derek onto her lap. "I know it must have been a shock seeing your parents like that, but it sounds as if it was a bigger one for them. I can hardly believe no one told them you'd come back to Larkin."

"I haven't exactly been hiding out."

But that wasn't strictly true. Fee had only seen the people she needed to see to get re-admitted to the university and arrange for financial aid. She'd only talked to the grad student who'd sublet Fee her seedy apartment, and the manager at the Food-4-Less when she applied for her job.

"Answer the phone when your mom calls again," Casey urged her. "She needs to know you're all right. *She needs to know about Samantha.*"

Fee nodded, more in acknowledgment than assent.

She hated having to admit how right her mother and father had been about touring with Jared and the band. They'd tried to tell her how hard life was going to be, playing one-night stands. They'd warned her that leaving school was irresponsible, that it would undermine everything she'd ever wanted for herself. But midway through her junior year, she'd been restless, bored by the college routine, eager to be on her own. So she hadn't listened.

How was she going to confess to her parents the mistakes she'd made or acknowledge the consequences? She couldn't imagine how she'd ever find the courage to tell her mother about Samantha—because once she did, her mother would tell her *father.*

Dan DeCristo stepped into the kitchen doorway, his short, black hair gleaming wetly. "So . . ." he said, grinning at his wife, "is my best girl ready for her big night on the town?"

It was easy to see why Casey had fallen in love with Dan. He was big and rangy and so handsome that in high school most of the girls blushed and stammered when he talked to them. He'd played center on the Larkin basketball team and had been recruited by both KU and K State, but that wasn't the life he wanted.

He'd stayed home instead, joined his family's restaurant-supply company, and married Casey. Judging from the way they looked at each other after three years of marriage, Fee figured Casey and Dan were going to beat the statistics against high-school sweethearts staying together.

Casey rose, plopped Derek in Fiona's lap, and turned to her husband. "Am I ready for dinner at Finelli's Pizza and a movie, you mean?"

"That's what passes for a night on the town in this burg," Dan said with a laugh. "Besides, neither of us has eaten a meal that wasn't interrupted by spilled milk in weeks."

"Go," Fiona urged them and cuddled Derek in her arms.

Casey took a shawl and purse from the jumble of toys and keys and bills piled on the kitchen counter. "Derek goes to bed at eight o'clock," she said in her mom's-going-out-for-the-evening voice. "He can have animal crackers and juice before bed. But don't give him a great big glassful or we'll be changing the sheets at two A.M."

"I know the drill," Fee assured her.

"You can call if you need me."

"I won't," Fee answered. "Now get out of here—and have a good time!"

Dan took his wife's hand and the smile Casey gave him in return would have lit up a coal mine.

Fiona followed them down the hall to the front of the house and stood at the screen door so Derek could wave "bye-bye" to his parents.

She and Derek had barely gotten back to the kitchen when the phone rang. The sound rippled through Fee like an electric current. She gathered the toddler more tightly in her arms and stood waiting for the answering machine to pick up the call. That took three more rings.

Fee stood motionless as her mother spoke. "Casey, hello."

The sound of her mother's voice sliced through Fiona, opening a raw, weeping wound.

"This is Avery Montgomery again."

Was there an unusual hesitancy in her mother's voice? Was it tinged with the same uncertainty and reluctance Fee was feeling?

"I—I'd appreciate it if you'd call me back as soon as you have a chance."

There was a pause, a moment when Fee could hear her mother reordering her priorities. Or maybe abandoning her pride.

"I—I saw Fee at the grocery store this afternoon," she explained, and Fee could tell by the waver in her tone that she was more upset than she wanted to let on. "I know she's back in Larkin, and I'm sure you can tell me how to get in touch with her. So would you call me, Casey, please? I need to talk to Fee. I know you understand now that you're a mother just how important that is to me."

It was a plea that would have melted Casey's heart. A plea Fiona appreciated on a level she could never have understood before. She acknowledged that her own heart would be broken if anything ever came between her and Samantha.

Fiona shifted Derek onto her hip and reached for the receiver, but before she could close her hand around it, fear froze her where she stood. What would she say to her mother once she picked up the phone? How could she account for the life she'd lived these last eighteen months? Where would she find the words to tell her mom about Samantha?

And what would her mother say once she had?

"Well, then, Casey," Avery ended the pause that had been filled with fruitless expectation and hope. "I'll expect to hear from you tonight no matter how late it is when you get home."

Her mother broke the connection, and Fee stood for a very long time with her palm poised above the telephone. Finally, she clenched her fingers into a fist and drew it close against her body.

※

Mike barreled his truck down the narrow dirt road, a banner of thick tan dust lofting in its wake. He roared into a sharp left turn, trying to outrun the disillusionment he'd seen in Avery's eyes when he dropped her off at the house.

She'd accused him of keeping Fiona's return to Larkin from her. *And, of course, he had.*

He'd been installing bookcases in the provost's office at Larkin University when he glanced out the window and saw Fiona striding across the quad. Or at least he'd thought it was Fiona. He hadn't expected that *his* daughter would ever dye her hair the color of grape Kool-Aid. Or that *his* daughter would be seen in a T-shirt so short and tight it looked spray-painted on.

Mike tromped on the gas pedal. The truck fishtailed, sending up another plume of dust.

He hadn't wanted it to be Fiona that day at the college, but as she climbed the Ad Building's steps, he'd seen her up close. He could tell by the square of her shoulders and the set of her head that Fee hadn't changed. She was exactly what she'd always been: a headstrong girl so bent on getting what she wanted that she didn't care what her thoughtlessness or her ambition did to anyone else. He and Avery were the ones who'd been torn apart and transformed by her leaving—not Fee herself.

Right then, he'd decided that telling Avery about Fiona being back in Larkin couldn't bring anything but heartache. His wife had been devastated by the note Fee left. He'd watched hope flicker in Avery's eyes every time she got a phone call or a three-line e-mail from their daughter—and he'd watched that hope die when Fee once again fell silent.

He'd held Avery weeping in his arms more nights than he could count, but he was helpless against her grief. He was far too angry at his daughter to give Avery the comfort she'd needed.

He'd worked so hard to build a safe, strong life for his family. They'd had their moments of triumph and tragedy; every family did. But for more than twenty years the life he'd made with Avery had come very near to being perfect. Then Fee had run away and ruined everything.

In leaving the way she had, Fee had betrayed both Avery and him. She'd driven a wedge between them in a way nothing else ever could. Every word he and Avery exchanged on the subject of their daughter threatened the solidity of their marriage. Finally, Mike refused to discuss Fiona at all, and once he stopped, he and Avery had less and less to say to each other.

Especially today.

Avery had glared across the truck at him, her sage-green eyes iced with accusation. "You knew Fiona was back in Larkin, didn't you?"

Mike hadn't been able to defend himself or explain he'd done what he'd thought was best. So he'd gunned the Silverado's engine and peeled out of the Food-4-Less parking lot like a rowdy teenager. They'd made the ten-minute ride back to the house in absolute silence: with Avery staring fixedly ahead and Mike's guts boiling. He still hadn't figured out what to say to her when they pulled into the driveway, so once she got out of the truck and slammed the door behind her, he bolted for the farm.

Now, as he dipped down the road into the lush, tree-shaded valley cut by Little Apple Creek, he passed the rambling farmhouse that had sheltered the Montgomery clan for four generations. His brother Ted's truck was parked by the back door, but Mike was too intent on getting where he was going to do more than slow down.

The Silverado's wheels spit gravel as he climbed the grade that rose behind the house. Not five minutes later, he parked beside a tall, barn-red shed at the top of the hill. He clambered out of the cab, braced his hands against his knees, and sucked in air as if he'd run, not driven, all the way from town.

"Jesus!" he gasped, not sure if the word was a prayer or a curse.

He closed his eyes and stood wavering. He hadn't seen Fiona close-up that day on the quad. He hadn't felt her gaze touch him, hadn't seen it ice over and slide away. She'd dismissed him this afternoon as if he were nothing, as if the time they'd spent together when she was growing up meant nothing. As if the plans they'd made for her future meant nothing.

God knows, he'd worked so hard to make a life with Avery and Fiona. He thought he'd sited the future he'd hoped to build on solid ground. He thought he'd laid down a firm foundation and formed a life worthy of his family. He'd poured everything he had into doing that, thinking it would last forever. But it hadn't lasted.

Bitterness burned beneath his breastbone. First Fiona had run away. Then Avery had turned away from him. Now Fiona's return was threatening all he had. *All he had left.*

Mike stood hunched over until his hands stopped shaking and he caught his breath. Then he pushed resolutely upright and headed toward the stout, metal-banded door at the back of the shed. He unclipped the wad of keys from his belt and twisted one of them in the padlock. With a creak he pushed open the door to the observatory, the only place he still felt completely himself.

It was pitch-black inside, the air cool and a little stale with being shut up. He stepped into the dark, flipped on both the computer and exhaust fan, then reached up and unfastened the row of safety latches that held the roof to the walls. He grabbed one of the aluminum struts and pushed it hard. To the grumbling accompaniment of a dozen casters, he rolled the corrugated top of the shed backward, opening the observatory to the autumn sky.

From the highest point on the Montgomery farm, Mike savored the subtle beauty of eastern Kansas. Striped cornfields lay gilded by the last raking light of sunset. Hay, shorn and gathered into shaggy bales, squatted on the hilly fields like herds of grazing mastodons. Squares of earth lay harrowed and turned, ready to be sown with winter wheat.

Mike raised his gaze from the rich, opened soil to the clear, darkening sky, and finally to the telescope that would allow him to probe the heaven's secrets.

He went about the preparations for viewing with the ease of long practice. While he waited for the temperature of the air inside and outside his small observatory to equalize, he climbed the rolling ladder and carefully removed the dust cap from his big sixteen-inch Newtonian reflector telescope.

He did the same with the smaller finder scope, which was attached along the side. Finder scopes were used to sight the particular object the astronomer meant to study before focusing the larger scope on a narrower field of view.

Mike carefully cleaned the eyepieces on both the telescopes, then swung the whole thing around to sight on one of the easy-to-see guide stars just becoming visible as the sky shifted from turquoise to navy blue.

Once he'd checked the alignment between the smaller and larger telescopes, Mike prepared the computer on the battered desk for tonight's observing run. He double-checked the connections between the CCD—the charged-coupled device—camera mounted on the larger scope and the program that would record, store, and eventually print whatever images he made.

Odd as it seemed, working in the observatory he and his daughter had built together was the single thing that settled the turmoil inside him.

Thinking back, Mike remembered the exact moment when Fee fell in love with the stars. She was eight and the two of them had been "camping out"—sleeping in their sleeping bags in the backyard—when she pointed to a slash of light streaking across the midnight sky.

"What was that, Daddy?" she'd asked him.

"A falling star," he'd answered.

"So what makes stars fall?"

Fee had always been so full of questions that Mike had to work to stay ahead of her. Back then, he hadn't been able to recognize more in the sky than the moon and the Big Dipper.

"I don't know," he'd been forced to admit. "They just do sometimes."

"But *why* do they?" she persisted, being bright and curious—and unrelenting.

Being Fee.

"We'll look it up tomorrow," he'd promised her.

And they had. What they'd seen wasn't a falling star; it was a meteoroid burning up in the Earth's atmosphere. What they also discovered was that they'd been out during the Perseid Meteor Shower, a yearly occurrence that happened when the Earth's orbit passed through the tail of a comet.

"So what's a comet?" Fiona wanted to know. That had been the beginning of his daughter's obsession with astronomy.

And his own.

In the next few months they'd pored over every astronomy book in Larkin's town library. They'd driven to Kansas City and seen a show at the planetarium and visited the observatory in Topeka. When her grandfather had heard about Fiona's burgeoning interest in astronomy, Jonathan Parrish had used his position as president of Larkin University to arrange for them to spend an evening with the science department's telescope and one of the grad students.

Those experiences had whetted Fee's appetite, so for her next birthday Mike bought her a telescope. That telescope led not only to a series of prizewinning science projects, but to contact with other amateur astronomers. He and Fee had gone to star parties all over the Midwest, observing everything from the rings of Saturn to the elusive Horsehead Nebula.

Eventually the two of them started making plans to build their own observatory, and Fee had decided to pursue a degree in astronomy. Of course, that all happened before

Fee got so involved with Jared Hightower and his rock band.

Now that it was full dark, Mike slewed the telescope toward a familiar piece of sky. He was up on the ladder working to refine the focus when he heard the crunch of footsteps on the gravel drive.

A moment later his brother's voice echoed up to him. "Can I talk to you a minute, Mike? It's not like those stars are going anywhere."

Mike grimaced. He wanted so much to be alone right now. He wanted to forget about everything but the pin-pricks of light that originated in galaxies millions of miles away. He wanted to lose himself in the cosmos.

"Come ahead," he called back in spite of himself.

Ted's tread was ever so slightly unsteady as he ambled into the observatory.

"Woo-ee!" he hooted, bracing one hand against the wall and staring upward. "The stars are sure out tonight! How come they're so much clearer here than down at the house?"

Ted asked that question every time he came up to the observatory.

Mike gave him his standard answer. "There isn't any light pollution to wash them out."

Ted nodded as if he was actually listening. "You looking at anything in particular?"

"I thought I'd start by looking in on Mars. Just give me a minute to finish setting things up, and you can have a look."

"Nah!" Ted backed off, shaking his head. "How come you're here on a Sunday night? Don't you have to work in the morning?"

"I've got some data to collect," Mike hedged. He wasn't

about to admit he and Avery had argued, that he was here cooling off. Or hiding out.

He especially wasn't going to admit that to his brother.

"It's not like you to be home on Sunday night, either," Mike observed. "Didn't you have the kids today?"

Ted dipped his head. "Nancy wanted them dropped off early."

Which had given Ted the chance to stop for a beer—or probably a couple of beers—between Nancy's folks' in Lenexa and home. He had that sour, yeastiness about him, a smell Mike had learned to recognize—and hate—in childhood.

"Well, I'm glad you're here," Ted went on. "There's something I've been wanting to talk to you about."

Immediately Mike's guard went up. If his brother had sought him out, it was because he wanted something. He braced his palms against the cement pier the telescope was mounted on and tried not to say anything judgmental.

He did anyway. "So what kind of trouble are you in now?"

"Aw, Mike!" Ted protested. "How come you always have to put it like that?"

Mike couldn't pretend he didn't know what his brother meant. "Because that's how it almost always is."

It was this time, too. It took Ted a while to get around to it, but he finally admitted why he'd come.

"I've got taxes to pay on the farm by the end of the month," Ted told him. "What with the support I'm giving Nancy and all, I'm having a little trouble keeping up. Janice couldn't spare anything on account of Rich being cut back at work, but Ma gave me—"

"*Ma gave you?*" Mike roared.

Their mother lived in a one-bedroom apartment in Kansas City, not much more than a block from their sister's house. She just barely made ends meet with her Social Security check and what he and Janice managed to add to it.

"Ma doesn't have the money to bail you out of this!" he all but growled at Ted. "You've got no business asking her!"

"She doesn't want us to lose the farm," his brother defended himself. "It being the Montgomery home place and all."

As if the memories they'd made here were ones any of them would want to cherish.

"I swear, Mike, it's the last time I'll ever ask you..."

Mike took a breath, knowing he'd have to help, knowing he couldn't let Ted pester their mother. Knowing with Ted, there'd never be a "last time."

"How long have you let this slide?"

Ted shifted his shoulders the way he did when he was trying to avoid something unpleasant. "A couple months is all," he hedged. "When Nancy comes back with the kids, I'll be able to manage better."

Mike wished he believed Nancy and the kids were coming back to the farm. Or that Ted would sprout a sense of responsibility. Or stop drinking.

But no matter how much Ted was deluding himself about the future, Mike couldn't let him lose the farm. He might not have had the happiest childhood here, but the eighty acres left of the homestead their great-grandfather settled had given all of them space and quiet and fields to roam.

Besides, Mike couldn't give up the observatory; it was his last tangible link to his daughter.

"So how much money do you need?" he asked his brother.

Ted ducked his head. "About thirty-five hundred would catch us up."

Mike imagined he could hear a sneer in Ted's voice, like he knew he'd won. His only satisfaction came in making Ted wait for the capitulation.

"I've got my checkbook in the truck," he finally said.

Ted followed him outside and waited as Mike dug his checkbook out of the glove compartment. He wrote the check by the light of one of his cherry-red flashlights and handed it over to Ted begrudgingly.

"Thanks," Ted said, but Mike heard no gratitude in his tone. They'd played these roles too long for him to expect it.

It was the pattern they'd perfected in childhood. Mike was the dutiful older brother, cleaning up whatever mess Ted made, covering for him with their mother, the teachers at school, and even once with the sheriff. Ted was the screwup, forever resentful of Mike's help, but dependent on it anyway.

Mike reached through the truck window and shoved the checkbook back into the glove box. He turned back to his brother, as aggravated with himself as he was with Ted.

"You need anything else?"

Ted shook his head and headed down the road toward the house. Mike watched him go, seeing how lost and displaced Ted seemed, how alone and disconnected. For the first time in years, Mike understood that feeling.

Chapter 2

✳

Avery recognized the deep-throated mumble of Mike's pickup as it crept down their silent street toward home. She lay poised and listening as its tires crunched on the gravel in the drive, as the truck's door closed with a solid *whump,* as her husband's footsteps approached the house.

She pushed up on one elbow and peered at the clock. It was three twenty-six, which meant she'd been lying here half the night waiting for Mike to come home.

She hadn't worried much about where he'd been; she knew once he left her at the house he'd hightail it out to the farm. He'd go out to his star guides and his telescope, out to where he could put everything except the circle of sky in the eyepiece out of his mind.

Avery understood that working in the observatory he and Fiona had built together had been Mike's way of grieving when their daughter ran away. But after those first few months, Avery began to think the hours he spent studying the stars was his way of avoiding her. It was his way of evading the question festering between them.

That question had come to a head yesterday afternoon: Were she and Mike going to have a relationship with their daughter, or weren't they?

Avery glanced at the clock again. She didn't have the energy to argue with Mike about Fiona tonight, not when they could just as well fight about her in the morning. So when she heard Mike padding up the stairs, Avery burrowed deeper into her pillow and pretended she was sleeping.

Still, she couldn't help hearing Mike undress: the spill of change as he emptied his pockets onto the dresser, the whisper of friction as he tugged the tails of his shirt from his waistband, the scrape of the zipper on his jeans. His belt buckle jingled as he dropped his clothes over the chair in the corner. The bed dipped downhill behind her as he climbed aboard.

Mike usually didn't wake her when he came home from an observing run. He'd drop a kiss on her bare shoulder or caress her hip, make just enough contact to let her know, even in sleep, that he was there with her.

That's what Avery expected now. But instead, Mike rolled up tight against her back and wrapped his arm around her. She squeezed her eyes even more tightly closed and tried to ignore the solid warmth of his chest and belly.

He slid one hand up her side and cupped her breast. He grazed the side of her neck with the tip of his tongue, moistening what he knew was a particularly sensitive spot. Avery exhaled through gritted teeth.

After being married to this man for twenty-three years, she knew exactly what he wanted. With his kisses and caresses, he meant to span what had suddenly become an unbreachable rift between them. *How could Avery let him get away with that?*

Mike had known Fiona was back in Larkin and deliberately kept it from her. When she'd accused him, he hadn't offered so much as a word of either explanation or apology. Then, in the middle of what might be the most significant crisis of their married life, he'd dumped her in the driveway and driven away.

Damn him!

Yet as determined as Avery was to ignore Mike's touch, it was no less potent now than it had always been. The instant he put his hands on her something shivered to life, a frisson that could have been electrical or chemical or magnetic. Avery had never been able to explain what it was, this spontaneous awakening, her cell-deep awareness of this particular man.

He stirred a mysterious, earthy part of her, a part that prudent, unperturbable Avery had never dreamed existed until Mike Montgomery kissed her. Her response to him was instinctive, almost organic, the way sunflowers knew to turn to the sun.

Tonight was no different from a thousand other nights when Mike had reached for her. Avery responded in spite of herself.

Over the years her husband had made a thorough inventory of what she liked and how she liked it. Tonight he used that knowledge to court and seduce her. He teased a shiver from her with nothing more than a nip on the lobe of her ear. He slid his big, warm hand down her belly and squeezed her mound. He lifted her nightgown and brushed his erection against her buttocks to show how ready he was to give her pleasure.

Her body constricted in anticipation.

Yet even as it did, Avery recognized that Mike was never

going to forgive Fiona. He was never going to allow their daughter back in their lives. He wasn't going to agree to Avery having a relationship with Fiona on her own.

He was making love to Avery tonight by way of apology.

A sob swelled huge and hot at the back her throat. Her chest ached; her muscles tightened. She willed herself to wrench out of his arms, to rise from their bed and leave him alone in it. Yet when Mike skimmed his palms up along her body and tossed her nightgown aside, all Avery could do was tremble.

Gently he pulled her over onto her back and, as he did, he must have seen the sheen of tears on her cheeks. With a murmur of contrition, he cupped her face in his big hands and kissed her. He kissed her as if he had dedicated himself to soothing her, to salving her hurts. Even if he was the one who'd wounded her.

He whispered apologies between the kisses, and those whispers washed over her in a breathless, hopeless tangle of words. They were words Avery could never allow herself to believe or accept, and that made her cry harder.

Yet as his lips dipped and clung to hers, she began to kiss him back. She slid her arms around his neck and surrendered to the slow, sinuous brush of his mouth. To the heated exchange of breath, to the glide of tongues. As she slicked her own tongue against his, he cupped her breast and circled gently.

Avery arched against him, the moan she stubbornly refused to surrender, trapped in her throat. Still, her response streamed through her, becoming a sweet, pulsing pool between her legs.

Mike kissed her more deeply and teased her tightly pearled nipple with his thumb. She gasped against his mouth, letting the sensation he awoke melt into her. Trapped beneath his broad, hard body, she shuddered and squirmed.

She felt the faint curl of his lips against her own, and recognized the pleasure he was taking in being able to stir her. Quick, hot anger spiked along her nerves, but it was instantly blunted by the sweep of his hands and the mesmerizing power of his kisses.

After a restless, breathless, mindless time of stroking and twining skin to skin, Mike broke off his kiss. He raised his hand from the swell of her breast and replaced it with his mouth. He suckled her, circled her nipple with his warm, wet tongue. All the while, his palms gathered her in, tracing the length of her spine and curling around her derriere.

Inexorably he claimed every inch of her. And when he sought to explore her most intimate self, Avery twisted and sighed and opened her legs.

She went liquid at his touch and, no matter how much she'd tried to rein in her response to him, she was lost. Willingly so. With a shivery sigh, she gave herself over to loving him and letting him love her. She gave herself over to believing, for the moment at least, that this delicious tenderness could heal the broken places in their life. That this sweet, deep communion could mend the past and make a promise to resolve the difficulties that lay ahead.

She reached for him and scaled the contours of his broad shoulders and back with her fingertips. She breathed the sharp, familiar tang of fresh-cut wood that was so much a part of him. She shivered beneath the worship in his hands, the adoration of his mouth, the reverence with which he'd always touched her.

This was how she had defined love and intimacy and

permanence, masculinity, loyalty, and strength for more than twenty years. She couldn't bear that in the months Fiona had been gone, her definition had changed, that her belief in Mike had changed, that her love for him had changed. She couldn't accept that all of that had shifted again today. So she clung to her husband not wanting anything—even Mike himself—to remind her how wrong things were between them.

She closed her hands around the taut muscles of his buttocks and drew him to her. Mike came, opening her as if he were seeking the delicate heart of a flower. He sought her soft, heated core and, with a gliding stroke, made himself one with her.

Avery shuddered, overwhelmed by the pure, physical power of being with him. They'd come together like this more times than she could count and, as always, there was a rightness to their joining, an immutable fulfillment in sharing herself with her husband.

Still, she swallowed her need to tell him how much she still loved him, to speak the words she'd whispered freely in other moments as uninhibited and overpowering as this. Mike was silent too, as if he realized this was a respite in the midst of a reckoning, an instant to cling together before the need to make terrible, destructive decisions tore them apart.

Then, as if to sweep all their reservations away, he lifted his hips and drew her more and more deeply into the blaze of carnal intensity. Bound as one, they rose and glided together in a slow, slithery dance. They lost themselves in fervent and overwhelming voluptuousness. Their ragged breathing shredded the silence of the night. They clung together, seeking unity and surcease, connection and forgetfulness.

Avery surrendered herself to him completely as pleasure swelled through her, raced up the midline of her body, spilled in tingles along her limbs. Filling her and overflowing, rising and overflowing again and again.

The pleasure carried her far away, and when she came back to herself, she and Mike were sprawled across the rumpled sheets, sweaty and replete, shivery and spent. Neither of them moved as they cherished the last sweet moments of a connection that had been almost unbearably perfect.

But as their bodies cooled and their breathing took on a more regular cadence, Avery squirmed beneath her husband. Mike pressed a lingering kiss to her mouth, rolled to his own side of the bed, and fell instantly asleep.

Avery lay beside him staring into the dark, and slowly the reality their loving had kept at bay settled over her. Her heart beat heavily inside her, each stroke more leaden than the last. Tomorrow she would beg Mike to make peace with Fiona, to allow their daughter a place in their lives. And Mike would refuse.

Making love tonight hadn't changed anything. It had been an elaborate dance, one they'd perfected through long, sweet years of repetition. They'd come together so often and so well that they'd refined every movement, choreographed every kiss and every sigh. It was a dance that brought both pleasure and release, but tonight those strokes and kisses hadn't opened them to each other.

Through most of their married life coming together had been a measure of their love, of the strength of their commitment and their true accord. Tonight it had been an apology Mike hadn't wanted to make, and one Avery couldn't bring herself to accept.

Once she'd admitted that to herself, Avery couldn't lie beside her husband a moment longer. She squirmed toward the edge of their big bed, searched out and donned her nightgown, then pushed to her feet.

She slipped silently down the stairs and put the kettle on, took out her favorite mug, and filled the tea ball. As she waited for the water to boil, she did her best not to think about Fiona, but that was impossible.

They'd only shared that single shocking moment of recognition before Fee turned away, but Avery had combed over it a hundred times. The way the Food-4-Less smock hung from Fee's shoulders made her realize how thin her daughter was. She'd seen the pale mauve smudges beneath those defiant eyes, recognized the wary tension in Fiona's stance, and read a truculent set to her mouth that was harsh and new. Those things stirred a nameless dread, something Avery needed to pin down, evaluate—and rectify.

If Fee had looked healthy and happy, Avery tried to tell herself, she might have been able to accept Mike's judgment and leave well-enough alone. But as it was, she needed answers, explanations.

Not five minutes after Mike had dropped her off at the house and fled, Avery had called Casey DeCristo. If anyone knew why Fee was back in Larkin, her best friend would. Avery called and called, but the answering machine had picked up every time.

Avery thought about driving back to the grocery store, but she had been too afraid of what she and Fiona might say to each other to do that. She thought about going to the DeCristo's house, but she didn't want to burst in on Casey and Dan and risk alienating the only ally she might have in reconciling with her daughter.

At its first wheezy tweet, Avery snatched the teakettle off the burner and poured steaming water into her cup. As she waited for the tea to steep, she reached among the clothes hanging on the back of the kitchen door for something to keep her warm.

Mike's work shirt came under her hand and, as she slipped it on, she was wrapped in his scent again. She petted the well-washed fabric thinking of Mike, thinking of the choices they had to make, and the scope of the conse-quences. Her throat constricted all over again.

She wrapped her hands around the cup and carried it into the dining room. The window seat that overlooked the drive and the thick row of brightly blooming zinnias by the fence was one of Avery's favorite perches. She settled there among the plants, took a fortifying sip of tea, and watched as the first grainy hint of daylight brought the world to life. She listened to the birds stir and chatter in the trees. She tasted the astringency of fall in the breeze that set the gauzy curtains fluttering.

Avery set her cup on the windowsill, wrapped her arms around her knees, and squeezed them close against her chest.

Fiona had turned their world upside down when she ran away. The arguments they'd had about leaving school and risking her future to tour with Jared Hightower's rock band had been fierce and full of anger. Avery did her best to un-derstand her daughter's need for adventure, her yearning to be out on her own. But the way Fee had severed their rela-tionship, the tone of the note she'd written, and the pearls she'd taken when she left, made it hard for Avery to accept

Fiona's leaving for what she believed it really was: a child asserting her independence, a child making an impulsive grab at the life she thought she wanted. A child making a child's mistakes.

Mike hadn't made any attempt to see Fee's leaving in that light. He'd been wounded and disillusioned, shaken to his bones that the daughter he loved so fiercely could shatter their family. And he wasn't about to forgive Fiona doing that, even now.

Avery expelled her breath on a sigh and took up her tea.

For the past twenty-three years, Mike had been her home, the bedrock of her life, the other half of herself. She knew the kind of man he was, the compassion and the strength in him, his capacity for tenderness, the depth of his love. Hadn't he convinced her that being who she was *was* good enough? Hadn't he given her the strength to take chances in her life and risk making mistakes along the way? Wasn't he the best and most vivid part of every memory she'd ever made?

Yet Fee was her living flesh—the baby she'd carried beneath her heart, the closest bond she'd ever have to anyone. Fee was her only living child, her life, her most significant accomplishment, and her promise to the future. She'd given Avery the deepest joy she'd ever known—and twenty-one years of challenges and worry.

And now that Fiona was back in Larkin, Mike was going to make Avery choose between them. *How in God's name could she let him do that?*

She dashed away fresh tears with the back of her hand. Somehow before she slept again, she needed to see and talk to her daughter. She needed to find a way to make Mike understand that when Fiona ran away, she hadn't deliberately done it to hurt them.

Avery stared out at the lightening sky and swore she'd find a way to reunite her family, to make it whole again. But sitting here drinking tea in the dawn, she had no earthly idea how she was going to accomplish that.

⚜

November 1982

Avery Parrish was stuck in the Kansas City Airport.
Literally.

The big, flat presentation case she'd brought with her from Chicago had snagged sideways near the top of the up escalator. In spite of her best efforts to twist the huge thing free, the movement of the stairs kept wedging it tighter.

That same inexorable movement was pushing it, pushing her, toward the edge of the stair she was standing on.

Hanging tight to the case, Avery backed down.

She figured her best chance to break the stupid thing free was to throw every ounce of her weight against it. With a quick glance to make sure there was no one behind her on the escalator, Avery released the handle of her suitcase and the strap of her purse. As they *thud*ded down behind her, she shoved at the corner of the black leather case with all her strength.

The case shoved back.

It nudged her nearer the brink of the stair she was standing on. It nudged her off.

Avery made a vain grab for the escalator's moving handrail as she toppled backward. The stainless-steel walls whisked past her. The sharp, grooved stair treads nipped at her as she fell.

Then, midway down the escalator, she collided with someone solid enough to catch her and hold her as she fought to find her feet. When they reached the top of the escalator, that same solid someone twisted the presentation case free, then lifted it—and her—to safety on the main floor of the terminal.

"You all right, miss?" her rescuer asked, still steadying her.

Avery looked up at the man who'd come to her aid. It might have been adrenaline, or that his hand was clamped tight around her ribs, but a tingling sensation she'd never had before danced through her, like spangles shimmering in her blood.

The man holding her was tall; Avery barely reached his shoulder. Thick hair the color of black coffee fell in a wind-blown cascade around a face that was long and sharply cut. It was a strong face with a kind of enduring architecture that meant he'd still be a knockout when he was eighty.

"You all right, miss?" His voice was insistent, deep with concern.

Avery looked up into his eyes, the gold-flecked blue of lapis lazuli, and nearly lost herself.

"Yes," she finally managed to say and wriggled free of the stranger's grasp. "Shaken up is all." She twitched the slim skirt of her business suit back in place. "Thanks for coming to my rescue."

He dipped his head and slid her a grin that pinched a dimple into one lean cheek. "Glad to help," he said.

And her knees went weak.

Just then, a young woman dressed in a work shirt and

jeans hopped off the escalator. "I brought up your bag and
your purse," she said, parking Avery's trim tapestry suitcase
beside her and plopping her handbag on top of it.

"Thank you for coming to my rescue," Avery told them
both, then looked at the woman more closely. "I know you,
don't I?"

"I'm Janice Montgomery."

Avery nodded, though the name didn't mean a thing to
her.

"We went to high school together," Janice prompted her.
"I labeled pictures for the Larkin High yearbook when you
were the editor." Janice gestured to Avery's rescuer. "This is
my brother Mike. He would have been a couple years ahead
of you in school."

And I never noticed? But that would have been eight or
nine years before, and Mike Montgomery didn't look like
he'd spent much time with the student council crowd. He
looked dark and dangerous and...

Oh, my. Oh, my!

"I'm home from Villanova for Thanksgiving," Janice was
saying. "Mike came to pick me up."

Avery felt compelled to share her plans. "I'm spending
the holiday with my folks on my way to a meeting in
California." Avery patted the big leather case, now badly
scraped along one side. "I hope none of my presentation
materials were damaged."

"Your folks coming to pick you up?" Janice asked, glancing around.

Anyone who'd grown up in Larkin would have recognized Avery's parents. The president of Larkin University
and the chairman of the English department seemed to get
their pictures in the *Larkin Chronicle* every couple of weeks.

"I was supposed to catch the shuttle"—Avery hastily gathered up her things—"but my plane was late."

"Why don't you hitch a ride with us?" Janice offered.

Avery hated it when people did her favors because of who her parents were. "I wouldn't want to put you to any trouble."

"No trouble at all," Mike Montgomery said.

He didn't have much else to say for himself on the two-hour drive to Larkin, but squeezed elbow-to-elbow on the bench seat of Mike's battered pickup, Avery was monumentally aware of him. Even with Janice between them, Avery could smell the wind on him. Fresh, tinted with cedar and pine. She could see his profile—a wide forehead, straight nose, and strong chin—black against the moonlit landscape. She could hear his quiet breathing and found something inexplicably settling about the rhythm, perhaps because it so perfectly matched her own.

Janice did the majority of the talking, mostly about school in Philadelphia and the trials of being one of the few women in the engineering department.

"I studied commercial design at Parsons and Rhode Island," Avery ventured. "When I graduated, I took a job at a graphic design firm in Chicago. I design packaging, everything from Essence perfume to Scentinal mouthwash."

"I've bought that," Mike spoke up. They were the first words he'd spoken since he'd refused to let her pay for parking as they left the airport garage.

"You get to many Cubs games?" he asked her.

"Is that the Chicago baseball team?"

Mike chuckled and pulled out into the passing lane. "Yeah, one of them."

"I'm not much of a sports fan," Avery said and felt herself

flush. The fact was, she'd lived in Chicago for more than two years and hadn't gone much of anywhere but to her office. She'd hear her co-workers talk about meeting at this bar or that restaurant, going to this gallery opening or that concert. With her close focus on her projects, her accelerated move up the corporate ladder, and her almost weekly trips out of town, Avery hadn't made many friends.

This conversation with the Montgomerys, she realized, appalled, was as personal as any she'd had in weeks.

"Mikey's a carpenter," Janice volunteered when Avery didn't seem to have anything more to say about Chicago.

"Have you been at that long?"

Mike kept his focus on the dark streak of road and the red necklace of taillights strung out ahead of them. "I started doing clean up at construction sites when I was in high school. I knew most of the guys pretty well by the time I graduated, and one of them got me into the carpenters' union."

Gorgeous *and* handy, Avery found herself thinking. Not that that would impress her mother; Miriam Parrish only barely tolerated people who worked with their hands.

"Mike specializes in custom cabinetry," Janice volunteered. "He's making Mama the most beautiful buffet for Christmas."

"I built the trophy cases in the new student union." Mike gave the words a buff of pride.

Avery usually didn't spend much time wandering the campus when she was home, but this time she thought she'd have to take a look at Mike Montgomery's work.

He didn't have to ask Avery for directions once they hit town. Everyone knew the imposing cut-stone house at the crest of University Hill was where Larkin's president lived.

Mike pulled up at the head of the circular drive, unloaded Avery's bags, and carried them across the wide, white-columned porch.

While she rummaged for keys to the fan-lighted front door, Mike stood over her. "So," he said after a moment, "you go out much while you're home?"

Avery's heartbeat picked up speed, and she glanced up at him in surprise. Was Mike Montgomery going to ask her for a date?

"Sometimes," she hedged.

"*For Your Eyes Only* is at the Bellevue this weekend."

Avery said she liked James Bond movies.

"I could pick you up at seven on Saturday," he suggested. "And maybe we could catch a burger afterwards."

Avery flushed like a high-school girl. "I'd like that," she said, though she knew her mother was going to have a fit when she found out she was going out with a carpenter; Miriam thought her daughter ought to confine her dating to corporate magnates and Rhodes scholars.

On Saturday night, Mike Montgomery showed up looking like her mother's worst nightmare: long-limbed, masculine, and decidedly working class. Avery was lucky her mother wasn't home to pass judgment, and she and Mike sped off together to enjoy the evening. James Bond was innocuous and lots of fun. Mike was, too, until he pulled into Charney's crowded parking lot after the movie.

"You're not planning to take me in *there*, are you?" Avery gasped, staring at the ramshackle building crouched at the edge of a cornfield.

The roadhouse was the most notorious place in Larkin, a townie bar that was forbidden territory for anyone even remotely associated with the academic end of the university.

Every fall a few freshmen felt obliged to take their fake IDs and challenge that taboo, but all they ever got for their trouble were scuffed knuckles, black eyes, and a night in the pokey.

"The burgers are the best in Larkin," Mike cajoled as he helped her out of the truck.

"My parents will have you strung up on the quad," she warned him, "if they ever find out you brought me here."

"You know"—Mike gave her a cocky grin as he opened the Plexiglas door and ushered her inside—"I'm not that scared."

The burgers were wonderful, grilled crusty along the edges and pink inside. So, in its way, was Charney's wonderful.

The long, knotty-pine room glowed phosphorescent with Budweiser neon and pulsed to the beat of the rainbow-hued jukebox. Stuffed deer heads hung antler-to-antler on every wall and the floor was filled with a milling logjam of work-shirted bodies. Smoke from hundreds of cigarettes hovered like storm clouds, mingling with the yeasty bouquet of beer, cooking grease, and honest sweat.

"Want to play some pool?" Mike asked when they had finished their burgers and fries.

"I don't know how to play pool," Avery demurred.

"I figured I could teach you," he offered. So they ambled into the larger room at the back of the tavern where more than a dozen pool tables squatted beneath low-hanging fluorescent lights. Mike piled quarters on the lip of one of the tables, then won possession by racking and clearing the table in a single run.

"We're going to play eight ball," he said instructively and selected a cue stick for her from the rack on the wall.

Avery discovered that teaching her how to play apparently involved Mike putting his arms around her and leaning in close against her back. It involved his breath fluttering against her neck in a way that raised gooseflesh along her ribs. It involved being wrapped in what she was coming to recognize as his scent, the sweetness of sawdust and the tang of some gingery aftershave.

It involved his hips nudge-nudge-nudging her backside in a way that lit a simmering sexual heat low in her belly.

While his sure, square hands molded hers to the proper grip on the cue stick, every instruction he breathed in her ear made it harder to concentrate. With him snugged up close against her behind, Avery couldn't seem to focus on the green baize table in front of her.

What Avery really wanted to do was turn her head and nuzzle Mike's clean-shaven cheek. What she wanted was to tangle her fingers in that thick, soft hair and see what it was like to kiss him.

Would that kiss set off sparks in her the way everything else about Mike Montgomery did? Was he as aware of the hot, crazy current flowing between them as she was?

"Okay, now," Mike coached, leaning in to adjust the angle of her stick. "Just let the cue slide through your fingers."

With his right hand guiding hers, Avery slowly drew back her cue, then jabbed it forward. It connected with a solid *thunk* that sent the cue ball rocketing toward the opposite end of the table. It smacked into the cushion with force enough that it hopped a foot in the air, then dropped to the floor and skittered away beneath the table adjoining theirs.

Avery straightened abruptly, nudging Mike back. "I don't think I have an aptitude for this game," she told him.

"Sure you do," he reassured her, though he might have been more convincing if he hadn't been grinning. "Pool is about geometry and finesse."

"I never much liked geometry." She set her cue diagonally between them and looked up at him from beneath her lashes. "Besides, I don't want to play pool with you."

Mike seemed to get her drift; his voice dropped half an octave. "So," he asked, "what is it you want to do?"

Her cheeks went hot just thinking about it, thinking about him. As she stared up at him, she could see the color come up in his face, too.

"Would you like to get out of here?" he asked softly.

Avery nodded.

Mike replaced their cues in the rack with exaggerated care, helped Avery into her coat, and headed for the door.

They were elbowing their way through the crowd when someone staggered into her. As Avery turned to apologize, she recognized one of the men who worked in the maintenance department at the university.

He recognized her, too, and grabbed her arm. "What the hell do you think *you're* doing at Charney's?"

Mike insinuated himself between Avery and the man who'd clearly had too much to drink. "It's all right," he said. "She's here with me."

"And who the fuck do you think you are?" he slurred.

Mike's voice remained deceptively quiet, but his frown was menacing. "I'm someone who thinks you should let go of Ms. Parrish's elbow and apologize."

"The hell I will," the man bellowed and swung at Mike.

Mike brushed off the blow and shoved the man back.

The fellow stumbled, careening into the group behind

him. The people he'd collided with turned, snarling and yelling.

For a moment, the whole room steamed and seethed like a pot about to boil. Before it could, Mike gathered Avery against him and bulldozed his way to the door.

The roar of the brawl erupted behind them, all but blowing them into the parking lot. They clasped hands and sprinted toward where Mike's truck was parked, what seemed like a quarter of an acre away in the darkest corner.

They arrived breathless and panting and leaning on each other.

"I've got to hand it to you, Mike," Avery gasped, giving in to laughter, "you take me to the most *interesting* places!"

"New drinks, new games, new friends," he quipped and bundled her against him. "Did you have a good time?"

Odd as it seemed, she had. She'd liked the movie and Mike's company. Charney's had been exciting, disreputable, and more than a little exotic. Like exploring an alien culture in her own hometown.

"I *did* have a good time," she admitted, nestling in his arms.

That contact stirred her awareness of him, her need to touch him and have him touch her. Bolder than she ever dreamed she could be, Avery reached up to cup her hands around Mike's jaw. She stretched along the length of his body and pressed her mouth to his.

With a groan deep in his throat, Mike hugged Avery against him and kissed her back. His lips were warm, in contrast to the cold night air, yet as they brushed hers they were respectful and gentle. Avery leaned closer, kissed him more deeply, savoring the bite of malt on his breath and the dark, wet sweetness of his mouth.

His lips glided over hers, as if he were experimenting to find what it was that pleased her, to learn the rhythm of her breathing, and the texture of her mouth.

Avery shivered, luxuriating in that delicate exploration. She opened to him, inviting the touch of his tongue. When he answered, Avery tightened her hands on the lapels of his pea jacket and tugged him closer.

Mike mumbled something deep and appreciative and leaned into her, pinning her against the door of the truck.

Avery took pure, carnal delight in the feel of that long, lean body crushing hers. She liked the substance of him, the bulk of his shoulders and the breadth of his back. She liked the firmness of his thighs against her own and the way his hips nestled into hers. She liked knowing how much he wanted her.

They leaned against the side of the truck and kissed for a very long time. They kissed unperturbed when the sheriff arrived with his sirens blaring. They kissed while he and his deputies broke up the fight and loaded the county's two paddy wagons with brawlers. They kissed as the crowd at Charney's dispersed, pulling out of the parking lot with engines revving and tires spitting gravel.

Mike and Avery kissed until their blood was roaring in their ears, until they were languorous and muzzy-headed—and hungry for more than they could have tonight.

Mike finally raised his head and looked down into Avery's eyes. "So," he whispered, "you're coming home for Christmas, aren't you?"

✳

Every couple argues in their own way. Some shout loud enough for the neighbors to hear; some seethe for days in

poisonous silence. Some rake up offenses from years before; some speak their minds and get it over with. Some
partners explode spontaneously, while others lie in wait.

True to her pattern, Avery lay in wait for Mike to come
striding into the kitchen the following morning. True to
his, Mike pretended there was nothing wrong.

He was freshly showered and shaved, and looked aggra-
vatingly well rested for someone who'd been making love to
his wife until after four A.M. In spite of the extra time she'd
taken with her hair and makeup, Avery knew she looked
haggard and threadbare. But then, *she* hadn't slept at all.

Oblivious to the trap Avery had laid for him—a bowl
and spoon, milk and a box of Cheerios laid out beside her
at the kitchen table—Mike headed for the coffeemaker. He
filled his big ironstone mug and braced his hips against the
edge of the counter.

Avery glared across at him, resentment seething beneath
her sternum. Why did *she* always have to pick the fight
when there was something that needed to be settled between them? Why was it *her* responsibility to address their
problems when this was as much Mike's marriage as it was
hers?

But then, Avery had never been able to let things lie. She
hated secrets, hated the undertone of things unsaid and unresolved. She detested the reserve that grew between a husband and wife once they'd agreed that maintaining the
facade of a perfect marriage was more important than being honest with each other.

Since Fiona left, Avery had learned far more than she
ever wanted to know about what could undermine a perfect marriage.

Every couple disagreed about money and time and household chores. She and Mike were no exception, but they'd weathered the hard times together, too. They'd lost their second baby at full term, dealt with Myra Montgomery's cancer, and pulled together so Avery could launch the Holding Company. Never had they faced anything as devastating as their daughter running away.

What frightened Avery was that Fee's return to Larkin promised to be more difficult and dangerous than anything they'd faced so far. That's why Avery's throat knotted at the prospect of broaching the subject with Mike, but she couldn't think of any way to avoid it.

She wrapped her icy hands around her coffee cup, drew a breath, and opened negotiations. "We need to talk about Fiona."

Mike's head came up, his mug poised halfway to his mouth. "I thought we settled that last night."

A scorching wave of anger surged through her. "What we did last night was have sex. We didn't *settle* anything."

Mike shrugged, negligent and infuriating. "I think I've said pretty much everything I have to say about Fiona."

His obstinacy made heat flare in her cheeks. "You haven't said anything at all."

Mike stared at her, stubborn, obdurate. Silent.

But Avery had decided what she meant to do, and she refused to lie about it. "For my own peace of mind, I need to track Fiona down and find out why she's come home."

"She hasn't come *home*," Mike pointed out, his tone bitter.

The distinction stirred up Avery's own doubts and fears. No, Fee hadn't come home, but she was back in Larkin. Avery couldn't function, couldn't concentrate until she found out why.

"I didn't want to see her behind your back." What she wanted was his permission to see their daughter, permission he wasn't likely to give her. "I didn't want to keep what I was doing a secret."

The moment the words were out of her mouth she heard the edge of reproach in them.

Mike shifted—his shoulders, his feet, then the direction of his gaze.

Suspicion blared in Avery's head. "Is there something else you haven't told me, Mike?"

"I don't have any idea why Fee's back in Larkin," he said, but she could see the color rising in his face. "I haven't talked to her. All—all I did was see her one day on the quad."

"When?" she demanded.

"Three weeks ago."

Avery hissed with the singe of another betrayal.

"I knew I ought to tell you she was back—"

"But it served your purpose better not to?"

He slammed his mug down on the countertop and faced her. "I held back because I knew you'd do exactly what you're doing, run after her like you did when she was little. I knew you'd have to see her, talk to her. You'd try to make peace with her. How can you want to do that, Avery, after how she left?"

"She's our daughter, Mike!" she declared. "Our only child."

Even after fifteen years, Avery was still staggered by the loss of their stillborn son, the ache of knowing that as much as they'd wanted to, they could never have another child. Avery could no more ignore Fiona's return to Larkin than she could stop breathing.

"Don't you think I know that?" he shouted at her, his

voice gone hoarse. "What you don't seem to grasp is that Fee made it perfectly clear the day she left that she doesn't want anything to do with us. She doesn't want to be our daughter anymore."

Avery opened her mouth to deny that, but Mike went on.

"She turned her back on college and the future she claimed she wanted. She turned her back on us to head off on some punk-rock odyssey with Jared Hightower."

Avery and Mike and Jared's parents tried to prevent Deer in the Headlights from signing a contract with Starburst Productions that was little short of indenture. They tried to convince the kids to stay in school, but it was too late. The band had gone ahead and signed on the dotted line.

Mike strode across the kitchen toward where Avery was sitting at the table. "Just look at how Fee left; she slipped away in the night like the thief she is. Except for the note she left, she's only been in touch with you a time or two."

More than that, Avery conceded silently. There'd never been enough contact between Fee and her, but there was more than Mike knew. It was Avery's own guilty secret.

"Fee's been back in Larkin for the best part of a month," he went on, "and she hasn't made any attempt to contact you. Doesn't that make her intentions clear? She doesn't want any part of us."

Avery heard the torment in Mike's voice. Fiona had been her daddy's little girl, camping out with him, playing in his workshop while he was building things, spending hours with him peering up at the stars. Sometimes Avery thought that Mike had been even more devastated than she was when Fee ran away. But though she'd been nearly as hurt and outraged as Mike, she'd been willing to put that aside in order to maintain some semblance of contact with her daughter.

"Damn it, Avery!" He braced his hands on the table and leaned over her. "How can you open your arms to Fiona after she stole from you?"

Fee had taken her pearl necklace, the one Mike had given Avery on their sixth anniversary. Every time Avery put those pearls around her neck, it had been like Mike was caressing her. Every time she wore them, she walked a little taller, felt a little more beautiful. But as much as she loved those pearls, as much as they meant to her, she loved her daughter more.

"Fee's *our child*," Avery reiterated and reached to cover his hand with hers. "That makes her unspeakably precious. So how can what she stole or how she left possibly matter?"

"Well it matters to me!" he roared and jerked his hand away. "It matters that you and I have barely had a conversation since the day she left that didn't begin or end with Fee. She's infected every moment of our lives—and now you mean to make that worse."

Avery understood that this family had always been Mike's security, their marriage had been his bedrock. It was the reason he'd worked so hard to be a good husband and caring father.

Next to Fiona, that security was the most precious gift Avery had ever been able to give him. But she couldn't give him what he wanted now, even if refusing split their marriage in two.

"Mike, please," she whispered. "Please don't make me choose between you."

"I can't forgive her, Avery," he said in a rasp. "How can you?"

She rose and cupped her hand to his cheek. "Because I never invested my hopes and dreams in her, because I never expected as much of her as you did. Because I knew she was bound to fail, to make mistakes."

She saw fear kindle at the backs of his eyes in the instant before he jerked away.

"I don't want you talking to Fiona!" he ordered. "I don't want you making peace with her."

"You did what you thought was right when you kept Fee's return to Larkin from me." She looked into his eyes. "Now I'm doing what I think is right—finding out why our daughter has come back to Larkin." She pushed past him on her way to the door.

He followed her into the back hall. "Avery!" he shouted after her. "Don't you do this!"

Avery slammed the door behind her. She could face Mike—and the consequences of what she was doing—later. She could face anything once she'd talked to her daughter and knew she was all right.

Chapter 3

✳

Avery pulled her red Forester into the parking lot behind the building that housed the Holding Company, and turned off the ignition.

"Damn you, Mike Montgomery!" she whispered fiercely, swiping her eyes. "How can you turn your back on your only daughter? How can you expect *me* to do that too?"

For more than twenty years, she and Mike almost never argued, never spent much time apart, never turned away from each other in bed. They'd agreed on which house they were going to buy and how they were going to decorate, which of them would do the laundry and who would clean. They agreed on brownies without nuts, who they'd vote for in the next election, and nature versus nurture. They'd taken turns driving Myra Montgomery to her chemotherapy appointments, applauded at Fee's piano recitals together, cried in each other's arms when they lost the baby. They'd weathered everything together—and then Fiona ran away.

Between one day and the next, Avery and Mike lost their common ground, went blind to each other's point of view.

They forgot what they believed in. They were both so deso-
late at Fiona's leaving, so wrapped up in their own anger
and regret that they couldn't turn to each other for comfort.

They'd been stunned and bewildered when their marriage started unraveling—and didn't have any idea how to
stop it. Now that Fiona was back in Larkin, portents of
disaster loomed like thunderheads.

Avery sniffled and rummaged for tissues in her purse.

Fighting with Mike was like being at war with herself.
Every word she spoke in anger cut her as deeply as it did
him. Every victory she declared, tasted of defeat. But how
could she do what Mike was asking? How could she know
that her only child was living here in Larkin and not see her,
talk to her, take her in her arms and hold on tight? How
could she turn her back on her husband so she could rebuild her relationship with her daughter?

At the sharp rap on the driver's side window, Avery
nearly jumped out of her shoes. She turned with a jerk and
saw her secretary, Cleotis McCracken, peering at her.

Cleo's soft, honey-brown face was crinkled with concern. "You all right, hon?"

Avery jammed the tissues in her purse and got out of the
car. "I'm fine," she said.

The older woman bowed her wide scarlet-lipsticked
mouth in an expression of disbelief, then chose not to question Avery more closely. *At least not now.*

Instead, they crossed the parking lot to the Holding
Company's bright purple door. The logo above it was one
Avery had designed, crisp and clean, with a bit of whimsy.

Cleo pulled keys out of her voluminous handbag, unlocked the back door, and flipped on the lights in the wel-

coming tangerine-colored stairwell. "Guess we're the first ones here," she observed with the same throaty laugh she laughed every morning.

"Not a surprise," Avery mumbled as she followed Cleo up the broad, metal stairs to the Holding Company offices on the second floor.

She and Cleo were always the first to arrive because it was Holding Company policy that employees put their children on the bus before they came to work. In the early days, Avery had built her business around school-bus hours for her own convenience. Eventually she added vacation breaks and sick-kid days to the schedule. Those benefits extended to everyone who worked for her, which attracted a loyal workforce of nineteen women from Larkin and the surrounding communities.

Avery had begun the Holding Company on her dining-room table not long after they lost the baby, cutting out and sewing copies of the stuffed animals she'd designed and made for Fiona. A year later she was selling enough of the animals to start farming out the sewing to three women who had answered when she'd advertised for seamstresses in the newspaper.

The company had grown slowly at the start as Avery groped her way through the intricacies of marketing the cute, squeezable creatures to upscale specialty stores. As the business expanded, they moved to a heated garage, hired someone to do the cutting, and bought five industrial sewing machines secondhand. From there they expanded into a warehouse at the edge of town.

Then, during a flurry of urban renewal in downtown Larkin, Avery bought and rehabbed three adjoining cut-stone buildings that fronted on Main Street. She rented out the quaint tin-ceilinged shops at street level, expanded her company to fill the buildings' three adjoining second floors, and used the attic for storage.

As Cleo turned on the rest of the lights, Avery headed into her glass-fronted office and grabbed up the telephone. She didn't care what Mike wanted; she had to talk to her daughter. She started by calling information. If Fiona was living in Larkin, the phone company would have her number and street address.

"Do you have a new listing for Fiona Montgomery?" she asked.

The operator didn't.

"Do you happen to have one for Fiona—" Avery ignored the sharp twitch of distress. "Fiona Hightower?"

"No, ma'am, we don't."

Avery let out her breath. At least Fee and Jared hadn't up and gotten married behind their parents' backs.

She called Casey DeCristo's house and got her answering machine—again.

She slammed down the receiver and chewed thoughtfully on her lower lip. If Mike had seen Fiona on the quad, the chances were good that she was attending classes at the university.

Just as Avery reached for the phone to call the registrar, Cleo came in carrying two steaming mugs.

"I'm perfectly capable of getting my own coffee," Avery grumbled, grateful anyway.

Cleo found a level place amid the piles on Avery's desk to set the cup. "I figured us taking a coffee break before everyone else came in would give you a chance to tell me what's wrong."

She perched on the chair in front of the desk, serene,

sweet-faced, and waiting for Avery's confidences. She'd get them, too, Avery reflected, just like she did everyone else's. The comforting thing about telling Cleo your troubles, was that she'd lived long enough and hard enough that she never judged.

She was a big, soft woman suspended, the way black women often were, in the inexact gulf of years between forty and seventy. She had a wide face with a few dark brown freckles speckling her cheeks. Cupid would have envied the shape of her mouth, and Cleo made the most of it, keeping it slicked with colors that had names like Persimmon Rose, Cinnamon Sand, and Candy Apple Crimson. She wore skirts and hose every day and swished a little when she walked. Her long nails were always perfectly manicured, and when she wore her hair down instead of bound in a corona around her head like it was today, she had a thick salt-and-pepper braid that hung nearly a foot past her ample behind.

The best thing about Cleo was that she had a heart to match the rest of her, big enough to accommodate her own vast family, the parishioners at her church, and all of them at the Holding Company. That she was sharp, insightful, and completely organized kept them all on track. Her being a computer whiz was frosting on the cake.

Just like everyone else, Avery adored her, and had accepted long ago that it was Cleo, not she, who was the true soul of the Holding Company.

So when Cleo adjusted the hem of her flared georgette skirt across her knees, Avery knew it was time to tell her what was going on.

"Fiona's back in Larkin," she began baldly and watched for any sign that Cleo had known about Fee's return.

Instead, Cleo's dark eyes widened. Her jaw dropped. She drew breath, but couldn't think of a thing to say.

It was a very satisfying reaction. At least Avery knew Cleo hadn't been keeping secrets.

"Fee was working the checkout at the Food-4-Less yesterday afternoon," Avery continued. Her heart picked up speed at the memory of looking up from a handful of coupons and seeing her long-lost daughter not ten feet away.

"Oh, hon," Cleo breathed, "I'm so glad your little girl's back. But I know seeing her out of the blue like that must have been a terrible shock for you. Did you get a chance to talk to her?"

Avery retreated behind the rim of her coffee cup, hiding from the concern she saw in Cleo's eyes. "Mike was with me."

Cleo lifted her chin. "He feel any different about Fiona now that she's come back?"

Avery shook her head and suddenly had to blink back tears. "Mike saw Fee on campus three weeks ago and he didn't say so much as a word to me."

"Oh, Avery, girl," Cleo moaned.

"I was so furious last night"—her voice broke and her tears spilled over—"I could have... could have smothered him in his sleep!"

Cleo would have swept her up in a warm blossomy hug if Avery had given any sign that's what she wanted. The older woman compressed her Soulful Scarlet mouth instead and offered her a crisp, lace-edged handkerchief.

Avery looked at it, gave a hiccupy little laugh, and tugged a tissue from the box on her desk. "Mike insists Fiona has no place in our lives after what she did," she continued after she'd blown her nose. "We had a terrible argument this morning. He's forbidden me to contact her."

Cleo reached across the desk and clasped Avery's hand in hers. "You mean to go ahead and see Fiona anyway?" It wasn't really a question. Cleo had daughters of her own and knew how mothers felt.

"Of course I am."

Cleo nodded, bestowing the approval Avery needed.

"Going after Fiona is what's right," she pronounced. "Mike's wrong to think he can keep you from her."

Avery nodded, wishing she could sit there all day basking in Cleo's warmth and reassurance. But Avery hadn't had much practice being either mothered or approved of, and pulled her hand away.

"I'll just have a word with the Lord," the older woman promised her, "about sending your Mike a change of heart."

If only Avery believed prayer worked like that. If only you could tell God what you wanted and your fears would be assuaged or your fondest wishes realized.

"Thank you, Cleo," Avery offered on a sigh. "That would be lovely."

She might have said more except that there was the clamor of women's voices and the *thump* of footsteps on the stairs. The early-bus mothers were arriving.

The women waved to Cleo and Avery, tucked their purses into the brightly painted lockers along the back wall, and punched in. Someone slid open the big, metal door that led into the second building where cutting, sewing, and stuffing of the animals took place. Beyond it, through another metal door, was the finishing department and the area that tagged and shipped the toys.

As the machines throughout the building began to hum, Cleo rose. "Anything I can do for you, Avery, honey..."

Avery thanked her and reached for the telephone as Cleo went back to her desk. She dialed the university's main number by memory and asked for the registrar's office.

"I'm trying to contact one of your students," she began when someone answered. "Do you have an address and telephone number for Fiona Montgomery?"

"I'm sorry," the slightly nasal voice on the other end of the line informed her. "It's against university policy to give out that information on any of our students."

Avery hadn't been expecting that. "It's all right," she assured the woman. "I'm Fiona's mother."

"We don't give that information to *anyone*," the woman reiterated and hung up.

Avery called right back. "Look, I'm grateful that the university is so adamant in protecting the students' privacy, but this is an emergency. I need to contact my daughter right away. Her name is Fiona Montgomery."

Avery heard the clatter of computer keys and waited.

"I'm sorry," the voice answered. "Ms. Montgomery has put in a specific request that her information remain confidential."

Avery went cold all over. Why had Fee gone out of her way to see that her files remained closed? But then, the answer seemed simple enough; Fee didn't want anyone knowing where she lived, what courses she was taking, her marital status, her financial status. She'd done it because she didn't want her parents interfering in her life.

But then, why had she come back to Larkin when she could have finished her degree anywhere?

"Thank you for your help," Avery managed to say before

she hung up. She sat there shaking, trying to get her breath back, trying to marshal her thoughts.

Finally, she pushed to her feet and stepped out to Cleo's desk. "Is your niece still working in student records at the university?"

Cleo looked up from invoices she was recording. "You mean Shoshona?"

"Fiona has re-enrolled at the university, but they won't tell me anything. Do you think Shoshona can find out how I can get in touch with Fee?"

Ten minutes later, Cleo sashayed in and stuck a note to the edge of Avery's drawing board.

Avery looked up, surprised. "Did you get her address already?"

"They can't give her address or her grades to anyone," Cleo answered. "But Shoshona was able to get me something better."

"'Something better'?" Avery echoed and reached for the paper.

"Where Fiona will be at two o'clock."

✳

At two o'clock, Avery was pacing outside the Wexler Science Building lecture hall like an expectant father. She'd arrived nearly half an hour before Fiona's class let out, which had given her a chance to rehearse what she was going to say to her daughter at least a dozen times. Every time she did, she was less and less confident in what she had to say, less and less sure of what Fee's reaction would be when she saw her.

By the time Avery heard the scrape of chairs and the

shuffle of feet that signaled the class was over, anxiety was wrapped around her ribs like a straitjacket.

The doors to the auditorium blasted open, and college kids tumbled out like third graders headed for recess. Fiona was one of the last to leave. She came stalking toward the door with her head down and a backpack dragging at one shoulder.

Avery's throat knotted up at the sight of her. Beneath the mangy mat of magenta hair and sulky expression, Avery recognized the apple-cheeked darling Fee had been when she was four; the eager, toothy nine-year-old; her sleek, coltish beauty the year she'd turned fourteen.

But beyond those hazy images of her daughter's childhood, Avery recognized in Fee's sharp features and purposeful stride, that she was headed for pressing appointments elsewhere.

Avery took a long breath and called out to her.

Fee jerked around, scowling as if whoever wanted to talk to her was an unbearable inconvenience. When she recognized her mother, an expression of what might have been either suspicion or dread came into her face.

Avery's heart withered at her daughter's reaction, but she hurried toward her anyway.

"I should have known you couldn't leave well enough alone," Fiona greeted her.

Her daughter's tone whisked every calm, diplomatic thing she meant to say right out of Avery's head. "Why wouldn't I come looking for you, Fiona?" she snapped. "Aren't you still my daughter? Isn't it conceivable that after all this time I might want to be sure that you're all right?"

Avery gritted her teeth, trying to hold back the anxious, impatient, angry words boiling in her throat. She was stunned by the bitter tone she'd taken with her daughter, ashamed of the way her voice shrilled with reproach.

She saw a shadow of what might have been regret skim across Fee's eyes in the instant before her stance turned belligerent. "I'm perfectly fine. You can see that for yourself, right?"

But to a mother's eye, Fiona didn't look "fine." Skin that had once been flushed and flawless, was sallow and dull. Fee looked weary, as if she'd been pushing herself too hard. Beneath the fashionable torn neckline of her T-shirt, Avery could see the bony arc of her daughter's collarbones and noticed all at once how knobby her wrists suddenly seemed.

Why, she must have lost twenty pounds, Avery fretted, but stopped short of asking her if she was getting enough to eat.

Instead, she asked the only question that mattered. "Why didn't you tell me you were back in Larkin?"

Fiona lifted one shoulder in a negligent shrug. "I guess I didn't want you to know."

The words might as well have been a body blow. Avery staggered back a step, the wind knocked out of her. What had she done, she wondered, to make Fiona hate her?

She was frantic to take Fee somewhere, pin her down, and demand that she explain. She wanted an accounting of every day since Fee left Larkin, where she'd gone, what had happened, and what she thought about it. She needed to know why Fee had come back. Had she and Jared argued? Had the band broken up? Was Fee in some kind of trouble?

Avery swallowed the most invasive questions, trying to make talking to her daughter less of an interrogation. "So, are you staying with Casey? I hear her Derek's quite a handful."

"He is." The lines around Fee's mouth softened. "I stayed with her and Dan the first week I was back."

"So you've got your own place now?" Avery inquired.

"Yes."

An answer deliberately without details.

Frustrated, Avery reacted without thinking. "But how can you afford a place of your own? Surely your job at the Food-4-Less doesn't pay enough to cover an apartment *and* school."

"I'm doing okay," she insisted.

Though she knew better, she made the offer anyway. "If you need money, Fee—"

"I don't want your money," Fiona all but snarled at her.

Avery stepped closer, trying to convince her. "Your father wouldn't need to know..."

Fee retreated, her eyes sparking with anger. "So Dad's still being an asshole about me leaving, huh?"

Not once in the three times they'd spoken on the telephone while Fee was gone, nor in the half-dozen precious e-mails they'd exchanged, had Fee asked about her father. Not once had Avery hinted that Mike had responded to her leaving like a lion with a thorn in its paw.

"Your father was as hurt and upset as I was when you left," she said, skirting the truth.

"He's pissed that I took the pearls, isn't he?" When Avery didn't answer, Fee went on. "They were your pearls, after all. If you're not all that upset about me taking them, why is he?"

Of course Avery was upset that Fiona had taken her pearls. She'd always loved wearing them, loved that Mike had saved for months to buy them for her. She loved that her husband and her daughter had picked them out together. But knowing Fee had the pearls with her had given Avery some small comfort; if Fee needed money to live on, she wasn't completely without resources.

Avery shook her head. "I'm not entirely sure why your father's so angry about the pearls."

"I could tell by the way he looked at me yesterday that he hadn't forgiven me. I was right not to let you know I was coming back to Larkin." Fee's narrow-eyed gaze ran over her. "Did he know you meant to track me down today?"

"Yes."

"And what did he have to say about it?"

"It doesn't matter what your father said."

Fee expelled her breath in a mirthless laugh. "He doesn't want you to have anything to do with me, does he?"

Fee surmised entirely too much about how she and Mike had dealt with her leaving—and how each of them had greeted the news of her return.

"You and I kept in contact before, even though he didn't approve," Avery argued. "We can do that again."

"See each other behind his back, you mean?"

Fee had put the worst possible spin on what her mother was proposing. Avery felt heat creep up her jaw. "I'm your mother," she said quietly. "I need to know you're all right."

"I *am* all right," Fiona assured her, her expression softening. "You shouldn't worry. I negotiated a pretty good financial aid package, and with what I make at the Food-4-Less, I'm going to be fine." Fiona took a step away. "Now I've got to go."

Panic soared through Avery's chest. "Fiona, wait! Where are you living? How do I get in touch with you?"

Fee took another step. "I have a class, Mom."

Hearing Fiona call her "Mom" all but dropped Avery to her knees. "Meet me later," she whispered.

Fee shook her head. "I need to be at work at four, and I have to stop home first."

Home.

Fee wasn't talking about the pretty Victorian cottage where she'd grown up. She meant a room in one of the dorms or a student apartment at the edge of campus. Even after all these months, Avery wasn't ready to admit Fee had left the nest forever. She wasn't ready to accept that there was no going back to the halcyon days when they'd lived together, done things together. When they'd been that perfect family.

The last of her illusions collapsed around her like the walls of Jericho.

"Fee..." she entreated.

"I'm busy these days, Mom. Really busy." She paused and, just before she turned and strode away, Avery thought she heard Fee say, "I'm sorry."

Avery stood and watched her go. As her daughter approached the glass doors at the far end of the hall, her silhouette narrowed, wavered, and disintegrated into the blinding glare of daylight as if she were gone forever.

※

Avery stopped her car in front of her mother's house. She didn't know why she was there. Not for comfort, certainly.

Maybe she'd stopped because she hadn't had the energy to drive farther than the edge of the Larkin University campus after confronting Fiona. Maybe she couldn't imagine going back to the office and wasn't ready yet to go home.

Or maybe the idea of facing Mike after what they'd said to each other this morning scared her more than her mother did.

Resigned, Avery climbed out of the driver's seat, feeling more her mother's age than her own—though somehow Miriam managed to make eighty-four look like seventy.

Avery eased her way up the walk toward the tall brick Tudor affair Miriam Parrish had bought after Avery's father suffered a fatal stroke in his office at the university. Avery had never particularly liked the house, but she supposed that had more to do with her father not being there than anything else.

The place did have certain advantages. It was solid and trim and easy for her mother to maintain. It was close enough to campus that Miriam could walk to the Emerson Language Building where, as professor emeritus of the English department, she served tea and tortured grad students twice a week.

As Avery approached the front door, she admired the way the lushness of her mother's late-summer garden spilled around the corner of the house and frothed to the very edges of the flagstone stoop. Though the arched inner door stood invitingly open, Avery knocked on the screen anyway.

Miriam Parrish wasn't the kind of woman you popped in on, even if she was your mother.

As Avery waited, she peered down the dark tunnel of a hall toward the blare of light from the back of the house, which was provided by the wall of French doors that opened onto the terrace. In due course her mother came trotting toward her, frowning a little as if Avery had come in the midst of something important.

"Good grief, Avery!" her mother greeted her. "Whatever are you doing here at this time of day?"

Trust Miriam to make her feel welcome.

"May I come in?" she asked with some asperity. "Or am I interrupting you?"

Her mother laughed. "I was just making notes on what has to be the most dreadful master's thesis I've ever read!"

Which explained the reading glasses nestled into the breaker of milk-white hair that rolled back Gibson-girl fashion from Miriam's high forehead. She must have been on campus today because she wore a dark skirt and a soft, cream-colored blouse, her string of pale, perfectly matched pearls just visible at the open throat.

Once Avery had stepped into the foyer and bussed her mother on the cheek, Miriam turned toward the kitchen. "Since you've taken it into your head to stop over, I'll make tea."

Tea was the glue that held her mother's world together. She served it strong and hot, and she claimed her students lost a full letter grade if they added either sugar or cream—though lemon was tolerated.

After Avery's conversation with Fiona, a cup of strong tea sounded wonderful. She followed Miriam into the cheery yellow kitchen with its glass-fronted cabinets and row of African violets blooming their hearts out on the windowsill.

"I got to the English Shop while I was in Kansas City last weekend for the symphony, and stocked up on Jaffa Cakes. Those orange and chocolate cookies your father used to like so well, remember? Why don't you put some on a plate?"

They were Avery's favorite cookies, too, but her mother never seemed to remember that.

"I never taste those cookies but what I think of my dear Jonathan," Miriam said on a sigh.

Avery did as she was told, wondering if her mother could possibly miss her father as much as she did.

Miriam didn't bother getting the chintzware pot from the china cabinet the way she did when the faculty wives were summoned to visit. She brewed Earl Grey in the sturdy old brown one from the kitchen, instead. Then she put it, their cups, and the plate of cookies on a tray and took it out onto the terrace.

The yard was *House and Garden* perfect. A pale purple froth of sedum defined the edge of the showy rose garden. The delicate pale-flowered stalks of the Japanese anemones bobbed in the breeze, and the chrysanthemum buds were swollen and ready to burst.

Her mother put the tray on the table and settled herself in one of the wrought iron chairs. She poured tea for both of them with the practiced motions of a dowager queen. Her pale, knobby-fingered hands were sure on the cups and saucers, and she conveyed a patrician air that belied her humble beginnings.

Avery had never been sure if that's just how her mother was—a royal foundling left under the wrong cabbage leaf—or if her gentility was an illusion she'd cultivated for the sake of her husband's career. Whichever it was, the persona had served her well—a lady who was Emily Post proper, yet more than a little intimidating.

"So what brings you by at this time of day?" Miriam asked once she'd handed Avery her cup. "Shouldn't you still be down at the *factory*?"

Avery bristled at her mother's emphasis on the word, though her attitude was nothing new. Miriam viewed people who worked outside of academia with a certain contempt, as if having a job in the real world was somewhat less than admirable.

She'd considered the job Avery had taken out of college in commercial design as a personal affront. She had been even more scandalized when Avery started the Holding Company. That Mike worked with his hands, as Miriam's own father had, put him completely beyond the pale. It was the reason, Avery thought, that Miriam had always treated her son-in-law with a certain disdain.

Miriam was a snob and proud of it—but education and what you did with it, was where she drew the line. Success, money, and renown weren't part of the equation as far as Miriam was concerned. But today Avery refused to get sidetracked into arguments they'd never resolve, and hopes of acceptance that had been crushed to smidgens years before.

She sipped her tea and decided that maybe the reason she'd come to her mother's house was to let Miriam know that Fiona had come home to Larkin.

"Something's come up," she began, trying to think of the best way to broach the subject with her mother, "that I thought you ought to know about."

"Oh?" Her mother's eyebrows rose.

"Fiona's back in town," she said. "Mike and I ran into her at the Food-4-Less out by the highway yesterday. I tracked her down at the university and had a word with her this afternoon."

Miriam gave a placid nod. "Oh yes, dear. I know about Fiona being in Larkin."

The air in Avery's lungs seemed to evaporate. Her head went muzzy, and she was too astonished to conjure words.

"How—how do you know?" she finally gasped.

"Fiona came by and asked me to intercede on her behalf with the university's financial aid office," her mother said and took a cookie from the plate. "I do still have *some* influence, you know. Though you'd think they'd have had sense enough not to try to do Jonathan Parrish's granddaughter out of a scholarship she earned fair and square."

"They gave Fee's scholarship back?" Avery asked, astonished.

"Once I had a chat with them." Miriam preened with satisfaction.

Avery stared at her mother, trying to catch her breath. Then her shock gave way to a hissing wave of black betrayal. She leaped to her feet, sending her cup and saucer crashing to the flagstones. "You knew Fiona was in Larkin and didn't tell me?"

"My granddaughter was quite adamant"—Miriam's mouth went prim—"that this be our little secret."

Avery's brain began to sizzle. Blood roared through her veins and a trembling started in her hands. She stared at the woman sitting there calmly sipping tea and wondered who the hell she was. Not her mother, surely. Not someone who cared about Avery's welfare and peace of mind.

"You know how worried I've been about Fiona," she cried, her voice as shaky as her hands. "You knew how frantic I was to be sure she was all right. How could you know that she was back in Larkin and not say so much as a word to me?"

Her mother straightened from the tailbone as if she didn't appreciate being chastised. "This is between my granddaughter and me," she sniffed. "I did what Fiona asked."

An even worse suspicion coursed like venom through

her veins. "You haven't been keeping in touch with Fee, have you? You haven't known where she was all this time and kept it from me?"

"Of course I haven't!" Miriam denied hotly. "Fiona called me because the financial aid people were giving her trouble."

As outraged as she was, Avery believed her.

"Do you know why she came back?"

Miriam fingered the string of pearls. "If you want to understand Fiona's reasons for returning, you really ought to ask her yourself."

Avery glared at her. "I want to know about Fiona, Mother; I want to know now."

"Fiona is a grown woman." Miriam glanced away as if she were disengaging herself from emotions she found distasteful and a conversation she didn't want to have. "I can't do anything but abide by her wishes."

Her mother had cut her off just the way Fiona had half an hour before. In that moment Avery felt alienated from everyone who mattered to her. She'd been betrayed by her mother, her daughter—and by Mike.

Heartache overtook her anger, bringing a terrible singe of hopelessness and the burn of coming tears. She needed to get out of there.

"This isn't over!" she shouted and whirled toward the door. Toward her car, toward the house and the devastating loneliness she'd come here—of all places—to avoid.

※

Avery and Mike's neighborhood took up six square blocks just north of campus. But then, every place in Larkin was measured against the university yardstick. Distances were calculated from the perimeter of the college; directions were given using the campus buildings as landmarks. From the air, the town ruffled out from University Hill like dependencies around a medieval castle.

The historic district, which in Larkin meant anything built after the Civil War, was an enclave of homes that gave lip service to nearly every Victorian building style. In the 1980's, when the neighborhood was being threatened by an unruly influx of frat houses and off-campus housing, young couples like Avery and Mike had swept in and begun rehabbing.

In the next few years, decrepit Carpenter Gothics sprouted new gingerbread. Second Empire homes regained their grandeur while Queen Anne and Eastlake houses brought newfound charm to the brick-paved streets. The rehabbers' success was measured in the skyrocketing property values and the reclaiming and replanting of the neighborhood's lush central square.

Now the houses nestled along the wide, tree-shaded streets like bonbons in a candy box. But as Avery drove home in what the weatherman on the radio was promising would be the last day of September heat, even the most brightly painted homes looked listless and faded. The whole place would revive with the first whisk of autumn wind, but for now, even her own buttery-yellow Eastlake cottage looked tired and forlorn.

As tired and forlorn as Avery felt.

She breathed a sigh of relief when she pulled in the drive and saw Mike's truck wasn't there. He must be working on-site today instead of in his workshop out back—which meant she'd have the house to herself for a while, at least.

She needed that. She needed peace; she needed quiet.

She needed a chance to recoup from her fight with Mike, her rejection by her daughter, and her mother's betrayal. Her life felt like sand being washed away beneath her feet, and she needed this one solid bit of ground where she could stand.

She pushed through the back door and climbed the steps to the back hall and the kitchen. She dropped an armload of sketchbooks and fabric samples on her desk in what had once been the butler's pantry and heaved a sigh. She'd been mulling over a new line of toys for babies, but her brain was too scrambled right now to concentrate.

She might dutifully have drunk tea at her mother's house, but now that she was home, she needed something stronger. There was half a bottle of Reisling in the refrigerator, and Avery poured herself a generous glassful. Sipping as she walked, she headed through the dining room toward the big comfy rocker in the parlor. But there lying on the floor beside the window seat was a big branch from her Christmas cactus.

From Great-Grandma Letty McIntire's Christmas cactus, Avery corrected herself. By tradition, cuttings from the original plant had been handed down through the four generations of McIntire women as each of them proved themselves.

Avery's plant, given to her as a sprig when Fiona was born, was enormous now, spanning three feet from one branch of deep-green, paddle-shaped leaves to the ones on the opposite side. Come Christmas it would be covered with glorious fuchsia blossoms. At the moment though, it seemed spindly, graceless, it's branches oddly akimbo.

"Oh, you poor thing," she murmured, setting her wine

glass aside as she bent to pick up the broken branch. "Did the cat try to share your pot again?"

She carried the branch into the kitchen and laid it carefully at the edge of the sink. It took some rummaging in the back of the cupboard for Avery to find her favorite narrow-throated rooting vase.

Thankfully, Christmas cactuses were easy to grow. All you needed to do was to trim the bottom of the stem, put it in water that had been spiked with a few drops of rooting compound, and let nature take its course. If she was lucky, this new plant would be putting out blossoms by Christmas.

Avery set the vase on the windowsill above the sink, then stood for a moment and simply stared at it.

The women in her family had been growing Christmas cactuses from the same stock for more than a hundred years. She knew the story well enough. The first plant had been a gift from Gilbert McIntire to Letty Swanson on the eve of the Spanish-American War.

But who will I give this cutting to? she wondered. All her life she'd been waiting to give a cutting to her daughter, but Avery couldn't imagine how that could ever happen now.

The weight of Fiona's rejection, of Miriam choosing to stand against her—the outright burden of Mike's betrayal—pressed up beneath her sternum like steam in a geyser. The pressure swelled and grew until her head throbbed with the force of it and her throat ached with holding it back. She bent above the sink with a gulping sob and wept into her hands.

Letty

❋

December 10

I am a bride. Just this morning, Lieutenant Gilbert McIntire and I were married at city hall. It was the briefest of ceremonies, just a few vows spoken before a judge, but it has changed my life. We are bound forever, my Gill and I. We have made promises to each other, to the future. Promises I am eager to begin fulfilling.

As I write this, I am sitting in the window of my room at Mrs. Boetcher's boardinghouse, waiting for my darling to return to me. He will be shipping out in the next few days, and he has gone down to the navy yard to see if his orders have been posted. While he is on about his business, I am writing in the journal he gave me as a wedding gift.

"I want you to write in it every day," he told me when he presented the book to me at our wedding breakfast. "When I return, I will read about everything you did and saw and thought while I was gone."

"But I'll write letters," I protested.

"And I will cherish every one," Gill said, taking my hand. *"But I want to know everything, Letty. Everything."*

So I am doing as you ask, my love. I am putting down all my thoughts, knowing that before you return from the voyage you are embarking on, I will fill many of these clear, creamy pages with my musings and the secrets of my heart.

I suppose by rights I should begin with my recollections of the day we met, nearly a year ago now. I will always remember the weight of the stack of books in my arms as I returned them to the library shelves. I will always remember the scent of dust and leather bindings, and how the light from the window played across your face when I looked up and saw you watching me.

I knew right then that you were someone special.

As close as the library is to the navy yard, we have any number of sailors coming in. But in all the time I've worked in the place, I was never so struck by how handsome a man in uniform could be. I could do no more than stare as you rose from the table where you'd been sitting and came toward me.

"Please, miss," you said. *"Can you help me find a book of Keats's poetry?"*

I stood there caught by the light in your eyes, my heart knocking so hard against my ribs I could barely speak.

"Just this way," I finally managed to murmur and led you down one row of library shelves and up another.

"Wonderful," you said when I put the volume in your hands, but you were looking not at the book, but at me.

I didn't see you again until later when you came to the desk to apply for a library card.

G-i-l-b-e-r-t M-c-I-n-t-i-r-e, I typed on the first line. "And what is your address, Lieutenant?"

"*I'm assigned to the USS* Maine.*"*

"*Will you want extended borrowing privileges?*" *My fingers were poised above the keys, but my gaze seemed locked on you.* "*Lots of sailors like to take our books when they ship out, and this service provides for that.*"

"*That seems wise," you said and smiled again.* "*Do many of the sailors who come to the library also ask the pretty librarian to take a turn with them on Sunday afternoon?*"

I remember how the hot flare of a blush rose in my face.

"*Or is it necessary for me to arrange a proper introduction before I call? Or request your family's permission?*"

"*I have no family, sir," I said, "but Mrs. Boetcher at the rooming house keeps as close an eye on me as any mother.*"

"*Shall I bring her chocolates, then, when I come to see you on Sunday?*"

That was how all this began. Odd as it sounds, I knew in those first few moments that you and I were meant to be together.

As I glance up from my writing now, I see you at the head of the street, striding along in the evening twilight, magnificent in your dress uniform. You are carrying something in your arms, something large and wrapped in tissue. I like that you are so eager to give me things. What woman wouldn't like that? But don't you know, my darling Gill, that you are all the gift I'll ever need?

December 11

Today I am your wife in every way.
And today you are gone.
While the sky was still dark, you rose and kissed me good-bye. You left me with your warmth still lingering

*in the sheets and the scent of you on my pillows. You left
me the taste of your sweet kisses on my mouth and the im-
print of your body against me. You left me alone and
changed by the love that can grow between a man and a
woman in a single night, changed and consumed by delicious dreams of the life we will make together when you
return.*

*I slip out of our bed and glide to the window, hoping to
catch one last glimpse of you. But you are gone, long out of
sight.*

*I look down at where the Christmas cactus you brought
me sits on the windowsill. The plant is in full bud, each
plump whorl edged with fuchsia and bursting with promise. It is waiting for Christmas to reveal its beauty, just as I
must wait for your return so that our true life together can
bud and blossom.*

December 20

*Today I received the package you mailed from Key West.
As much as I enjoy getting gifts, a lieutenant's pay is mea-
ger and I fear you will ruin us with your extravagance. Besides, the only gift I want is your safe return.*

*Last night Mrs. Boetcher and I decorated the Christmas
tree down in the parlor. She brought out her collection of
blown-glass bells in a rainbow of colors her mother had
given her. I had crocheted dozens of lacy snowflakes and
filled shiny paper cones with candied almonds, so we had
lots of decorations. Once we draped the branches with
cranberry and popcorn chains and lit the candles on the
tree, the parlor looked quite festive.*

I put the gift you sent beneath the tree, so I can unwrap

it when we return from Christmas Eve services. I find anticipation makes any gift seem all the sweeter when it is opened at last.

December 24

It is very late, so this entry must be brief. I opened the package you sent to me, and I am rendered speechless by the beauty of the pink coral necklace. The color is exquisite and each of the beads seems to glow with its own inner light.

When I put it around my neck, it is as if you are touching me. I am going to wear the necklace to bed tonight and pretend that you are here to admire how well I look in it.

December 25

I should tell you first, my darling Gill, that when I awoke this morning the Christmas cactus you gave me had burst into full and glorious bloom. It is covered with the most exquisite tiered, fuchsia blossoms. They hang at the tips of the stems like strings of exotic bells. Their color is so vibrant and intense, it brings a kind of vivid and wondrous life to my room and to the day that Christ was born. As beautiful as the Christmas cactus is today, the myriad of buds still left unfurled promise more of these glorious flowers in the days to come.

Christmas has passed pleasantly enough with singing, feasting, games, and reading here at the house. But no matter how congenial the day, with every breath I took, I missed you.

After my years at the orphanage and living as an independent woman, I thought I could bear the loneliness of being a sailor's wife. But now that I have sipped the *sweetness of being with you, I know what I am missing and yearn for more. I want to be with you every day, build a life with you, and start a family.*

Yet we must wait. The days and weeks and months that lay between today and the future we have planned, make me feel unsettled, restless, as if we are wasting time. I want all the things we talked about, a place of our own, nights spent in each other's arms—and children. Oh, how I long to have children with you.

You, darling Gill, have proved yourself a very wise man. By giving me this journal, I can tell you of my impatience and the longing in my heart. And yet, when I write to you tonight, I will be able to tell you things are going well. Only here I can admit how desperately I miss you.

January 12

The newspapers are full of talk of war with Spain. Indeed, Mr. Hearst's yellow-dog journalism stirs everyone up. His warmongering political cartoons and inflammatory editorials have brought people into the library in droves. We have ordered additional copies of the New York Journal *to try to keep up with the demand, but I will order even more tomorrow.*

And of course, all this talk of war makes me fear that if we engage with our enemies, you, my darling, will be in harm's way.

January 24

I have not been at all well for several weeks. I've been queasy in the mornings and have barely been able to hold down my breakfast. I have suffered dizzy spells at work and, no matter how much I sleep, I always seem tired. But today I have begun to suspect there is a very good reason for these maladies.

I believe I am with child. A child, my darling Gill, a child. I can barely contain my joy.

Just writing those words makes me shiver with astonishment and fear and anticipation. How can I be in a family way after lying only one brief night with my new husband? Yet I am pleased and happy to be carrying our child.

This is a dream come true, a wondrous promise of what lies ahead for us. I long to write and tell you the news, but you are so far away that I hesitate.

I want to be in your arms when I tell you you're about to become a father. I want to see the surprise spark in your eyes and watch a satisfied smile dawn across your face. I want you to hold me close and tell me I've done well. I want you to kiss me and cosset me and promise never to leave me.

So I have chosen not to tell you this miraculous news until the doctor has confirmed that we have begun a new life together. I hate myself for keeping this secret, but I am convinced that it is best for all of us.

All of us...

Imagine.

January 27

The newspapers are reporting that the USS Maine was ordered from Key West to Cuba and is now anchored in the Havana harbor. The articles claim this assignment to Cuba is part of a diplomatic mission. They say you are in

Havana to protect the Americans living there from any violence that might break out between the Spanish and the revolutionary forces on the island.

But is that true? Is there to be rioting in the streets of Havana? If there is, will our government order bombardment of the town? And if the Maine fires on Havana, how will the Spanish retaliate?

After months of worsening relations between the United States and Spain, has the Navy put you, my darling, and the Maine in harm's way? I can barely contain my distress. How can I help but fear for your safety when I love you so and our life together is just beginning?

February 9

Dr. Grover has confirmed it; I am with child. You will be glad to know that he also expressed the opinion that I am healthy as a horse and should have no difficulty delivering a living child. Though I am still suffering bouts of nausea, he has eased my mind considerably. He says that is to be expected, and the sickness will pass.

I cannot help but wish that you were here to experience the beginning of this miracle with me. To speculate about whether the child that grows inside me will inherit my curly hair and the color of your eyes, my love of reading or your skill at hitting a baseball.

I lie in bed at night and rub my belly trying to sense some change in me, some proof that this is happening. Have I grown fatter from one day to the next? When will I be able to feel the stir of this new life in me? The doctor assures me that will come, but with this, like so much else in my life right now, I am impatient.

February 11

I wrote tonight to tell you you are going to be a father. I tried so hard to wait, but I couldn't hold back a moment longer.

Mrs. Boetcher noticed the change in me. "Goodness, Letty," she said as she passed the bowl of carrots to me tonight at dinner. "You're glowing like a new-minted penny. Did you have a letter from Lieutenant McIntire in the post?"

I said I had; but I knew very well that if I was "glowing" it was from more than having another letter to read until I have committed it to memory. In time I will have to own up to deceiving her, but it made me realize that I didn't want anyone to guess my secret before I had a chance to tell you that you are going to be a papa.

I shall wait with bated breath to read your response to me—or will I hear you whooping with joy even up here in Baltimore?

Still, I had such hopes that I could wait until we were together to tell you about our child. But as the situation in Cuba worsens, it does not bode well for your imminent return.

Every day you are anchored there in the harbor at Havana, my concern for you grows. Please, my darling, take care of yourself and come home whole to me.

February 16

As I walked toward the library this morning, I found the newsboys on every corner hawking papers.

"USS MAINE *SUNK IN HAVANA HARBOR*," the headline said.

I paid for the paper with shaking hands and began to read: "Yesterday at nine-forty in the evening, the second-class battleship USS Maine exploded and sank in Havana harbor. The thunderous blast appears to have been the result of sabotage, and nearly all the sailors aboard are believed to be dead."

That was all I saw before the newspaper slid from my trembling fingers, before the world swirled around me, and the sun went dark.

One of Mrs. Boetcher's other borders saw me faint and carried me back to the boardinghouse. Mrs. Boetcher has been sitting with me all day, but I barely stirred until someone came in with the evening papers. The news of the Maine is not much better than it was this morning. Of the three hundred and fifty men aboard when it exploded, nearly three hundred are believed to be missing or dead.

As I read those figures I pray to God, "Please don't let Gill be one of them. Please don't take him from me. Please let him live to hold me in his arms again, to hold his child."

Even as the words run through my mind like a litany, a numbness rises inside me. It baffles me like dense fog, protecting me against the torture of waiting, against the news I fear is inevitable.

Against the terrible unfairness and the grief.

February 19

The telegram came today—not from the War Department, as I expected, but from Mrs. Mary McIntire, Gill's mother. Because we were so recently married, the War Department notified her of Gill's death instead of me.

Her telegram has extinguished the last of my hope. It has turned my fear to grief. It has dimmed my world to black.

March 3

Mrs. McIntire will arrive on the train tomorrow evening, traveling from a place called Hamilton, New York. Her telegram arrived not an hour ago, but I fail to understand why she is coming all this way.

There is nothing for her here. In these last weeks I have become aged and useless, a bedridden wraith, a sorry, endlessly weeping bag of bones. I aspire to nothing else.

I look no further than the Christmas cactus standing silhouetted on the window ledge; nor do I care to. The plant is barren of all its gay blossoms now, just as my life is barren without my Gill. It still lives, as do I, but it is shorn of its gaiety.

If I continue to live and breathe it is only because I carry my darling Gilbert's child.

March 12

Mary McIntire is the most stubborn, infuriating woman I have ever encountered in my life. Though I telegraphed her, telling her in no uncertain terms that she need not come to Baltimore, she arrived yesterday and rented a room just down the hall from me.

She is tall and solid as a block of granite, with the kind of strong, square features that looked infinitely better on her son. Her energy and impatient manner makes me want to shriek, when all I wish is to be left alone.

How could my darling Gill ever have had such a woman for a mother?

March 13

Gill's mother and Mrs. Boetcher have conspired against me. They ordered an open carriage for this afternoon and insisted that I go with them out to Fort McHenry so that Mrs. McIntire can see the place that inspired Francis Scott Key to write his marvelous poem. Of course, it was common for the orphanage to have outings at the fort when I was a girl, and I was quite bored at the thought of driving all that way.

Still, the day proved to be uncommonly fine for March and the sun felt good. It reminded me that there are things growing in secret beneath the earth, just as there are in me.

Mary wants to attend the memorial service for the men who died aboard the Maine, to be held in a church downtown on Saturday. Since Gill was interred in Cuba with the rest of the dead, his mother has it in her head that we must attend.

March 18

Mary has discovered I am with child.

In the midst of the memorial service, I was taken by a fit of light-headedness, and as she stood pressing my head between my knees, I heard her whisper. "You're pregnant, aren't you?"

That she expressed it in such a vulgar manner, made me want to deny the accusation, but I could not.

"Three months along," I whispered as the church organ swelled into the first bars of "Amazing Grace." As the voices *soared around us, Mary McIntire sat down in the pew as if someone had cut her off at the knees.*

"Then Gill lives on," she whispered and began to weep loudly and with an intensity of grief I had never seen. Somehow, as the words of the song washed over us, I ended up comforting her. She ended up comforting me. We ended up weeping in each other's arms and comforting each other.

March 21

Today is my last day in Baltimore, the place where I was born and raised, where I worked and loved and conceived my child. But it is good to go, good to be starting a new life.

I am traveling back to this place called Hamilton, New York, to live with Mary and have the baby Gill and I conceived. It is a place I've never seen, but one Gill spoke of so fondly while we were courting.

Going to live with Mary is both a personal and a practical decision. Once my pregnancy begins to show, the library board will ask me to resign my position. Once I do, there will be no money to live on. With no family to call on to look after my child, how would I work? How would I support us? How would we live?

Mary has promised me a fruitful future in the place my Gill called home, a place more alive with who he was than this one small room could ever be. So I have packed up my bags, my Christmas cactus, and my treasured memories. It is hard to leave, but Mary and I will board the nine o'clock train tomorrow.

And my life will start again.

Chapter 4

✳

Sometimes life took the most unlikely turns.
    Her mother had turned into a stalker.

Fiona had spotted her parked near the science building
Wednesday afternoon and ducked out the loading dock
door to avoid her. Casey said she'd seen Avery cruising past
their house off and on for days. Now her mom's red
Forester was parked two rows back and three cars over in
the Food-4-Less parking lot.

Fee shifted the bag of groceries on her hip and, instead of
heading for her own car, she strode determinedly toward
her mother's. Better to confront her here on her own terms,
Fee told herself. Better to keep her from approaching the
Neon where she'd be sure to notice the baby seat. Better to
get things over with rather than having her mom trail her to
Casey's—or worse yet, back to the apartment. The idea of
her mother being able to drop in on her any time she liked
made Fee itch all over.

As she closed in on her mother's car, she saw Avery's eyes
widen and her jaw drop, as if she was surprised at getting
caught.

Her expression made Fee grin in spite of herself. "Don't take a job with the CIA, okay, Mom?"

Avery had the good grace to flush. "You 'made' me, huh?"

"More than once this week," Fee said and stepped up close to the door of the car so her mother couldn't get out.

Avery leaned into the open window and stared up at her. "Well, how else am I supposed to behave? You came back to Larkin without letting me know. You won't talk to me, won't tell me where you're living, or why you came home."

"I came back to Larkin so I could finish my degree." It was the unvarnished truth, and Fee hoped her mother accepted it wholesale.

"Yes," her mother acknowledged, her eyes narrowing, "but why? I've known you every minute of your life, Fiona Montgomery, and things with you are never that simple."

Fee gave an acknowledging shrug and looked away.

I ought to tell Mom about Samantha and get it over with, she conceded with a hot twitch of dread. But not just yet.

She wasn't ready to admit to her mother how completely she'd screwed up her life. And if her father never discovered Jared had gotten her pregnant, it would be aeons too soon.

"It's ridiculous that you're living right here in town," her mother argued, "and I don't even know how to get in touch with you. The university won't tell me anything!"

Fee could hear the frustration in her voice and was swamped with contrition. Just not nearly enough to tell her mother the truth.

"I've called the phone company," Avery went on. "I've tried running your Social Security number on the Internet."

Fee retreated half a step, surprised at her mother's resourcefulness. She might have found the information she was looking for except that Fee couldn't afford a telephone and was subletting her apartment from a grad student who'd moved in with her boyfriend.

"I'm thinking about hiring a private detective."

That got Fee's attention. It made the hair bristle on the back of her neck.

"Oh, don't do that, Mom," she advised, a chill creeping into her voice. "I promise once I get my life together, I'll tell you everything. Right now, I need to concentrate on school."

"I can make that easier," Avery tempted her.

"I don't want it to be easier!"

Fee saw her mother's eyes glaze with tears at the rebuff. Her own throat tightened. They used to have such a cool relationship; Fiona had told her mom almost everything.

"Look," she said and clutched the groceries tighter. "I've got some things I need to prove to myself. Can you understand that?"

Something shifted in her mother's face.

"Things happened in L.A.," Fee went on, "that I'm just not ready to discuss with you."

Avery reached to catch Fiona's wrist and looked up into her eyes. "You don't—you don't have HIV or anything like that, do you?"

Fee stared at her. Her mother's imaginings were so much worse than what really happened. That should have made talking to her about Samantha and Jared easier, but somehow it didn't.

"No, it's nothing like that." Fee stepped far enough away to slip out of her mother's grasp.

"It makes me crazy," Avery fumed, "that after having you under my roof for nineteen years, there are things in your life I don't know anything about. Secrets you're deliberately keeping from me—as if I can't be trusted!"

"It isn't that I don't trust you," Fee began. *It's that I can't face you with the mistakes I've made—or admit to the consequences.*

Fiona tried a different tack. "Isn't there anything going on in your own life right now that you're not willing to talk to me about?"

Her mother lifted her chin and looked away.

That tacit admission jolted Fiona in a way she didn't expect. She'd always accepted that her parents worked, went places and did things without her. She knew they had friends and interests and obligations, but she'd never much considered what their lives were like beyond the times and places where they intersected her own.

Now, with that single acknowledging glance, her mother stepped from behind the cardboard cutout Fee had made of her. In that instant, Avery became real in a way Fee had never seen her before. She became a person in her own right, a separate entity with a history and motives, failings and dreams.

She became a woman Fee knew intimately—and not at all. The notion stunned her, and because she couldn't think how to respond, she took one step backward and then another.

"Look," she offered hastily, "I have to go."

"Fiona."

Fee refused to acknowledge the long, slender hand that reached out to her—the hand of a stranger.

"I'll make a deal with you," Fee bargained hastily, off balance and feeling threatened. "If you stop following me, stop trying to dig into my life, I'll call you at work once a week."

"Fiona, please."

Fee settled back on her heels and made her stand. "If you don't stop making me feel like I'm under surveillance, I'll leave Larkin for good. You'll never see or hear from me again."

It was a completely empty threat, but Avery had no way to know she was bluffing. Instead, Avery paled, and her face twisted with a kind of torment Fee had never seen, never dreamed her mother could feel.

"Someday, Fee, you'll be a mother"—Fee's heart turned over with guilt and fear—"and you'll know what this is doing to me."

Fee couldn't think of a word to say in her own defense, so she turned and marched back across the parking lot. Behind her she heard the Forester's engine roar, but she kept right on walking. She reached the Neon, stowed her bag of groceries in the backseat, and slammed the door. Only then did she dare to turn and look.

Her knees went wobbly, and she slumped against the side of the car in relief. Her mother was gone.

※

Avery bent over the drawing board in her office at the Holding Company and tried to concentrate. Usually it wasn't difficult for her to lose herself when she was working on something new, but today a scrim of worry swam between her and the work at hand.

Getting "busted" by her daughter the previous afternoon in the Food-4-Less parking lot had been nearly as humiliating as it had been frustrating. Fee was being Fee at her stubborn, independent worst.

Avery hadn't gotten an explanation of why Fee had come home, or even the most basic information about how to contact her. The one thing she did have was Fee's promise that she would be in touch on a regular basis—and Avery supposed that was something.

With an impatient sigh, Avery leafed through the sketches she'd been fiddling with all morning. They were designs for her first line of toys for newborns, simple squeezable shapes in colors babies would respond to. But she couldn't nail down an approach that would make them special, make them "huggable." She was looking for something so unique and adorable that moms and grandmas would find the toys irresistible.

"A tall order," Avery muttered and reached for her fabric samples.

Just then, Cleo popped into her office.

"I thought I told you I didn't want to be disturbed," Avery grumbled. "So what is it this time?"

"You've got a call." Cleo's Kiss Me Coral mouth drew up in a smile. "And I think it's one you'll want to take."

Is it Fee? Avery almost asked.

"It's James Marshall," Cleo informed her.

"The Special Promotions Manager for Elite Cards?"

"The very same."

Elite Cards was the biggest card and gift store chain in the Midwest. They dominated the market from the Canadian border to the Gulf of Mexico. Avery had been introduced to James Marshall during a cocktail party at the Toy and Gift Expo in New York last spring. Since the Holding Company couldn't possibly be on Elite Cards's radar, she was stunned that he remembered her. Even more stunned that he had called.

"Did he say what he wanted?"

Cleo lifted her eyebrows. "To talk to you."

"Then we'd better oblige him."

The phone rang through to Avery's office, and she took a moment to tug at her blouse and smooth her hair before she answered.

"Good morning, Mr. Marshall," she said crisply. "What can I do for you?"

"Good morning, Ms. Montgomery." His voice was silk-suit smooth and heads-will-roll powerful. "I have a problem I'm hoping you'll be able to solve."

"I'd certainly like to try."

"We don't usually go outside our studios for promotional products—" Marshall went on.

Avery knew Elite maintained a number of in-house studios for designing everything from cards to candles, from wrapping paper to ribbons. Most recently the promotion design studio had come up with Ber-r-r-nice the Polar Bear, last Christmas's premium with purchase. It was so cute, it had brought customers into the stores in droves, and according to the industry press, nearly half a million Ber-r-r-nices had gone home with satisfied customers.

"Recently, however," James Marshall went on, "we decided to run a special Easter promotion for our five-star customers. We haven't time to develop the premium ourselves, but someone remembered seeing a lamb in your booth at the Toy Expo that might be appropriate."

Avery knew exactly what lamb that was. "We call him 'Sheepish.'"

"Cute," Marshall snorted.

Sheepish *was* cute. He was the most huggable sheep Avery had been able to dream up. His curly hair, black faux-leather hooves, and demure expression made it almost impossible for people to pass without stopping to cuddle him.

"Is Sheepish in production?" Marshall asked.

"We're just gearing up for Easter," Avery hedged.

In truth, producing Sheepish required far more expensive materials than they usually used, and Avery didn't have the capital to commit to the project.

"I'll need to see the prototype first," Marshall went on, "and your figures on the materials. But if Sheepish passes muster here at Elite, we'll want to buy the design outright and put him directly into production."

Avery hesitated, then inched forward in her chair. "Sheepish has a special significance for me personally," she said, hoping he wouldn't hear the sudden quaver in her voice.

Sheepish had been the main character in the ongoing stories she used to tell Fiona when she was little. Sheepish belonged to the two of them, and the idea of giving away anything that tied her to Fiona right now made Avery's chest ache.

"I'd prefer to maintain the copyright on the project and the vision I have of him. We'll produce Sheepish ourselves if that's what it takes to maintain control."

Avery knew what she was risking by demanding that. The Holding Company was probably just one on Marshall's list of places to call. But she also had a hunch that it would be worth it in the long run to keep the Sheepish copyright. She might even turn the stories she'd told Fee into books someday. But at the moment, maintaining the connection to her daughter was most important.

The silence that stretched between her and Marshall resounded with his displeasure. "That isn't how we usually do business," he warned her.

"You don't usually go outside Elite Cards for products, either," Avery countered, holding her ground.

"If we go with this, we'll need a little more than fifty

thousand units shipped to our stores for arrival by New Year's Day. Can you promise us that?"

Avery sucked in a deep breath of exhilaration at the same time her stomach dropped into her shoes. Even if they suspended production on all their other products, they couldn't deliver even half that many Sheepishes by New Year's.

"Of course we can," she said with a show of bravado that made her palms sweat. "But it will mean a major commitment of our resources."

She was getting in over her head and she knew it. But how could she pass up this opportunity? "I'd need a firm order before I can even start putting the project together."

"Then get me the prototype and figures," Marshall told her. "If everything's in order, we can turn this over to the lawyers by the first of the week."

Her thoughts spun, organizing, prioritizing, trying to figure out how they were going to manage what she'd committed to.

"I'll get Sheepish off to you this afternoon," Avery promised. "And thank you for this opportunity."

Marshall's voice darkened. "I hope you'll make the most of it, Ms. Montgomery."

"We will," Avery promised.

Panic set in the moment she hung up the phone. What in the name of heaven had she gotten them into? Doing this project with Elite Cards would bring the Holding Company to national prominence. If Sheepish was successful, she'd get the infusion of money it would take to change what was barely more than a cottage industry to an entirely new kind of enterprise.

Avery's head swam with the risks and possibilities. They

were either poised on the brink of fabulous success or utter disaster.

"Cleo!" she shouted.

The older woman materialized in the doorway and, from her grin, she'd been eavesdropping.

"Elite wants fifty thousand Sheepish the Lamb shipped off by the first of the year." Just saying that out loud made Avery's heartbeat lumber. "Do you think we can do that?"

"Of course we can!" Cleo nodded decisively. "But we're going to need some help."

"I know," Avery agreed. "Get me information on who we can hire to produce Sheepish for us, what it will cost to finance that. And if you have any ideas about how in heaven's name I can come up with that kind of money, I'd appreciate hearing that, too."

✻

Mike's heart sank when he pulled into the driveway and saw the light was still on in the bedroom. Avery had left a message on his voice mail that she wanted to talk, but he'd been doing his best to avoid that. He had a very good idea what she wanted to talk about, and he was trying to avoid making Avery any madder than she was already.

So he'd deliberately stayed late at the farm, going about his observations and making his images with meticulous care. He was building a catalog of the sky around Andromeda. He liked doing that, visiting familiar places, imaging things he knew, objects he and his daughter had found for the first time together.

He parked his truck in front of the garage, and once inside the house, he opened the refrigerator. He was hungry and hoping to be inspired. He wasn't.

Since Fiona left, Avery had more or less given up cooking. He never came home these days to the smell of sauce bubbling or a pot roast in the oven. Avery never baked bread anymore and the cookie jar was always empty. But then, since he wasn't home for dinner all that often, what right did he have to complain? Still, he missed her cooking, missed sitting down with her at dinner, missed hearing about her day. He missed feeling like she was looking after him, as if once Fee left they'd ceased to be a family.

He took an apple from the crisper instead and ate it while he leafed through the mail. But even as he ate, his mind was on the conversation Avery seemed so determined to have with him—which probably meant it was about Fiona.

After they lost the baby the year Fee turned five, they'd talked and talked. They'd talked for hours at a time and hung on to each other. They hung on tight to Fiona, too. Knowing she was the only child they were ever going to have, made her all the more precious.

That their son had been stillborn and Avery had to have an emergency hysterectomy had extinguished the dreams they'd harbored of filling the house with children and plunged them both into months of grieving. Avery had finally thrown herself into getting Fiona ready for kindergarten, then focused on starting the Holding Company.

Mike had more trouble moving on—but then, he'd almost lost Avery, too. Sometimes, even after all these years, he'd dream about the night the baby died. He'd dream about clinging to Avery's hand and pleading with her not to leave him, too. Then he'd jerk awake panting and drenched with sweat. Only watching Avery sleep, only creeping into

Fiona's room in the dark to assure himself that they were safe could quell that panic.

All Mike had ever wanted was to protect his family. Somehow, losing that baby made him feel as if he'd failed at that. Fiona's leaving the way she had, made him feel as if he'd failed again. It ended the happiest, most complete and settled years Mike had ever known—and he resented the hell out of losing them.

With a curse, he fired his apple core into the trash. He understood Avery wanting to reconcile with their daughter; she and Fee had always been extremely close. Hell, they'd all been close. They'd been such a wholesome, picture-perfect American family they could have sold goddamn cornflakes.

But that time was gone; there was no going back. *Why didn't Avery get that?*

She was in bed reading when he got upstairs. "Good seeing?" she asked him.

Mike nodded and emptied his pockets onto the dresser. "It's been really clear these last few nights. I've been getting some nice images."

"Of anything in particular?"

He just shrugged. "What're you reading?"

"A romance novel Cleo gave me. It's really good."

He could be having this conversation with a stranger and hated that he was having it with his wife. He stalked into the bathroom, washed, and brushed his teeth. Avery was waiting when he came out. Judging from the way her mouth was drawn up tight, she had something to say he wasn't going to like.

When he climbed warily into bed, Avery set her novel facedown on the quilt and turned to him. With the glow of the bedside lamp behind her, her hair seemed alive with filaments of copper and gold. Her face, bare of makeup, looked soft and incredibly touchable. So touchable, he longed to reach out and caress the slope of her cheek, skim that long, smooth throat, curl his fingers around the curve of her shoulder. He wanted to draw her to him and kiss her instead of arguing.

Mike willed himself not to flinch when she sucked in her breath to speak.

"The most amazing thing happened today."

That wasn't at all how he'd expected the conversation to start. "Oh?"

Avery shifted to sit cross-legged facing him, her flowered pajamas drawn taut across her knees. "Elite Cards called. They want to make Sheepish the Lamb one of their Easter promotions."

"Good old Sheepish!" he exclaimed and reached across to squeeze her thigh. "How'd that happen?"

Avery told him. "Elite wanted to buy the design for Sheepish outright."

Mike heard the hesitation in her voice. "But?"

Avery sighed. "You know the inspiration for Sheepish came from the stories I used to tell Fiona."

Mike nodded, remembering how many nights he'd stood outside Fee's bedroom door taking delight in watching the two of them. They'd lie nose-to-nose on Fiona's sunflower sheets sharing hugs and laughter and mother-daughter secrets.

Remembering how the two of them looked lying in that bed together sparked up an acrid glow just north of his solar plexus.

After Fee had quieted, Avery would tell her a story, a new

one every night, and Sheepish had been the star in her cast of characters.

"I'd always kind of hoped I'd be able to collect those stories in a book someday," she said wistfully, "so I wanted to hang on to my copyright."

"Is there an alternative to them buying Sheepish outright?" Mike wanted to know.

Avery lowered her eyes. "Well...we could produce Sheepish ourselves and sell them the finished product."

"Are they amenable to that?"

"I've sent them some preliminary figures."

But he could see Avery wasn't telling him all of it. He fumbled through a list of possibilities, problems the Holding Company might face in doing that.

"How many lambs do they want?" he finally asked her.

"A little more than fifty thousand in three months' time."

Mike whistled under his breath. "Can you produce that many?"

She shook her head. "Even suspending all other production, we might produce ten or twelve thousand. Our only hope of meeting Elite's demand is to contract with someone who's better equipped to deal with orders that size."

"And who would that be?"

She looked up at him. "Cleo's found two companies in China—"

"'China?'"

"I talked to the stateside representatives for both companies this afternoon," she went on, and he could see her excitement growing. "I faxed them our specs, so they'll be able to give me a solid price tomorrow."

My God! Mike found himself thinking as he watched her. How far she'd come since she'd begun stitching and stuffing her funny animal designs on the dining-room table. And how proud he was of what she'd accomplished.

"All these years you've resisted sending work overseas," he said, concern drawing his brows together. "Wouldn't doing that with Sheepish undermine the manufacturing operation you've set up here?"

"It could," she conceded. "I deliberately built the Holding Company with a commitment to its employees, and somehow I've always managed to keep us in the black. But we've never had the resources to introduce more than one or two new products a year. We've never had the chance to explore new markets. We've never had any kind of financial cushion if things went wrong. The offer from Elite would give us an opportunity that may never come our way again."

Mike could see she was trying to convince herself as much as she was him.

"Besides, this is the only way to give Elite what they want and protect my copyright."

She might have reservations about the course ahead, but Mike could see that she'd thought things through. He reached across and clasped her hand. "You've proved you're a good businesswoman, Avery. Do what you think is right."

She let out her breath. "I'm so glad you agree, because I need your help."

Mike warmed with the knowledge that she'd turned to him, trusted him with her worries and her problems. It was the first time she'd done that in ages.

"So what do you need, sweetheart?" He would have promised her anything.

"I need you to go with me to the bank."

"'The bank?'"

"If Elite Cards agrees to the price I asked for Sheepish, I'll get what's called a firm order. With that in hand, I can approach the bank for an international letter of credit."

"What's that?" He hated asking, but no one needed an international letter of credit if they were putting up a new garage.

"It guarantees the Chinese company we select to do the manufacturing that I have the money to pay them."

Mike's throat went tight. "And how do we secure this letter of credit?"

Avery looked up and held his gaze. "We'll have to put up the Holding Company as collateral, the stocks my father left us, the money in our accounts—and the house."

The house. The house they'd rehabbed board by board. The house he'd worked double shifts to pay off early.

"That's pretty much everything we have," he said, trying not to sound completely horrified.

"Yes."

Did Avery have any idea what she was asking him to risk? But then, how could she understand? She hadn't grown up on a farm that was always one step ahead of foreclosure. She hadn't had a father who drank up every paycheck. She hadn't gone to work at fifteen to make sure there was food on the table.

Their house with its whimsical shingle trim and ornate front porch, this house they'd bought and filled with love and life and family was not just their home. It was the only place Mike ever felt like he belonged. It was the only financial security he'd ever had. The only place he'd ever felt as if he were safe. Now Avery was asking him to sacrifice that safety.

"I wish there were another way," she apologized softly.

This was why she wanted to talk, Mike realized with a sting of disillusionment. She hadn't been waiting up because she'd been bursting with news she wanted to share with him. She hadn't wanted his advice; she needed his cooperation. She needed his signature at the bank in order to commit every penny they had to this business proposition.

The hope he'd momentarily harbored that things were getting better between them seeped away. Things hadn't gone back to the way they'd been before. There was still a gulf between them, and the only reason Avery had spanned it was to finance this business deal.

He abruptly let go of her hand.

"So, will you go with me to the bank?" Her voice sounded breathy and uncertain.

Mike knew that once they started laying out their finances Avery would discover things he hadn't intended her to know, commitments he'd made and deliberately hadn't told her about. Still, he couldn't refuse her the help she needed and live with himself.

"Of course I'll go to the bank with you," he promised.

"Thank you," she said and leaned across to kiss him.

He kissed her back—but for a moment he almost wished she'd wanted to talk about Fiona.

⚜

The diner on the outskirts of Larkin was already crowded when Mike arrived at just before seven A.M. He shouldered his way past the line gathered at the cash register and scanned the room for Ted. He'd seen his mail truck parked out front, so he knew his brother was here somewhere.

Mike finally spotted him on the second-to-last seat at the far end of the stainless-steel counter. As he slid onto the stool beside him, Ted looked up from where he was crouched over his coffee.

In a glance Mike saw Ted's eyes were red. His hair was mussed, and he'd missed a patch of stubble on the side of his chin. He looked like someone barreling down the road to hell who'd just gone breezing past the last turnoff.

Mike compressed his lips and tried to keep from saying what he thought.

"I'm sorry," Ted offered in an undertone as the waitress set a cup of coffee down in front of Mike and slid him a smile.

"Didn't you know there'd be late charges?" Mike asked him.

Ted's head sagged even lower. "I guess not."

Mike let out his breath in a sigh that started at his diaphragm. He dipped into the breast pocket of his work shirt and pulled out the check he'd promised his brother. He held it between two fingers until Ted looked up.

"This is the last time," he said and meant it.

"I know. I know." Ted wagged his head as he deposited the scrap of folded paper in the pocket of his jacket. "If I saved a little out of every paycheck, I'd have the money when the taxes come due. But after paying support to Nancy and the kids—"

"No, Ted," Mike said quietly and distinctly. "I mean it. This really *is* the last time."

At his tone, Ted looked up. "What's going on? You and Avery aren't—"

"No." But Mike's mouth went dry. Even Ted had picked

up on the tension between Avery and him and thought the worst.

"Avery has an opportunity to expand the Holding Company," he felt compelled to explain. "In order to take advantage of it, she has to invest a lot of her own money up front. She's applying for financing this week, and we're going to have to put everything we own on the line at the bank."

"So what you're saying is that there won't be anything extra."

"That's right." Mike was glad Ted understood. No matter how much he disapproved of the way his brother was living his life, when Mike had money to spare, he'd done his best to help Ted out.

They sat for a moment over their coffee before Ted spoke. "Does Avery know you've been lending me money?"

"Lending" was a polite name for what it was, but Mike let the euphemism slide. "Avery hasn't needed to know."

Ted glanced sideways, his brows drawn together. "But she'll find out now, won't she? She'll find out that you've been helping me keep the farm?"

"Yeah, probably."

"What will she think of me when she finds out?"

Mike could barely hear his brother's weary voice above the clatter of dishes and silverware. He knew Ted was miserable at the course his life was taking, but he couldn't seem to find the gumption to do anything about it. Still, telling Ted the truth seemed unnecessarily cruel.

Mike shrugged. "She'll understand."

What Avery wouldn't understand was why Mike had continued to give Ted money to hang on to the farm, a place that was a constant reminder of their unhappy childhood.

A place that had become a symbol of Mike's own broken relationship with his daughter.

"Are you putting up the house, too?"

"Of course we are," Mike snapped back.

He hadn't been able to admit to Avery last night how hard it was going to be for him to risk the only place in the world he'd ever cared about. Every shingle he'd nailed, every cabinet he'd built and installed, every wall he'd plastered had one purpose: to shore up the haven and the life he'd made for himself and Avery. Yet in a few days time, she was going to expect him to sign the papers that would put the only place he ever felt settled, in jeopardy. He'd hoped she knew him better than to ask him to do that—but obviously she hadn't.

Just thinking about the possibility of losing the house made his palms sweat. It made him feel hollow and rootless and out of control. It made him feel like one more piece of the bedrock he'd built his life on was crumbling beneath him.

He wanted to wrap his arms around what was left of the life he'd loved and hold on tight. But how could he deny Avery his support when such a genuine opportunity to expand the Holding Company had come her way?

Mike couldn't do anything about risking the house, couldn't do anything about the discoveries Avery was going to make, so he swallowed down the last of his coffee and pushed to his feet. "They'll be waiting for me on the job site."

He put down money enough for two coffees and a hefty tip. "Aren't folks along your route going to be looking for their mail?"

"I'm going to have one for the road." Ted's mouth quirked as he raised his cup to signal for a refill.

"I wish you wouldn't make a habit of that," Mike muttered as he turned to go.

Ted must have heard him, because Mike felt his brother's glare burning between his shoulder blades as he strode the length of the diner to the door.

Chapter 5

❋

The reckoning came sooner than Mike expected.
Avery had picked up loan papers from the bank that afternoon and insisted they sit right down after supper to fill them out. By ten o'clock they'd listed every asset they had.

Everything but the gold in our teeth, Mike thought irritably as he rose from the paper-strewn dining table to get them both another cup of coffee.

When he set Avery's mug beside her, he found her tapping her pen at the bottom of their most recent bank statement. "I thought we'd have a lot more money in our accounts than this."

Mike felt his face get hot. He'd taken over their personal finances when Avery started doing the books for the Holding Company.

"I mean—" She scowled down at the papers as if that could change the figures printed there. "—you've worked steadily for the last two years. I've finally started taking a salary at the Holding Company."

Mike's palms began to sweat.

"We haven't had house payments or college expenses since Fiona left. We even got a tax refund this year, didn't we?"

He took a breath. The time had come to own up to what he'd done. "Remember when we talked about helping Ted out with things at the farm?"

Avery looked up, her gaze wary. "We agreed to give him the money to meet his mortgage payment."

"Well, I've had to do that more than once."

Her wariness gradually ripened into suspicion. "We talked about that ages ago. How often have you had to help him?"

"I've been writing checks to him pretty regularly," he hedged.

Avery's focus on him sharpened. "Exactly how much money have you given Ted?"

Even Mike hadn't realized the total until he'd added everything up tonight. He swallowed, took a breath, then met Avery's gaze head-on. "All together it amounts to about twenty-three thousand dollars."

"Twenty-three thousand dollars!" Avery gaped at him. "My God, Mike! What were you thinking?"

Mike paced to the far end of the table, shaking his head. "You know Ted's been having a rough time. How could I refuse to help when he asked me to see him through the worst of it?"

"'The worst of it?'" Avery echoed. "Ted's always been a mess. He's never been able to hang on to a job. He doesn't have any idea how to manage money. Right now I bet he's drinking up half of what he earns!"

Mike hated admitting it, but Avery's assessment probably wasn't all that far off the mark.

"After Nancy and the kids went to live with her folks," Mike went on, trying to explain himself, "Ted was in a bad way. I had to do something to keep him afloat."

"But how could you have given him so much of *our* money?"

"It wasn't like I handed him piles of hundreds," he said, trying not to think of all the checks he'd written. "I added a little to his mortgage every month or two, and when he didn't have enough to cover the taxes—"

"Oh, Mike!"

"Jeez, Avery, try to understand." He scrubbed a hand through his hair. "I couldn't stand by and let him lose the farm."

"The farm!" she exclaimed, facing him down the length of the dining-room table. "Why should you give a damn about that farm? It's not like any of you have happy memories of the place."

"Avery."

She hesitated just long enough to acknowledge the warning in his voice, then continued anyway. "Your father was an alcoholic. When he drank too much, he came home and beat your mother. When he was done beating her, he beat the rest of you!"

Mike turned his face away. *Maybe it was the memories of the helplessness he'd felt when he was growing up that kept him shackled to that little valley.*

"Your father couldn't make the farm pay; neither can Ted." Avery's gaze was intent on him. "You wouldn't have been able to do it, either, Mike, if you'd chosen to stay."

Maybe the money he'd given Ted had been a ransom, what he owed for having made good his escape.

"That farm has been Montgomery land for four generations," he insisted. "I couldn't stand by and see Ted lose it for taxes."

He could see the color come up in her face. Avery's family had always been careful, prudent. She might have been born with a silver spoon in her mouth, but it was one her mother had bargained for in a thrift shop.

Except for him, none of the Montgomerys had been able to hold onto two nickels long enough to rub them together.

"Explain to me"—Avery shoved angrily to her feet— "exactly how maintaining your family heritage is worth the twenty-three thousand dollars you've spent on it?"

Her words echoed in Mike's head like the indictment they were. She thought he'd been a fool to keep writing checks to Ted, but even now he couldn't see how he'd had another choice.

Avery swallowed, straightened, took a breath. Mike could see she was trying to get control of herself, trying to be reasonable.

"Elite Cards has offered me this opportunity, Mike," she began calmly enough, though her voice was shaking. "They've given me a chance to make the Holding Company into everything I ever dreamed it could be. They've made me an offer that might never come again. If we don't qualify for this letter of credit, that chance will be lost."

He saw how much making this happen meant to her.

Regret made his throat go tight, turned his voice soft and raspy. "Oh, sweetheart," he murmured, stepping closer. "If I had any idea that helping Ted pay a few of his bills would jeopardize the future of the Holding Company, I'd have found the money somewhere else. It never once occurred to me that giving Ted a few mortgage payments would make such a difference in our lives."

"You've given him a whole lot more than a few mortgage payments, Mike. What if we don't get the letter of credit from the bank because of this shortfall?" Her voice wavered. "What if the profits from the Sheepish deal with Elite could have made the Holding Company a presence in the marketplace and because of what you've given Ted it never has a chance to grow?"

Mike felt himself bristle.

"You know, Avery," he began. "Over the years I've done more than my share to keep the Holding Company afloat. Without me paying the bills here at home, you wouldn't have had the money to reinvest in the company. You wouldn't even be on Elite Card's radar."

"Yes," she conceded. "You're right. I couldn't have built the business without your help, and I thank you very much for all you've done." Avery sucked in a long, slow breath. "But do you know what's even worse than us not qualifying for that letter of credit, Mike?"

He didn't know how to answer.

"What's worse"—she leaned toward him for emphasis —"is that you gave Ted that money without once consulting me. You gave it to him behind my back because you knew that if you told me what you were doing—"

"I should have told you," he conceded with a nod. But he'd just been doing what he'd always done, taking care of his brother. "I never meant—" Mike reached for his wife, needing her to understand.

Avery stepped back, avoiding his touch.

Mike saw the censure in her expression. For the very first time in their married life, Mike saw her mother in her.

Avery wasn't going to forgive him for this. She wasn't going to forgive him, just like Miriam Parrish had never forgiven him for who and what he was. Just like she'd never forgiven him for thwarting the plans she'd made for her daughter.

Mike faced Avery sharing the same space, breathing the same air—but he didn't know how to reach her. He didn't know how to make her understand what he owed Ted, or how much more that farm had come to mean to him after Fiona went away.

He didn't know how to make Avery understand how sorry he was that he'd put her dreams in jeopardy. A weary desolation settled over him.

Slowly Avery straightened. Her chin came up. A fierce, silvery glint sparked in her eyes. "So," she challenged him, "you didn't tell me about Fee. You didn't tell me about the money you've been giving Ted. Is there anything *else* you're keeping from me?"

Bitterness rose sharp on the back of his tongue and he spoke before he thought. "Not that I'm willing to own up to."

There wasn't anything for him to do after saying that but leave. In three long strides he'd brushed past where she stood at the head of the table. He stormed across the kitchen, bent on escape.

But Avery, being Avery, couldn't just let him go. She trailed him into the back hall. "Going to the farm?" she guessed.

He snatched his jacket from one of the pegs and jerked open the door. "Do you really give a damn where I'm going, Avery?"

Then, not sure he'd like her answer, he made for his truck.

❉

February 1983

Chicago, Illinois

Any guy who'd drive eight hours through blowing, drifting snow to take a woman out for Valentine's Day, Mike Montgomery reflected with a snort of derision, must have it bad.

Yet here he stood in the lobby of Avery Parrish's apartment building, waiting while the doorman called her on the intercom so he could be approved of and verified. Mike spent the time staring up at the soaring stone arches a story and a half above his head, admiring the tall mullioned windows, and gleaming banks of elevators.

Somehow he'd never pictured Avery living somewhere quite so grand. Not a place with rows of polished mailboxes, a shoe-shine stand, and tenants who bustled across half an acre of marble floor to limousines idling beneath the portico.

Parked behind that sleek, mile-long car, Mike's battered pickup looked like a panhandler crouched in the cold and hoping for a handout. If he'd needed proof that a guy like him had no business dating Avery Parrish, here it was.

He probably should have taken the hint when Avery's mother met him at the door the night of their third date. Just the lift of those disapproving eyebrows made it clear that Miriam Parrish didn't think he was good enough to be going out with her daughter.

Those thin, judgmental eyebrows might have scared

some guys off, but Mike was stubborn, not sixteen any-more, and pissed off enough by her attitude not to be in-timidated.

And, yeah, he *did* have it bad for Avery Parrish.

Mike was getting pretty tired of the doorman's suspi-cious glances, when Avery burst out of the elevator. She gave a peep of excitement at seeing him, threw her arms around his neck, and kissed him full on the mouth.

"I'm so glad you called from Moline!" she said, beaming up at him. "I'd have been frantic if I hadn't known where you were. Was the driving terrible?"

"Not so bad," Mike lied.

"I've arranged for you to have a parking space in the un-derground garage," she informed him. "I'll show you where the entrance is, and we can take the elevator up from there."

The doorman handed her a parking tag. "Space thirty-three, Ms. Parrish."

As they turned toward the front door, Mike saw Avery slip the man some folded bills. The poise with which she ac-complished that, and the wink the doorman gave her, made Mike flush. *He should have known enough to tip the door-man.*

Avery's apartment on the ninth floor was bigger than Mike had imagined and built with the same attention to de-tail he'd seen in the lobby. The bookshelves that lined one wall of the living room were well proportioned and well built. A pair of big, deep-set windows looked out to the south, and Mike suspected that if it wasn't snowing, he'd be able to see the lake.

"The apartment's a sublet," Avery explained as she took his pea coat. "When one of the university alumni was transferred to Europe, he and Dad worked out a deal on the rent."

Mike immediately recognized her mother's stamp in the decor. The mossy velvet couch, tapestry chair, and gate-leg table looked like they'd been hijacked from the Parrish's parlor. So did the Oriental rug in shades of brick and green.

Yet Avery had made the place her own. She'd painted the walls a soft terra-cotta color and tumbled big, exotic pillows everywhere. Embroidered, quilted, and needle worked, they were plumped across the width of the couch and heaped on the floor. Her bookcases overflowed with art books, an assortment of small marqueterie boxes, and some kind of blue-green pottery Mike admired the moment he saw it.

"The couch is a pullout," Avery went on, dashing the hope Mike had been harboring for four hundred snowy miles that they were going to be sleeping together.

Of course, they'd really only had three dates, he reminded himself. Still, he'd seen enough of Avery Parrish to know that he liked everything about her, that kissing her made his insides liquify. That their bodies fit together— even through layers of sweaters and coats—in a way that hinted at all sorts of delicious possibilities. Mike got hard just thinking about what they were.

He'd prepared for the weekend by buying Avery the biggest heart-shaped box of chocolates he could find—and himself a fresh pack of condoms.

After giving him the news about the couch, Avery led him down the hall toward the back of the apartment. "You can put your bag in my studio," she said and opened the first door on the left.

Chaos reigned beyond it. A drawing board and taboret wrestled for floor space with a sewing machine and quilting rack. Beneath the window a row of blue plastic milk crates exploded with skeins of yarn and swatches of cloth. Bolts of fabric stood three deep in the corners and paper samples were tacked up on the walls like a collection of butterflies.

"Oh, dear!" Avery flushed and hastily shut the door. "I didn't realize it had gotten so out of hand."

She led him hastily past an apricot-and-white bathroom, and into her bedroom at the end of the hall. Because it was at the corner of the building, the windows faced west and south, bathing the room with light even on so dark a day. But it was the rich rosy paint of the walls that made the room so welcoming.

Mike sensed Avery's hand in every detail. He recognized the proper young woman he'd known in Larkin in the selection of traditional mahogany furniture. But the plush plum-gray rug, the swathe of filmy fabric at the windows, and the intricately worked quilt on the four-poster bed hinted at an Avery he hadn't seen.

A deeply romantic and hedonistic Avery. *An Avery he looked forward to knowing better.*

Mike set his duffle on the painted chest at the foot of the bed and eased closer to take a look at that remarkable quilt. Made from fabrics with dozens of different colors and textures, it was patched and stuffed and stitched together, unified with ribbon and lace, and bound by rippling streams of bright embroidery. It made him think of his great-aunt Esther's crazy quilts, only this was brighter, bolder, and more complex.

"You made this, didn't you?" he asked and turned to her.

Avery shifted her shoulders. "It's just what I do."

When she wasn't designing seductive packaging for perfume or clever ways to display and market cookware, Avery was cutting and stitching bits of beautiful cloth, creating something exotic enough for use in a sultan's harem or for a wizard's overcoat.

In the last ten minutes, Mike had learned more about Avery Parrish than she'd ever let him glimpse in Larkin.

"I've never seen anything like this," he said, running his hand over the soft, beguiling surface of the quilt.

Avery lowered her gaze and shrugged again.

He recognized the pride and embarrassment in the simple gesture. He'd been every bit as flustered the day they stopped at the farm and Janice had taken it upon herself to show Avery the sideboard he'd made for his mother.

"I donate the quilts to local charities," Avery mumbled. "They raffle them off."

For thousands and thousands of dollars, Mike would bet. He could hardly believe a woman who poured every bit of herself into making these marvelous works of art could turn around and give them away.

"This quilt is beautiful and extraordinary, Avery," he whispered and cupped his hand to her cheek. "Just like you."

Avery's eyes widened, and her cheeks went rosy with pleasure.

Tenderness for her grew in him, and he leaned close to kiss her.

At the very last moment, Avery stepped back. "There are hangers in the closet," she told him. "Once you've unpacked, come into the kitchen so we can talk while I fix dinner."

They ate beef stroganoff, drank wine, and, because it was snowing, nestled on the couch in front of the TV. They cuddled and kissed a little, but to Mike's immense frustration, every time things started heating up, Avery got all stiff and skittish.

He understood her reticence—they were alone here, and she didn't want anything to happen she wasn't ready for— but it didn't make sleeping that night any easier. While he shifted and squirmed on the sofa bed, he kept thinking about Avery snuggled beneath that exotic quilt just down the hall. He kept thinking about how that thick, auburny hair would be rippling across her pillows, and how her pale, coral mouth would bow in sleep. He couldn't keep from imagining climbing into bed beside her, kissing her awake, and making love to her.

By the next morning the snow had stopped and the sun was out. Since Mike had never been to Chicago, Avery had made plans to take him places she thought he'd like. They headed for the Field Museum, the Sears tower, and finally one of the galleries along Clark Street.

Mike had told Avery to make reservations for dinner at somewhere she liked, and by quarter to seven, he was dressed and ready. He'd put on his corduroy slacks, tweed sports coat, and knitted tie; it was as dressed up as he ever got.

When Avery came swishing into the living room a few minutes later, it was all Mike could do to keep from drooling on the rug.

Her dress was deep sea-green and so bare and sheer it looked like a gust off the lake could blow it away. The short ruffling skirt showed the impressive length of her legs, and she had on the sexiest shoes he'd ever seen. They were wispy things, spiky and black, with half a dozen delicate straps that fastened with rhinestone buckles.

The dinner at the little Italian bistro a few streets west of the apartment was excellent, and as they ambled home the air was cold, yet heavy with the promise of a distant spring.

"It's been a wonderful day," Avery enthused and slipped her hand through Mike's arm as they walked. "It's the most fun I've had since I moved to Chicago. What did you like best?"

Being with you, Mike almost said.

"The gallery with the woodworking show." He'd never seen wood laminated and pressurized until it was all sleek and fluid. He'd gawked at the huge richly grained bowls turned from trees that grew only in South America. His favorite pieces, though, were the classic tables and chests made whimsical and wry by having objects, gloves or keys or a book, carved to look as if they were resting on the surface instead of being part of it. Just looking at those made his fingers twitch with the need to feel his tools in his hands.

"I think you're capable of doing things every bit as fine as those," Avery encouraged him.

"Maybe," he conceded and steered her around a patch of ice. "But that kind of woodworking isn't practical. It would take years to master the techniques and longer still to find galleries to represent your work. Then you'd only get paid when something sold.

"Besides," he went on, "I like building homes and barns and offices, things that touch people's lives. And I could never leave the job I have."

"Why not?"

Mike wondered how honest he could be with her. "Well," he said, "my dad didn't leave my mother very well off."

He didn't come right out and say his father spent every dime he earned on liquor, though everyone in Larkin knew it. Until Mike started working construction, the

Montgomerys were only ever one step ahead of going hungry.

"You're making pretty extraordinary quilts," he said, turning the tables on her. "Why aren't those hanging in a gallery?"

Walking close beside her, he felt Avery shrug. "I make the quilts for me, because I like manipulating fabric and color. Maybe someday I'll design something more commercial, something I'll want to show and sell. But this is what makes me happy today."

Still, he could see how easily she'd be absorbed into the gallery scene, glittery openings and one-woman shows. That was one more thing he and Avery didn't have in common. She was the princess from University Hill; he was the son of the town drunk. She was a talented and sophisticated artist; he was a rube in a pickup truck. She'd been steeped in the social graces; Mike hadn't even known enough to tip the doorman.

But knowing they didn't belong together didn't change the way Mike felt about her.

They were nearly back to the apartment when Avery caught the toe of her shoe on a rippled patch of ice. She flailed, trying to regain her balance. Mike grabbed at her, but she pitched forward anyway, sprawling headlong on the sidewalk.

Mike immediately dropped to his knees beside her and started checking for broken bones. "Jeez, Avery, are you all right?"

"I'm fine," she wailed and swatted his hands away. "How could this happen when I was having such a wonderful time? I should never have worn these stupid shoes!"

"Why did you?" he asked, seeing that her injuries weren't all that serious.

"Have such a wonderful time?"

"Wear those shoes."

She glanced at him from beneath her lashes, changing suddenly from a lady in distress to a practiced coquette. "I wore them because I wanted you to think I looked sexy!"

"Oh, I did think that!" Mike assured her and scooped her up in his arms.

In spite of her protests, he carried her back to her apartment building, carried her right past the gaping doorman and into the elevator. He kicked the apartment door closed behind them and headed down the hall to the bathroom.

Once he'd settled her on the lid of the commode and flicked on the lights, Mike knelt to take a closer look at her bumps and bruises. His throat went a little thick when he saw her knees were badly scraped and bleeding.

"Where do you keep the first-aid supplies?"

"In the medicine cabinet," she told him, pointing.

While he rummaged for peroxide, salve, and bandages, she stripped off her shoes and ruined panty hose.

"I had lots of practice bandaging Janice when she was little," he assured her as he stanched the steady seep of blood. "She was always tripping or falling out of trees...."

He rambled on as he bathed her knees with peroxide, dabbed them with antiseptic ointment, and taped big gauze pads over Avery's scrapes.

"You okay now?" he asked when he was done.

"Much better. Thank you."

When Mike would have pushed to his feet, Avery caught his face between her hands and held him where he was. Her palms were warm against his winter-cold skin, her touch soft and beguiling. Mike couldn't have moved if he'd wanted to. Then, very slowly, she leaned forward and kissed him.

Her lips were plush on his, warm and astonishingly gentle. She tasted of tenderness, appreciation, and—ever so slightly—of garlic.

That made Mike smile.

As Avery leaned in closer, Mike curled his hands around her arms and drew her toward him. It was the least romantic situation Mike could imagine—Avery sitting on the lid of the toilet and him kneeling on the bathroom floor—yet the kisses that blossomed and deepened between them were as tender and intimate as any they'd ever shared.

He touched the seam of her lips with his tongue, and she granted him access to her mouth. He circled slowly, and she circled back. He shifted closer and she opened her legs to accommodate him.

Though he knew she hadn't meant it as an invitation, heat soared through him. A flush scoured his skin; his scalp rippled.

He reached inside her opened coat, closed his hands around her hips, and pulled her against him. She arched her back, her ribs rising, her breasts nudging the front of his Oxford shirt.

He raised one hand and cupped her breast with no more than the silky swish of fabric to bar his way. His blood began to boil as he took the fullness and weight of her breast in his big palm, memorizing the shape with the tips of his fingers. Her nipple budded at his touch.

His breathing roared like a blowtorch and his heart was thudding in his ears.

"Mike," she whispered and shifted away. "Mike?"

He swallowed a curse and forced himself to loosen his hold on her. "What is it, sweetheart?"

"This isn't a very comfortable place to be"— a flush rose in her cheeks—"doing what we're doing."

He chuckled low in his throat. "I'd noticed that."

"I thought"—he saw that flush intensify—"maybe we could move to the bedroom."

"Are you sure?" he asked, doing his best to be solicitous. "You got pretty banged up when you fell."

"I skinned my knees!" she said and laughed away his concern. "Besides, I know you'd never do anything to hurt me."

Now what had he ever done for her to have such faith in him?

"I never will, Avery," he whispered. "I promise."

As they rose, she slipped off her coat and dropped it over the edge of the bathtub. Once he'd done the same, she took his hand and led him into her bedroom. Her erotic rose-colored bedroom with its tall poster bed and magical coverlet.

The quilt came to even more exotic life once as she'd lit half a dozen candles. In the candle glow, with the scent of sage and sandalwood drifting around them, she began to undress him. She slid his tweedy sports coat down his arms, demolished the knot on his tie. The one it had taken him five minutes to get tied exactly right.

She pinched open the buttons down the front of his shirt, then leaned in to nuzzle the base of his throat. "How come you always smell so good, like fall and sawdust and outdoors?"

"Do you like that?" He'd never imagined the smell of sawdust could turn a woman on.

She was nibbling kisses down his breastbone, his heartbeat resounding against her mouth.

"I've never known anyone who smells like you do."

He caught her face in his two hands and tipped her chin so he could kiss her. As they kissed, he caught one strap of her dress with his forefinger and lifted it free of her shoulder. When he did the same with the other, her bodice drifted downward, baring her breasts, catching on the flare of her hips.

He'd never seen a woman so lush yet finely made, a woman who all but glowed in the candlelight. A woman with skin the color of cream and whose nipples rose sweet and pink, budding like fairy roses, and begging for his touch.

He took her breasts into his hands, and as he caressed her, he lowered his head and claimed her mouth. For a time they stood wound together, half-dressed and luxuriating in the slow, sweet graze of kisses. They swayed together, dancing to some low, smoky melody no one else could hear.

Their hands strayed in sinuous glides, undressing each other bit by bit. Change from his pockets spattered onto the floor. His belt followed. Her dress drifted downward, his heavy trousers and socks, a whisper of panties.

They came together flesh to flesh, hissing with the power of that first full contact, shivering in its aftermath.

Mike eased Avery backward and spread her across the coverlet. Her body was pure and pale amid the shimmering colors, an island of beauty and calm in that sea of pattern and lace.

He lay down beside her and stroked his palm down the length of her. He skimmed the flush that rose beneath the surface of her skin, traced it down the flesh of her throat to the arc of her ribs. He claimed her hipbone in the curve of his big hand and pulled her to him.

"You're so beautiful, Avery," he breathed against her mouth. "I want so much to make love to you."

He could tell that she was well beyond words, so when he saw her nod, he traced the curve of her belly and ruffled the curls at the juncture of her legs.

She moaned and opened to him. Very slowly and very gently he unfurled her secrets, fold by fold, layer by delicate layer. He touched her in ways that made her writhe, made her lift her hips against his hand. Made her surrender herself to him.

The way she stroked him in return, the way she kissed him as if she were pouring hot honey into his mouth, over his chest and belly and loins, made his own surrender inevitable.

He rolled over her, looked down into her face, and smoothed back her hair. "Avery," he whispered, needing to be sure, "are you a virgin?"

"I'm not, Mike," she whispered back, "but it's sweet of you to ask me."

He went hot with humiliation. He hadn't wanted to be sweet. He wanted to be smooth and sophisticated, like the other men she probably dated.

As if she knew what he was thinking, she lifted her head and kissed him until nothing mattered but the taste of her, the feel of her beneath him.

"Do you have a condom?" she asked him softly.

Mike nodded and reached for his pants.

When he eased over her again, he was ready. She reached for him, drew him close, drew him home. For a moment they lay fully joined, looking into each other's eyes. He recognized the surprise in hers, the mounting pleasure of having him inside her.

Mike had never made love with someone he cared for so deeply. Being with Avery seemed so right, so much where he belonged that he could barely keep from telling her how he felt. He whispered her name and pressed deep into her flesh instead.

She moved with him, rose against him, took him deeper. They lifted and swayed together, lost in a haze of sensation. They kissed, languorous and openmouthed. They stroked backs and breasts and buttocks. Slid skin on skin, their bodies tangled close.

They came even more intimately together, rising, gasping, shivering in a foretaste of pleasure. Their breathless sighs chorused as they danced nearer to the edge. They took up the age-old rhythm of hunger and fulfillment, each seeking to please the other.

Mike felt her trembling begin deep inside as the frenzy took her. He heard her cry out his name as she shivered, soaring toward the crest of her pleasure. He pulled her to him, feeling closer, more connected to her than he had ever been to anyone. With a moan low in his throat, he lost himself in her.

The crest rolled over them, drowned them in sensation, left them gasping and spent in each other's arms. They curled and melted together, whispered sleepy, sated endearments, and in the soft flickering glow drifted to sleep.

They spent all day Sunday in bed together. And before Mike left early Monday morning, he told Avery that he loved her.

※

Mike was running away.

He was running away from the bank statement and loan

papers, the truth he'd hidden from Avery. *Running from Avery herself.*

As he jolted across the railroad tracks gleaming silver in the moonlight, as he roared along the dusty, rutted roads, he was trying to outrun all the things in his life and his marriage he didn't want to deal with, didn't want to face. The loans he'd made to Ted were only part of that.

God knows, he'd been slipping his brother money for as long as he could remember: a dime for a Popsicle when their dad took them into town, five bucks here and ten bucks there once he started working regularly and was feeling flush. So when Ted came to him needing help with his mortgage, Mike reached for his checkbook.

He braked hard as the truck swept through the tunnel of old trees that led down to the farm. As he roared along the narrow road, leaves swooped and swirled across the beam of his headlights like blackened bits of char.

How did Avery think he could refuse to help his brother and still face himself in the mirror? Hadn't Mike always had work? Wasn't his house paid for and Avery's business growing? Hadn't Fee—until recently—been an almost perfect daughter?

His brother's life hadn't turned out nearly so well. Even after he'd passed the civil service exam and started working at the post office, Ted was always short of cash. He was forever scrounging to keep his truck running and his bills paid. Ted never seemed to have money for school clothes for his three girls or shingles to patch the farmhouse roof or Nancy's tuition at the community college where she was studying nursing.

When Nancy and the kids moved out six months ago,

Ted's finances had collapsed completely. And what could Mike do but bail him out?

Mike exhaled in sharp relief when he rolled past the farmhouse and saw the windows were dark. He just couldn't deal with his brother tonight.

At the top of the rise, he parked the truck beside the observatory and killed the headlights. As his eyes grew accustomed to the dark, he could pick out row upon row of ridges rising off to the south —with not so much as a pinprick of light to spoil the seeing.

They'd chosen the perfect site for Fee's observatory.

But then, how many times had he and Fiona hauled her telescope up to the top of this hill to debate the exact location? How many months had they spent laboring over their plans, turning down the corners in astronomy catalogs, arguing about how to stretch their budget so they could get the equipment they wanted?

Mike's throat thickened when he remembered how excited both he and Fee had been about the project, how close it had brought them.

They'd started excavating for the observatory on a warm spring day at the end of Fee's junior year at Larkin High, not long before he'd started lending Ted money. Avery had packed a lunch and, while he and Fee staked out the foundation, she'd crept around taking pictures to document the project.

Ted came to help with the digging. Nancy and the kids arrived at noon with another basket of food. They'd all shared a picnic on blankets in the grass, the sun beating warm on their backs and a cool breeze wafting over them.

The only photograph Fee had taken with her when she left was the one Nancy had taken of the three of them:

Avery, Fee, and Mike sitting with their arms around one another, looking like the happiest family in America.

Mike sagged back against the seat of the truck. How had he let what they had that day slip away from him? What had happened to destroy his perfect family?

To begin with, Fee left. She'd stolen away in the dead of night taking with her her parents' trust and unity and peace of mind. Her note had broken her mother's heart; the thievery and the betrayal they'd discovered later had sliced so deep that Mike didn't even want to talk about Fiona much less have contact with her.

He had expected Avery to feel the same way, or at least understand how he felt—but she hadn't understood anything. All Avery thought about was Fee; all she wanted to talk about was Fee. All she seemed to be able to do was blame herself for Fiona's leaving. She didn't have room in her life for anything but Fee—not even for him.

All Mike wanted to do was put what had happened with Fiona behind them and get on with their lives. When they lost their baby years before, he and Avery had done that—somehow.

Wearily he'd tipped his head against the headrest and closed his eyes. Dear God! How different things might have been if their son had lived. He'd have played catch with him, taught him to hit a ball and how to ride a bike. He'd have shown him how to fix things, build things, taken him fishing and camping. Instead he'd done those things with Fiona, made her both his son and his daughter. He'd poured so much of himself into her, all the things he'd learned, all the dreams he'd dreamed, all the wisdom a father had to give. And when she'd left she'd thrown everything back in his face. She'd rejected him, rejected everything he had given her.

She'd rejected both of them so coldly and completely that he wondered if Fiona had ever really loved Avery and him at all.

That he'd been shocked, disillusioned, and furious with Fee. That he hadn't shared Avery's obsession about where their daughter was and whether she was safe traveling with four guys she'd known since junior high had driven a wedge between his wife and him. It led to more and more disagreements, more uncomfortable silences. It led to sleepless nights when he and Avery had lain side by side in their big bed without speaking or touching or holding each other.

Mike shifted his gaze to Fee's observatory, sitting hunched and waiting at the lip of the hill. He ought to get out of the truck, throw back the observatory roof, and prepare the telescope. Making a few observations and some CCD images would take his mind off what he and Avery had said to each other tonight.

But he couldn't seem to move.

He just sat there in the truck rubbing the tight, hot place at the base of his breastbone and wishing he could make Avery understand about the money. He wished he could make her understand about Fiona and the farm—and himself. He wished he could admit to her that there was a whole lot more behind giving Ted money than his concern for his brother's welfare. He wished he could explain that doing that was the only way to hang on to the Montgomery land, to hang on to the observatory he and his daughter had built together.

To preserve the single place in the world where the Fiona he adored was still alive to him.

Chapter 6

✳

A very stopped at the bank to initial the last of the loan papers, and got to work late on Tuesday. They finally had the Sheepish project under control, she reflected as she parked her car out back of the Holding Company; now maybe she could breathe again.

That sense of well-being only lasted until she reached the top of the stairs and saw her employees milling around in the big, glass-fronted coffee room.

"What's going on?" she asked.

Cleo followed her into her office, her Cinnamon Sand mouth puckered and grim. "I tried to talk them out of this, but they just don't want to hear."

"It's about Sheepish, isn't it?" Avery guessed.

She and Cleo had been working night and day for two full weeks to put the Sheepish deal together. Once Avery had secured a firm commitment from Elite Cards, she'd hocked everything she and Mike owned to get the financing approved. While she'd arranged for the letter of credit they needed to do business in China, Cleo had found a company that agreed to produce Sheepish to Avery's exact specifications and negotiated the contract. They'd also signed with a shipper on the West Coast who'd take delivery of the lambs when they arrived and distribute them to the Elite stores across the Midwest.

They'd accomplished a lot in a very short time, but as Avery glanced toward the coffee room, she realized she'd overlooked one of the most important details. "I should have talked to everyone about this sooner," she mused.

"They're just being foolish," Cleo huffed.

"No, they're not. Considering how many jobs American companies have shipped offshore in the last decade, they have every right to be worried."

"But you don't mean to do that," Cleo insisted.

"Of course not, but our ladies don't know that," Avery said on a sigh. She should have known better, should have found a way to head this off. "They're running on speculation and fear. I need to explain to them what's happening and convince them their jobs are safe."

When Cleo didn't argue, Avery snatched the prototype for Sheepish from the corner of her desk and headed for the coffee room.

The hum of conversation died the instant she stepped inside. Avery paused for a moment and looked at women who, over the years, had woven themselves into a kind of second family. She'd hired Marta Petrovich as a seamstress when she was still cutting out patterns on her dining-room table. Julia Stevens, who ran the shipping department, had been a year or two ahead of Fee in school. Mary Dorn was newly widowed and had been keeping to herself since Walter died. Phyllis Nordstrom had a severely retarded child her husband Pete looked after during the day. Once she got home from the Holding Company, Pete took off for his job as one of the night janitors at the university.

How could these people—people with whom Avery had shared the joys and sorrows of all their lives—think she'd do anything to hurt them?

Clutching Sheepish tight against her midriff to keep her hands from shaking, Avery crossed to the center of the room and looked out across the rows of worried faces.

"I want to apologize to each and every one of you for not keeping you up to speed on what's gone on these last two weeks," she began. "As cute as this little guy is, it never occurred to me that he'd cause you so much concern."

"Didn't it, now?" Shirley Witkowsky snapped from over by the coffee machine.

Avery squeezed Sheepish tighter. "I should have explained to you right off what an opportunity we've been given."

"Isn't 'opportunity' just another word for, 'We put yer pink slip in with yer check'?" Nora O'Malley snorted from the front table.

"Sometimes that's true, Nora," Avery admitted. "But not this time. Not with the Holding Company. I screwed up by not telling you what was going on, but I'm going to fix that now.

"Two weeks ago Elite Cards called wanting to make Sheepish one of their special Easter promotions. In order for them to do that, I had to promise to produce and ship more than fifty thousand units of Sheepish the Lamb by Christmas."

A low mumble rippled through the room.

"You know as well as I do that we don't have the manpower—womanpower—to meet that kind of demand." Avery scanned the familiar faces and saw that the women were listening. "So when I got the call from Elite, I had to decide whether to refuse the opportunity they were offering us, or look for another way to meet their deadline.

"I'm so sorry I didn't talk to you about this then and save

everyone a lot of worry." Avery dipped her head for a moment in contrition, then raised it again. "My only excuse is that Cleo and I were so preoccupied trying to figure out how to make the Sheepish project happen, we weren't thinking about much else."

"Why did you decide to take this on?" Julia Stevens wanted to know. "The Holding Company's doing well enough as things stand, isn't it?"

"We're doing okay, Julia," Avery said with a nod. "The Holding Company makes a steady profit, but we don't have money to reinvest. You all know that besides Sheepish, we showed several other prototypes at the Toy Expo last spring. Yet in spite of the interest they generated, we haven't put them into production. One reason is because we've had orders to fill. Another is that those new toys require more expensive materials, and we haven't got the capital for start-up costs."

Avery glanced toward where Cleo was standing in the doorway, for confirmation. The woman gave a nod of her elegantly coiffed head.

"What producing Sheepish for Elite Cards will do," Avery went on, "is give us the capital to expand, to open new lines of products. I accepted Elite's offer because I think the Holding Company has room to grow."

"But once Sheepish has been produced in China, how do we know you won't fire all of us and outsource everything?" June Federson wanted to know.

Though June never said much, she was well liked and skilled in every aspect of production. Both the veterans and the newbies looked up to her. Naturally, she'd be the one to speak their gravest fear.

"You don't know that," Avery admitted solemnly. "When

it comes right down to it, all I can give you is my word that your jobs are safe."

The women in the coffee room stared at her, wanting to be convinced, reassured. And Avery owed them that. "All of you know that I founded the Holding Company as the mother of a young child," she went on, thinking of Fee. "I've done my best these last sixteen years to build a company with the needs of mothers like me in mind.

"We accommodate our schedule to the school-bus runs. We have days built in so you can stay home if your kids are sick. The school bus will stop right outside the building and drop your kids off if you need to work late. There's a playroom where you can keep an eye on them until you've finished up.

"We have a safe and pleasant working environment, and the best medical benefits we can afford to give you."

A murmur of assent ran around the room.

"I understand the pressures and problems you all face," Avery continued, squeezing Sheepish even closer. "God knows, I faced them, too. But hasn't the Holding Company done its best to accommodate working women's needs? Haven't I proved my good intentions?"

She scanned the faces of the women around her.

"I know this is a scary economic time. I know that what's happening with Sheepish makes you wonder if your jobs are safe. But considering how I've run this company and the history we have together, I don't think it's too much to ask that you trust me on this. That I've made the best decisions I can for all of us."

She stood for a moment waiting for more questions, more challenges. And when none came, she nodded.

"Well, then, thanks for listening. If you have anything

you'd like to talk to me about privately, you know I'm available in my office from seven-thirty in the morning until six at night. Now why don't you all have a second cup of coffee before you get to work."

With that, Avery turned and made her way toward the ladies' room. Once inside, she locked herself in one of the cubicles and tossed up her breakfast.

⁂

Sometimes the past just came right up and bit you on the ass. It took a good big chomp out of Fee's behind as she was climbing out of her car in front of her apartment building.

"Hey, Fee-oh-na!" someone shouted.

Fee recognized the greeting immediately, but she had to blink twice before she managed to reconcile it with the tall, rangy guy ambling toward her from across the street. For a moment all she could do was stare at him.

Had David Lowery ever *changed!*

Because they'd both been light-years ahead of the rest of the class in the sciences, Mr. Baker, their high-school chemistry teacher, had assigned them to be lab partners. The pairing should have worked, but instead David's unrequited crush on Fee had made the experience excruciating for both of them. Dave had been the class geek back then and looked the part. He'd been small for his age, worn dark-rimmed glasses, had nappy hair. The only thing that saved him from living up to the stereotype was that he never accessorized with a pocket protector.

"Dave?" Fee greeted him once she'd regained the power of speech. How could those broad shoulders and that wide grin belong to the same skinny kid who'd lit her Bunsen burner? "I thought you were at MIT."

David resettled the ball cap on his head. "I finished up the course work for my B.S. this summer and came home for a couple of months because my mom's been sick."

"I'm sorry to hear that."

"She's doing better now," he said with a shrug. "While I'm here, I'm working on a project with Dr. Buchanan."

"On string theory?" Fee asked, impressed. The project was a hot ticket with Larkin's science crowd.

"Yeah," he acknowledged with a bob of his head. "My folks are glad to have me back. But after being away for a couple of years, living at home is way too—you know—confining."

Fee could guess how it would have felt if she'd moved back into her parents' house after being on her own in L.A.—like being caught and reeled in after living in the wild.

"I heard you were out touring with Jared Hightower's rock band for a while. Guess that explains that purple hair, huh?" Dave asked and grinned again. "So how'd that go?"

"I decided I wasn't cut out to rock and roll."

He leaned an elbow on the roof of the car. "So, you came home to finish your science degree?"

"Sort of," she answered shortly. She wasn't eager for someone who'd liked and admired her before she screwed up her life to know how low she'd sunk.

"So, do you suppose we could go out for pizza sometime, and you can tell me about all that?" David suggested. He'd sprouted a certain easy confidence along with those linebackers' shoulders.

Once, Fee wouldn't have considered being seen with David in public, but a stylist somewhere had tamed his thick, tufty hair, and he'd grown into that broad, bony face.

He had a sort of smart-guy kind of cool about him, and Fee was astonished by the transformation.

But before Fee could agree to have pizza with David, Samantha started to squall.

Dave jumped like he'd been goosed, then peered into the Neon. From the expression on his face, he couldn't have been more shocked if somebody had lobbed a bomb into the backseat.

"You have a kid?" he asked in horrified incredulity.

Fee's cheeks went hot. "Seems like." There wasn't anything for her to do but open the door and liberate her daughter from her car seat.

"I suppose she's a cute kid when she's not howling," David conceded, already backing away.

"Yeah, she is."

David bobbed his head. "Well, look," he muttered. "I'd better let you go take care of your..."

"Samantha," Fee put in.

"Samantha," Dave repeated, still head-bobbing. "Hey, well, maybe I'll see you around the science building. You're still doing astronomy, right?"

Fee gave a distracted nod as she gathered up her knapsack and Samantha's diaper bag. David had escaped by the time she started up the walk to the U-shaped block of apartments.

Built of bricks the color of dried blood, the Windsor Arms was of pre–World War II vintage and had once been considered a nice place to live. But gradually the original tenants had been supplanted by hoards of university students looking for off-campus housing. Once they left, the narrow strip of garden that ran between the wings of the apartment building had gone to seed, just like the rest of the place gradually had.

But even if the pipes moaned and roaches scurried when

you opened the cupboards, the Arms was the best Fee could afford. She climbed the stairs, noticing the halls were rife with the smell of beer and cats and the SpaghettiOs someone had heated for supper.

When she reached the third floor, the light in the hall was out, and she had to fumble for her keys in twilight. She fit the right one in the lock and shouldered open the door to the apartment. It was only marginally brighter than the hall.

She carried Samantha inside, swaying as she walked and tickling her daughter's drooly chin. Samantha giggled and wiped one spitty hand down Fiona's cheek.

Fee scrubbed the wet off with her shoulder, settled Samantha in the swing Casey had lent her, and wound the crank. As Samantha swung, Fee went back to drag in her knapsack and Samantha's diaper bag. She closed the door and snapped the dead bolt. She had started locking up after she'd found some drunken frat boy passed out on her couch at three A.M.

Though it would be dark in an hour, Fee went around raising the roller shades. The apartment consisted of a living room and a bedroom, a tiny outdated bath, and a galley kitchen. Though the walls had been painted before she moved in, they were scabby with an accumulation of double-sided tape from the posters college kids had been sticking up on them for a decade. The linoleum that had been laid down over the hardwood floors was chipped and of the army-surplus variety. The couch that came with the place was so far gone in mange that the idea of upholstery-to-skin contact had made Fee itch, so she'd rummaged around in Gran's basement until she found a pink chenille bedspread to drape over it.

With a sigh, Fee leafed through her mail hoping for the check Jared had promised her. It wasn't there, but her electric bill was. So was the one from Samantha's first visit to Doctor

Isaacs, the pediatrician who'd shepherded Fee herself through strep throat, chicken pox, and all her inoculations.

She tossed the bills aside, made a bottle, and fed Samantha. After she put her daughter down for a nap in the tiny bedroom the two of them shared, Fee reheated spaghetti and made a salad from a globe of not-too-wilted lettuce Brian, the produce manager, had set aside for her. Once she got her degree and teaching credentials, Fee swore she was *never* going to eat spaghetti again.

As she ate at the card table set up at one end of the living room, she couldn't help wondering what her mom was making for supper. Was she putting together the rice and chicken casserole Fee loved so much? Was her father grilling steaks out in the yard? Fee's mouth watered at the thought. She hadn't turned vegetarian by choice; meat cost too much.

While she was eating, her cell phone chirped. She hadn't been able to afford a telephone until the week before, and when it rang it startled her. No one had the number except Casey, so Fee didn't have to wonder who it was. She pulled the phone out of her pack and took the call.

"Hi," Casey greeted her. "I'm sorry I was busy giving Derek a bath when you came to pick up Sami. How was your day?"

Casey had begun calling Samantha "Sami" and Fee wasn't sure she liked that someone else had picked her daughter's nickname.

Fee slumped over her spaghetti. "Well, hey, it was a day."

"You get back that chem exam you were so worried about?"

Casey would be able to hear the lie in her voice, so Fee told the truth. "I got a C plus," she admitted. "Maybe motherhood has made my brain go spongy."

In her other life, Fee had made straight A's without even trying.

"Did you have a chance to study?"

Fiona left her half-finished plate of spaghetti on the table and threw herself down on one end of the couch. "Samantha was running a fever the night before the test and— Well, I couldn't just give her Tylenol and let her cry..."

Casey knew how it was when your baby needed you. "You'll ace the next one."

Fee hoped so, but there were so many more demands on her now than in the days when she was blithely acing tests.

"Hey, I ran into David Lowery today," she said, not wanting to think about how her classes were going.

"Where? At the Food-4-Less? I heard he was back in town."

"Here, out front of the apartment."

"So how is he?"

"You wouldn't believe how much he's changed. He's grown about a foot and filled out in a most interesting way."

"David?"

"Yeah, that's what I thought," Fee said, smiling as she remembered how good Dave looked. "He said he was in town because his mom's been sick."

"Colon cancer is what I heard from someone at church." Casey filled in the details. "But she responded to chemo and things look good."

Fee had only ever seen Mrs. Lowery at school events, but thought the woman should be flogged for letting David wear the clothes he did to school.

"Dave asked me out for pizza."

"Really?"

"Then he kind of reneged when he saw I had a kid."

"I'm sure that's not what it was."

But Fee *was* sure. She'd tried not to acknowledge how much his reaction to Samantha had deflated her. There was a time when Dave would have forfeited his pocket calculator to talk to her outside of class.

"It kind of made me realize how far I've come. How different my life is from what either David or I thought it would be when we were in high school."

Casey's voice was gentle. "Are you sorry?"

"Yeah," Fiona admitted after a moment. "Things would be so much simpler if I'd stayed in college. I'd be applying for graduate programs now. I'd be logging time on the university telescope instead of cramming in extra classes so I can graduate with a teaching certificate."

She wouldn't be working part-time. She wouldn't be waiting for checks from Jared that never seemed to come when she needed them. She wouldn't be living in this dinky apartment with the roaches.

She wouldn't have Samantha. Fee squeezed her eyes closed against a sudden burn of tears. She loved Samantha. No matter how much she wished she hadn't gotten pregnant, once she held her daughter in her arms, Fee had been overcome by feelings of connection and love so intense she wasn't sure she could explain them to anyone.

But with those feelings came fear: that she couldn't care for her baby properly, couldn't keep Samantha safe, couldn't raise Samantha to be a more sensible and responsible individual than her mother was. Fee was torturing herself these days wondering if she was too busy with work and school to be the kind of mother Samantha needed.

"Am I crazy for trying to do this?" she asked, and hoped her voice didn't sound as frightened and small as she felt.

"Of course not." But not even the conviction in Casey's voice made Fee feel better.

"I could give up on my degree and work full-time at the grocery store." Fee had been thinking about that a lot lately. Her mother had been home when she was growing up; she hadn't dumped Fiona with a baby-sitter for ten hours a day like Fee was doing with Samantha.

"Is dropping out really what you want to do?" Trust Casey to ask the right questions. If she ever wanted to do it, she'd make a terrific counselor.

"Not really," Fee conceded. "But it's only October and I'm already exhausted trying to work and go to school and take care Samantha."

"Being exhausted is part of motherhood," Casey put in sagely.

"Yeah, I know." She knew how hard Casey worked looking after the kids and keeping house for Dan. But then, that was all Casey had ever aspired to.

Fee had wanted more than that—so much more.

"You could go to your parents and ask for their support." It wasn't the first time Casey had suggested that.

Remembering the heat in her father's glare that day at the Food-4-Less, Fee gave a snort of bitter laughter. "Like my father's going to forgive me and fork over next quarter's tuition."

Like he was going to overlook that she'd defied them and run off with Jared's band. That she'd stolen her mother's pearls, knowing how much they meant to her. And to her dad.

"I think your mother has already forgiven you," Casey prodded.

Fee knew that was true—and it made her squirm. But then, her mother didn't know everything yet. She didn't know Fee had been dumb enough to make love with Jared without using birth control. She didn't know about Samantha because Fiona had deliberately kept her baby's birth a secret. Fee wasn't sure her mother would forgive her for that. She wasn't even sure she *deserved* to be forgiven after the mistakes she'd made.

When Fee remained silent, Casey pressed on. "Have you talked to your mom since that day in the parking lot?"

"No."

"Have you told her about Samantha?"

"You know I haven't."

By keeping Samantha a secret, Fee knew she was deliberately hurting her mother, depriving her of the grandchild she'd always looked forward to having. But once Avery knew, she'd start interfering in Fee's life. Her mom would insist on helping out, and Fee would lose the adrenaline edge their estrangement gave her.

She'd gotten herself into this situation, and she had to get herself out. She needed to do that by herself or she was going to lose every last gram of her self-respect. Not that she had any to spare right now.

Fee sank lower into the couch. "If I told my mom about Samantha, she'd be knocking on my door a minute and a half later, her arms full of diapers and frilly little outfits."

"What's wrong with that?"

"She'd also feel obliged to tell my father." Fee did her best to swallow the quaver that rose in her throat. "I need to prove to him—to both of them—that I can manage on my own."

The only way to show them how responsible and mature she was, was to make a life for herself and her daughter without their help.

"You're spreading yourself pretty thin right now, Fee," Casey offered gently.

Fee ran a hand through her unruly hair. "I'm not spread nearly as thin as I would be if you weren't taking care of Samantha."

"Sami's a joy." Casey's voice went soft. "She makes me want another baby."

Fee jumped at the chance to talk about something besides her own doubts and her relations with her parents. "So are you and Dan working on that?"

Casey laughed and Fee imagined her glancing from the kitchen into where Dan would be watching TV in the living room.

"He'd like to be working on it right this minute," Casey admitted.

"Then I ought to let you get at it. Besides, I've got reading to do for child psych."

"Well, then, I'd better let you go."

Fee almost hung up before she remembered what she'd meant to ask Casey this afternoon. "Oh, speaking of child psych, can you keep Samantha until about ten tomorrow night? I get off work at eight, but I need to do research in the library for the paper that's due next week."

"Why don't you let me keep Sami for the night," Casey offered. "That way you can take all the time you need at the library."

Fee knew she shouldn't start letting Casey do that. Her daughter was her responsibility. She accepted anyway. "You're a pal, Case."

Fee disconnected and closed the phone. She left her unfinished dinner on the table and rummaged in her knapsack for her child psychology book and highlighter.

Samantha woke up yelling not ten minutes later.

Engraved pens
American postage stamps
Water purifier tablets
Low heeled shoes
Woolite packets and clothesline
Computer and adaptor
Hair dryer and adaptor
Antibacterial hand wash
Toilet paper
Book on doing business in China

Avery put a few more of the things from her list in the suitcase that lay open on Fiona's bed. She was leaving for China on Wednesday, and she could see she wasn't going to get away with packing light.

Not that she'd ever been good at that.

The manufacturer outside Beijing was starting production on Sheepish on Monday, and she needed to be there to approve the final fabric and stuffing selections. She also intended to oversee the layout of the pattern pieces so they'd waste as little fabric as possible in the cutting. She'd stay until a few thousand of the lambs came off the assembly line, to make sure she was happy with the quality and workmanship. She expected that would take the best part of two weeks.

Not that she could afford the time away. They'd be shipping out their Christmas orders while she was gone. Though she knew Cleo could oversee that, Avery always fretted until she saw the very last carton of her Christmas babies go out the door.

Like everyone in toys, Christmas was the Holding Company's make-or-break season. Because of the size of the loan Avery had taken out to finance Sheepish, strong Christmas profits were essential. Their orders had been up from last year, so that was promising. But it was impossible to predict from year to year what would sell and what wouldn't.

Of course, Avery couldn't truly let out her breath until every last one of those lambs arrived at the individual stores and Elite wrote her the last big check. But until then . . .

Her palms began to sweat.

The phone on the bedside table rang, making her jump. She snatched it up hoping—as she had been for well over a year—that she'd hear her daughter's voice on the other end of the line. It was Mike instead, checking to make sure she'd gotten all her errands run.

This had been her day to tie up loose ends: pick up engraved pens and postage stamps, small things that were popular as gifts for the people she'd work with in China, get her dry cleaning, make sure she had extra pairs of stockings, and some granola bars to put in her carry-on. She'd also arranged for her traveler's checks to be issued in yuan, and had a thousand dollars in Chinese money tucked into her purse.

"Since you got everything done," he said once she enumerated what she'd accomplished, "I thought I'd head out to the farm."

Avery sank down on the side of the bed and rubbed at her eyes. "So you won't be home for supper?"

"You need me there for something?"

I wish we could settle at least some of the problems between us before I leave, Avery almost said. She had been appalled when she went back through their bank statements and looked at the checks Mike had written to Ted. There must have been more than a dozen, each for well over a thousand dollars, and Mike hadn't once asked if she minded subsidizing his brother's lifestyle.

What had he been thinking? How could he imagine she wouldn't mind? And were there other things he wasn't telling her?

"I *can* come home," Mike offered reluctantly, "if there's something you need."

She needed to talk to him about Fiona. With Avery's close focus on the Sheepish project, she hadn't had time to track Fee down. She hated going so far away without knowing where her daughter was living or how to get in touch with her. Avery wasn't sure Mike would be any more effective at finding that out than she had been, but she wanted him to try. She could just imagine what he'd say if she asked him to do that while she was gone— and wasn't sure how she'd react if he refused.

"It's going to be really clear tonight," he cajoled, breaking into her thoughts.

Maybe it was better not to ask him. Maybe she was too frazzled and exhausted tonight to start an argument she probably couldn't win. Maybe she didn't want to traipse halfway around the world while she was in the middle of a fight with her husband.

Avery let out her breath in a long-drawn sigh. "Go enjoy your telescope," she told him.

After she hung up the phone, Avery tucked a tiny sewing kit into the side pocket of her suitcase, added another high-necked blouse to the pile, and closed the top. She didn't want Caleb inside depositing cat hair on everything.

The very last thing on her list of things to do was to plant the piece of Christmas cactus she'd been rooting these last few weeks. She picked up the cutting on her way through the kitchen and went out to her potting shed, the lean-to at the side of the garage where Mike had his woodworking shop.

She washed the cream-colored ceramic pot she'd bought the day before with soap and water and dried it carefully. She scooped a double handful of tumbled stones from a plastic container and spread a layer over the bottom.

Her grandma Ada had taught her that since Christmas cacti were succulents, they needed good drainage.

She troweled a good, thick layer of potting soil on top of the stones and carefully eased the thick knot of fibrous roots out of the vase where the broken piece of cactus had been sprouting. Settling the sprig in the center of the pot, she added more dirt. The cactus settled in immediately, standing straight and tall, its handsome links of paddle-shaped leaves draping gracefully over the edge of the pot.

Since the turn of the century, when Gill McIntire had given his new bride a Christmas cactus before he sailed off for Cuba on the *Maine,* the women in the McIntire line had been passing cuttings from Letty's plant from mother to daughter. Receiving one of Letty's Christmas cactuses from your mother, or passing one on to your daughter, was as potent a sign of approval and love as one McIntire woman could give another.

Avery wanted with all her heart to give this plant to Fiona for Christmas, to use it to rebuild the bond between them. But she wasn't sure she would even be seeing Fee over the holidays. She wasn't sure Fee would welcome a renewal of their relationship or accept the cactus as a gift, knowing what it had meant to the last four generations of McIntire women.

And yet...

Avery reached resolutely for the watering can.

Ada

*

DECEMBER 1965

I love Christmas—always have, always will. I like it especially now that my granddaughter Avery comes to visit as soon as school lets out. It gives us a few days together before the rest of Tom's and my hooligans arrive on Christmas Eve.

Avery's eight now, all teeth and eyes and knees. Helpful as she can be. And, Lord, so full of questions! I don't remember any of my children asking something new every five minutes. Not even Miriam.

"So, Grandma," Avery would ask, "where'd you learn to make so many kinds of Christmas cookies?"

"Are Christmas trees a different species, or are they pine trees that get cut before they grow too tall?"

"How did Grandma McIntire's special ornaments get here safely all the way from Germany?"

So I tell her the story.

"Your great-great-grandma Mary McIntire, brought those glass ornaments in her own little suitcase when her family emigrated from Germany. She wrapped them up in her extra pantaloons so they'd be safe all the way across the ocean."

I smile to myself remembering that stiff-jawed old woman. "She loved Christmas almost as much as I do. We used to do all our baking and decorating together."

Avery nodded, "Mama said Great-Grandma Letty was busy working at the college, so she didn't have time for household things."

That sounded like Miriam. She and Letty always loved learning, loved being out in the world, loved making something of themselves. And both of them had succeeded.

I give Avery a big special hug because I know it's not easy having a mama who's bent on making something of herself like Letty and Miriam.

"My grandma Mary, your great-grandma Letty, and I all lived in the big house over on Maple Street here in Hamilton, where I was born," I tell her. "Letty worked in the Colgate University library and Grandma Mary took in boarders, mostly students."

I can see them still, sitting around the dining-room table after supper studying, the room wreathed in smoke. Grandma Mary didn't approve of smoking, but she put up with it to keep the boarders. But I remember how she used to go around and open up the windows when they lit up their cigarettes and pipes, even in the dead of winter.

"Now that we've got the last of the cookies iced," I say, screwing the caps on the bottles of colored sugar, "we've got one last Christmas project to see to."

"What's that, Grandma?" Avery asks.

"We've got some cuttings from my Christmas cactus to pot."

"You mean, from Great-Grandma Letty's Christmas cactus?"

"Did your mother tell you about Letty's Christmas cactus?" I'm surprised by this; Miriam isn't much for passing on family lore.

"She told me," Avery explains, "when we were talking about the Cuban refugees in school. Mama said Great-Grandpa Gill got blown up on that ship in Havana harbor."

"The *Maine*, you mean."

Avery nods. "She told me about him giving Great-Grandma Letty the cactus before he left."

I start covering the kitchen table with newspaper, since it's way too cold to work outside. "Passing the Christmas cactus along in the family helps keep memories of Gill and Letty alive. Did your mother tell you that it's one of the ways the mothers in our family let our daughters know we're proud of them."

Avery looks at me wide-eyed.

I start laying out the things we'll need: the pots, good, heavy ceramic ones freshly washed; the bucket of earth I've been mixing and turning for the best part of a week; my favorite trowel; and a coffee can of broken china.

"Putting broken china in the bottom of a pot is the secret to good drainage," I tell her. Besides I figure using pieces of the china I've broken passes on another piece of myself with the plants. "Christmas cactuses are succulents and need good drainage."

While Avery is busy placing the bits of china in the pots, I take the mason jar from the windowsill. Through the greenish glass I can see that the branches I've been tending have all sprouted thick white knots of roots.

"When did you get your Christmas cactus, Grandma?" Avery asks.

I carry the mason jar back to the table. "I got my Christmas cactus the Christmas I was nineteen. Only, your great-grandma Letty didn't give it to me directly."

"Who'd you get it from?"

I smile, remembering rolling over in bed this morning and seeing my sweet Thomas's face on the pillow beside me.

"I got it from your grandfather."

Avery looks up from the colorful pattern she's laid out in the bottoms of the pots. "How come you got it from him?"

My heart takes a slow, melancholy turn. I miss my mother in this moment more than I have in a decade.

"You know I told you that giving a Christmas cactus is a way of showing a mother's approval of something her daughter has done?" Avery nods her head. "Well, with my mama, it was her way of showing me she approved of something I wanted to do."

"What did you want to do?"

"Marry the boy next door," I tell her and smile. "I fell in love with Thomas Avery the day he moved in."

"How old were you then?"

"I was six and he was eight. I wanted to see the new peo-ple who'd bought the house next door, so I went and peeked through the picket fence. Your grandpa was out in the backyard shooting crab apples with his slingshot. You know what a slingshot is, honey?"

"Like in David and Goliath?"

I nod. "Your granddad must have seen me looking through the boards because he shot right at me and pinged every single one those pickets. I was so impressed, I ap-plauded him."

And he grinned in a way that thrills me still.

"Were you always friends with Grandpa?"

"Well," I say, scooping dirt into the first of the pots, "you know how kids are. Sometimes you do everything together."

Like hunting fireflies on a summer night. Like roasting potatoes in the burning leaves. Like being on the same side in a snowball war.

"And sometimes kids are just plain mean to each other."

Avery narrows her mouth as if she knows about kids being mean. "I thought Marie Lynch was my friend," Avery confides, "and then she blew milk through her straw on me at lunch!"

"That wasn't very nice," I console her. It just goes to show you children haven't changed in half a century.

"Your Grandpa and I were friends, and then we weren't for a while," I tell her. "We were in high school when we started noticing each other again."

"Did he walk you home?"

"He did sometimes, but your grandpa's family were bricklayers like he is now. He worked with his dad and uncles most afternoons."

"Did he take you to school dances?"

Avery seems to know a good deal more about dances and flirtations than I did at her age. But then, she's grown up around college kids, and probably knows more about what goes on between boys and girls than most children.

"He took me once."

I'd worn a pink chiffon dress and shoes with filigree buckles. My Thomas showed up in a borrowed suit that hung on him like he stole it from a giant's wash line. He was embarrassed by that, and never asked me again, though I knew he wanted to.

"Did he kiss you?"

"Give me my first kiss, you mean?" I ask her.

Avery flushes and nods, though all this must seem like ancient history to her.

"Yes, he did."

It happened right after I graduated from high school. I'd been on a date with one of the rich college boys my mother kept introducing me to. She hoped I'd marry one of them and never have to worry about money the way she and Grandma McIntire always did.

I'd gone to a movie with one of them and sat up in the balcony so he could smoke. That wasn't all he'd wanted to do while we were up there, either. Every time he tried to grab me I'd slap his hands, and when he went to kiss me I excused myself to go to the ladies' room. I walked home instead.

I was just coming up the walk when my Thomas came across from his front porch. He could see that I'd been crying. "What's the matter, Ada?" he wanted to know.

Since Thomas had been my friend since I was little, I told him. I was too upset to go into the house and face my mother, so we went and sat in the garden.

"Your grandfather kissed me sitting in the arbor out back of the house on Maple Street," I say and begin troweling earth into the rest of the flowerpots.

I can feel Avery looking up at me.

"Did you like it?" she whispers.

"Kissing him, you mean?" I ask and she nods. "I liked it very much."

What I liked was how gentle Thomas was with me. I liked how he dried my tears and smoothed my hair. I liked that I could tell by the tenderness in his touch how much he cared for me. I liked it when he turned my face to his and asked before he kissed me.

"And then you married Grandpa?"

"Not right away," I answer. "Your grandpa and I took long walks every Sunday afternoon. Sometimes he'd buy me a soda or an ice cream at Hibbards downtown. He was saving his money to buy me this engagement ring, though I didn't know it at the time."

I show the ring to her. The stone is small and the setting outdated. But I wouldn't trade that ring for anything.

"So Grandpa saved his money and bought you a diamond ring, and you lived happily ever after."

"Well, it wasn't quite as simple as that," I say, gently separating the first of the cuttings, roots and all, and settling it into its pot. "Your great-grandma Letty was determined that I should marry a college man, and because I was working at the university then, too, I met a lot of them."

"But you loved Grandpa and he loved you!" Avery protests.

"The first time he asked my mother for permission to marry me, she refused him." I plant the next cutting. "The second time he asked her, she again said no."

"No!"

"Mama thought she was doing what was best for me. She thought I'd be happier with a doctor or a lawyer or a businessman."

"Did you run away to get married?" Avery asks, her eyes gone even bigger than usual.

I shake my head. "We kept walking out together, kept spending time together. I went places with the boys I met at the college and the ones Mama introduced me to, but I was in love with your grandpa, and he was in love with me."

"So what happened?" Avery demands, handing me another of the pots. She's as impatient to know the end of the story, as I was then.

"Your great-grandma Letty saw how much in love we were. She realized that I was never going to marry anyone else. So not long before Christmas in 1917, she potted a cutting just like the ones we're potting today and took it next door.

"Your grandpa says she stared at him over the top of that cactus like she was taking his measure once and for all. 'You love my Ada?' she wanted to know.

"'Yes, Mrs. McIntire,' he told her.

"'Do you want to marry her?'

"'I want to take care of her for the rest of our lives,' is all he said.

"'Did you buy her a ring?' she wanted to know.

"'Indeed I did,' he said.

"Your grandpa told me later that your great-grandma Letty sighed deep and long, like she was putting what I wanted ahead of what she'd always wanted for me.

"Then she said, 'You come over to the house on Christmas Eve. You bring that ring and you ask my Ada to marry you right there in front of all our friends and relatives.'

"Your grandpa said he was scared to do it. He never figured he'd have to ask me to marry him in front of a room full of strangers. But he agreed.

"'Then you give my Ada this Christmas cactus,' she told him, 'so she'll know it's all right with me to accept your suit.'"

"Did he do what she said?" Avery asks as she waters the four new Christmas cactuses lined up in a row.

"Indeed he did! He got down on bended knee right there in our living room on Christmas Eve. He did it in front of my mother and Grandma Mary, my uncle Henry and aunt Caroline, Mr. Franklin, Mama's special friend, and his son Fred.

"He said, 'Ada, I've known you since you were six years old and I've wanted to marry you since the day you turned sixteen. If you accept this ring and be my bride, it will make me the happiest man this side of paradise.'

"Then he brought out the Christmas cactus from where he'd been hiding it in the hall. It was in full bloom, trailing wonderful fuchsia blossoms just like these cuttings will be next year.

"I looked up at Mama and Grandma Mary before I gave him my answer. They were both crying, but I could tell they were happy tears. So I said, 'Yes' to your grandpa, and I've never been sorry a day in my life."

Avery sighs all dramatic-like, as if she's liked the story. "Will I get a Christmas cactus someday, too?"

"I expect," I say, carrying two of the plants we'd just potted into the dining room. Avery follows, carefully carrying the others. We put them on the plant stand in the window, four handsome new plants with flat green leaves and the promise of flowers.

"I'm going to give these to your aunties on Christmas Eve," I tell her.

"To show that you approve of them?" Avery asks, with the hint of a teasing smile.

"Of course I approve of them," I tell her, laughing. "I let them marry your uncles, didn't I?"

Just then I hear the rumble of a car coming up the drive, its tires crunching on the freshly fallen snow. It's my Thomas coming home to me, and my heart turns over in my chest.

"Is that Grandpa?" Avery asks.

"I'm sure it is." I tell her.

She runs for the door, as eager to kiss him hello as I am myself.

Chapter 7

Avery found the airline tickets to China on her desk when she got to the Holding Company early Monday morning. She picked up an e-mail from the manufacturer outside of Beijing confirming that a driver and a translator would meet her at the airport. She scanned a memo from Julia Stevens saying they were a day ahead of schedule in getting out their Christmas orders.

Avery let out her breath. Everything was working out; she'd be able to leave for China on Wednesday with a clear conscience.

Not more than ten minutes later, she heard Cleo come bustling up the stairs. Her high heels rapped out a staccato beat as she crossed the linoleum between the head of the stairs and Avery's office. When the older woman burst inside and closed the door behind her, Avery knew something was wrong.

Her stomach dropped into her shoes.

Cleo listened to the police scanner on her way to work. That's how Avery managed to get to the hospital ahead of the ambulance when Nora O'Malley's husband was hurt in a tractor accident. It's how everyone at the Holding Company had been able to come together and offer Marta Petrovich and her family clothes and toiletries and a place to stay when their house caught fire.

"Honey," Cleo began, crossing the room to Avery's desk.

Having Cleo call her "honey" in that particular tone of voice made Avery go cold all over. *Had Mike been hurt at the job site? Had Fiona wrecked her car?*

"What—what's the matter?" Avery managed to ask.

Cleo pulled the stool from Avery's drawing board up close and took both her hands. "Yesterday after church, my sister Vi and I went out to Liberty Lake Park for our Sunday constitutional."

Avery nodded, jumpy and impatient.

"And while we were there," Cleo went on, "we ran into Fiona."

"Was she—was she all right?"

"She was striding along in that way she has, like she's half gazelle." Cleo smiled big and broad, as if the memory pleased her. "But what purely took me by surprise"— her expression shifted; a cluster of lines gathered between her brows—"was that our Fiona was pushing a baby in a stroller."

"Was it Casey's Derek?" Avery guessed, wanting Cleo to get on with what she had to say. "It wouldn't surprise me if Fiona looked after him sometimes to give Casey and Dan a little time together."

"It wasn't Derek." Cleo shook her head. "This baby was lots younger than Casey DeCristo's boy. This was a pretty little blonde-headed girl."

"Maybe Fee's doing baby-sitting for extra money," Avery guessed, though her heartbeat had picked up speed.

Cleo pressed her full, Vibrant Vermillion lips together. "When Vi and I asked who this baby was, Fee said her name was Samantha."

"Samantha." Avery's throat tightened. "Fee always said if she ever had a little girl she'd name her..."

Roaring started in Avery's head. She looked up into Cleo's eyes. She wanted the older woman to laugh away the suspicion rising in her. She wanted Cleo to tell her the baby she'd seen in the park didn't belong to Fiona.

Cleo's wide mouth bowed with compassion. "I wanted to tell you face-to-face, Avery, honey," she said gently, "because I knew you didn't have any idea our Fiona had a child."

The very marrow of Avery's bones seemed to liquify.

Cleo clasped Avery's hands a little tighter, as if the older woman knew what she was thinking. "Fiona didn't say so, but the child we saw has to be hers. She looks just like our Fee did when she was little."

But Fee's too young to have a child of her own, Avery wanted to argue. *She's still my little girl.*

"But wouldn't I have known if Fiona had a child?" A feverish agitation ran through Avery's flesh. "Wouldn't Fee have told me?"

Maybe back before she ran away she would have come to you, Avery thought. Maybe back when she and Mike and Fee were still a family... But not now... Oh, God, not now...

"How—how could Fiona not tell me?" Avery whispered, shivering so hard to suppress the need to weep, she thought she might shatter.

Cleo reached out and wrapped Avery up in her arms. Avery leaned into the haven of the older woman's embrace—and came apart. She sobbed, trembling and openmouthed, shattered and hurt and furious. Tears scalded her cheeks.

Her daughter had turned her back on her, shut her out. Fee had betrayed the bond between them, the bond between mother and daughter that Avery had believed would last forever. Anguish ripped through her, searing along every nerve. How could the child she'd carried beneath her heart, the daughter she'd held and comforted, the little girl who'd been more precious to her than anything, shut Avery out of her life?

"How could my only child treat me as if I were a stranger?" she gasped, burrowing into the shoulder of Cleo's blouse.

"Oh, hon," Cleo crooned, holding Avery closer. "Children just don't have any idea how much they hurt us sometimes."

"Did she think I'd be ashamed of her if I found out she was pregnant?" Avery choked out. "Did she think I'd turn my back on her if I knew she'd had a child?" Outrage expanded inside her ribs, clotted hot at the base of her throat. "Why doesn't she want me to be part of this baby's life?"

For well over a year, Avery had been fighting for balance on shifting ground. She thought she understood Mike's feelings of betrayal, and shared some of his anger at the way Fee left. But she also saw that Fiona had needed to assert her independence and chase her dreams. Avery found that constantly weighing her love and loyalty to her husband and to her daughter was almost unbearably difficult. Yet she'd done it because she loved them, loved them both. But now that she knew how completely Fiona had shut her out of her life—shut her out of her new granddaughter's life—

Avery wondered if the struggle had been worth what it had cost her.

In the year and a half since Fiona left, Avery had lost her happy home; the warm, messy intimacy of family life; her daughter's trust; and her easy and tender relationship with Mike. Finally admitting that made Avery cry harder.

As she wept, Cleo offered the solace of those soft, broad hands patting her, of that low, rich voice murmuring that everything would be all right. Avery didn't believe that, but in time the spate of tears ran their course.

"Lord knows," Cleo murmured, still holding and patting, "how Fiona kept all this quiet—especially here in Larkin."

"Maybe *I* was the only one who didn't know she'd had a baby," Avery said on a sniff.

"It surprised the life out of Vi and me."

And Avery thought Cleo knew *everything* that went on in town.

Finally she straightened, swallowed hard, and scrubbed the tears from her cheeks. Cleo offered a linen handkerchief embroidered with daisies, and so starched it crinkled.

"I can't blow my nose on *that*!" Avery snuffled and fumbled for the box of tissues on the corner of her desk. She wiped her eyes, blew her nose, then smoothed back her hair.

"So why wouldn't Fee tell me she was pregnant?" she asked, doing her best to be rational.

"Maybe she thought you'd be disappointed in her," Cleo suggested.

"Well, I wouldn't have encouraged her to have a baby at twenty," Avery declared and wiped her eyes again. "But Fee ought to have known I'd stand by her."

Avery knew Mike was going to be even more shocked and disillusioned than she had been when he heard about the baby, and she hated having to be the one to tell him. He'd put it down as another black mark on the tally he'd been keeping against Fiona ever since she left.

"Do you think Fee would have wanted you to step in and look after her?" Cleo asked, breaking into Avery's thoughts.

Avery considered the question. Fee had always been independent and headstrong. From the time she drew breath, Fee had done things her own way. Everything from eating left-handed and throwing with her right, to hugging Avery good-bye the first day of kindergarten and whispering in her ear, "It's all right, Mama. I'm going to like school." She'd insisted on studying oboe in spite of the talent she'd shown for the piano, decked herself in outlandish outfits no one else could wear, and petitioned Larkin High to teach a class in Latin because she thought it would be useful for students going into the sciences.

"Do you think Fee kept her pregnancy from me because she was determined to handle it herself?" Avery wondered aloud.

"She's proud, our Fiona."

"Stubborn, too," Avery admitted on a sigh.

"I don't think Fee knew *how* to tell you about Samantha," Cleo offered quietly.

"Maybe not."

"I don't think she wanted to admit to you—and to Mike—that when she took off with the band she made a mistake."

Fee was never more stubborn, never more determined to fix things on her own, than when she realized she'd done something wrong.

Avery nodded in agreement and scrubbed at her face with her hands again. She supposed now that she'd found out about Samantha she'd have to confront her daughter. The very idea sapped her strength. But if she wanted a relationship with Fee, if she wanted the chance to hold her grandchild in her arms, if she wanted to be a part of that baby's life, Avery was going to have to be the one to force the issue.

"I guess I need to see Fiona and talk to her," Avery said with as much resolve as she could muster. "Could you call Shoshona and see if she's willing to do us one more favor? I need to know when and where Fee's next class is meeting so I can be there when she gets out."

While Cleo went to talk to her niece, Avery paced to the window that overlooked Main Street. Seeing Fiona came first. Explaining what she'd discovered to Mike would come later. She wanted to believe that telling him about Samantha would bring about a change of heart, but she didn't think that's how he'd take the news that he'd become a grandfather. She was so tired of being at odds with him about Fee and, rather than making relations between them better, this was going to make them infinitely worse.

With a long sigh, she turned, put her laptop and the files on Sheepish into her briefcase then tucked her plane tickets and boarding passes into her purse.

Avery had less than forty-eight hours to try to straighten things out with Fee before she left for China—and then she'd have to deal with Mike.

❋

Avery paced outside the chemistry lab in the Wexler Science Building, catching glimpses of Fiona each time she passed the door. Inside, her daughter was weighing and measuring some kind of residue she'd collected and taking notes. In the safety goggles and an oversized lab apron, she looked skinny and intense—and far younger than her twenty-one years.

Avery's stomach churned just watching her.

How could this person who seemed—at least to her mother—to still wear the sharp, pure features of the child she loved, have a baby of her own? *And what in the world was Avery going to say to Fee about it once this lab let out?*

"Mrs. Montgomery?" The woman who addressed her had paused at the head of the intersecting hall. "You *are* Fiona Montgomery's mother, aren't you?"

Avery looked long and hard at the woman in the lab coat. She seemed familiar, but Avery couldn't quite place her.

"I'm Dr. Margaret Gunderson," the woman said with a smile. "I'm Fiona's academic advisor."

Avery wasn't surprised she hadn't remembered; she'd only met the woman twice.

"I'd like to have a word with you about Fiona," Dr. Gunderson went on, "if you don't mind."

Avery didn't want to be distracted, but she wasn't going to miss out on anything this woman might have to say about Fiona, either. "All right."

Dr. Gunderson drew her a step or two away from the laboratory door, before she continued. "I know Fiona's of an age where she's making her own decisions and, as a parent, you might not have much say about what she's doing with her life."

None at all.

"What I wondered, though," Dr. Gunderson continued,

"was if you could have a word with her about returning to her original major."

" 'Her original major'?" Avery echoed, not willing to admit how ignorant she was about the life her daughter was living these days.

"Astronomy," Dr. Gunderson prompted, as if reminding her.

Fiona had changed her major from astronomy? Avery stared, speechless.

"It's been years," Dr. Gunderson went on, raking a hand through the fashionable drape of her ice-gray hair, "since anyone here at Larkin has seen a student so clearly meant to have a career in astronomy. It didn't take me long to spot Fiona's natural aptitude, Mrs. Montgomery, when I had her in intro to astronomy freshman year. She has a gift."

Small wonder, Avery thought. Her daughter had probably logged more hours at a telescope than some of her professors—thanks to Mike. Thanks to the telescopes he'd bought for her, thanks to the star parties they'd gone to together. If Fee had a gift, it was because she'd spent hours at the observatory she and Mike had planned and built together.

"Everyone in the department agrees it's a shame to waste all that ability and passion on something she might be far less suited to doing. But as you no doubt know..."

Avery felt the heat rise in her cheeks. She quite obviously didn't know *a thing* about her daughter's life these days.

" ...when Fiona came back to the university this fall she changed her major to"—Dr. Gunderson sniffed—"secondary education."

"To education," Avery mumbled, trying not to sound surprised.

"It's practically criminal for someone with Fiona's potential to waste her talent teaching general science to gaggles of hormone-crazed high schoolers."

Dr. Gunderson made it sound tantamount to skydiving without a parachute.

"A good teacher is never wasted," Avery observed sagely, still struggling to process the news that Fee had changed her major. Fiona had been obsessed with becoming an astronomer ever since the first star party she and Mike had attended.

"All of us here in the science department know that Fiona has a child to raise," Dr. Gunderson continued, "and because she does, aspiring to the advanced degrees she'd need to move up in astronomy must seem daunting."

Avery's face went hotter. This woman, this *stranger,* knew more about Fiona's child than she did. How could Dr. Gunderson be so aware of Fee's baby when Fee hadn't so much as *mentioned* Samantha to her grandmother?

"There are programs, grants Fiona could apply for," Dr. Gunderson went on, "that would give her a stipend to live on while she works toward her doctorate. Or there are internships and teaching assistant positions I'd be happy to recommend her for that pay a salary."

Dr. Gunderson stepped closer; Avery could feel the conviction in her.

"Bright, gifted young women like Fiona," she went on, "are the future of science, of astronomy. We can't afford to lose her both for the sake of the discipline, and because her abilities could advance the cause of women in all realms of science."

Avery did her best to listen to what Dr. Gunderson was saying, but outrage was circulating fast and feverish through her veins. How could Fiona have drawn so far away from the people who loved her? How could she have changed the course of her life without even letting her parents know?

"What I'm hoping you'll do, Mrs. Montgomery," Dr. Gunderson pressed ahead, "is talk to Fiona about the choice she's made. And if you and Mr. Montgomery are in a position to do it, perhaps you could offer her a bit of financial support..."

Avery fought down the urge to tell Dr. Gunderson that she'd be more than happy to chat with her daughter about the folly of changing her major and to offer her money to live on.

She'd do it right after she dressed Fee down for keeping Samantha a secret. Right after she got Fee's address and phone number so she wouldn't have to hang around the science building to have a word with her daughter. *Right after she saw and held her first grandchild.*

Avery gritted her teeth and nodded. "That's exactly what I'll do, Dr. Gunderson," she managed to answer before she said something she might regret. "I'll have a chat with Fiona about her major first chance I get. Thank you for your concern."

Avery had barely gotten her breathing back under control when the bell rang for the end of the hour. The lab door burst open, and Fee's classmates rumbled out.

Fee lagged behind like she always seemed to these days, finishing her notes and putting things away. She traded a few words with the teaching assistant as she headed toward the door—then stopped in her tracks when she saw her mother.

"We've got to stop meeting like this," Avery said without a trace of humor.

Fee must have sensed the moment of reckoning had come and didn't resist when Avery led her down the hall to a bench in front of a bank of windows.

"So Cleo told you about Samantha," Fee said, perceptive as always.

"My question is why *you* didn't see fit to tell me," Avery kept her voice low and reasonable with an effort. "Didn't you think I'd be interested in knowing you were pregnant? Didn't it occur to you that I might want to know that my first grandchild had been born?"

Fee flinched at the rebuke, but she didn't make any attempt to get up from the bench and leave. Maybe she knew Avery wasn't going to tolerate that, wasn't going to let her get away before she got what she'd come for.

Instead Fee shrugged with a negligence that made Avery want to shake her. "I wasn't sure how you'd feel about that news."

"You knew exactly how I'd feel," she snapped. "And you were afraid to face me."

"I wanted to take care of this on my own."

You wouldn't be back in Larkin if you'd been able to do that, Avery wanted to say.

Yet how like Fee it was to refuse to ask for help unless her back was against the wall. Fiona had gone to her grandmother only because she was having trouble with the people in financial aid and knew Miriam would handle them. Somehow figuring that out made Avery breathe a little easier.

"So is Jared Samantha's father?" she asked instead.

"Yes."

"And did Jared help out while you were 'taking care of this on your own?'"

Fee colored up. "Jared stuck by me all through pregnancy and delivery," her daughter snapped, defending the boy she'd been dating since junior high. "And he took a regular job to pay off the hospital bills."

Because rock bands didn't carry medical insurance.

"And when was Samantha born?"

"In May, the twelfth."

"Five months," Avery murmured, her voice tattered with regret.

Five months of Samantha's life had passed before Avery even knew she existed. She'd missed five months of bottles and gurgles and burping. Of waving fists and toothless smiles. Of the soft, mewing sighs babies gave when they were sleeping.

To Avery, Fee's first five months had been so very, very precious. She'd spent hours and hours rocking and holding and feeding her. She'd cherished the way Fee's small, warm body would nestle in the crook of her shoulder as she slept. She'd breathed the smell of her hair and skin. It had been a special time, a time Avery had used to discover what kind of mother she wanted to be.

Losing those five months was one of the things Avery regretted most when their second baby died, and now she'd missed that time with Samantha, too. Regret twisted inside her, stealing her breath.

"Did—did you take care of yourself when you were pregnant?" she asked, shifting her questions to safer ground. "Did things go okay when Samantha was born?"

Avery made sure she ate right, exercised, and taken

Lamaze classes a second time—and they'd lost little Jonathan anyway.

"Everything went fine," Fee answered shortly. "Jared was with me in the delivery room."

"I'm glad you weren't alone," Avery said and silently blessed Jared Hightower for standing by her Fiona. "How did things go after the baby was born?"

"We got by," Fee answered with a dismissive toss of her head. "I stayed home after I had Samantha, instead of going to gigs with the band. But when the guys had been out playing half the night, they didn't much appreciate having a baby start yelling at dawn."

Avery heard the bitterness and disillusionment creep into Fiona's voice. The future she'd risked so much for hadn't turned out at all the way she thought it would.

"Is that why you decided to come back to Larkin?" Avery asked quietly.

"There wasn't any future for me in L.A."

And she had Samantha to think about.

Fiona didn't say that outright, but Avery knew that's what she meant. Even through the morass of her own emotions, she felt a sharp tang of pride that, when it counted, her daughter had put Samantha first.

"Look, Mom," Fee's jaw hardened. "I've set things up here so I can be independent. I don't need you to look out for me, or worry about how Samantha and I are getting along."

"I heard you changed your major to education."

Surprise flickered across Fee's face, but she didn't ask how Avery knew. "It was the right thing to do."

There wasn't a hint of regret in Fiona's voice, but Avery

could see that her daughter's dreams of becoming an astronomer still lingered at the backs of her eyes.

It *had* been the sensible thing for Fiona to do, Avery acknowledged. A teaching job would give Fee a stable income, teachers' hours, and summers off. Hard as it must have been for her, Fee had made the prudent choice—at no small cost to herself.

But then, pretty much every mother made that kind of choice at one time or another.

"Look, Fee," Avery said, getting to the heart of the matter. "Why don't you just let me help you—"

"No!" Fee jumped to her feet and stood glaring down at her. "I've got to do this on my own."

With the light from the windows falling full on Fee's face, Avery realized suddenly how sharp and delicately drawn the line of her jaw had become, how pale and worn out she looked.

"Please, Fee," she began, trying to sound reasonable. "I only want what's best for you and Samantha. Let me write you a check. It's not like you have anything to prove—"

"Look, I really screwed up this time." Fiona admitted, her mouth narrowed with obstinacy. "So of course I have things to prove—to you and Dad especially. But also to myself. I'm never going to prove any of them if I let you give me money."

As if she thought that settled things, Fee bent and grabbed up her backpack. "Now, if you'll excuse me, Mother," she said. "I have another class to get to."

Avery jumped up from the bench, caught the pack's dangling strap, and pulled Fee to a halt. "You're not moving another step, Fiona Montgomery, until I know where you're living and how to get in touch with you. I'm going to China day after tomorrow, and I—"

"'China'?" Fee echoed.

"For something at work," Avery said, refusing to get side-tracked. "I'll be gone about three weeks, and I want to know that if I take it into my head to check on you and that baby while I'm gone, I can do it.

"What's more, when I get back, I want to meet my granddaughter. I want to be a part of Samantha's life, Fee. That's nonnegotiable."

Fee seemed to know her mother meant what she said. She tore a page out of one of her notebooks and wrote down her address and phone number.

"You live at the Windsor Arms?" Avery asked incredulously. For all the building's faded glory, the place was an undergraduate ghetto with dingy halls and probably roaches in the cupboards.

"I keep my phone turned off most of the day," Fee explained, "because I'm in classes or at work. But you can always leave a voice mail."

Both of them heard the clock in the university's bell tower chime, signaling the start of the next hour's classes.

Fee stirred restively, then asked. "So are you going to tell Dad about Samantha?"

"Don't you think he has a right to know he has a grand-child?"

Fiona snorted in derision. "As if he'll care."

Oh, Mike would care. He might not admit it, but he'd be every bit as shocked and devastated as Avery had been when she found out about the baby. What she didn't know was what he'd say, how he'd react to the news that he'd become a grandfather.

"You leave your father to me," Avery said with far more confidence than she felt.

"Yeah, I'll be glad to let you do that, Mom," Fee said on a sigh. For just a moment it felt like old times. Then Fee adjusted the strap of the knapsack and turned to go.

"If Samantha is half as beautiful as you were when you were a baby, Fiona," Avery called after her, "she's really something."

Fee looked back over her shoulder and shot Avery a grin that made her heart turn over.

"Oh, Samantha's something all right, Mom. She's really something special."

※

Avery skidded her Forester to a stop in front of her mother's house and snapped off the ignition. Once she'd spoken to Fiona, Avery was able to look beyond their confrontation to the other people who must know about Samantha. Casey DeCristo knew and, though Avery wished she'd been more forthcoming the times they'd talked, she understood why Casey had kept Fee's secret. People at the college must know about the baby, too: Ms. Gunderson and the other professors in the science department, the clerks at the registrar's office, in enrollment and financial aid.

And, of course, her mother.

Avery jumped out of the car and marched up the walk to Miriam's front door, her blood sizzling in her veins. She'd come to her mother's house intending to demand answers.

Avery's hands were shaking as she jabbed the doorbell.

Just exactly how long had Miriam known about Samantha? And why in God's name hadn't her mother seen fit to tell Avery about Fee having a child?

Frustrated and impatient, she punched the doorbell even harder. From inside she could hear the cool, staid notes of the Westminster chimes tumbling over and over each other.

Miriam jerked open the heavy, arched door as if she were ready to give someone a piece of her mind. Her eyes widened when she saw Avery standing on the stoop. "Whatever are doing here at this time of day?"

"May I come in?"

"Well"— Miriam glanced hastily over her shoulder— "you've caught me at a rather inconvenient moment."

"I can see I didn't get you out of the bath," Avery said, not about to be deterred. "Are you in the middle of an assignation?"

Miriam actually blushed. "Good heavens, no!"

"Well, I'm sorry to insist, but I have something I need to discuss."

Accuse you of.

Berate you for.

Miriam peered nervously down the hall and finally swung open the door. Avery stepped into the entry, slung her jacket and purse over the newel post, and trailed her mother into the kitchen. The water in the kettle must already have been hot, because it only took a moment for it to come to a boil. Once it had, Miriam got down her sturdy brown teapot and a pair of mismatched cups.

Never anything fancy for *her*, Avery thought, the observation firming her resolve.

But as she watched her mother lay out the tea tray, she noticed how gnarled Miriam's fingers suddenly seemed, and that her hands trembled ever so slightly as she filled the strainer with tea. Her mother might be just as sharp and caustic as she'd always been, but she was getting old.

A cold seam of dread opened somewhere inside of Avery.

Once she'd wet the tea and laid out a few crumbly short-bread cookies, Miriam took up the tray and lead Avery back down the hallway to her study at the front of the house.

"It's so cozy in here with the fire going," she offered by way of explanation. "I thought we'd have our tea in here."

The Indian Summer heat had long since broken, and the air had taken on that blue, sharp-edged crispness that made a person appreciate a fire. Avery settled into what had always been her father's chair. Tall and wingback, it was nearly as comforting as his embrace, and she fancied she could still smell his pipe smoke in the upholstery. Being so near him calmed her, but only a little.

She accepted the cup of tea her mother offered her, sipped it and set it aside.

"So, Mother," she began, "did you know Fiona had a baby while she was in California?"

Miriam's cup rattled in its saucer; she looked up, non-plussed.

It was all the confirmation Avery needed. "You *do* know all about Samantha, don't you?"

Miriam retreated into the depths of her overstuffed chair, fingering her pearls. "Of course, I know."

Though it was the answer Avery had been expecting, a tarry ooze of disillusionment settled at the base of her belly. *How could my own mother have kept this from me?*

"One of the forms Fee asked me to help her fill out," Miriam admitted now that she'd been caught, "was for a grant that provides financial assistance so single mothers can finish their degrees."

"And you knew when I came to talk to you about why Fiona had come back to Larkin that she'd had a child."

"Yes."

"Yet you didn't say a word to me."

"Fiona swore me to secrecy."

Avery sucked in a breath that burned all the way to her diaphragm. "Didn't you have any compunctions about keeping that secret from your own daughter? Surely you know how precious Fiona is to me—especially after we lost our little Jonathan. Didn't you realize that Fee's baby would be every bit as precious as she is?"

Her mother lifted her chin, a gesture Avery immediately recognized; Miriam wasn't backing down. "I thought it best to keep Fee's secret so she'd have *someone* in the family to turn to if she needed help."

Even when her mother was in the wrong, Miriam always managed to find a way to make what she'd done seem right and virtuous. To make herself sound both unfairly accused, and unaccountably aggrieved at having her motives questioned.

"If I'd known Fee was back in Larkin," Avery shouted, "don't you think I'd have given her all the help she'd need?"

Miriam lifted her eyebrows in the kind of unspoken rebuke that had terrorized Avery all through childhood. *We Parrishes never raise our voices in anger,* that gesture said.

"Fiona didn't want your help," her mother continued with a sniff. "I tried to convince her to call you, but she absolutely refused. And I can hardly blame her. Her *father* is never going to forgive her for leaving the way she did."

Avery had been married to Mike for twenty-three

years—twenty-three years in which Mike had proved himself a fine husband and exemplary father, but Miriam's disdain for him had never wavered. She couldn't forgive Mike for being a townie, blue collar, and the son of the man who had played his role as Larkin's town drunk with consummate skill. Nor would she ever forgive Avery for choosing a husband Miriam believed was unworthy of her, one who *worked with his hands.*

To accept Mike would mean acknowledging Miriam's own humble beginnings and destroying the illusion she'd spent years creating: that she'd been born into Jonathan Parrish's world instead of having to work long and single-mindedly to earn her place.

Still, Avery had too much yet to say about Fiona to let her mother divert her by attacking Mike. "No matter what your intentions were, Mother"—Avery did nothing to hide the outrage in her voice—"you should have told me the truth about Fee and Samantha. I *am* your daughter."

"And Fiona is my only grandchild," Miriam countered stubbornly.

They glared at each other for a moment, then Miriam turned and reached for her teacup. "So how did you find out about Samantha? Did Mike tell you?"

"'Mike'?"

The tea Avery had drunk backed up in her throat. Was her mother saying that Mike had known about Samantha, too? But, no...She loved Mike; she trusted Mike. Mike would have told her about Samantha if he'd known.

Yet, hadn't Mike admitted that he'd seen Fiona on campus a full three weeks before they ran into her at the Food-4-Less? And hadn't he been giving Ted money without consulting her?

No, Mike wouldn't have kept *this* from her. *Would he?* Suspicion bubbled hot in her chest.

The night they'd been working on the loan applications, the night he'd told her how much money he'd given Ted to save the farm, she'd asked him outright if he was keeping anything else from her. And he'd said...

From the corner of her eye Avery caught her mother's faint, almost furtive movement. It was an attentive stiffening, a tilt of her head as if she was listening—

Then Avery heard it too.

A baby crying.

"Must be next door," Miriam mumbled hastily.

But the crying wasn't next door. It was here, right in this house—and Avery knew immediately whose child it had to be.

She pushed to her feet and hurried out into the hall. She followed the sound and found Samantha squalling and kicking her feet in a playpen set up in Miriam's living room.

Avery paused at the sight of the baby, and for an instant all she could do was stare down at her. Then she bent, took her first grandchild into her hands, lifted the little girl against her shoulder, and clasped the soft, sweet weight of her close against her heart.

"Oh, Samantha," she whispered.

With tears in her eyes she nuzzled the child, breathing in that familiar sleepy warmth, the sweetness of milk and baby powder and No More Tears shampoo. Avery breathed deep, the closeness and contact settling both of them.

Here in her arms was her Fiona's little girl. Her daughter's daughter. A miracle of innocence and perfection. *Her very first grandchild.*

Avery looked down into Samantha's round, pink face

and laughed as her tears spilled over. She had Fee's beautiful mouth, all pouty and full at the bow, and her same frank, inquisitive regard for the world around her. In this case, her grandmother.

The baby's pale fluff of hair was the exact same color Jared's had been when he was little, and her hands were Miriam's, long-fingered and capable.

She laughed down at her granddaughter again, and this time, Samantha smiled back. As she did, Mike's single misplaced dimple crept into her cheek. Seeing it froze Avery's breath in her throat, made her heart twist hard with regret inside of her.

Would Mike ever even see this baby? Would he ever know that Samantha had his dimple in one chubby cheek? Would he ever get to see that Samantha had his smile, Avery's eyes, and Myra Montgomery's delicately arching eyebrows?

Or did Mike know already?

Avery pushed that thought away and allowed herself to be engulfed by a love that was primal and soul-deep. Though she sensed what lay ahead, for now she was content to hold and cuddle Samantha.

Wordlessly Miriam came, brought a bottle for the baby, and left again. In the silence of her mother's house, Avery fed her granddaughter. She burped her, changed her, and sang to her until she slept. She stared down into that new and yet familiar face as the clock on the mantel ticked and the afternoon sun crept across the living room.

But as she held Samantha close in her arms, her thoughts returned to Fiona's secrets and Miriam's betrayal. How could they have denied her contact with this precious little girl? How could they have thought she wouldn't love this child on sight?

Yet in spite of her anger, the tight, hard ache beneath her breastbone, Avery knew she was going to forgive them for what they'd done.

It was Mike—if he'd really kept this secret from her— who'd be impossible to forgive.

Tears swelled in her throat and burned beneath her downcast lashes. Mike was the only man besides her father that Avery had loved and trusted completely. How would she ever look at him again, ever lie with him again if she found he'd betrayed her in such a devastating and intimate way?

But then, Mike had changed when Fiona left. He'd refused to talk about their only living child, refused to sanction any contact between her and their daughter. He'd withdrawn from Avery bit by bit, become distant, secretive. He'd lent money to Ted without telling her. He deliberately hadn't let her know that Fiona had come back to Larkin.

And now this.

Avery had to confront Mike and find out if he'd kept this last and most monumental secret. The very idea of facing him with such damning accusations made fresh tears rise in her eyes. The very idea that Mike would lie to her—or worse, not tell her the truth—frightened her beyond all bearing.

But for the few hours between now and when she had to face her husband, Avery meant to lose herself in the pleasure of watching her granddaughter. She meant to hold this beautiful child, feed her, change her, and adore her.

And later, Avery thought. Well, later would have to take care of itself.

Chapter 8

✳

Avery stayed and cuddled Samantha until Fee was due to arrive, then turned the baby over to her mother. She had just pulled away from the curb when she saw Fiona's purple Neon round the far corner. She'd said everything she had to say to both Fiona and Miriam, so she kept on going.

Only confronting Mike remained.

The idea of facing him with this secret, this accusation, made her throat ache and her eyes swim with tears. She'd lived with Mike for twenty-three years and never once questioned his intentions. She'd slept curled against him every night and shared soft, sleepy kisses every morning. She'd made his bed, made his doctor and dentist appointments, made his breakfast and dinner. She'd made love with him more times than she could remember and lain safe in his arms afterward. *Or at least Avery had always thought she was safe.*

She'd trusted Mike Montgomery with her life, with her daughter's life, with her hope, with her grief, and every dream she'd ever had. Had she been wrong to have had such faith in him?

How could he have known about Samantha and kept it from her?

She pulled into her own driveway and sat waiting for an answer. When there wasn't one, Avery went inside and started to clean. While she was waiting for Mike to come home from a meeting at the Carpenters Local, she scrubbed and Lysoled both bathrooms, dusted every stick of furniture upstairs and down. She vacuumed every rug and mopped every floor. She stewed and cursed and got her crying out of the way.

When she heard Mike pull into the driveway a little after nine, Avery was waiting. From her perch on the windov seat in the dining room, she watched as he parked the truc and came into the house. He called her name. When s didn't answer, she heard him shuffle through the mail p on the counter. He washed his hands at the sink, took a from the refrigerator, and popped the top. He padded past where she was sitting.

She rose without a sound, deliberately stepping doorway, cutting off his escape.

Mike must have sensed the movement, be turned to her. "Hi," he said, tilting a smile in her "How come you're sitting here in the dark?"

She stood there smoldering, her chest on breathing ragged. Mike was completely oblivi

"So," she accused, "when were you going t Samantha?"

Mike blinked at her. "Who?"

"Cleo saw Fee in the park with her."

"Saw Fee in the park with who?"

Avery never suspected her husband v ing liar.

"You know who," she prompted him. "Samantha. Fiona's baby."

He hesitated and glanced away. "Fiona's baby."

That he said those two words without a hint of surprise confirmed every one of her suspicions. Her heart squeezed hard inside her.

Though part of her still wanted to believe that Mike, her Mike, couldn't have kept this from her, here was proof. *He couldn't even look at her.*

Avery shivered at the depth of his betrayal. "How could you do this?" she demanded and heard how her voice was shaking. "How could you know about Fiona's baby and never say a word? How could you know that we had a grandchild and keep that from me?"

Mike stood staring, his expression gone truculent, stony.

"Didn't you think I'd find out about our granddaughter?" She stepped toward him, furious and determined that he answer her. "I discovered that Fee was back in Larkin, didn't I? I found out about the money you were giving Ted."

Even in the dimness she saw his face darken with an acknowledging flush. "I'm the one who told you about the money."

"But you put that off until you had no choice. You didn't admit you knew that Fiona was back in Larkin until we saw her at the grocery store. Now you've done your best to keep me from knowing my own grandchild!"

He settled back on his heels, gathering himself, shoring his own anger.

"Yeah, Avery, sure." he admitted, his voice rife with sarcasm. "I own up to all of it. I drove Fiona away. I refused to you when she came back. I squandered our money saving my brother's ass. And just for spite, I thought I'd keep you from knowing your grandchild."

"Damn you, Mike!" she hissed at him. "I used to believe I could trust you. What happened? When did all that change?"

"You don't listen, Avery," he shouted at her, "and you don't believe me when I tell you the truth. Sometimes I wonder why I try to talk to you at all. All you ever want to discuss is Fiona. You don't give a damn about me, what I'm doing from one day to the next, or what I think about besides our daughter."

A flush flared in Avery's cheeks. "And you can't forgive her because she defied you. You're disappointed in her because she dropped out of school. You're furious at her because she decided there was more to life than studying astronomy."

"God damn it, Avery!" He stepped toward her, his eyes narrowed and his scowl fierce. "I'm furious with her because she took your necklace. Don't you wonder what kind of kid we raised that Fee can lie to us and steal from us and throw everything we ever tried to give her back in our faces? Hell, yes, I'm disappointed in her; she ran off as if you and I didn't matter. She betrayed every bit of the trust we put in her. She tore this family apart. Don't I have a right to be angry with her?"

"Isn't it your fault that our family has been torn apart?" she blazed at him. "Aren't you the one who refused to let me keep in touch with her?"

"But you did keep in touch with her anyway behind my back, didn't you, Avery? And you've talked to her more than once since she's been back in Larkin, even though you knew I didn't want you to."

Avery lifted her chin in defiance. "Having a little conversation with my daughter is hardly as heinous as refusing to tell me about my grandchild!"

A kind of change came over him. He straightened from the base of his spine; his features hardened. "You think what I've done is 'heinous,' huh?" he asked her. "Well, maybe before you decide to add 'intolerable,' 'uncaring,' and 'loathsome' to that list, I'd just better go."

"Don't you dare walk out on me, Mike Montgomery!" Avery warned him. "Not when we have something so important to discuss."

"I'm through 'discussing,' Avery. I don't have another word to say about Fiona." He strode right at her, forcing her backward.

Avery grabbed both sides of the doorjamb, refusing to let him pass.

"Get out of my way," he ordered, then caught her around the waist and lifted her out of his way.

The moment Avery regained her feet she scrambled after him. She followed him across the kitchen and out of the house. She stood in the driveway shouting at him as he gunned the truck's engine and roared right past her.

He tore up the street, his tires squealing as he shifted gears.

Avery stood staring after him. Then, with a sob, she ran back into the house and cried until her tears were gone.

※

Avery knew where Mike was, and she didn't think twice about dialing the number. She could hear the phone ringing in the dawn, imagined someone stirring, stumbling half asleep through those gray, silent rooms, fumbling the receiver off the phone on the wall. A rotary phone, long outdated and sticky with grease, it's cord curling and knotting around itself.

"Hello?"

Mike's voice was as ragged as Avery felt. She hesitated, imagining him standing in the farmhouse kitchen in nothing but his jeans, his shoulders hunched against the chill.

"We need to talk," she said.

She sat on the side of the bed and did her best to endure the silence that followed. She hadn't slept; the adrenaline buzz of anger had given way to a terrible restlessness and endless recriminations.

She wondered if his night had been any better than hers. She wondered how he would answer her.

"Yeah, all right," he finally agreed.

She knew better than to ask him to come to the house. After the things they'd said to each other last night, they needed to meet on neutral ground.

"At the Sunny Spot?" she suggested.

She could almost see his mouth narrow the way it did when someone pushed him. She could almost see the crease tighten between his eyes, the way he'd cup the phone a little closer to his mouth before he spoke. How well she knew this man, the man she'd lived with almost half her life—and how much of a mystery he was to her still.

"Seven-thirty," he countered on a sigh. "I have a meeting with one of the other subcontractors at eight-thirty. This won't take longer than forty-five minutes, will it?"

He didn't want to meet with her, but she wasn't giving him a choice. "I'll see you there."

"Avery," he said.

She paused, going breathless, thinking of all the things she wished he'd say to her. "Yes?" she answered, holding her breath.

"Could you bring my toothbrush?"

Unfortunately, that wasn't one of them.

"Of course," she assured him and hung up before he could say anything else.

※

Everyone met at the Sunny Spot: business people from the nearby shops and offices, stay-at-home moms with offspring in tow, professors between classes at the university, farmers in town to pick up supplies, ladies who lunched, Larkin's finest, and folks from the hospital across the park.

The place, two linked storefronts on a side street just off Main, was always cheery. Its butter-yellow walls were set with panels of mosaic sunflowers that would have made Van Gogh feel right at home. The Sunny Spot served breakfasts hearty enough to satisfy lumberjacks, soups so thick you had to chew, Dagwood sandwiches worthy of the name, and the best desserts for miles around.

But today, all Avery could do was push her spinach omelette around on her plate and watch Mike eat his way through a tower of pancakes.

Why didn't *Mike* ever lose *his* appetite in a crisis? Avery thought this qualified: for the first time in their married life, her husband hadn't come home to her.

Not that she entirely blamed him.

After everything she'd accused him of, she supposed he had good reason to stay away. She'd made up her mind that Mike knew about Samantha. She'd decided his refusal to tell her about the baby was meant to keep her and Fiona apart. And Avery had been too angry, too fired up by her own suspicions, to entertain any other possibilities.

Only later, as she prowled that empty house, did she begin to suspect the truth: that Mike hadn't kept anything from her. He hadn't lied to her. He really didn't know who Samantha was.

Curled up alone in their big bed fruitlessly waiting for Mike to return, Avery relived every nuance of their confrontation. She remembered how his wide shoulders had sagged when she told him who Samantha was. When he'd turned away, she realized in retrospect, the expression on his face had been one of sorrow and resignation—not guilt.

If she hadn't been so sure about what he'd done, Avery might have noticed those things. She might have read his reactions differently. *She might have recognized his anger and his sarcasm for what it was.*

She loathed herself for the things she'd said to Mike. She'd called his cell phone at least a dozen times to apologize, but he hadn't answered. She'd left him voice mails, but he never called back.

As darkness eased toward dawn, she felt the weight of her regret built up behind her sternum: Mike wasn't going to call; he wasn't coming home to her. She began to fear that by staying away, he was severing the last tenuous threads holding their marriage together.

So she'd called out at the farm and asked him to meet her and talk—but so far, neither of them had said a word except to order breakfast. Avery set her fork aside and faced him directly. She'd been the one who insisted they meet, so it was up to her to open the conversation.

"I want to apologize for the things I accused you of last night," she began. "I was wrong to think you knew about Samantha."

He glanced up from his plate. "So you figured that out, did you?"

She could tell by the set of his mouth he was still mad at her.

"Maybe you should have had a little faith in me."

"Maybe I should have," she conceded. "But I think I had some pretty compelling reasons for losing faith in everyone I care about. My daughter refused to tell me she has a baby. My mother knew the truth and never said a word to me. And you, Mike—you haven't been all that forthcoming, either."

She saw a flush rise in his face.

"I should have come right home the day I saw Fiona on the quad," he conceded, "and told you she was back in Larkin. I should have let you know I was giving Ted money. I was wrong; I admit that."

He compressed his lips before he went on. "But last night, Avery, before I even set foot in that house, you had your mind made up that I'd lied to you. You'd judged me and found me guilty, and nothing I said or did was going to change your mind."

She deliberately lowered her voice. "So you owned up to something you hadn't done, and jumped on the first excuse you had to run away."

"I told you what you expected to hear." Mike's expression went truculent. "And frankly, Avery, sometimes you make it easier for me to leave than it is to stay."

His words sent a chill rippling along her nerves because she recognized the truth in them.

He scrubbed a hand through his hair, then let out his breath in a sigh. "We've wandered so far from where we were, Avery, that I don't know how we can ever get back."

He sounded as bewildered as she was by everything that had changed between them. As frightened, as confused, and as filled with regret.

She reached across and took his hand, offering him what comfort she could. Trying to find a little reassurance and consolation for herself. Though his fingers tightened almost reflexively, she felt more like they were children lost and fumbling in the dark than two adults who loved each other and had problems to solve.

"Sometimes, Mike," she said, her voice gone thick, "I don't think there is any going back. I think there's only going ahead."

"Going ahead to where?"

"I'm not sure."

The instant they found the note Fee left when she went away, they'd gone from parents united in raising their daughter to strangers at odds over what to do next. They'd gone from a couple content with their life, to individuals who questioned everything—including each other.

"If we want to move ahead," Mike ventured, "I don't think there's anything to be gained by talking about Fiona."

"I think talking about Fee is the only way to settle what's dividing us," Avery insisted.

Mike scowled and opened his mouth to argue, but before he said a word, Avery broached the thing she'd been trying to find the courage to ask him for days. "Then I suppose I'd be wasting my breath if I ask you to keep an eye on Fiona while I'm in China."

"Jesus, Avery! How can you ask me that?" Mike pushed back in his chair and stared at her. "You're the one heading for the back of beyond in the middle of all of this."

"I know I don't have any right to ask you," Avery conceded.

"No. You don't," he snapped at her. "And, anyway, hasn't

Fee spent the last year and half pretty much looking after herself?"

Avery refused to back down. "The fact remains, Mike, that I'm leaving for China in a matter of hours so we don't lose the Holding Company, the house, and the shirts off our backs."

He cursed under his breath.

"All I'm asking you to do is drive past Casey's or the Food-4-Less once in a while," Avery told him. "Or maybe cruise by the Windsor Arms in the evening—"

"She's living in that dump?"

"—and be sure her car is there. I've been keeping an eye on her myself ever since I found out she'd come back to Larkin."

"You've been stalking Fee for six weeks," he asked incredulously, "and you didn't know about her kid?"

Avery's cheeks burned. She didn't have any idea how she had missed finding out about Samantha.

"All I've been doing is making sure Fee's all right. Come on, Mike," she pressed him. "Who else am I going to ask to do this?"

When he didn't answer, she took a carefully folded note card out of her purse. "Here's her address and her class schedule. At the bottom of the page is the number for her cell phone. . . ."

Mike made no move to take the paper. "You didn't say I had to talk to her."

"Don't you want this information just in case?"

"There isn't going to be a 'just in case.'"

Avery didn't say a word. She just held the note card out to him, staring at him with her heart in her eyes.

He finally gave a snort of bitter laughter and took the

card. "I'll drive by once a day," he conceded. "But I'm only letting you talk me into this because you won't give me any rest unless I agree."

That was far more than she'd expected. "Oh, Mike, thank you! I can't begin to tell you how much this will ease my—"

He held up his hand, halting her. "There's something else we need to talk about."

"Is there?"

His mouth narrowed ominously. Avery's heartbeat picked up speed; she wasn't going to like what he had to say.

"I've decided to move out to the farm for a while."

For a moment she could do no more than stare at him. "But—but I said I was wrong," she finally managed to stammer. "I—I said I was sorry."

He shifted uncomfortably. "I figured it'd give each of us time to think."

A sharp tang of panic rose in her throat. "Won't me being away in China give us time enough?"

"It might," Mike conceded. "But then you'd come back— and things might be the same as they are now. Besides, there's something I need to take care of out at the farm."

"Ted, you mean?"

"Yeah," he admitted reluctantly. "I think he's been coming home drunk pretty much every night. The place is a wreck, and all I could find in the cupboards was instant coffee and Oreos."

Avery could just imagine: Ted had never been very good at looking after himself. He'd been a completely hopeless bachelor until Nancy moved in to settle and organize him. Even after they got married and the children started coming, he'd had trouble holding on to a job until he started at the post office. Ted had completely lost his tether when Nancy and the kids moved out.

"You don't have to do this, Mike," she said, knowing he wouldn't welcome her opinion. "Ted isn't your responsibility anymore."

"Ted will always be my responsibility," he said with the shake of his head. "Besides, it's what's right. Maybe if I'm staying out there I can help him get back on track."

Avery doubted that, but she'd said all she could say.

Because Mike's father had been an irresponsible drunk, Mike had grown up to doing his father's job. He'd worked all through high school so his mother could put food on the table. He'd made sure Janice had money for college, and he'd been pulling Ted out of one scrape after another since they were kids.

Now he was ready to help again—no matter how much Ted loved and resented him for doing it.

"Are you sure this is what you want to do, Mike?" she pressed him. "How can you and I work things out if you're living out there?"

"It's what I'm doing, Avery." His tone was obdurate.

He glanced down at his watch, then shoved to his feet. "I've got to go. I had a meeting at the job site ten minutes ago."

"But you *are* going to keep an eye on Fee while I'm away?" Avery needed to be sure.

He nodded distractedly as he pulled a few crumpled bills out of his pocket and dropped them on the tabletop. "Have a good trip, sweetheart," he said as he turned to go. "And thanks for bringing my toothbrush."

With a knot in her throat, Avery watched him leave. She watched him cross the street, climb into his truck, and pull his battered ball cap down on his forehead. She watched him until he drove out of sight.

Once he was gone, her energy drained away. She'd won an important concession; he was going to check on Fee. But she'd lost something infinitely more vital. Mike was moving out to the farm—out of her house and out of her bed. Much as he'd tried to dismiss it as time to think, the truth was they'd be separated, living apart. It was the very last thing in the world she wanted.

Besides, she was leaving for China tomorrow, and Mike hadn't so much as kissed her good-bye.

❋

Avery called Mike from the international terminal at Chicago's O'Hare. Huddled close to the window that overlooked the tarmac, she turned her back to the other passengers and watched as the ground crew loaded the last of the luggage onto the plane she'd be taking to China.

All she wanted was a modicum of privacy and a few last minutes when she could talk to her husband. But instead of Mike himself, his voice mail picked up her call.

She hung up without saying a word, sick with disappointment. Though she told herself she was being silly, Avery needed to hear Mike's voice just one more time before she boarded the flight that would take her halfway around the world.

She glanced at her watch. She knew Mike intended to come by their house on Prospect Street and pack some things to take out to the farm. Was there any chance of catching him there? she wondered, and dialed the number.

But if Mike was at the house, he didn't answer.

As a last resort, she called out at the farm. The phone rang and rang again.

As it did, the first boarding call for the flight to China blared over the loudspeaker in the waiting area. Avery checked her seat assignment on the boarding pass, and hung on as the phone at the farmhouse rang a third, fourth, fifth, and sixth time.

On the seventh ring an answering machine whirred and picked up. Ted's voice came on the line. "So leave a message at the beep, asshole."

Avery hesitated, both disconcerted by the greeting and taken aback at the thought that Ted might be picking up whatever message she left for Mike.

Through the loudspeaker the ramp agent announced that the next rows were boarding. If Avery was going to leave Mike a message, this was going to be her last chance.

"Hi, Mike, it's me," she began, sounding a little breathless even in her own ears. "I just wanted to call before I left O'Hare..."

A hot swell of regret pushed up from her diaphragm.

"...to tell you again how sorry I am about what I said the other night. I should have known—" Tears gathered in her throat, and she swallowed hard. "I should have known you wouldn't do what I accused you of, and I'm so very, *very* sorry for doubting you."

Her voice wavered on the "very, very," and she had to swallow again.

"Oh, Mike," she went on miserably, cupping her hand around the mouthpiece. "I know things haven't been very good between us for a while"—tears burned beneath her downcast lashes—"but we can work this out, can't we?"

She hesitated, hoping to hear her husband's suede-soft

voice, hoping Mike would come on the line and tell her they'd settle everything when she got back.

Instead the silence lengthened and disappointment swelled inside her.

"Anyway," she said as the tears she'd been fighting spilled over. "I couldn't go all the way to China without telling you—without telling you that I love you."

"Seating is now open for all rows aboard Flight 7712 to Beijing," the ramp agent announced, sounding officious, sounding impatient. "All passengers please board Flight 7712 at this time."

"I'll call you, Mike," she whispered before she hung up. "I'll call you from China."

❋

Mike heard the answering machine pick up just as he was hauling the last of his belongings into the farmhouse. Ted's greeting made him snort with laughter, then shake his head. What stopped him in his tracks was the sound of Avery's voice.

"Hi, Mike, it's me. I just wanted to call before I left O'Hare..."

With a *thud,* Mike dropped the duffel bag he was carrying and started toward the olive-green phone mounted on the wall at the far side of the kitchen.

"...to tell you again how sorry I am about what I said the other night. I should have known—"

He caught the waver in his wife's voice and reached for the handset.

"I should have known you wouldn't do what I accused you of," she apologized, "and I'm so very, *very* sorry for doubting you."

The distress in Avery's voice tore into him. Yet even as he stood with his hand curled around the receiver, he couldn't bring himself to pick it up.

"Oh, Mike," she went on at the other end of the line. "I know things haven't been very good between us for a while—"

He heard her hesitate.

"—but we can work this out, can't we?"

He could sense her apprehension right through the phone lines, sense her hope and fear as if it were a charge of electricity rippling from her to him.

Pick up the phone, you jerk, he told himself.

But somehow he couldn't do it.

Instead the silence stretched high-pitched and thin between his wife in Chicago and him standing in the farmhouse kitchen. His stomach balled and his palms began to sweat. He wanted to tell her that things were going to be fine between them, but he was as uncertain about the future as she was.

"Anyway," she finally said. "I couldn't go all the way to China without telling you—without telling you that I love you."

In the background he could hear them announcing her flight to China. He heard a rustle as if she were gathering up her things to board the plane.

"I'll call you, Mike," he heard her promise. "I'll call you from China."

He stood there with tears in his eyes and listened as she broke the connection.

"I love you, too, Avery," he whispered when it was too late—and knew just how badly he'd failed her this time.

Chapter 9

✳

Sometimes when you're up to your neck in alligators, someone will throw you a lifeline. David Lowery flung one to Fiona about eight-thirty Thursday night.

Fee was sitting cross-legged on the couch cramming for Monday's foundations of education exam, when someone came knocking on the door of her apartment. Muttering over the disruption, she dislodged the books and papers on her lap and padded sock-footed down the hall. She peered warily through the peephole to find Dave standing outside—carrying a pizza box.

Fee shrank back from the door. She hadn't washed her hair this morning. She'd pulled on a pair of industrial-gray sweatpants and one of Jared's castoff T-shirts when she came home from work. She didn't have on a scrap of makeup. Fee wasn't generally vain about her looks, but David *was* someone who'd had a crush on her in high school. Did she really want him to see her looking like this?

Just then the sharp tang of tomato sauce came wafting right through the door, bringing with it the promise of gooey cheese, pepperoni, and maybe mushrooms. Saliva flooded Fiona's mouth.

She slicked back her hair with her hands, then snapped the dead bolt. David grinned when he saw her—proof positive that she looked as scruffy as she felt. A hot flush crept up her jaw.

"Hello, Fee-oh-na," he greeted her.

"Hello, David," she said, stepping aside to let him in.

"We never got around to setting a time to go out for pizza—" She noticed he didn't actually use the word "date." "—so I brought the pizza to you. Is the kid asleep, or will we need to split this three ways?"

"Samantha's asleep," Fee answered and scowled at him. "And just so you know, I'm only letting you in because you come bearing pizza."

"Whatever works," he said with a shrug and slung his jacket over one of the coat hooks in the hall.

He stood holding the pizza box as she bustled around stacking books and gathering up the papers strewn across the couch. Just having him here made her nervous.

The frank appraisal he was giving the apartment made her nervous, too. She wished the place conjured up adjectives like "funky" or "eclectic." "Tired" was more apt; worn, shabby, messy. Littered with toys. She didn't have the time or energy to make it more than that.

"Studying, huh?" he asked as she stuffed the last of her notebooks into the backpack.

"Midterms."

"Already?"

"And I'm behind." She heaved a sigh. "I'm always behind these days."

"Then it's a good thing I brought pizza to help you keep

up your strength." He put the pizza box on the wobbly coffee table and settled into one corner of the couch like he belonged there.

Fee stood looking down at him. She wasn't sure what to think about David Lowery. He kept surprising her by not being who she thought he was, not who he'd been in high school. Though peer pressure had prevented her from admitting it, she'd always kind of liked Dave, or at least liked the way his mind worked. He had a quirky kind of logic, a slightly skewed approach to the problems they'd worked on together in chemistry that stirred Fiona's own imagination. She liked that being with him made her synapses fire faster to keep up. They might even have become friends if he hadn't been such a geek—and Fee hadn't been so terrified of being labeled a "geek by association."

The Dave who'd showed up tonight with pizza in hand confused her with his easy grin and masculine confidence. He kept her off balance by being interested and friendly when single moms like her were anathema to guys his age. He unsettled her by being nice when Fee had never once in her life made an effort to be nice to him.

Fee didn't one bit like being unsettled. But then, David had brought a pizza and that mitigated a lot of things.

"I can offer you iced tea, water, or beer," she said.

"Are you old enough to be buying beer?" he asked, grinning up at her.

Being nearly three years younger than everyone else in her graduating class had been a drag when it came to most things, but especially when it came to buying beer. She'd never once found a clerk at 7-Eleven who was duped by her fake ID. Although she finally was old enough, she hadn't bought this six-pack, either. The single bottle in the fridge was left from when

Casey and Dan came over last week. Of course, she wasn't about to admit that to David.

Instead she crossed her arms against the faded Insane Clown Posse logo on her chest and scowled at him. "I turned twenty-one in August."

"I wouldn't have pegged you for a day over nineteen," he smirked. "I'll take iced tea."

Fee returned from the kitchen with drinks, paper plates, and napkins. They dug into the pizza.

"Oh, my God!" Fiona moaned, sucking sauce from her fingertips. "This is so good!" She couldn't remember the last time she'd spent money on anything so frivolous as pizzeria pizza.

Once David had scarfed down a couple of slices, his attention wandered back to her. "By the way, I like your hair."

"Yeah, well," Fee conceded with a shrug, "the grape Kool-Aid thing just didn't play as well here as it did in L.A."

It had taken her and Casey three hours and two boxes of L'Oreal to get her hair back to its original color, a dark auburny brown a few shades darker than her mother's.

Dave took a swig of his iced tea. "Yeah, I've been wanting to ask you about L.A. How'd that come about?"

Fee nibbled her way through a piece of pepperoni and tried to decide how much to tell him. "You knew Deer in the Headlights had a regular gig at The Shingle Shack out on the highway, didn't you?"

"My sister said you guys were really good."

Fee's face warmed with pleasure. The five of them had been playing together since high school. Jared was the front man. He played a little guitar and sang in a voice so rich and ragged it could melt you to a puddle. Max drummed like pounding on things made him happy. Jimmy played lead guitar and wrote some of the best songs Fee had ever heard. Devon on bass and Fee on keyboard sang backup and filled out the sound.

"One night," she said, tucking her feet up under her, "a producer for Starburst Records caught our last set out at The Shack and was waiting for us when we finished. He said Starburst was a 'small but ambitious label' looking for a breakout band to take them to the top of the charts. He thought Deer in the Headlights was it."

Fiona would remember that night for the rest of her life: the rush of euphoria when they found out what the producer wanted, how Jared kept laughing and squeezing her knee under the table as the guy talked about the plans he had for the band, the way the five of them had whooped and hugged one another once he was gone. They'd sat up speculating about their future until almost dawn, convinced, now that they'd gotten their big break, that their lives were going to be exciting and extraordinary. Even knowing how things turned out, Fee wouldn't have traded that night for anything.

"The Starburst producer offered us a contract on the spot."

"That's so cool!" Dave hooted and clicked her glass with his.

Fee sat back and sipped her tea. "We signed the contract for five CDs with Starburst right then and there. But there were lots of things the producer wasn't all that up front about. One of them was that we were going to have to play our way to L.A."

"'Play your way'?"

"We spent the next six months touring, doing gigs Starburst set up for us. They told us we were building our name by playing at every dive and county fair between here and the coast."

Sometimes Fee could still smell beer and cigarette smoke in her hair. Some nights she woke up sweating from dreams about the afternoons they'd stood on makeshift stages in the sun, their music drowned out by the shrieks from the thrill rides on the midway.

"All those months, we were barely earning enough to cover our expenses—and only if we stayed in places that made Motel 6 look like the Taj Mahal."

The money she got from hocking her mother's pearls was all that kept them alive.

"It must have been tough," David sympathized.

Fiona shrugged, but a thread of bitterness crept into her voice. "We told ourselves we were professional musicians. We told ourselves every artist has to pay his dues."

They'd lived on the belief that once they reached L.A., Starburst would record and release a CD. They'd start opening for bigger and bigger bands, and watch their career take off from there.

Fee especially wanted everything to work out for Jared's sake. He had the looks, the talent, the kind of voice and range that made him special. He—and Jimmy's songs—were what had gotten them noticed.

"You sure you want to hear all this?" she asked.

David nodded. "What other chance does a geek like me have of brushing up against the world of rock and roll?"

Fee made a face at him, then went ahead. "When we got to L.A., there were more open-air festivals and gigs to play. Starburst kept assuring us that this was how we got exposure. What they didn't tell us was that they were getting sixty percent of our gate every time we played.

"When we asked how soon we'd start recording, they put us off. When they heard we meant to make a CD on our own so we'd have something to sell, they waved the contract in our faces. We'd granted them exclusive rights to record and distribute our material."

Fee turned and set her plate aside. "We'd heard horror stories about bands signing contracts that kept them hamstrung for years, but we didn't think we were dumb enough to get caught like that. Turns out we were."

Fee lowered her lashes, embarrassed all at once to admit that that wasn't the only way she'd screwed up her life. "I didn't think I was dumb enough to get caught, either," she said softly. "But the next thing I knew, the pregnancy test I took turned out positive."

When she looked up, she could see neither censure nor pity in David's eyes. "Is Samantha Jared's baby?" he asked her.

"Yes, she is."

"Did Jared stand by you?"

Fee bristled a little at the question. "He didn't ask me to marry him, if that's what you're asking. But after they fired me from the band—"

"They fired you!" Dave's outrage on her behalf sent a delicious tingle of satisfaction dancing along her nerves.

"Once I began to—to show, the producer took me aside and said pregnant mamas weren't sexy enough to rock and roll. He told me Starburst had found someone to replace me."

"My God, Fee!" David was incredulous. "Did you sue his ass?"

"To be honest," Fiona said, "that never occurred to me. Besides, if I'd fought them, Starburst might have stopped booking gigs for the band, and that's all we had to live on."

David receded into the corner of the couch and folded his arms across his chest. "So what happened?"

Odd how understanding he'd been about Samantha, and how disapproving he was that she hadn't stood up for herself.

"Starburst hired a sexy girl singer to take my place," Fiona went on. "I retired to keep house for the guys and wait for the baby to come."

She didn't tell him what pigs guys that age could be. She didn't admit how she'd seethed every time she saw the skanky redhead who took her place come on to Jared. She didn't confess that she felt alienated from the guys who'd been her friends and bandmates for years.

"Jared took care of you, didn't he?" The timbre of David's voice deepened; his words rang sharp with disapproval.

"Jared was great. When he wasn't rehearsing, he went with me to my appointments at the clinic. He stayed with me all through labor and delivery. He got to hold Samantha even before I did." Fee's throat ached, remembering the awe and absorption in Jared's face when he held their daughter. "He took a second job to pay off the medical bills."

Dave's expression remained stony.

"Jared's a good guy, David. Really he is. He stepped up when I needed him."

"So are you in love with him?"

No one had asked her that. Certainly Jared hadn't. Neither had her mom nor her grandma. So why did David want to know where things stood with Jared and her? He wasn't still carrying a torch, was he?

Talking about her feelings for Jared wasn't all that easy— at least not for the Fiona she'd become. "I can't afford to be in love with Jared," she said, looking down at her hands. "I needed to come back to Larkin and finish my degree so I'd be able to support Samantha. Jared needs to be in L.A. playing clubs and singing backup in recording sessions until he gets his break."

"You think he will?"

"Jared's really very good, he and Jimmy." Fee flashed David a self-conscious smile. "They're the ones with talent; the rest of us were just along for the ride."

Since that was all she had to say on the subject of the band and L.A., Fee climbed to her feet and began gathering up their plates and napkins.

"You want to take the rest of the pizza home?"

"Nah," Dave said.

Which meant Fee would have leftover pizza for dinner a couple of nights this week.

He followed her into the kitchen with the pizza box.

"Casey told me about your mom being sick," she said, wrapping the pizza in foil. "So how's she doing?"

"They've started her on another course of chemo." David said, slumping against the counter, his hands tucked into his armpits. "She's losing her hair again and that really pisses her off."

Fee didn't know that much about either cancer or David's mom except that she'd seemed nice enough when she'd volunteered for events at the high school. Her having a second round of chemo didn't sound all that promising, though.

"And how's the string theory stuff going with Dr. Buchanan?" she asked, heading back to the couch.

David settled on his end before he answered. "You know, Fee, it's the most interesting stuff I've ever worked on. You know anything about string theory?"

"Not a lot," Fiona hedged.

David started to explain. He was barely six sentences in when Fee's cell phone rang. She reached for it and heard that familiar husky voice in her ear.

"Jared!" she exclaimed.

"So what are you doing, sweet baby," he purred, and the rich, buttery cadence of his voice made her toes curl.

"I'm stud-stud-studying," she fibbed and climbed to her feet.

"So how are my girls there in Larkin?" Jared asked, a chuckle in his voice.

"We're doing fine."

Fee was almost unbearably distracted by David being there, by knowing he was listening to their every word and calibrating her responses.

As much as she hated to admit it, she was responding to Jared the way she always did. Beneath the soft, faded cotton of his T-shirt her nipples tightened. She went soft and melty inside, remembering far too clearly what it was like to go to bed with him.

She turned her back on David, not wanting him to see how flushed she was, how mesmerized she became at the sound of Jared's voice. But David must have known.

He rose from the couch, stepped into her line of sight, and waved good-bye.

"Thanks for the pizza," she mouthed to him.

Fee couldn't properly concentrate on what Jared was saying until she heard the door close and knew that David Lowery was gone.

"So what do you think?" Jared was asking when she shifted her focus back to him.

Fee heard the suppressed excitement in his voice and

knew she'd missed something important. "I'm sorry," she apologized. "I was just—shutting the door into the bedroom so I wouldn't wake the baby."

Jared sounded miffed as he repeated himself. But then the announcement, when it came, was probably worth repeating—at least for him.

"Starburst is releasing Deer in the Headlights's first single for radio play next week," Jared all but crowed. "Isn't that great, Fee? Isn't that great?"

⁂

His cell phone rang before it was full light, but Mike was awake. He'd spent most of the night trying to fold his six-foot-two-inch frame into the bed he'd slept in when he was a boy. Though Nancy had painted the walls Pepto-Bismol pink to please her younger girls and carpeted the rough wooden floor, the room felt the same when he closed his eyes. Tucked up under the eaves, it was all angles and dormers, close as a clamshell. Safe and suffocating.

He rolled over, snapped on the Hello, Kitty lamp beside the bed. He caught the phone on the third ring.

"Hello," he mumbled, wondering where Ted was. Had he gotten home all right last night? Was this the hospital calling?

"Hi." It was Avery's voice, surprisingly clear considering she was half a world away. "Did I wake you?"

He settled a little deeper into the pillows. "It's just after five A.M. here. What time is it where you are?"

"It's six in the evening, and I've just gotten into the hotel." She sounded exhausted.

"Long flight?"

"You have no idea," she answered on the hint of a sigh. "I'm going to bed as soon as we hang up."

There was something comfortable and familiar about talking to Avery in bed. Mike nestled into his pillow and pulled the blanket higher against the morning chill.

"I'm going over to the plant first thing in the morning," she went on, "to make the final fabric selections."

"How are you getting around over there? Have you hired a car and an interpreter?"

He probably should have asked more about the arrangements before she left, but he'd been preoccupied with Ted's drinking. He and Avery hadn't exactly been on the best of terms, either. And though he knew why it was necessary, he hadn't been thrilled about putting up everything they owned so Avery could get that letter of credit. Besides, he hated that she'd dumped Fiona and the baby in his lap before she left.

"The toy company arranged for the car and the interpreter," Avery answered. "He speaks pretty good English except that he spelled my name 'Mountgummy.'"

Mike chuckled.

"So, did you get my message?"

Silence unfolded, a silence as gray and cool as the dawn. The truth was, he didn't know what to say to her about the message she'd left. The message he'd intercepted on Ted's answering machine. He hadn't known what to say to her when it first came in, and he'd erased the message as soon as she hung up.

"I wasn't sure I should leave it," her voice went all soft and tentative, "especially there at the farm. But I'd tried your cell phone, and it just seemed wrong for me to head off for a couple of weeks without telling you—you know—how I felt."

Mike knew he should reassure her. He should tell her that he loved her, too. He'd never had trouble saying that before, not since that morning in Chicago. He swallowed, took a breath, and finally managed to push out those four little words: "I love you, too."

He said them a second time, not just for Avery's sake, but to reassure himself.

Still, she must have sensed his reticence. "You needn't say that if you're having doubts. I know you're still angry with me—and you have a pretty good reason."

"Listen, Avery—" he began, wanting to make things right with her, but still not knowing what to say. When she cut him off, he was almost glad of it.

"Have you looked in on Fiona?"

The idea of following Fee around still made Mike squirm. "I figured that you'd talked to her before you left, so I'd have a couple days' grace before I—"

"It's the one thing I asked you to do while I was gone." He heard the aggravation that darkened Avery's tone.

"I know." He offered up the semblance of an apology, though he wasn't a bit sorry.

Now that she knew Fee had a child, Avery was going to be even more intent on getting their family back together. Asking him to keep an eye on Fee was her way of forcing him to confront his feelings for his daughter.

Mike hated being manipulated. Avery had done that to get that damned letter of credit, and now she was trying to make him deal with Fee, if only at a distance. She used to understand why he needed to make his own decisions;

she used to take that into consideration. What he thought and felt, used to be important to her.

"If you're not going to do this, Mike, just say so." She sounded gruff, tired, and out of sorts.

"Yeah, okay." He didn't want to argue with her anymore, especially not when she was so far away and clearly exhausted by her trip. "I'll look in on her."

"You promised," she reminded him.

"I remember."

"Good, now I'm going to bed. I'll call you again when I get a chance."

He hesitated for what he thought might be a heartbeat too long. "Avery, I really do love you."

"Prove it," she challenged and disconnected.

✤

Mike felt like a stalker.

He'd been parked up the block from Casey DeCristo's house for the best part of an hour waiting for Fee to come out. He'd caught up with her in the Food-4-Less parking lot at the end of her shift and followed her here.

Shadowing her turned out to be ridiculously easy. She got up at six, dropped the baby off at Casey's by seven, and studied in the campus library until nine. She had back-to-back classes three days a week, with labs the afternoons of the opposite days. Her job at the Food-4-Less began at four. On Saturdays and Sundays she worked from noon to six. She was usually in bed by ten.

Exhausted, probably.

On one hand, Mike was relieved that Fee hadn't seen him tailing her; the last thing he wanted was a confrontation. On the other hand, Fee *should* have noticed. If he'd picked up on her schedule so easily, so could someone else. The very thought of that made Mike sweat.

He glanced at his watch and shifted uncomfortably in the Silverado's cab. What was Fee doing in there? How long did it take to pick up a kid, anyway? Or was Casey feeding them supper?

He could imagine them all clustered around the table in Casey's bright kitchen: Casey and Dan, their kid Derek, Fiona, and the baby. He wondered what Casey was serving. Something kids liked probably, spaghetti, chicken strips, macaroni and cheese. When Fee was little, they'd eaten so much macaroni and cheese, Kraft's profits should have gone right through the roof.

Mike remembered what dinnertime was like: trying to get food into Fee, jumping up and down to wipe up spills, hoping you'd manage a bite or two yourself before something else happened.

Sitting there in the dark, he chuckled to himself. But when he realized what he'd done, that chuckle became a curse. This was Avery's doing, damn it! She'd asked him to watch over Fee and that baby hoping it would soften him up, hoping it would change how he felt about his daughter and make reconciliation possible. That wasn't going to happen.

Instead he kept thinking about how Fee's leaving had destroyed all the hopes he'd poured into her, all the dreams and aspirations he'd harbored for her future. He kept thinking how she'd disappointed him, how she'd broken Avery's heart.

Mike's job in life was—and always had been—taking care of his family. He'd worked at it for as long as he could remember, helping his mom, looking after the younger kids, making sure he lived up to the unexpected gift of love and home Avery had given him. The morning they'd gone into Fiona's room and found her gone, he'd been devastated. He felt worthless, lost—*as if he'd failed again.*

He'd felt like that the night Avery went into labor for their second child. He and Avery had been in the delivery room holding hands and fighting their way through stronger and stronger contractions when something went terribly wrong. Avery started bleeding and, before Mike could ask what was happening, the doctors and nurses bundled Avery up on the gurney and ran her out of the room.

They'd left Mike standing in the middle of the hospital corridor watching helplessly as the doors to the operating suite swished closed behind them.

After that, all Mike could do was sit and wait. Finally, after what seemed like forever, someone came and showed him into a small, dim cubicle at the end of the hall. Once inside, the nurse came in, murmured how sorry she was for his loss, and put their stillborn son into his arms.

He'd stood there winded, as if he were trying to balance in midair. He didn't know what to do, what he was supposed to feel beyond a profound sense of confusion and loss.

"Jonathan," he'd finally whispered, gently cupping his and Avery's child in his two hands. The baby was tiny and utterly perfect. He had a dusting of Avery's reddish hair and Fee's pouty mouth. Seeing that connection to the people Mike loved more than life, he drew the child closer, nestled him up against his chest.

The baby was still warm from Avery's body, and, as Mike stroked little Jonathan's cheek, he could hardly believe that instead of having years ahead to watch him grow, Mike would only ever have this brief time with the son he and Avery had hoped and prayed for.

He'd held little Jonathan for as long as they would let him, doing his best to pour a lifetime of love, a lifetime of dreams and promises into this child they'd lost. Finally, because Avery was still in surgery, Mike alone was left to say good-bye to their small, sweet boy.

Hours later, when Mike finally staggered home numb with worry and grief, Fiona had come running to him with arms outstretched. He'd knelt right there on the floor in the front hall and crushed her to him. He'd buried his face against her rumpled hair, breathed the milk and Cheerios scent of her, and let her yellow-ducky pajamas absorb his tears. There, bathed in the morning's sunny warmth, he'd poured all his love, all his hopes and dreams for the children he and Avery would never have, into this one precious little girl.

Mike swallowed hard and shifted in the truck seat. He swiped at his eyes. *What the hell was keeping Fiona?*

His stomach grumbled, and he realized he hadn't had lunch. What he ought to do, he told himself, was leave. What he ought to do was swing by the Food-4-Less on his way to the farm and get something for Ted to eat that didn't come from McDonald's or Taco Bell.

But just then the DeCristo's front porch light flicked on, it's soft glow banishing the deepening blue twilight. Casey emerged first carrying Derek, with Fee's blue knapsack slung over her shoulder. Dan came next and hefted a big, old-fashioned stroller into the Neon's trunk. Fee brought up the rear, cuddling the baby in her arms.

Mike strained toward the windshield, hoping to catch a glimpse of her. Of Fiona's baby. Of his little girl's little girl.

His granddaughter.

The weight of that connection settled over him with equal measures of grief and joy. Samantha was a responsibility he'd never voluntarily shoulder, but she was a part of Fee, a part of Avery. And of himself.

For an instant he stared at the child bundled up in his daughter's arms. Did she have the same hint of red in her hair that her mother and grandmother did? Did she have Fee's green eyes? Was there so much as a hint of him in Samantha?

Mike muttered a curse, his voice strained and gruff.

He hated the way everything had turned out. Samantha was flesh and blood to him, yet he might never feel the soft weight of her in his arms. He might never tickle her until she writhed and shrieked with laughter. He might never read to her at bedtime, or teach her to throw a ball.

He might never lift Samantha to peer through the eye-piece of a telescope for her first real look at the stars. He hated not being able to share that with his granddaughter the way he had shared it with Fiona. Mike squeezed his eyes closed to shut out the image of those lost opportunities.

Damn Fiona, anyway!

He kept expecting he'd get past the pain of her betrayal. He kept thinking he'd finally put his anger and disillusion-ment in their proper place and get on with his life. But then, memories would unexpectedly overtake him and the pain would roar over him again, burying him so deep he couldn't breathe.

He wasn't going to let that happen tonight. He was going to make sure Fiona got safely home, then he was going to the observatory and lose himself in the stars.

Four houses down, he saw that Fee had finished strap-ping Samantha into her car seat. She wrapped Dan and then Casey in enormous hugs, then climbed into the purple Neon he and Fiona and Miriam had picked out together as Fee's high-school graduation gift.

He heard the Neon's engine purr to life, saw Fee signal and pull away from the curb. Once she was a good way down the street, Mike cranked the truck's ignition and followed.

※

When the cell phone rang, Mike was pouring his second cup of coffee. He'd been awake and waiting six mornings in a row, but Avery hadn't called. Though it felt way too much like high school, he let the phone ring three times before he picked it up.

"Hi, sweetheart," he greeted her.

"Hi, Mike, did I wake you?"

"M-m-m," he muttered noncommittally. "How are things in China?"

"Going remarkably well." Avery sounded a little amazed by that. "The materials were exactly what I specified. The workmanship is every bit as good as what we do at the Holding Company. The ears were crooked on the first few Sheepish off the assembly line, but we worked that out."

Though Mike chuckled, he was acutely aware of just how much of their future—and the Holding Company's future—Avery had put at risk to finance this project.

"I'm glad you got that straightened out," he told her. "Since things are running so smoothly, do you think you'll be home earlier than you thought?"

Even though he was living out here at the farm, Mike missed her. His life felt off balance knowing she was on one side of the world, and he was on the other. He hated not being able to call her if he wanted to, see her if he wanted to. He hated stopping at the house to pick up the mail and feed the cat as if he was some kid she'd hired from down the block. He resented that in some odd, subtle way, wandering around those familiar rooms felt like trespassing.

"No," Avery said on a sigh, "I think I need to stay on until they're finished with production."

She sounded lonely, as if she missed him, too. Or maybe that was wishful thinking.

"I'll probably get home Wednesday or Thursday of next week."

He let his voice warm, soften. "It'll be nice to have you back, sweetheart."

In the beat of silence that followed, he sensed both confusion and a new wariness in her.

"So how *are* things in Larkin?" she asked, abruptly shifting the subject from anything that might get personal. "Have you been keeping an eye on Fee?"

Her first question when she was away on business was, and always had been, about Fiona. Why hadn't that rankled him until now?

Mike pushed away from where he'd been leaning against the counter. "So, you want a report, do you?" he snapped at her.

The faint companionable glow between them abruptly dimmed.

"*Is* Fee all right? Is that baby all right?"

"As far as I can tell she is."

She exhaled sharply. "You mean, you haven't gotten a good look at Samantha?"

He paced the length of the farmhouse kitchen. "I'm afraid your plan to throw Fiona and me together hasn't worked out quite the way you hoped."

Avery didn't even bother to deny her intentions. "Oh, Mike! You mean, you haven't gotten close enough to see what a beautiful baby she is? Samantha's absolutely adorable, tow-headed like Jared always was, and she has Fee's mouth."

"She has your mouth, you mean," he said quietly.

"And your dimple."

His fingertips grazed the stubbly crease in his own cheek. "When did *you* get such a close look at Samantha?"

Avery hesitated, and he could tell by the hitch in her breathing she had something to tell him he wasn't going to like. Instinctively, he braced himself.

"There are some things I didn't have a chance to talk to you about before I left," she said.

He set his cup down on the counter and shifted the phone a little closer to his mouth. "What things?"

"Well," she began tentatively, "when I stopped at my mother's the day I found out about Samantha, Mom was baby-sitting."

Mike drew in his breath and stared out into the farm-house yard where the last of the oak leaves were kiting past the window like flakes of gold.

"I got to hold her, Mike." Avery sounded awed and breathless. "I had a chance to feed her and change her and play with her. And you know"—he imagined that she was leaning a little closer to the phone to share the moment with him—"she sucks two fingers just the way Fiona always did, and she makes that same little snuffling sound when she takes her bottle."

The memories of Fiona swamped him, hitting him so hard he couldn't think, couldn't say a word. He just stood there, feeling as if his heart was shriveling in his chest.

How could Avery have seen and held their grandchild and not said a word? How could she tell him about that baby now—a child he might never hold, never know—as if hearing about her wasn't going to scour him raw?

Mike hunched over the sink and tried to dredge up something to say so Avery wouldn't guess—

"Mike?" she asked uncertainly.

"Yeah, I'm here."

He heard her let out her breath.

Mike pushed himself to speak. He didn't want Avery asking questions he had no way of answering. "Maybe the reason Fee's stopped at Miriam's twice this week is that your mother's been baby-sitting. Though it looked to me like Fee was there to help with the garden."

Avery snorted in disbelief. "Mother never lets anyone near her flowers. What else has Fee been doing?"

She didn't ask about Ted. She didn't ask about the house he was working on, or how he liked living out at the farm. She didn't ask about her mother, the weather, or the cat. She didn't apologize for not telling him about seeing and holding Samantha.

Granted, he'd kept some secrets of his own along the way, but that was different. He'd kept them to protect Avery, to keep her from being hurt.

He made his voice deliberately curt when he answered her. "Pretty much all Fee ever does is go to school. She goes to work and then to Casey's to pick up Samantha. After that she pretty much always goes home. Is that comprehensive enough for you, Avery?"

He was acting like a jerk, but couldn't seem to help himself.

"But you know what's odd," he went on, trying to redeem himself, at least a little. "Fee doesn't seem to be logging any time on the university telescope. Shouldn't she be up doing that? Doesn't she have to have a certain number of hours of observation each semester to complete her major? Do you think she isn't meeting her requirements because of the baby?"

On the other end of the line, Avery went quiet. Mike suddenly felt the weight of that silence in the pit of his belly.

"Um, Mike," she said tentatively. "There's something else I didn't get a chance to tell you before I left."

"What?"

"Fiona changed her major."

"From astronomy?" he asked, incredulous.

"I ran into Fee's faculty advisor." Avery's voice was gentle. She might not have anticipated how he'd react to hearing that she'd seen and held Samantha, but Avery knew very well how he'd react to this. "Fee's taking education classes; she's decided she wants to teach."

"Teach!"

"I know you're disappointed…"

Disappointment didn't even come close to what he was feeling.

"But Fiona loves the sky," he protested. "She was born to be an astronomer. It's all she's ever wanted."

Hadn't the two of them spent hours bent over star atlases, hours more making observations? Hadn't they visited every planetarium and observatory within driving distance? Hadn't they crept from telescope to telescope at star parties so they could peer at objects too far away for them to visualize with their own equipment? Hadn't they planned the observatory out at the farm, then built it with their own hands? Fiona giving up astronomy after all of that was one more betrayal.

"Fiona's doing what's practical," Avery consoled him.

Mike shook his head. He'd learned everything he knew

about the stars because he'd wanted to share Fiona's love for
the sky. Hadn't the hours they spent studying and observing together been some of the most precious he'd ever had
with anyone?

"She has that baby to raise all by herself," Avery insisted,
trying hard to convince him this was best. "If Fee can pick
up enough credits for an education major before graduation, she'll be able to walk right into a teaching job."

Avery paused as if she were testing the silence, and when
Mike didn't say anything, she pressed ahead. "Mike, just
stop and think. Fee's a single mother. She needs a job that
comes with reasonable hours and medical benefits."

Mike turned his back on the crisp October morning. He
understood what a sacrifice Fee was making for the sake of
her child. The practical part of him applauded that. The
dreamer in him cried out, bitter and disillusioned.

Hadn't he worked all these years so Fee would be able to
make the kind of choices he had never had an opportunity
to make? Hadn't he done everything in his power to en-
courage her to set ambitious goals for herself? Hadn't he
hoped to fulfill some of his own thwarted dreams through
her success?

Knowing his daughter had turned away from everything
he'd tried to give her made him feel like she was rejecting
him, betraying him all over again.

"The professors in the science department aren't very
happy about her changing her major, either," Avery admitted. "They all think she has a future in the sciences."

Mike nodded; he thought that too.

"I haven't had a chance to talk to Fiona about her decision," Avery went on, "but it seems to me she's doing what's
sensible."

But ambition wasn't about making sense, he wanted to say. Dreams didn't answer to practicality.

"Yeah, sure," he finally agreed, sarcasm searing the back or his throat. "We always raised Fee to settle for sensible."

Though dawn was only just creeping across the yard, Mike ached with exhaustion. He felt like he was watching his own life replay itself, watching his daughter's aspirations being crushed by a sense of duty. How could Fee have turned her back on the only thing she'd ever wanted to do with her life?

How could Avery have kept that and so much else from him?

He remembered a time when they'd shared everything. Sometimes they'd lie curled together after making love and talk for hours. Sometimes she'd bring his lunch to the job site so they could have more time together.

What happened to that? he wondered. What happened to them? How had they lost the ability to share what they were thinking? Was his move out to the farm the first treacherous step toward something more permanent? Was this the beginning of the end for Mike and Avery?

A chill of dread shot down his back.

"Look," Avery said, breaking into the lengthening silence. "I've been invited out to dinner with the president of the manufacturing company tonight, so I need to shower and get ready."

"Right," Mike nodded. "Right."

"I'm sorry I didn't tell you about this before I left, but there were so many other things I needed to say..."

Like accusing me of knowing about our grandchild, and keeping it from you, Mike almost said.

"Yeah, well, you'd better go. Have a nice evening," he told her and disconnected.

He didn't realize until he'd hung up the phone that he hadn't told her that he loved her. But then, she hadn't said it, either.

⁂

If he ever got tired of being a carpenter—Mike told himself as he watched from the opposite row in the parking lot as Fee wrestled the bulky, old stroller out of the back of her Neon— he might make a pretty damn good private investigator.

In a matter of days, he'd charted the route Fee drove from the Windsor Arms to Casey's house and from Casey's to school. He discovered where she parked on campus, which table she liked to study at in the library, what ATM she frequented, and the brand of diapers she bought Samantha.

So maybe he'd gotten a little obsessed with this.

This morning he'd followed Fee and Samantha to Liberty Lake Park, where it seemed they strolled pretty much every Sunday. Once Fee had belted Samantha into the stroller and pushed it a fair way down the paved path that circled the lake, Mike climbed out of his truck and went to stand at the edge of the parking lot.

From up here on the rise, he could see Fiona striding along in that way she had, as if she enjoyed stretching her legs. Somehow in the year and a half she'd been away, she'd grown from a gangly girl into a graceful young woman. From a headstrong child to a responsible adult.

A responsible adult, he admitted grudgingly, who was living up to the choices she'd made for herself.

He couldn't account for one frivolous moment in Fiona's life, and when he thought about it, that made him sad. She spent every waking moment either attending classes, working at the grocery store, or taking care of Samantha. She was tending to what was important, making the kind of sacrifices any good parent would make, but she didn't have a social life. And she'd given up her dreams of becoming an astronomer.

He might not approve of that decision, but his daughter had garnered his respect.

Halfway around the lake, Mike saw Fee stop and come around to the front of the stroller. The distance made it impossible to see if something was wrong, so he went back to the truck and got his field glasses.

What he saw when he focused on the two of them made him smile. Fiona had lifted Samantha out of the stroller and moved to a bench at the edge of the path. She rummaged in the diaper bag, pulled out Samantha's bottle, and began to feed her daughter.

Watching the two of them through the glasses, Mike could see the pure angles of his daughter's face, thrown into light and shadow by the angle of the sun. He could see Samantha's wide-eyed expression as she nursed, and the way she stared up at her mother.

And what a good mother Fee had somehow become. He'd noticed how attentive she was, how comfortable she was holding Samantha, how she talked to the baby as if they were friends.

He and Fiona had been such pals once. They'd taken their sleeping bags and spread them on the grass in the yard on summer nights when the fireflies were out. They'd feasted on burgers and root beer at the A&W Drive-in when Avery was working late. He'd taken Fee floating on the river south of the farm more than once, and taught her how to bait her own hook when they went fishing.

They'd spent hours exploring the sky together—and, God, how he missed that.

He sharpened the focus on the field glasses and noticed how the light glinted in Fee's newly darkened hair, how Samantha's tiny, perfect hands were wrapped around the bottle. How his daughter was smiling down at his granddaughter.

It was an almost unbearably intimate scene; it turned him all soft and squeamish inside.

"Oh, Fee," he whispered, his throat gone raw with regret. "If only you'd listened." *If only you'd been sensible. If only you hadn't run away. If only you hadn't stolen your mother's pearls.*

He remembered the day he bought those pearls like it was yesterday. He and Fiona had stopped at the jewelry store on their way back from one of the first birthday parties she'd ever attended. Fee couldn't have been more than four or five, a wide-eyed little charmer in a frilly peppermint-pink dress.

The man everyone in Larkin knew as "Irv the Jeweler" had been instantly captivated. He'd picked Fee up and set her on the display case so she could see what they were doing.

"So, you're looking for pearls for your wife?" Irv asked once Fee had crossed her ankles and arranged her skirts.

Mike nodded. "For our anniversary."

Irv smiled, his dark eyes warm. "Which one?"

"Our sixth."

Mike had intended to buy Avery a string of pearls for their fifth anniversary—until he found out how much good pearls cost. Over the next year he'd worked as much overtime as he could and saved his money, determined to get Avery pearls *this* year.

"There are two styles of necklaces," Irv told him instructively as he took out a gray velvet tray. "Ones where the pearls are matched and ones with graduated sizes."

Mike had looked at them, baffled. He wanted something comparable to the ones his mother-in-law seemed to wear with everything but her bathrobe.

"Do you remember which one of these necklaces looks like Grandma's?" he asked Fiona.

Fee "tried on" Gran's pearls every chance she got and probably knew a good deal more about them than her father. After Fee studied the necklaces for a moment, she pointed to the one at the top of the tray.

"Your daughter has a good eye," Irv told him and draped the necklace between his hands. "This is a very nice strand. The pearls are matched in both size and color, and they have an eighteen-carat-gold clasp."

Mike touched the pearls, liking the way they shimmered softly in the light.

"Or we have these," Irv said, taking out another necklace. "As you can see, the pearls in this necklace are a little pinker."

"Does that mean they're more expensive?" Mike asked.

"Color in pearls is more a question of taste and skin tone."

"I see," Mike said, confused again.

"What about those?" Fiona asked, pointing down through the glass countertop to a necklace in a box all by itself.

Irv's eyes crinkled at the corners. "Your daughter *does* have good taste."

The minute Irv brought out those pearls, Mike could see they were something special. They were flawless, perfectly round, perfectly matched. They glowed, catching the light and reflecting back soft, luminous shimmers of color.

Mike was almost afraid to ask. "How much are these?"

"This is a strand of what we call heirloom pearls, pearls fine enough to be handed down from one generation to the next." Irv reached across and patted Fiona's hand. "They're pearls that will not just hold their value, but appreciate as the years go by."

"How much?"

Irv shrugged and smiled. "Eight thousand dollars."

Mike felt himself pale. He'd managed to save five thousand in an account he'd opened when he decided Avery ought to have a strand of pearls at least as nice as her mother's. The five thousand was more money than he'd ever had in one lump sum, more than he'd spent on anything except his truck and their house.

But the pearls were wonderful, lustrous, exquisite, spectacular enough to be noticed and remarked upon.

Maybe if he emptied his checking account, Mike found himself thinking, he might clear another thousand. The pearls were every bit as special as Avery was, and he wanted so much for her to have them.

"How much are you prepared to spend?" Irv asked him gently.

Mike told him.

"I don't usually do this, Mr. Montgomery, but if you want these pearls for your wife," Irv offered, "I'll let you pay the balance off a little at a time—and at very low interest."

Though owing anyone money made him uneasy, Mike took the pearls and walked around for days afterward feeling like a man who'd licked the world with one hand tied behind his back.

On the morning of their sixth anniversary, he and Fiona had served Avery breakfast in bed. Once she'd exclaimed over the last bite of French toast and sip of coffee, he set the narrow velvet box on the corner of her tray.

"What's this?" she asked.

"Open it, Mommy!" Fiona crowed, bouncing on the bed in excitement. "I can't keep this secret a minute longer!"

Avery lifted the lid of the box and stared at the pearls, openmouthed—then burst into tears. "Oh, Mike!" she'd gasped as she draped the pearls around her throat. "These are exquisite!"

Because her hands were shaking, Mike had to fasten the necklace in place. His hands were none too steady, either, but he didn't let her see it.

Avery whisked off to look at herself in the bathroom mirror. Mike watched her from the doorway, seeing the way she caught her breath, how she touched the pearls lying luminescent and vital in the hollow of her throat. Mike went warm inside just watching her.

Once she'd finished admiring herself, she turned and threw her arms around Mike's neck.

"Thank you," she whispered, her voice soft and a little teary. "I never expected anything so—so wonderful."

"I helped him pick them out!" Fee crowed and insinuated herself between them.

Finally, after giving Avery those pearls, Mike felt like he had proved himself. That he deserved to have Avery as his bride. While he might not be rich or highly educated, he could provide for his wife. He could take care of her as well as any man. He could make her happy.

When Fee had taken those pearls from their special place in her mother's dresser, she might not have known in dollars and cents what they were worth, but she knew how Avery treasured them. He knew she'd seen the pride in his eyes every time Avery wore that necklace.

And she'd stolen them anyway.

Mike refocused his field glasses and saw that Fee had put Samantha back in the stroller and that they were moving this way. Fee's pace as they completed their circuit of the lake sent him hustling back to the truck. He slumped down as she wheeled past the Silverado to where her Neon was parked in a space almost directly behind him.

Once she'd passed, Mike adjusted the rearview mirror so he could watch her. He saw Fee unbelt Samantha from the stroller and duck inside the car to put her in the car seat. Then Fee came around back, unlocked and raised the trunk.

The stroller, a battered old thing that looked like Fee had bought it at Goodwill, wasn't all that easy to operate. As Mike watched, Fee set the brake and reached around to pinch the releases on either side of the body.

But as the stroller collapsed, one of the mechanisms grabbed the cuff of Fee's jacket and jerked her forward and down onto her knees.

Mike jumped out of the truck before he thought. He crossed the parking lot in three long strides and bent over his daughter. In an instant he'd freed her sleeve and lifted her to her feet.

"Thank you," Fiona said before she'd even turned to him, "for your help with..."

Then, when she saw who'd rescued her, she paled. Her eyes went wide with shock.

"Fiona," Mike whispered, his hand still clasped around her arm to steady her.

He recognized the exact moment when the surprise in her face turned to panic. With a strangled cry, she jerked out of his grasp and spun away. She scrambled into the car, and he heard her lock the doors against him.

Against him, her father.

Mike barely remembered walking back to the truck or climbing inside. His hands were shaking as he shoved the key into the ignition. He gunned the engine, squealed out of the parking space, and roared out of the park in a cloud of dust.

He pulled into the first gas station he came to and parked around back. He pressed his fingers against his eyes until colors swirled behind his eyelids, but he couldn't block out the expression on Fee's face when she looked at him.

My God! How could this have happened? How could his daughter be afraid of him? How could she think he'd harm either her or Samantha? He was the guy who'd taught her how to fly a kite, drive a nail, and win at checkers. He was the guy who dried her tears when she fell off her bike and took her for ice cream after he'd bandaged her up.

He was the father who loved her—even now.

He rubbed his eyes and pressed harder, trying to stanch the sudden burn of tears.

Avery had been wrong to ask him to look after Fee while she was away. Doing that made him recognize the woman his daughter had become. It widened the scope of regrets and made him realize that the pain of rejection cut both ways.

From now on, if Avery wanted to know where her daughter was or what she was doing, she'd just have to spy on Fiona herself.

Chapter 10

✵

Sometimes life just knocked you on your butt! "I gotta tell you," Fiona declared, plonking her cup of coffee down on Casey's kitchen table, "seeing him like that really freaked me out."

Casey brought a plate of freshly baked sugar cookies to the table and settled herself in the chair across from Fee. "Your dad just showed up out there at the park?"

"Like he'd dropped out of the sky!" Fee took a bite of one of Casey's cookies. "I was having trouble getting Samantha's stroller folded up so I could put it in the trunk, and when the stupid thing finally collapsed, it caught on my sleeve. It pulled me off balance, right down onto my knees."

"And your dad came to rescue you?"

For a minute, Fee thought she was hallucinating. "I mean, I haven't seen him once since that day in the Food-4-Less, and all of a sudden he shows up in Liberty Lake Park trying to help me out. It was so weird. Just so"—Fee shook her head, perplexed—"damned strange."

"Did he say anything?" Casey asked and reached for a cookie.

"Just my name."

"Did you say anything to him?"

"I was too shocked at seeing him like that." Fee replayed the scene in her head: someone bending over her, releasing the fabric of her sleeve from the stroller mechanism, then lifting her to her feet. She didn't know who it was until she turned to thank the man who'd helped her—and saw it was her dad.

"I think I might have kind of yelped and backed away," she admitted. "I jumped into the car and..."

...locked the doors against her own father.

It wasn't that she'd exactly been afraid of him. She'd been more scared about what he might say to her or the accusations he could make. Or the shame he'd make her feel over what she'd done or the way she'd left.

Casey broke off a piece of the cookie and put it in her mouth. "What did he do then?"

Fiona wrapped her fingers a little more tightly around her mug of coffee, glad for its warmth. "He got back in his truck and drove away."

Fee was still locked in her car when Mike peeled out of the parking lot.

"I can't imagine how I missed seeing him," she went on. "He was parked practically across from me. I must have walked right past his truck!"

"So do you think running into him at the park was a co-incidence?" Casey ventured.

"Not a chance."

Casey nodded sagely. "Then he must have been keeping an eye on you."

"Now why would he be doing that?" Fee wanted to know. "He made it pretty clear he was disowning me when I left Larkin. He forbid Mom to even talk to me."

Fee saw Casey glance toward the living room where Dan was watching *60 Minutes* with his own sleepy kid in one arm and Samantha in the other. She was probably thinking that Dan loved Derek too much to ever disown him. To do what Mike Montgomery had done to Fiona.

Fee thought her dad loved her that much, too. Once. But she'd been wrong. So much for that unconditional love your parents were supposed to give you, she thought with a sniff. If she was honest with herself, Fee had to admit her mother's love had never wavered. But it was her dad she'd most provoked, her dad who must have felt the most betrayed.

She knew her mom had loved those pearls, but Fee had seen just how much they meant to her dad every time her mother wore them. And Fiona had stolen them anyway. Looking back, she wondered how she'd been able to live with herself afterward.

"I bet your mom asked your dad to look after you while she's in China," Casey suggested.

Fee took a sip of her coffee and considered that. "Mom has left a couple of messages on my voice mail about how well things are going in China. She said she was bringing home a stuffed Sheepish for Samantha."

"I remember how your mom used to tell us Sheepish stories," Casey said, "all those times when I slept over."

Fee remembered those times, too. She and Casey would be tucked in among their mounds of stuffed animals while her mom sat cross-legged at the foot of the bed and told them stories. It was going to be neat having the lamb her mother had made up for her turned into something she could snuggle and hold in her arms.

Fee reached for a second cookie. "Mom said she hoped

that once she got back she and Samantha and I could get together."

"So are you going to do that?"

"Yeah, I am."

Fiona missed her mother. She missed the house where she'd grown up, missed lying in her cozy bed and hearing the wind in the trees out back. She missed feeling safe. She missed feeling as if not everything in the world depended on what she said or did or decided.

"You know what else creeps me out?" Fee asked.

"What?"

"When my mother was following me around," Fee reflected, "I'd see her cruising the campus or parked at the Food-4-Less. With my dad, I never had a clue he was watching me. It's kind of unnerving to realize someone can follow you around, and you not know."

"So maybe you ought to be more careful," Casey suggested. "But there is one thing that's for sure in all of this."

Fee glanced across the table at her friend.

"Your dad wouldn't be doing this if he'd written you off."

"Not likely," Fiona snorted. But regardless of what she said, something warm and nourishing stirred inside of her—something that felt remarkably like hope.

✺

Mike couldn't wait for dark. As soon as dusk began to sift down over the rolling Kansas hills, he climbed the road to the observatory and threw back the roof.

For more than a week he'd been too busy watching over Fee and Samantha to come here, but tonight he needed the solitude and the silence. He needed to remind himself that in the vastness of space, a single moment in a single life was insignificant, inconsequential. He needed to flirt with the waning moon, lose himself in the shimmer of Saturn's rings, and peer deep into the dark where the heavens hid their secrets.

He came here as a diversion from the memory of how his daughter had withdrawn from him this morning, because he needed to focus on something he loved almost as much as he loved Fee.

Mike booted up the computer and prepared the telescope the way he always did. Like an athlete stretching out the kinks before a game, he slewed the telescope toward a familiar piece of sky. Orion popped into view; the three bright stars in his belt made the constellation recognizable to any schoolchild.

Mike focused on Rigel and its dimmer counterpart glowing at the hunter's left foot. As he turned the telescope to Betelgeuse glimmering in Orion's upraised hand, he did his best to turn his thoughts from Fiona and the way she'd rejected him this morning.

How many times, he wondered peering up at the sky, had she slid her hand into his when she was little? How many times had he sat on the edge of her bed and stroked her hair when she couldn't sleep? He always felt proud, privileged that his little girl put such trust, such faith in him. Until today—today when Fee had jerked away as if she hated him.

After all the months they'd been estranged, he shouldn't have been surprised by her reaction. Still, the shock and panic he'd seen in her face when she realized who he was, had caught him by surprise. But then, he'd only been trying to help, only been trying to make sure she was all right. He'd only been reacting the way he would have to anyone in trouble—much less his own daughter.

It hurt that she was more willing to accept help from a stranger than she was from him.

Mike's eyes stung and, jumpy and impatient with Orion, he flitted across the sky to pay his respects to Andromeda. Fee had always loved the soft, cloudy glow of that huge spiral galaxy. It was one of the first things she'd found with her own telescope, and he remembered how enormously pleased Fee had been with herself. She'd gone into the house and dragged Avery out into the backyard in her nightgown to look at it.

Stop thinking about Fiona, he told himself and swung the scope away from the objects they'd viewed so often together.

Mike needed something more challenging than star hopping to keep his mind occupied, so he plugged his CCD, charged-coupled device, into the computer. The advent of digital cameras for telescopes made it possible for rank amateurs to catch spectacular, amazingly clear images of the sky—if they were patient.

Setting up the CCD, the colored filters for the camera, and the computer were exacting work, just the kind Mike needed. He took a few test images, adjusted the focus on the telescope, took a few more, then typed the appropriate commands into the computer. He began imaging the ecliptic in Pisces.

He spent the best part of an hour doing that, then brought the pictures up on the computer screen. They were clear images, but Mike didn't see anything that interested him until he "blinked" through them, flipping from one to

the next in rapid sequence. As he did, one of the "stars" began to move.

"I got an asteroid," Mike said with some satisfaction. He
calculated the asteroid's course, then called up the Web site
listing all the known asteroids and their orbits to figure out
which one he'd "caught."

He made a notation in the notebook where he and Fee
had always kept a record of what they saw, and was about to
erase the images from the computer when he spotted something else—another fainter speck moving across the sky on
a tangent to the first.

He reviewed the images, made a few more calculations,
rechecked his work, and went to the Web site again. There
was no known asteroid in the position he'd recorded.

A bolt of excitement shot up his back. Was it possible the
spear of light shooting across the sky that he'd captured in
his images was a new asteroid, one no one had seen before?
He checked the data and the Web site four times before he
began to believe what he was seeing.

Instinctively, he reached for his cell phone wanting to
talk to Fiona. In spite of everything, she was the only person
who'd understand what he'd accomplished, the only one
who'd feel the same mix of uncertainty and euphoria he
was feeling.

But he couldn't call. Not with the way things were between them, not after how she'd backed away from him this
morning. And certainly not at this hour.

Besides, someone somewhere—some expert in astronomy with years of experience, advanced degrees, and hours
of course work, some *real* astronomer staring up through
one of the telescopes at Mount Palomar or Kitt—had already seen and verified his findings.

Who was he—a man with no pretensions and no degree—to have found something no one else had ever seen? Even if his observations and the images he'd make over the next days and weeks verified what he'd spotted tonight, how would he dare report it?

The very idea was laughable.

But he wasn't laughing when he saved the images and his page of notations. He didn't so much as snicker as he shut down the camera and computer, or as he put the telescope to bed and closed the roof of the observatory.

Mike went outside and sat in the cold and the quiet for a very long while. How could he possibly have made a legitimate discovery? A man like him?

He sat there caught between the earth and the cosmos, between new ambition and a horrifying fear of failure. Between hope that he'd found something no one else had seen before and overwhelming regret that he didn't have anyone he could tell about his discovery.

Chapter 11

✳

No one met Avery at the airport the day she came home from China. No one rushed out to carry her bags when the shuttle dropped her off at home. No one greeted her when she let herself into the house except Caleb the cat, meowing and wanting to be fed.

Avery dragged her suitcases in off the porch and stood for a moment in the dimly lit living room. The house felt empty, a little stale, and oddly silent. She'd been away just long enough to feel a certain detachment, as if she were entering an archaeological site where a happy family had lived once long ago.

Avery switched on lights as she crossed to the fireplace at the far end, and stood looking at the photographs on the mantel. They were pictures of that happy family, people with whom she felt compelled to reacquaint herself: Fee grinning toothless from the seat of her new first two-wheeler; Mike at the job site, hard hat on and hammer in hand.

Avery took down her favorite photograph, holding it in her hands like an artifact. Ted's wife Nancy had taken the picture the day they broke ground for the observatory. In it, she and Mike and Fee had wrapped their arms around one another and they were laughing as if they were glad to be together.

Avery hated how much things had changed from that day to this. She hated that neither Mike nor Fiona was here to welcome her home. They ought to be. They ought to have missed her enough to come to hug her hello, to have a salad made for supper and chicken ready to grill. They ought to be the family in the photograph, smiling and happy.

Her throat burned with a fine, fresh anger at all they'd lost, all they'd deliberately thrown away. She hated that Mike was still hanging tight to his anger and his hurt. She wanted to shake Fiona for being so determined to prove herself, so determined to deny her parents the joy of knowing their only grandchild.

Now that she was home from China, all of that was going to change. With the bulk of the Sheepish project out of the way, Avery wasn't going to stand idly by and let things go on the way they were. She meant to put the family in that photograph back together again—one way or another.

Avery set the frame back on the mantel and, as she moved through those empty rooms, the house seemed to embrace her, confirming her decision. Memories of the people she loved seemed to creep right out of the walls to strengthen her resolve. She trailed her fingers along the back of the rocking chair her father had given her so she could rock Fee to sleep and felt comforted. Grandma Ada's outrageously ornate breakfront in the dining room seemed to stand foursquare behind her decision. The fine linen tablecloth her mother had embroidered for Avery's birthday two years before seemed to bless her commitment.

And on the window seat, beside Avery's own cutting

from Great-Grandmother Letty's Christmas cactus, sat the potted plant she intended to give to Fee.

As she glided into the big, high-ceilinged kitchen, she felt Mike's love enfold her, sensed his care and craftsmanship, his commitment to this family in every board and nail and coat of paint. He was present in every inch of the house's plumbing and wiring, in the tile on the kitchen floor, in the tall glass-fronted cupboards he'd built for her. He was here in baseboards, in every spindle of the lacy gingerbread he'd turned for their front porch, in every shingle on the roof.

From the moment they'd climbed out of his truck and came up that broken walk, Avery had sensed Mike's need to turn this house into a home. They'd worked on it together for more than a year, transforming the place from a dilapidated shell into a haven for the two of them. *And then for the three of them.*

Because this house meant so much to both of them, it had been hard to fill out the loan papers that would put the place at risk. Avery had seen how difficult it was for Mike to sign his name to them and understood his reasons. This house was more than a place he'd built with his own two hands, it was the single place in the world where he'd ever belonged, ever been happy.

But now that the lambs were nearly finished and ready to ship to the distributor in Los Angeles, Avery could breathe a little easier. By Christmas the house would be theirs again free and clear—and when it was, Avery wanted Mike home again. She wanted Fee and Samantha running in and out. She wanted her family back together.

Now that she'd returned to Larkin, she had to make a start at that.

She made the easier phone call first. Fiona's voice mail picked up on the fourth ring.

"Hi, honey," Avery said at the beep, "it's Mom. It's about eight-thirty Thursday night. The airport shuttle just dropped me off at the house. As soon as I feed the cat, I'm headed for bed.

"I've got so much to tell you about the trip, and I have goodies from China for you and Samantha. Is there a time the three of us can get together? I thought lunch on Saturday or brunch on Sunday. Probably at the Sunny Spot. Let me know which of those times works for you. I love you both."

As she disconnected, the nervous fluttering in her belly started up. Talking to Mike wasn't going to be as easy as leaving a message for her daughter.

She dialed the farm anyway, hoping she'd catch him at the house. Ted answered instead, and she could hear the TV blaring in the background.

"Hi, Ted, it's Avery," she said. "Is Mike—"

"You back from—" Ted's voice was low and slurry. "Where was it you went again? Hong Kong?"

"China," she corrected him.

"Yeah, that's what Mike told me." He sounded like he'd been working his way through a case of beer.

"Is Mike there?"

"No, he's not. He's up at the telescope," Ted told her, sounding petulant. "He's spent most of every damn night up there. Why is that?"

Either Mike had decided to take advantage of being out at the farm to indulge in some intensive viewing, or he was running away from Ted the same way he'd run away from her.

"Is he imaging something in particular?" she asked him.

"He could be working on the next lunar landing, for all I know," Ted grumbled.

"I'll see if I can catch Mike on his cell. If you talk to him before I do, will you tell him I got home safe and sound?"

"Back from Hong Kong," Ted murmured. "I'll tell him that."

Avery hung up, knowing he'd never remember she'd called. Mike was right; Ted needed to do something about his drinking.

She punched in the numbers for her husband's cell and scowled when she got his voice mail, too. She'd wanted to talk to *him*, damn it, not dead air.

"Well, here I was," she began with an uncomfortable laugh, "expecting a big welcome-home celebration with balloons and noisemakers and cake. So where were you?"

The joke fell flat with no one to laugh at it. She pressed ahead, feeling foolish.

"I just walked in a few minutes ago. I had a long but totally uneventful flight. Thanks for coming by to feed Caleb and water the plants while I was gone. I'm heading for bed to try and beat this jet lag. Give me a call sometime tomorrow, will you?"

Before she hung up, she paused, feeling flushed and fluttery. "Hey, Mike," she said, her throat a little tight. "I missed you, okay?"

She puttered around for a few more minutes, fed the cat, and made a sandwich for herself, grateful that Mike had stocked the refrigerator. She took a halfhearted look at the mail. When she realized Mike wasn't going to call her right back, she trudged upstairs.

She put on pajamas, washed her face and brushed her teeth, then fell into bed exhausted.

Into her big, lonely bed; in her quiet, empty house.

She shut her eyes, wanting Mike home and back in bed with her, wanting Mike to snuggle up to. She wanted Fee and Samantha stopping by whenever they had a chance. She wanted her family back. She wanted the life she loved back again, and she wanted it all by Christmas Day.

Avery's last thought as she drifted toward sleep was that it was already very nearly Thanksgiving.

✶

The phone rang a little after three A.M.

Avery awoke with a start and bolted up in bed, not sure if she was in still in China or home in Larkin. The extension on the nightstand trilled again, and she groped toward it. By the third ring she managed to get the receiver to her ear.

"Hello?" she gasped, her heart thumping. She snapped on the lamp on the nightstand and was relieved to see her bedroom take shape around her—though a phone call at this hour was hardly going to bring good news.

"I'm sorry to disturb you, Mrs. Montgomery," the male voice said. "This is Deputy Dalton Miller down at the sheriff's office."

Cold doused Avery from head to toe.

Were Fee and Samantha all right? Had Mike had an accident?

"Is Mike there?" the deputy asked.

"'Mike'?" she echoed, still not thinking clearly.

"We picked his brother Ted up for DWI. He sideswiped a couple of parked cars coming out of Charney's."

"Is Ted all right?" Avery asked. He must have gone out after he talked to her, driven to Charney's, and gotten completely smashed.

"He's drunk as a skunk, ma'am, and puking up sock lint."

The deputy's colorful description made Avery smile in spite of herself.

"Mike's not available right now, but I'll have him call you as soon as he can," she promised and disconnected.

She knew small town law enforcement well enough to realize that that answer would set off a flurry of speculation about her and Mike. Still, Avery didn't owe anyone an explanation for why her husband wasn't in bed beside her at this hour.

She tried Mike's cell phone again and finally reached him on the farmhouse line.

"You calling me from China, sweetheart?" Mike sounded even more fuddled with sleep than she had been.

"I'm calling from our house on Prospect Street. I'm waking you up because I just got a call from the sheriff's office."

"Not about Fee."

Something about the way his voice sharpened with concern answered a question she hadn't dared to ask him.

"As far as I know, Fiona's fine," Avery assured him. "They picked up Ted for DWI."

"Oh, hell," she heard Mike say. "I knew this was going to happen sooner or later. Is he all right?"

"From what Dalton Miller said, he's fine but driving the porcelain bus right now. Apparently, Ted sideswiped some cars coming out of Charney's."

He whistled under his breath. "It's a wonder he escaped with his life after doing that."

"I told Deputy Miller you'd call him as soon as you could."

But both of them knew there was no rush; the sheriff was going to keep Ted until morning anyway.

Avery bent a little closer to the mouthpiece. "I'm sorry this happened, Mike. I know how much you've hoped Ted could get a handle on his drinking."

On the other end of the line she heard Mike sigh. "I just don't want to see him end up like my dad."

Mike never said much about his father's drinking, but Janice had told Avery how their father would drive them into town for church and be passed out in the backseat of the car by the time the service was over. Ted claimed he'd never once seen Ed Montgomery walk a straight line. Mike's mother Myra once showed Avery the scar on her forehead from when Ed had shied a jar of marmalade at her one morning at breakfast.

"Maybe this time Ted will listen to me when I talk about him going to AA," Mike said.

"I hear there's a pretty good treatment facility in Olathe," Avery suggested. "Do you think you could convince him to check himself in?"

She could almost see Mike scrubbing his hand through his hair. "It's residential, isn't it? And probably really expensive."

Avery didn't hesitate. "Whatever Ted needs, Mike. If he agrees to get help, we have to stand by him."

"I appreciate that." His voice went soft as he went on. "Especially after the way I kept writing him checks."

"You did what you thought you had to do," she murmured, not realizing until that moment that she'd forgiven him—for that at least. "What upset me more than the money was that you didn't tell me what you were doing."

"I should have," he admitted. "I just didn't want to argue with you about that, too."

There was a beat of silence between them, as if he

regretted opening a subject neither of them wanted to talk about. At least not now.

She could hear him moving around the farmhouse kitchen, could imagine him looking out the window above the sink to where the moon would be casting the shadows across the drive.

"So when did you get back from China?" he asked her.

"About eight tonight," she told him and turned out the light. "I told Ted to tell you and I left a message on your cell phone."

"I didn't think to check the cell before I went to bed," Mike murmured. "You pretty jet-lagged from the flight?"

"Pretty."

"You taking tomorrow off to get rested up?"

"Probably not," she admitted and settled back into the pillows. Now that the adrenaline rush of being awakened was wearing off, she was exhausted. "Work didn't stop at the Holding Company while I was gone. I need to go in and get caught up."

"Cleo took care of things."

The cadence between them was quiet and familiar, pillow talk, soft and comforting. It was surprising how quickly they fell back into the patterns of their regular married life.

"Um-hum. But I need to go in anyway. Restart things here. Have you been checking on Fiona?"

Mike went abruptly quiet; something about that silence disrupted the hazy drift of conversation between them.

"Not in the last couple of days," he finally said.

Before she could ask what Fee had been doing or why he'd stopped keeping an eye on her, Mike cut her off.

"Look, Avery, I probably ought to make that call to the

sheriff's office and see about Ted. Thanks for fielding this for me."

"I wish—" she began.

"I'm glad you're back," Mike said, then abruptly disconnected.

Avery sat for the best part of a minute cradling the receiver against her ear before she hung up too.

✵

Mike turned away from the high counter at the front of the sheriff's office as one of the deputies escorted his brother down the hall from the holding cells at the back.

Ted looked awful and smelled worse. His hair hung in strings around a face the color of skim milk. His shirt was rumpled and stained with vomit. He shuffled along clutching the waist of his pants because they'd confiscated his belt and shoelaces.

"Are you all right?" Mike asked, as his brother sorted through the envelope of belongings the deputies had taken from him when they booked him the night before.

Ted glowered at him just the way their father used to do when Mike had been the one to come and bail him out. Seeing that same expression on his brother's face made Mike's chest go tight, made him want to punch out all of Ted's teeth.

He hated that Ted was turning into their old man.

Instead, Mike stood over him as Ted plopped down on one of the chairs in the waiting area to relace and put on his shoes. Neither of them said a word as they crossed the parking lot, but when they reached the truck, Ted paused, unzipped his fly, and peed on the Silverado's front tire.

"Couldn't take a proper piss with all those guys watching," he smirked.

"Jesus, Ted, just look at yourself!" Mike hissed, then strode around to the driver's side. Ted was still fumbling with the seat belt when he climbed in.

"Just say whatever it is you've got to say to me," he snapped, "and get it over with. I need to get home and change; I'm already late to work."

Though he'd been preparing half the night, Mike wasn't ready to say what he had to say to his brother. "I already called in sick for you."

"'Sick'?" Ted sputtered, turning red-rimmed eyes toward him. "Why the hell did you call me in sick? I've gotten up and gone to work when I've been a whole lot more hung over than this!"

"Is that something you ought to be bragging about?" Mike asked him. "Haven't you just admitted your drinking's gotten out of hand?"

Ted leaned back against the door and shrugged. "So I stop for a shot and a beer after work. A lot of guys do that."

Mike had a fleeting vision of working men all over the country bellying up to a bar at five-fifteen for a sloop and a beer. Most of them downed their drinks, blew off a little steam with their buddies, and went home to their families.

Ted wasn't handling it that way—at least not since Nancy left.

"You're doing a whole lot more than having a drink on your way home," Mike insisted. "You either come home drunk, or plop yourself down in front of the TV and polish off a case of beer."

His brother snorted. "I knew I was going to regret letting you move in when things went south with Avery."

Mike swallowed the surge of anger that burned up his throat. Hadn't the money he'd been giving Ted paid for the privilege of staying whenever the hell he wanted to on that farm? And his relationship with Avery was none of Ted's damn business.

"Do you even remember what you did last night?" Mike asked.

Ted looked down at himself. "Puked all over my clothes?"

"You sideswiped four parked cars coming out of Charney's."

His brother's eyebrows drew together, then he nodded. "Yeah, maybe I did. You suppose they'll raise my car insurance rates?"

Mike hoped some smart judge would take his brother's license.

"Those cars you hit could just as well have been occupied," Mike pointed out. "You could have hit people who were crossing the road. You could have wrapped your car around a tree on your way home."

"I suppose I could have killed myself."

"Yeah, you could have," Mike agreed, hanging on to his temper with both hands. "If that thought doesn't bother you, just think about the fact that you could just as easily have killed somebody else."

Ted appeared to be thinking that over, then he turned to Mike. "Why don't you just go home and make up with your wife. That way I can go to hell in my own way."

Mike wished he could go home to Avery. He wished he could find it in his heart to forgive Fiona so they could be a family again. But it wasn't that simple. The way Fee had shrunk away from him when he tried to help with the stroller at Liberty Lake Park meant she wasn't all that anxious to make things up with him, either.

Besides, this conversation wasn't about Mike's family problems; it was about Ted's.

"Haven't you noticed," Mike said, not rising to the bait, "that instead of having you drive into Kansas City to get the girls, Nancy's insisted on bringing them out to the farm? Do you have any idea why she's doing that?"

"Because she still has the hots for me?" Ted guessed.

"Because she doesn't want the girls riding with you. Because she never knows if you're going to show up at her house drunk or sober. Because she never knows if you're going to leave the girls in the car while you go into a bar for a pick-me-up, or if you're going to need to 'take a nap' while you're supposed to be watching them."

Two bright spots of color rose in Ted's pale cheeks. "Did Nancy tell you that?"

"In so many words," Mike answered. He wished the truth wasn't so brutal, that he didn't have to use it so ruthlessly against his kid brother. "I called before I picked you up this morning to let her know you'd been arrested."

"Aw, shit, Mike," Ted whispered. "She didn't have to know about this."

"I'm afraid she did."

"Why? So you could humiliate me in front of my wife?" Ted shouted. The volume of his own voice seemed to make him flinch, but he didn't take any pains to lower it. "Did you call Nancy so she would know you were coming to rescue me again, like you always have? So you could convince yourself you're still Mr. Mikey Perfect?

"Well, you've hit a bumpy patch in your life now, haven't you, pal?" Ted's tone ate into Mike like acid. "You don't want to deal with your own problems, so you're going to give me the hand you're sure I need, huh? You're going to make old Ted feel worse about himself, so you can feel better."

Ted's accusation made Mike want to grab him by his filthy shirtfront and shake him until his teeth rattled. He wanted to get out of the truck, walk away, and let Ted take care of this mess himself. But what Mike felt for his brother went back to before either of them knew what the word "responsibility" meant.

If he could travel back in time, he'd go to the day they'd started the observatory. Things had been so good between Avery and him. Fiona had been his bright, happy girl. Ted and Nancy had been getting along, and his brother hadn't been drinking.

Instead of that, Mike was stuck with making his brother face what he'd become. He only hoped he had the resolution to convince Ted to do something about the hole he was digging for himself.

"You know, Ted," he spoke deliberately, metering out the words. "Coming here to pick you up today reminded me so much of Dad."

"Shut up, Mike."

"I can't tell you how many times I came to the sheriff's office to get him so Mom didn't have to."

How old had Mike been then? Barely old enough to drive, he figured. Not old enough to deal with his father's hostility.

"Did Dad hate you then as much as I do now?" Ted snarled.

Mike hesitated before he answered. "Probably."

The first time Mike had come to get him, Ed Montgomery had backhanded him right here in the parking lot. He'd hit him so hard Mike tasted blood, and when that didn't put him on his ass, his father hit him again. He kept hitting him, until Mike was on the ground and covering up to protect himself. When he refused to fight back, two deputies had grabbed his father and hustled him back inside. Ed had ended up cooling his heels in a cell for a full week. After that, it was what Ed Montgomery said to him on their drive home that drew blood.

"You remember what a hair-trigger temper he had when he'd been drinking," Mike went on, determined to keep Ted from turning into their father. "Remember how he threw away all your Matchbox cars because you left them on the floor."

"They were *garaged* under the couch," Ted said, still clearly angry with a man who'd been dead more than twenty years.

"And how he hacked off Janice's braids because he said no daughter of his was going to go around looking like a hippie."

Mike didn't have to remind Ted of the things their father had done to their mother, bringing her a bouquet of wildflowers one minute and slapping her around the next.

"God, how I hated him sometimes," Ted admitted. "He'd be so mean to Mom. She must have cried a river of tears over that bastard, and he wasn't worth even one."

When Ed Montgomery had been struck by lightning harrowing the south field, Mike hadn't mourned him. He just figured it was God's way of meting out justice.

"You don't want to end up like him, do you, Ted?" Mike asked quietly.

Ted's head jerked up. His bloodshot gaze met Mike's for the first time all morning. The impudence was gone. Mike felt Ted's desperation twist in his own guts.

"I'm not really like him, am I, Mike?"

As much as Mike wanted to spare his brother, he owed him the truth. "Not quite yet," he admitted. "But if you keep on the way you're going, Ted, your girls are going to remember you just the way we remember Dad."

"Oh, God!" Ted moaned and buried his face in his hands.

"You've got to do something about your drinking now, Ted," Mike insisted, "while you still can."

Mike's hand was shaking as he took a brochure out of his jacket pocket and handed it across to his brother.

"Hope House runs the best rehab facility in this part of the country. It'll give you a chance to dry out and get counseling so you can figure out why you're doing this. They'll teach you ways to cope with quitting and will help you find the support you'll need once you leave there."

Ted's face was gray and bleak as he looked down at the brochure, then up at Mike. "Do you really think I can do this?"

Mike swallowed his need to reassure his brother. "You've got to decide that for yourself, Ted. It's not something I can help you with."

Ted seemed to think that over, then looked at Mike again. "I don't want to live my life like Pa."

A bit of the weight he had been carrying seemed to lift off Mike's shoulders.

"I made some calls this morning," he said. "They're saving a space for you at Hope House if you're willing to start today. I've packed a bag of things I thought you'd need and put it in the back. We can go right there this morning and you can start—"

"But I can't just walk away from my job," Ted protested.

Mike's first impulse was to cajole and promise. Instead he did what the social worker on the phone had told him to do; he put the ball in Ted's court. "Do you want to do this, Ted, or don't you?"

"I want to do it."

"Then I'll find a way to square things with your boss. Hope House runs a twenty-eight-day program"—Mike allowed himself the slightest of smiles—"which means you'll finish up a week and a half before Christmas. Just when the post office needs you most."

Ted looked down at himself and asked, "Don't I need to at least go home and change?"

Mike started the truck. "They said they'd take you just the way you are."

Chapter 12

✳

When Avery bustled into the Sunny Spot for brunch on Sunday morning, Fiona and Samantha had already claimed the prime corner booth. She'd suggested they meet here partly because the Sunny Spot had always been Fee's favorite restaurant, but mostly because Avery refused to invite her daughter to the home where she'd grown up as if she were a guest.

Avery paused in the doorway into the dining room, knowing a new phase in her relationship with her daughter was beginning today. A rebuilding and reacquaintance, a new depth of love, a kind of equality daughters never truly achieved until they were mothers themselves. Avery wanted so much for this new beginning to lead to reconciliation between Mike and Fee, but she knew she mustn't count on that. So she sucked in a breath and breezed toward where her daughter and granddaughter were waiting.

Avery threw her arms around Fiona and hugged her hard, hugged her as she hadn't been able to in months. She clung to those broad, bony shoulders, rubbed her cheek against Fee's rusty-brown hair, and blinked back the sting of tears.

Then, giving her daughter a final squeeze, Avery slid into the banquette and spoke to the baby in the carrier. "And how's Miss Samantha this morning?" Avery cooed, stroking the baby's cheek with her fingertip.

Samantha gurgled and stared up at her grandmother, wide-eyed.

"She's eating so much these days," Fiona answered dryly. "I thought I'd order her her own stack of pancakes."

"You eat like that because you're growing, aren't you, sweetie?" Avery asked her granddaughter.

"So how was China?" Fee asked in what was clearly a pre-emptive strike, directing the conversation away from things she'd rather not discuss.

But Avery wasn't here to ask questions or make demands. All she wanted was time with her daughter and her grandchild.

"Things went very well in Beijing," Avery told her and began to rummage through her canvas tote. "I come bearing gifts."

"'Gifts'?" Fee asked.

Fee had always loved gifts, so Avery always looked for "prizes" when she traveled on business. Sometimes it was only a T-shirt from the hotel she'd stayed at or a snow globe she found at the airport, but Fee loved getting whatever she brought home, proof that her mother had thought about her while she was gone. It was an assurance, Avery supposed, people never really outgrew.

"What I brought Samantha," she began as she popped the gift out of the sack and onto the baby's belly, "is one of the very first lambs off the production line in China. Samantha, meet Sheepish."

Samantha crowed and reached for the cuddly, sweet-faced little sheep. She wrapped her hands around him, pulled him to her, and immediately jammed Sheepish's ear into her mouth.

Both Fee and Avery laughed.

"That's just the way I pictured Sheepish when you used to tell me stories!" Fiona exclaimed, nearly as pleased with the sheep as her daughter was.

"I'm glad you approve of him," Avery said, trading the teething ring Fee had given her for Samantha's hold on Sheepish's ear. "After all the years of telling you Sheepish stories, I think of him as your sheep, too."

Fee leaned a little closer and petted the sheep herself. "He must be something you designed after I left."

She tried not to think about what things were like after Fiona went away. Avery hadn't had a new idea in months until it occurred to her to turn the characters in the stories she used to tell her daughter into a toy.

"Elite Cards wanted Sheepish for an Easter promotion," she answered, bouncing the lamb on the baby's belly. "I wasn't happy about producing him offshore, but there was no way the Holding Company could finish more than fifty thousand sheep in three months."

"They wanted fifty thousand!" Fee gasped, clearly impressed.

"When I left China, nearly all the little guys were packed and ready to ship. Our West Coast distributor will pick them up in L.A. and send them directly to the Elite stores."

"This is wild, Mom!" Fee enthused. "Who'd have

thought the stuffed animals you made for me when I was little would turn into such a successful business?"

Avery just nodded. She could see that becoming a mother wasn't the only thing that had changed Fiona. She'd begun to see the world in a wider view. She'd learned the value of money, come to appreciate accomplishment. Maybe she'd discovered that success demanded focus and sacrifice.

Avery had protected her only child from reality for as long as she could, but once Fee struck out on her own, the life lessons must have come thick and fast. Wasn't Fee coming back to Larkin proof of that?

"I brought something from China for you, too," Avery said and delved back into her bag.

Fee made short work of the corded toggle around the beautiful, brocade-covered box. "Oh, Mom!" she gasped as she pulled out the shimmering embroidered kimono. She wriggled out of the booth and pulled it on right over her sweater and jeans. The brilliant sapphire blue brought out the tinge of red in her hair and warmed the tone of Fee's pale skin. But as she tightened the sash around her waist, Avery saw with a shock of concern how thin her daughter really was.

"This is beautiful," Fiona oohed, petting the lapel that had been embroidered with graceful cranes. "Thank you so much for thinking of me."

As if Avery hadn't thought about Fee every day, every hour and minute since she'd been born. "Have you ordered breakfast?" she asked.

"I was waiting for you," Fee said, then ordered as if she hadn't eaten in a month.

"Have you been seeing a lot of your grandmother?"

Avery asked, figuring the question fell on neutral ground, since it was where she'd finally seen Samantha.

"Gran's been great," Fee answered with a nod. "She's let me rummage through the attic and take things for the apartment. I do laundry there, and she keeps an eye on Samantha when Casey has stuff she needs to do. In return for her baby-sitting, I've been helping Gran with the yard."

"Your grandmother lets you work in her garden?" Avery asked in astonishment. Miriam Parrish never let anyone near her plantings.

"Gran's slowed down while I was gone," Fee observed with a shrug. "She's not keeping up with things the way she did."

A chill brushed up the back of Avery's neck. Why hadn't she noticed that? Was it because her mother's mind was still so sharp, or were there signs of her mother aging that Avery hadn't been willing to see?

"Gran's taught me how to prune the roses back for winter," Fee went on as the food arrived. "She taught me what needs to be mulched and where to plant the bulbs for spring. It's stuff that'll come in handy when I have a house of my own."

Avery looked at her daughter and projected her hopes for the future on to Fee: a job worthy of her skills and intellect, friends that she could count on the way she counted on Casey and Dan, a snug home, a husband who loved her, more children maybe, and a new relationship with her father. *A new relationship that reunited their family.*

While Avery picked at her omelette and wondered if there was any chance for reconciliation, Fiona tucked into her pecan pancakes and bacon as if she was starving.

Midway through breakfast, she unearthed a bottle from

the diaper bag and offered it to her mother. With that simple invitation, that gesture of trust, the last of the reserve between the two of them melted away.

Gently Avery lifted her granddaughter from the carrier and nestled Samantha in her arms. Sweet elation dawned in her chest as she held her baby's baby in her arms, her little girl's little girl. Letty's great-great-great-granddaughter. In this day and age when many children barely knew their grandparents, maintaining the connection through six generations of McIntire women with the gift of Letty's Christmas cactus seemed rare—and very special.

Contentment sped through Avery's veins like rays of sunlight as she offered the bottle to her granddaughter, who immediately drew the nipple into her mouth. It seemed impossible that this child had been conceived and born and cared for without Avery knowing, without her being there. But rather than dwell on what she'd missed, Avery took pleasure in what she had. As the baby nursed, she felt an aura of sweet serenity settle over them.

Only after Samantha had eaten and fallen asleep in the crook of her shoulder, did Avery turn to Fiona and ask, "Do you hear anything from Jared?"

She hoped she wasn't overstepping her bounds by asking that, but Jared had been in and out of their house since junior high. Avery had watched him grow from a sweet, compelling child to a talented and focused young man she genuinely liked and cared about.

"Jared calls when he can," Fee answered, refusing to meet her mother's gaze. "He sends money when he has it. He's as responsible a father as he can afford to be."

If he was really a responsible father, he would have married Fiona and come home, found a job, and put his family first. But that would mean Jared would have to give up his dream of having a career in music. And wasn't it bad enough that Fiona had sacrificed the things she'd always wanted, to provide for Samantha?

"Do you think you and Jared will ever get back together?" Avery asked hopefully.

Fee flattened her lips against her teeth and she shook her head. "Nope."

"Do you think Jared will ever want to have a relationship with Samantha?"

"I wouldn't count on it," she answered shortly.

Avery wanted to ask so many more questions: what Fee's life had been like during the months she'd been away, how she'd gotten pregnant when Avery knew very well she'd had access to birth control, and what finally happened between Jared and her that had set Fee running home. But she didn't ask any of that, because she knew that today she and her daughter were making a new beginning. And, as long as she didn't push, Avery would hear the whole story eventually.

Instead they talked about Fee's classes, Casey and Dan, her job at the Food-4-Less. Avery hadn't planned to say a word to Fee about her father until Fee brought him up.

"And just so you know, I didn't much appreciate having Dad following me around while you were away."

Avery paused in rubbing Samantha's back. "You knew your dad was following you?"

Fiona frowned around her last bite of Avery's omelette. "How could I not know? He came right up to me when Samantha and I were walking at Liberty Lake Park."

Mike had done that?

Fee must have read the incredulity in her mother's face. "You mean, he didn't tell you?"

Avery shook her head. She and Mike had talked twice since she got back from China. The first time they'd talked about Ted; the second about whether it was cold enough to put up the storm windows. *So why hadn't Mike told her about Fee?*

"I was having trouble getting the stroller folded," Fee explained, "and he showed up out of nowhere to help."

Avery could imagine that. Mike was always rescuing people: opening the door at the post office for a man with an armload of packages, stopping for a kid at the side of the road whose bike chain had broken. *Rescuing a strange woman tumbling down the escalator at the airport.*

"He's a lot better at following people than you are, Mom; I didn't even realize he was there until he came to help with the stroller."

Avery was still trying to imagine Mike and Fee coming face-to-face. "What did you do?"

Fee shrugged and scowled as if she wasn't pleased with how she'd responded. "I kind of freaked. He helped me with the stroller and I—" She shook her head. "—I pulled away from him."

Avery compressed her lips. She understood, as Fee might not, how much Mike had risked in approaching her. He must have done it only because Fee was in trouble, done it because it was natural for him to help. That Fiona had rejected him, explained Mike's silence.

"Mom?" Fiona's voice broke into her thoughts. "Mom, would you tell him I'm sorry. He surprised me is all; I didn't mean to pull away from him."

"Of course I'll tell him." But even though Fee's apology

was genuine, Avery knew Mike would never accept it. He wouldn't believe that Fee hadn't meant to pull away, that she hadn't meant to reject him. Mike believed that actions spoke louder than words, which at least partially explained why Mike took Fiona stealing the pearls as such a personal betrayal.

Out at Liberty Lake Park, Mike Montgomery would have known rejection when he saw it, and he wouldn't accept either her apologies or her excuses for what had happened.

Avery drew the sleeping baby close against her chest. She looked across at Fee, who she could see was working so hard to make up for the mistakes she'd made. She thought about Mike and the hurt still eating away at him, and realized how hard it was going to be to find a way to bring her family back together.

And she didn't have any idea how to do it.

⚜

Were the CCD images he'd captured an undiscovered asteroid, or the perfect chance to make an ass of himself?

Mike leaned closer to the computer screen and blinked through the entire sequence of photographs he'd made over the course of the week. Yet as compelling as the pictures seemed, he couldn't convince himself that the small, dark fleck moving steadily across the stationary background of stars was what he thought it was.

He hadn't had much experience looking at Near Earth Objects like comets and asteroids. Fee's fascination had been with planets, constellations, star clusters, and nebulae. After Fee left, Mike had taken comfort in visiting those familiar objects as if they were friends.

What he'd caught with the CCD more or less by accident

last Sunday night wasn't on any of his star charts. It wasn't on the list of known asteroids he'd downloaded from the Minor Planet Center at the Harvard-Smithsonian site. It wasn't anything whose orbit had been recorded and refined.

Could the misshapen speck he'd been doggedly tracking all week possibly be something no one else had seen?

The hot quiver at the base of his belly said it was. His backlog of experience studying the solar system said it might be. His lack of accreditation said he was probably kidding himself.

He knew other amateur astronomers had made remarkable discoveries. When Thomas Bopp had come to speak at Larkin University about his part in discovering the Hale-Bopp Comet, Mike and Fee had gone to hear him. Bopp had given a fascinating lecture, but what impressed Mike more than Bopp's ability, technique, or his astonishing good luck, was that he wasn't a scientist.

He worked an ordinary job ordering material for a construction company. Bopp hadn't warranted an article in *Time* magazine and interviews on CNN until he'd been part of one of the twentieth century's most astonishing astronomical discoveries.

Mike flipped on the radio to keep himself company and took a swig of his cooling coffee.

What he was looking at on the computer screen wasn't anything anywhere near as interesting as a bright new comet. But if this turned out to be an asteroid no one else had ever seen, he'd get the credit for finding it. Which meant he could claim it, name it, and leave his mark on the universe.

Not bad for someone without a degree or a speck of formal training. But then, that would only happen if he reported what he'd seen and his findings were eventually verified.

Mike sighed and scrubbed a hand through his hair. If only he knew someone at the university he could call, someone who could look at the images he'd made and warn him off if he was wrong.

Fiona.

Someone whose judgment he knew he could trust.

Fiona.

Someone who wasn't his estranged daughter.

Yet how much he wanted to share all this with Fee. He could very nearly taste the sweetness of the words in his mouth as he told her about his discovery. He could almost hear her voice spiral with pride and excitement.

Or at least that's the way things might have been if she hadn't run away, if he hadn't disowned her. If he hadn't followed her to Liberty Lake Park and discovered she was every bit as angry at him as he'd been at her.

Mike sat back and glared at the computer screen. Without Fiona to verify his discovery, how was he supposed to get up the nerve to report a new asteroid to the Center for Astrophysics?

Just as he was pondering that for the dozenth time, someone tapped him lightly on the shoulder. Mike all but catapulted out of his chair. He spun around and found Avery standing not two feet away. "What the hell are you doing here?" he demanded. "How come you snuck up on me?"

"You have the radio on so loud," Avery told him, a grin tugging at the corners of her mouth, "you wouldn't hear a buffalo stampede until they ran over you."

Mike snapped off the radio just as Bob Seger swung into

the second verse of "Night Moves." As an afterthought, he shut down the computer screen, too.

Like Avery would have any idea what she was looking at.

He hadn't seen her since she'd come home from China, and he took a moment to drink her in: her sleek hair, the sunny flush in her cheeks, the way her skirt and sweater set followed her every curve.

Belatedly, Mike remembered his manners. He offered her the observatory's second rickety chair, unscrewed the top of his thermos, and poured her coffee. Avery accepted it, sat down, and crossed her legs.

And nice legs they were, too, Mike acknowledged as he folded himself into the chair opposite hers. Nice legs, soft skin, kissable mouth.

He'd missed Avery a lot while she was away—and he was missing her even more now that she was back. He missed coming home and finding her with her feet up watching the news. He missed the sweet, crisp smell of her skin and hair. He missed their house, their bed, and having her in it with him. He missed the comings and goings, the innocuous conversations, the unexpected touching that was part of married life.

He was missing her even now, when she was sitting not three feet away.

"I had brunch with Fee and Samantha this morning," she said, surprising him.

Though she'd said she meant to resume her relationship with Fiona, he hadn't expected she'd do it quite so soon. "Oh?" he managed to mumble.

Avery leaned toward him, her eyes intent. "Why didn't you tell me you tried to talk to her out at Liberty Lake Park?"

Mike flushed at being caught and glanced down at the battered *Star Wars* mug in his hands. "I didn't deliberately keep that from you."

"Didn't you?"

Well, maybe he had, but since Avery hadn't made the words an accusation, Mike told her about it. "While you were gone, I kept and eye on Fee and the baby, just like you asked me to. Last Sunday they went for a walk at Liberty Lake Park. When they got back to the car, Fee had trouble with the stroller. Is that what she told you?"

"Yes."

"While she was folding it up, she got caught up in the mechanism somehow. It dragged her down onto her knees." As simple as he tried to make the incident sound, his gut tightened remembering how she'd been caught and helpless there on the ground. "I went to help is all that happened."

"Is that what you were doing?"

Mike looked up. "She didn't think I meant to hurt her, did she?"

Though Avery had swatted Fee's behind a time or two when she was being naughty, he'd never once laid hands on his daughter. No matter how deep the rift was between them, surely Fee couldn't think...

"You startled her is all," Avery said carefully, curling her hands around her cup as if she needed something to focus on. "Fiona understands now that all you meant to do was help, and she wants you to know how sorry—"

"'Sorry'?" Mike echoed, wounded and angry at his daughter all over again. How much of an ogre did Fee think he was?

"She didn't expect to see you." Avery's voice was soft,

almost cajoling. "She knows how angry you still are at her for stealing the pearls, then leaving the way she did."

"She gave me reason to be angry, Avery," he reminded her. "She gave you reason to be angry too."

He'd been telling her that since the day Fee left, only now the words rang hollow even in his ears. It was as if the time he'd spent watching over Fiona and Samantha while Avery was gone had begun to dilute that old, stiff brew of anger. The realization startled him, but before he had a chance to think it through, Avery leaped to her feet.

"Damn it, Mike!" she snapped, looking down at him. "It's time you come to grips with the mistakes Fiona made, forgive her, and put all this behind us. She's our only child. Samantha is our only grandchild. Stop and think about whether the feelings you've been harboring all these months are more important than making the two of them part of our lives."

He heard the quaver of what might have been regret or conviction in his wife's voice and wished he could do what she was asking. He'd known that if Avery heard he'd approached Fiona it would give her hope that his feelings for his daughter had changed, hope that he and Fee could reconcile. That was precisely why he hadn't said a word about what happened in the park.

Mike pushed to his feet and stepped toward her. "I know you've got this picture in your head, sweetheart, a picture where Fee and I forgive each other and we all live happily ever after. But that isn't going to happen. Fee's every bit as angry with me as I am her."

Avery threw up her hands in frustration. "So where does that leave us, Mike?"

He saw the pain in her eyes, and he wished he had it in him

to do what she wanted. He still couldn't deny how badly his daughter had disillusioned him. He couldn't ignore that the child he'd adored had betrayed his trust. He couldn't pretend that after all the time they'd spent studying the stars, he wasn't devastated when Fee turned her back on college and on astronomy. He couldn't lie to Avery about how deeply all that hurt. And he sure as hell couldn't lie to himself.

Mike shook his head. "I guess it leaves me here, you there, and Fiona someplace else."

"And that's the way you want it?"

Of course it wasn't the way he wanted it. He wanted to go back to a time when Fee was eight, when the two of them were buddies, and things were simple.

"Yeah, I guess it is," he said, feeling flippant and, for the moment at least, unrepentant.

Avery called him a name Mike hadn't even known was in her vocabulary, then spun on her heel and stalked away.

He followed her as far as the observatory door and watched as his wife climbed into her car and gunned the engine. He watched as the love of his life wheeled around in the drive and shot down the hill as if devils were chasing her. And maybe they were.

⁑

AUGUST 27, 1983

Larkin, Kansas

It looked like a wedding between the princess and the pauper. From where Mike stood with Ted in the arched doorway at the side of the Larkin University Chapel, he had a clear view of the guests gathered to see him and Avery make their vows.

Glancing down the bride's side of the aisle, he saw the men wore suits of blue or gray, ties were striped and impeccably tied, shoes beneath the needlepointed kneelers were polished until they shone. The women all had fashionable haircuts and wore trim suits or flowy dresses. A few sported hats for the occasion; others had artistically draped shawls around their shoulders. To any observer, the people on Avery's side of the aisle were examples of good breeding, good education, good taste, and good dental care.

On Mike's side the women's dresses were of the Sunday-go-to-meeting variety, and the men were universally outfitted from the JC Penney's catalog. His family and friends were sturdy folk with chapped hands and windburned faces. The men were tall, broad shouldered, like Mike was himself—and mostly hardworking. The women tended to be small, curvy, and used a little too much eye shadow.

"Ma looks pretty, doesn't she?" Ted whispered, diverting Mike's attention from the disparity between the guests on either side of the aisle to where their cousin Curtis was easing Myra Montgomery into her seat.

His mother had always looked nice in pink, and the dress Janice and Avery had helped her pick out was as frothy as cotton candy and with some kind of draping at the collar that set off the graceful length of her neck. She'd had her hair cut short and in a style that took years off her age. Or maybe it was burying her husband the previous spring that had made that difference.

"Make sure you tell her how nice she looks," Mike agreed, proud of her in a way he hadn't been in a very long while, "when you dance with her."

"I have to dance *with my mother*?" Ted whispered, appalled.

Though Mike nodded, he had turned his attention to Miriam Parrish. She was gliding down the aisle on the arm of another of the ushers. Tall and graceful, her gray hair beautifully coiffed, Miriam wore a shimmery silvery gown that rippled when she walked and her usual strand of luminous pearls. She seemed highborn, patrician, almost regal.

Mike glanced from Miriam to where his own mother was seated. As lovely as Myra Montgomery looked today, he could see in a glance the difference between Avery's family and his own.

Between Avery's life now and the one he was offering her.

From where he was standing in the vestry doorway, Mike felt the cold-eyed glare Miriam Parrish shot at him as she took her seat.

You're not good enough for Jonathan Parrish's daughter, it said. *I tried to warn her, but she wouldn't listen.*

Mike felt the chill of Miriam's disapproval to the center of his bones, but Avery had made her choice. When Mike asked her to marry him, she'd said yes—so what her mother thought obviously didn't matter.

Once Miriam was seated, the music changed.

Ted gave Mike a nudge in the direction of the altar and, as the two of them stepped up before the pastor, the bridesmaids, dressed in violet, began gliding down the aisle. Once all of them had taken their places, the congregation rustled to its feet in anticipation of the bride.

Mike anticipated Avery's arrival, too, sensing his new responsibilities settling over him. He went queasy with the weight of them, with a need to protect and care for Avery, to make everything perfect for her sake.

Then, as the opening notes of the wedding march soared

to the chapel's rafters, Avery stepped into the doorway at the back of the church on her father's arm.

She stood there smiling, serene, ethereal—and so damned beautiful she made his chest expand with pride that she was his. In that moment Mike realized the truth. While he might not be good enough, might not deserve the woman Avery was, no one in the world could love her more than he did.

When she looked up and saw him waiting at the end of the aisle, he saw the same love, the same commitment to their future pour into Avery's face.

It didn't take long for Avery and her father to reach the altar steps, and after Jonathan Parrish gave his daughter a fatherly kiss, he turned to Mike.

"I might have had my doubts about you at first, son," he said in an undertone that only Mike could hear, "but I can see how well you're going to care for my little girl."

"Yes, sir, I will," Mike promised earnestly.

"Then the two of you have my blessing," Avery's father said as he relinquished her hand to Mike. "May you have long and fruitful lives, a strong and enduring marriage."

Once Jonathan Parrish had settled himself in the pew beside his wife, the minister raised his prayer book and his voice circled toward the rafters.

"Dearly Beloved . . ."

Chapter 13

✳

Sometimes it's better not to know the truth.

Fee came puffing in the back door of her grandmother's house, the knees of her jeans grimy from kneeling in the dirt and her hands aching with cold. She'd finally planted the last of her grandmother's bulbs for spring, smooth oniony things that lay cool and inert in the hollow of her hand. Fee could hardly believe that something so innocuous would burst into exuberant, sunny daffodils by Gran's front door, or unfurl as tulips in a symphony of colors along the fence. But then, Gran said planting bulbs was like burying treasure, and that Fee would just have to wait and see if all the work was worth it.

Fiona toed off the Wellington boots her grandmother had given her to wear in the yard and padded sock-footed into the kitchen.

"The tea's almost ready, dear," Miriam Parrish sang out, glancing up from where she was filling the sugar bowl, a concession to Fiona's sweet tooth.

"Is Samantha all right?" Fee asked. When she'd gone out

into the garden more than an hour before, Gran was still
feeding the baby cereal.

"She's down for her nap," Miriam answered as she bent
to take a cookie sheet of perfectly browned scones out of
the oven. "You can check on her when you go wash up."

Fee took the hint and stopped in Gran's study to watch
Samantha sleep. Somehow she couldn't help seeing her
baby's father in Samantha's fluff of fair hair and the shape
of her chin. Though Jared hadn't called in weeks, she'd
found a check in the mail on Friday. It was a substantial
check and one Fiona desperately needed, but it had come
stuffed in an envelope without so much as a sticky note to
say hello.

Fee swiped at a tear with the back of one grubby hand
and tried to pretend that Jared's silence didn't hurt so
much. They'd been friends since the fifth grade, become
boyfriend and girlfriend when they were sophomores in
high school, and lovers the summer after. Drawn even
closer by playing in the band, they'd always had a great time
together and never ran out of things to talk about. These
days, though, Jared didn't have any more idea what to say to
Fee than she did to him.

He probably had a new girlfriend by now, she realized
with a stab of jealousy. God knows, he'd never lacked for of-
fers. And though the idea that he'd found somebody else
made her throat ache, Fee didn't begrudge him a future
with a woman who'd be willing to stick by him no matter
what.

Jared's music was taking him in new directions, and Fee
had deliberately chosen not to follow. She simply couldn't
keep up with the life he aspired to and be a good mother to
Samantha. She knew that even if Jared had offered to come

home with her, he'd have died a slow death playing at bars and roadhouses. He'd regret for the rest of his life that he hadn't taken his shot when he had the chance, and, one way or another, he'd end up blaming her and Samantha for his lost opportunities.

Fee would always love Jared, love his beauty and his talent, love the excitement he generated and the wildness in him. She'd always love him because he was the first guy she'd ever made love with and because he was Samantha's father. But she saw now that when he'd given her Samantha, Jared had given her the best of himself.

"Fiona?" she heard her grandmother call from down the hall. "I have tea set up in the dining room."

"Be right there."

Once she'd scrubbed the grime off her hands, blown her nose, and combed her hair, Fee took her place at her grandmother's perfectly laid tea table. Delicate plates decorated with forget-me-nots and recently polished silver rested on a creamy damask tea cloth. As Fee slipped the embroidered napkin from its ring, her grandmother offered the plate of scones.

Fee took just one, though she planned to eat a second later. No one made scones the way Gran did. "I'm way too grubby for all this elegance," she apologized and reached for the dish of clotted cream.

"I remember a time when you came to the tea table painted up like an Indian," Gran said with a smile.

Fee had gone through her Indian phase at six or seven when her father had given in to her whining and bought her a pair of deerskin moccasins. She'd made a fringed dress from a pillowcase to go with them, strung a necklace of feathers and beads, and wouldn't answer to anything but "Wild Buffalo Girl" for half the summer.

How was she going to provide Samantha with a childhood as idyllic as hers had been? Fee wondered. As filled with love and security?

She must have sighed, because Miriam glanced up from where she was putting a dollop of marmalade on a piece of scone and asked her what was wrong.

"Oh, I guess I've been wondering about Thanksgiving," she said, not quite able to keep the wistfulness out of her voice. "Are Mom and Dad having Grandma Myra, Aunt Janice, and Uncle Rich come from Kansas City like they usually do?"

Her grandmother set down her knife with a clatter. "I sincerely doubt that."

Something about Gran's pinched expression made Fee press for details. "Why?"

Miriam Parrish fussed with her pearls. "Didn't your mother tell you?"

Fee's throat went gummy with dread. "Tell me what?"

"That she and your father aren't living together?"

"What?" Fee asked, going cold all over.

"He moved out to the farm."

"W-w-when?" she whispered. "When did that happen?"

"Right around the time your mother went to China."

Right around the time her mom found out about Samantha, Fiona realized. Right about the time Avery swore she was going to be a part of her granddaughter's life.

"Your father's put it around," Miriam went on, "that he moved to the farm so he could keep an eye on your uncle Ted. Since his wife left, Ted has turned into a drunk, you know. Just like your Grandpa Montgomery."

Gran had never made a secret of how she felt about the Montgomerys.

"Maybe Dad was right to go out and keep an eye on Uncle Ted," Fee offered, hastily fumbling to make some sense out of the puzzle pieces her grandmother was laying out for her.

"Maybe he was," Miriam conceded. "But if that's all your father was doing, when Ted got arrested and went to rehab, why didn't he make an effort to move back into town?"

"Uncle Ted's in rehab?" Fiona echoed. Why didn't her mom tell her *anything*?

There must be other reasons for her father to stay out at the farm. Because there were animals to feed, things he had to attend to. Because her uncle Ted had asked him to. *Because it was hard going home once you turned your back on the people you loved.*

No one understood that better than Fiona.

Miriam lifted a carefully arched eyebrow. "I think your parents' marriage has been on the rocks for quite some time."

"How long?" Fee wanted to know.

Miriam shrugged evasively.

"How long have they been having trouble?" Fee persisted

"A year or more," her grandmother finally admitted.

Ever since she left. It confirmed what Fee was most afraid of. Certainly her mother and father hadn't had any trouble standing together to oppose her leaving with the band. They'd argued with her, then done everything but nail the doors and windows closed to keep her home and in school.

She *had* to be the cause of the rift between them. In spite of the way she left, her mother had been desperate to stay in touch with her. Her father had hung up on her twice when she called the house, and intercepted at least one of the e-mails she'd sent from a cyber-café in one or another of the towns where they were playing. Her dad must have made it as clear to her mother as he had to Fee that he didn't want the two of them having any kind of contact—but her mom wouldn't have accepted that. Avery Montgomery wasn't the kind of woman who responded well to ultimatums, not even from her husband.

No wonder her parents' marriage was in trouble. Guilt squeezed Fee's heart.

Finally, she'd begun sending e-mails and postcards to her mom at the Holding Company. She'd even passed messages through Casey once or twice. She did that until she found out she was pregnant. Once she knew, she was ashamed to admit she'd been stupid enough to make love without using birth control. She'd been afraid she'd lose Jared when he found out, or that he'd feel like she'd deliberately gotten pregnant to trap him into marrying her. She'd agonized over the decisions she had to make about keeping her baby and she knew that if she so much as spoke to her mother, Avery would hone right in on her turmoil.

Though it had scared her to break even that delicate tether, Fee deliberately fell silent. She'd have done that sooner if she'd know what strife she was causing between her parents.

Through all those months, Fiona had never once imagined she'd put their marriage in jeopardy. How could she have come between them when they'd always seemed to be of one mind when they'd dealt with her and had been so pathetically in love that sometimes she and Casey just looked at each other and rolled their eyes?

Fee had thought long and hard about how she was going

to handle coming back to Larkin, but she'd never once thought how her return might affect her mom and dad.

"...always thought your parents weren't the least bit suited," her grandmother was saying. "So it doesn't surprise me..."

Fee threw down her napkin and pushed to her feet.

Miriam stopped in midsentence and stared at her.

"I need you to take care of Samantha for another hour or so," Fee said. "Something's come up I have to deal with immediately."

"Fiona?" her grandmother asked as she rose and followed Fiona into the hall. "Where are you going?"

"To set a few things straight," she said and slammed out the door.

⁂

At the sound of a car pulling in beside the observatory, Mike looked up from the e-mail he'd been writing and rewriting for the best part of two weeks. He'd gone over his findings at least a hundred times and was trying to get up the nerve to send in his report on the asteroid he *thought* he'd found to the Minor Planet Center for verification.

Or humiliation, maybe.

Either way, he was pleased to have a diversion. Though they'd met for dinner just last night, he couldn't help hoping it was Avery who'd come by. Maybe she was out for a drive, maybe something had come up she needed to discuss with him—or maybe she just missed him.

He hoped she'd missed him.

Mike flipped off the computer screen, took a moment to smooth down his hair, then stepped into the observatory's open doorway expecting to see his wife. Fiona came blazing toward him instead.

"You asshole!" she bellowed and slammed the heels of her hands into the center of Mike's chest.

She hit him hard enough that it knocked him back on his heels, hard enough to drive the air out of his lungs in a *whoosh.* She shoved at him again, furious and aggressive in a way Mike never imagined his little girl could be.

"You dumb-ass jerk!" she shouted. "What the hell do you think you're doing?"

Mike back-stepped out of her reach. "What's going on, Fiona? Why are you here?"

She glared at him, her green eyes narrowed. "How come you and Mom are separated?"

This time Mike gave ground in surprise. Hadn't Avery told Fiona they were living apart? Shouldn't Avery be the one explaining to Fee that the two of them were…were working through a rough spot in their marriage? Mike sure as hell didn't want to do it, especially not when Fee had come roaring in to blame him.

"What goes on between your mother and me," he declared, trying to evade the issue, "is none of your damn business!"

"It *is* my business"—the belligerence in his daughter's face didn't fade—"if *I'm* the reason you're living here at the farm instead of home with Mom, where you belong."

Mike banded his arms across his chest and refused to explain. "You're not the reason I'm living at the farm."

"Besides me, what *else* do you and Mom have to fight about?"

Mike almost laughed. "Oh, lots of things."

Until he married Avery, he had no idea the kind of things

even happy couples fought about: money, friends, vacations. When and how much time they were going to spend together. Who cooked supper and what they ate. Whether he left the seat up or down. What he'd done recently to piss Miriam off, and who got to read the Sunday funnies first.

Though it was true that since September he and Avery had had a roiling, nonstop argument about whether she, he, or both of them were going to have a relationship with Fiona now that she was back in Larkin, Mike knew he wouldn't gain any ground by admitting it.

"I came out to stay at the farm because your uncle Ted needed me."

Fee snorted and paced away from him. "That's so bogus! Uncle Ted got arrested for DWI and went to rehab two weeks ago."

"How did you know about that?" Mike demanded. The incident at Charney's and Ted's arrest hadn't even made the paper.

"Gran told me."

Venomous old bat, Mike almost said. "Is your grandmother the one who told you your mom and I aren't living together?"

"Gran was surprised I didn't know." Fee faced him with her chin up and her eyebrows raised, looking remarkably like the woman she was defending. "She couldn't imagine that Mom hadn't seen fit to tell me. It never occurred to me when I took off with the band that my leaving would change things between the two of you—much less split you up."

After all the things he and Avery had been through together, Mike hadn't thought Fee's leaving could undermine their marriage, either. He'd never imagined it would put every facet of his oh-so-carefully constructed life in jeopardy.

The memory of that first terrible morning came back to swamp him. He could see his wife's hands shaking as she handed him the note, feel how her fingers dug deep into his forearm as he read what Fee had written. He heard her small broken voice, a voice that didn't sound at all like Avery, whispering over and over, "What are we going to do, Mike? What are we going to do?"

Fresh anger boiled up in him. "So what did you think would happen when you left?"

Fee lifted her shoulders in a shrug. "I guess I thought you'd be really pissed at me for a while, and then get over it."

As if she'd stayed out past curfew. Like she'd borrowed the car without asking.

Fee didn't have any idea what she'd put them through. Even now that she was a mother herself, Fee didn't get it.

"Well, you know, Fee," he said, his voice thick with sarcasm, "it didn't work out quite the way you thought. While she was sharing family secrets, did your gran tell you your mother wandered around like a ghost for months after you left? That she woke up every morning not knowing where you were, and cried herself to sleep night after night wondering if you were well, if you were safe?"

Fiona seemed to pale. "No, Gran didn't tell me that."

"Did you ever stop to think," Mike went on relentlessly, "that your mother had already lost one child? Did it even once occur to you how terrified she'd be of losing another?"

As he said the words, Mike saw how wrong he'd been to try to keep Avery from having contact with Fiona. He realized how wrong he'd been to keep Fee's return to Larkin from his wife. Avery had lost a child and, no matter how furious he was with their daughter, Avery needed to know that no matter where she was, Fee was okay.

Instead he'd tried to deny his wife the comfort that hearing from Fee would have given her. *How could he have been so goddamned selfish?*

"If I had any idea Mom would take it so hard—"

"She was frantic, Fiona," he told her ruthlessly. "Heartbroken. Terrified of losing you."

He hadn't been able to help Avery because he felt so betrayed himself. With a single stroke she had shattered the stable life he worked so hard to create for all of them. She'd exposed a need for security he'd never consciously acknowledged and couldn't bring himself to admit to his wife.

"And how do you think your mother felt the next time she went to wear her pearls and found that they were missing too?" Mike's throat ached when he remembered how shaken Avery had been when she discovered the necklace was gone. "How could you have taken your mother's prize possession, Fiona? You went with me when I bought her that necklace; you helped me pick it out. You saw how much she loved those pearls, how she glowed when she fastened them around her neck."

"What I saw was how proud *you* were of those pearls!" Fee answered back. "How good *you* felt when she wore them."

Mike felt a flush scald up his jaw. He wanted to tell his daughter he'd given Avery those pearls because it was their anniversary and he wanted to show Avery how much he loved her. Somehow Fee had come to recognize the dark side of the gift. That he'd given the necklace to Avery so he could prove—to her, her family, and himself—that he could provide for her. That he could provide for her every bit as well as Jonathan Parrish had provided for his Miriam.

Mike stalked away from Fee to where the telescope crouched on its pier in the center of the observatory. He pressed his shaking hands to the cool, nubbled barrel to ground himself and tried to clear his head.

"Your mother and I were always so proud of you, Fiona," he said once he'd caught his breath. "Of how smart you are, how well you did in school, and especially the goals you set for yourself. We wanted so much for you: a job you cared about, good friends, travel—maybe someday a husband and family. We did everything we could think of to make that possible."

Hadn't he and Avery volunteered at school, overseen Fee's homework, applauded her accomplishments at every school play, soccer game, and piano recital? Hadn't they focused their lives on being good parents to their daughter?

"Sometimes you wanted too much," Fee said, not quite able to look at him. "Sometimes you pushed way too hard. Sometimes you watched over me so intently I felt like a bug under a microscope. Sometimes all I wanted was to go my own way."

He recognized every teenager's lament in those words, the odd balance both parents and children struggled with. When did a child push away? When should a parent let go?

"We did our best, Fiona," Mike offered quietly, "to help you achieve the things you said you wanted. And then you turned your back on us as if none of that mattered, *as if your mother and I didn't matter.*"

"I—I recognized while I was away everything you and Mom did when I was growing up," Fee admitted, hunching her shoulders defensively. "But when Starburst Records offered us a contract, offered us a chance to record hit songs and play at sold-out rock concerts, all any of us could think about was signing on the dotted line and starting the adventure. We were all restless and ready to leave home, so we believed that what they promised was going to happen. It was tough when things didn't work out the way we thought."

"We tried to warn you," Mike reminded her, then wished he hadn't.

"I know," she acknowledged, but raised her chin another notch anyway. "Things would be so much different if I had listened—but then, I wouldn't have Samantha. I wouldn't have learned to own up to my mistakes or honor my responsibilities. That's why I came back to Larkin, so I could finish school and make the kind of life for Samantha you and Mom had made for me."

Mike nodded, pleased that Fee understood what he and Avery had done for her and that she wanted the same for her daughter. It made Mike breathe a little easier somehow.

"I'm so sorry I left Larkin the way I did." She compressed her lips before she went on, as if saying the words was hard for her. "I'm sorry I put you and Mom through so much heartache and worry. I'm sorry if I disappointed you. But I'm going to be even more sorry if what I did spoils the way you and Mom have always felt about each other."

"Are you apologizing, Fiona?" Mike looked down at her long and hard, seeing the sincerity in her eyes. "Are you asking me to forgive you?"

"Yeah, I guess I am."

Mike knew how he ought to answer, knew what Avery would want him to say. But the words lodged in his throat, a hard kernel of resentment he couldn't seem to swallow. How could he forgive Fiona after she'd torn their family apart? How could Fee expect him to welcome her back into their lives when she'd broken Avery's heart? How could he acknowledge even to himself that Fee's leaving had destroyed the only time in his life where he felt really safe?

He knew he ought to take Fiona in his arms and tell her everything was going to be all right, like he used to do when she was a little girl. But he was tied up tight inside. He still ached with the loss of everything he'd believed in, and he couldn't bring himself to grant her the forgiveness she was asking for.

"Sometimes, Fiona"—his voice faded a little as he spoke—"things have gone too far to fix by saying you're sorry. Sometimes you've hurt people too badly for them to be able to set aside their pain. Sometimes you've betrayed—"

He saw her eyes widen at his refusal.

"You always manage to forgive Uncle Ted when he screws up!" she protested, her voice soft and wobbly. "Why can't you forgive me?"

He looked down into her face, recognizing the child he'd been so proud of and so disappointed by, the young woman who'd showed him that the perfect family he'd thought he built for himself was—and always had been—an illusion. Discovering that had shaken the very foundation of his life, of who he thought he was. But he sure as hell didn't know how to explain that to his daughter.

"I've always expected so much more of you, Fee," he told her, answering with at least part of the truth, "than I ever expected from Ted."

Fee sucked in a breath and backed away, her face flushed and her eyes blazing. "Then you really are an asshole, and I don't see much point in standing here trying to convince you I'm doing what I can to make this right."

She spun on her heel and raced out of the observatory. She climbed into her Neon and gunned the engine, backing out so fast her tires split gravel.

Mike stepped into the doorway and watched Fee's car roar down the rise. He'd been wrong to let her go, but somehow he didn't have it in him to forgive her, to give his daughter the answer both of them wanted.

※

Sometimes Fee hated remembering how things used to be.

She swiped at her eyes as she wheeled her Neon along the steep gravel road that led down from the observatory. Her vision blurred as she zoomed past the farmhouse and up the rise that would take her out of the valley and off Montgomery land. But she couldn't outrun the deep, gut-wrenching pain of knowing she'd screwed up not just her life, but her parents' lives.

And that her father wasn't going to forgive her.

She'd confessed to her mistakes and apologized for how much hurt she'd caused her mother and him—then her dad had said being sorry wasn't good enough. He'd looked at her with such weariness and sorrow in his face and told her that after what she'd done, he didn't want anything to do with her.

Knowing how stubborn he could be once he'd made up his mind, made Fee cry even harder.

She and her dad used to have such a cool relationship. Just being there at the observatory, seeing the place they'd planned and built together, being close enough to touch the equipment they'd picked out, stirred up so many memories.

She'd been with her dad the night she'd fallen in love

with the sky. They'd been stretched out in their sleeping bags in the backyard, having a little adventure without straying too far from the house. The night had been alive around them. Cicadas shrilled in the treetops, and the sweetness of the blossoming honeysuckle had wafted over them. The thick, muggy heat of the afternoon had dissipated, and the dampness of the earth beneath them made Fee shiver.

"You warm enough, sweetheart?" her dad had asked, reaching over to rub his big, rough hand up and down her forearm.

"Yes, Daddy."

The sky had loomed over them, a huge, dark disk stippled with stars. Some of them beamed a bright, white light right toward where they were lying in the grass. Others were nothing but icy pinpricks in the blue-black expanse of space. The sky had been so clear that night, that Fee could make out hazy layers of even more distant stars, clouds of them too dim or far away for her to discern as individuals.

Then, as they watched, a bright, white spear of light shot across the sky. She sat bolt upright in her sleeping bag. "What was that?"

"A shooting star," her father answered, and by morning they'd seen a dozen of them.

Fee had barely been able to wait to go to the library so she and her dad could read about what they'd seen. And in the next weeks and months they'd read books, visited the Kansas City Planetarium and the observatory in Topeka. For someone who claimed he didn't know a thing about astronomy, her dad had taught her so much.

He'd bought her her first telescope, and they'd spent hours looking at the planets and learning the constellations together. They'd poured over star charts by the hour and kept an eye on the weather hoping for dark and cloudless nights.

Fiona remembered the way her dad always bundled her up before they went "seeing." Once they'd set up the telescope, she'd wait while he trained the telescope on the moons of Jupiter or the Ursa Minor or Andromeda, so eager and excited she could barely stand still.

She'd never forget the first star party he'd ever taken her to, off in the Flint Hills somewhere. They'd driven a good long ways, then jounced up something that barely passed for a road in the deepening twilight to a place that was no more than an X on the map. She remembered shivers bursting down her spine when they topped a rise and came upon a forest of telescopes.

They'd parked the truck, put on their sweatshirts, and gotten out their red flashlights. They'd joined the groups of stargazers milling around an odd mishmash of sleek store-bought and cobbled-together homemade telescopes.

Finally her dad had found the man who'd invited them, shook his hand, and then steadied Fee as she climbed the ladder to reach the eyepiece of his huge Newtonian telescope. When she reached the top, she'd seen Regulus pop into view, beautiful and clear, seeming close enough to reach out and touch.

That night Fee had looked through at least a score of telescopes, waiting her turn, listening to what the amateur astronomers had to teach her about what she was seeing, and becoming more and more beguiled by the wonders of space.

She didn't tell her father that she wanted to be an astronomer, at least not then, but somehow he'd known it.

Somehow he'd understood and done his best to guide her toward what became with every passing year more and more of an obsession.

Fee sniffled and swiped at her eyes again and turned back toward town.

Ungrateful twit that she was, she'd never thanked her dad for doing that. For spending so much time with her, for building her that wonderful observatory, or for the million other things—in the realm of astronomy and otherwise— she knew he'd done because he loved her.

After the things they'd said to each other this afternoon, Fee knew she was never going to have the chance to tell him. With her willfulness and bravado, she'd managed to alienate a man who adored her. She'd managed to hurt her parents and strain their marriage to the breaking point. After causing all that pain, how could she possibly deserve to be forgiven?

Knowing the answer made Fiona cry even harder.

Chapter 14

✳

"What I'm saying…" Avery scooped a heaping spoonful of sweet potato casserole into a sectioned Styrofoam food container and passed it to her mother. They were standing at the steam table in the slightly fusty basement of the Grace Lutheran Church where about twenty other volunteers had spent the morning preparing Thanksgiving dinner for the church's shut-ins.

"What I'm saying," she repeated, trying to work up the gumption to tell her mother something that had been gnawing at her for days, "is that you had absolutely no right telling Fiona that Mike and I are living apart."

Miriam spooned dressing into the box Avery had given her and added gravy. "I had no idea Fee didn't know about you and Mike."

Avery slid her mother a dubious glance as she took another Styrofoam box from the pile beside her.

"Now, how would Fee have known? We haven't exactly publicized our living arrangements, and I've only seen Fee once since Mike moved out. When I did, we had other things to talk about."

"It never occurred to me"—Miriam passed the container to the next woman at the steam table—"that you hadn't told her you and Mike are separated."

"We're not separated," Avery insisted, her voice pitched low. She didn't want the entire Women's Fellowship gossiping about Mike and her. "We're living apart."

"That's a very fine distinction," Miriam said with a sniff.

Was it? Avery wondered. She and Mike talked every day. Sometimes he stopped at the Holding Company after work, and they went out to dinner together. They got along well enough as long as they didn't talk about Fiona. To anyone observing them, they must have looked married. Except, of course, that they didn't share a house, didn't share a bed.

"Neither of us has done anything legal about the living arrangements."

On nights when she wasn't furious with Mike for refusing to resume a relationship with their daughter, Avery dragged around that empty house sick with loneliness, sick with longing. She missed whispering to Mike in the dark, missed waking up beside him, missed the way he'd reach out and touch her for no reason at all. She missed their lovemaking with a sharp, restless hunger she'd thought she'd outgrown.

She couldn't help wondering if Mike missed their lovemaking, too.

"You might as well go see a lawyer," Miriam observed. "Mike's never going to change his mind about Fiona."

Trust Miriam to know right where it hurt, right where Avery's deepest fears lay. When she'd asked Mike to keep an eye on Fee while she was in China, Avery had hoped it would be the beginning of a reconciliation between her husband and her daughter. It just might have worked that way, too, if Fee hadn't reacted so strongly when Mike approached at Liberty Lake. If she hadn't pulled away, hadn't rebuffed his offer of help. If she hadn't acted as if she hated him.

Avery spooned a dollop of the orange casserole into another Styrofoam tray. "I can't imagine ever divorcing Mike."

Her mother snatched the tray out of her hands. "You know as well as I do," she said in a quiet voice, "that Mike wasn't at all the kind of man you *should* have married. You're a smart, creative woman, Avery, coming up with all those cute designs and running that factory all by yourself. And Mike's never really amounted to much, now, has he?"

Avery turned her head to stare at her mother. "Never amounted to much—you mean, besides being a brilliant craftsman? Never amounted to much besides being a good provider, a wonderful husband, and attentive father?"

"If he's such an attentive father, why is he estranged from his own daughter?" Miriam snapped back. "If he's such a wonderful husband, why isn't he living with you?"

Avery felt anger flush her cheeks. "You started finding fault with him the day I brought him home."

But Avery had known what Miriam would think of Mike the night he'd rescued her at the airport. She knew the moment she looked up into that strong, lean face and those deep blue eyes, seen that flowing hair and don't-mess-with-me stance that her mother would never approve of him. But then, Avery told herself, what was one date with someone who was so... so darn hunky? She certainly hadn't planned on falling in love with Mike Montgomery.

"I always knew he was wrong for you," Miriam said with an authoritative lift to her brows. "The Montgomerys are, and always have been, the town scandal. Your Mike never

even aspired to go on to school. He never wanted to be anything but a common tradesman."

Avery was tempted to explain that Mike had never aspired to any kind of higher education because he'd taken it
upon himself to keep bread on the table in the Montgomery household.

"Mike's doing what he loves; it's what he's good at."
Avery said instead.

Miriam snorted in dismissal.

"Wasn't your own father a 'common tradesman,'
Mother?" Avery pointed out. "Are you ashamed of him because he was a bricklayer?"

"He was a *master mason*," Miriam corrected her. "He ran
his own construction company."

No matter what her mother said, Avery knew Miriam
was ashamed of her humble beginnings.

"From the moment I set eyes on your father," Miriam
said, her voice barely louder than a hiss, "I knew I wanted
more than what I'd had—and I worked very hard to get it. I
worked hard to fit into your father's world, to make my own
way, to be an asset to him in his career."

Avery knew her mother had struggled to be a perfect wife
to Jonathan Parrish because she adored him. And because
she wanted so desperately to be the woman she'd eventually
become, it hadn't mattered that always putting her husband
first had played havoc with her daughter's self-esteem.

"That's why," her mother explained, "I've always wanted
someone better for you than Mike has been."

Avery knew this wasn't the time or place to settle this.
They were in church. They were doing unselfish work. They
were surrounded by the members of the Women's Fellowship, each of them gossips to their last breath. But some-

thing about her mother's tone, her mother's curt dismissal of everything that made Mike special, uncorked the anger Avery had kept bottled up for years.

The outrage fizzed through her veins, sizzled up her spine like an electric charge. Her scalp shifted and her hands tingled. She went breathless and dizzy. She compressed her lips, doing her best to force down the angry words clamoring in her throat, but she couldn't hold back her feelings.

"What you mean to say," Avery accused, "is not that you wanted someone better for me, but that you wanted someone better for yourself!"

"I beg your pardon?" her mother all but squeaked, turning to her daughter, Styrofoam container in hand. "You know I adored your father!"

"I'm not talking about Daddy." Avery's voice shook with the effort she was making to maintain her control. "I'm talking about you wanting a son-in-law you could brag about, a doctor or a lawyer or a professor of—I don't know —*dead languages.*"

Avery sucked in a breath before she went on. "And you always wanted a daughter who's smarter than I am. Better than I am. More accomplished than I am."

"I can't imagine where you ever got the idea—"

"I got the idea because you spent pretty much every day of my life telling me I wasn't good enough to meet your expectations."

"Avery!" Miriam gasped.

Avery wasn't sure if her mother was appalled by the accusation or trying to shut her up.

"You found fault with every move I made. When I got straight A's, you said you expected A-pluses. My hair didn't curl and my anklets drooped. I never kept my room neat enough. I wanted to read Nancy Drew instead of the Hardy and Eliot and Thackeray you foisted on me years before I was ready to read them.

"You said I was wasting my time drawing and painting when I could have been doing something *useful*. You told me that because I was Jonathan Parrish's daughter people expected more of me than they did of the other girls, so I had a lot to live up to."

Avery dimly realized that the women in the church kitchen had fallen silent, that they'd all turned to stare at her and her mother. But Avery couldn't seem to stopper the words, couldn't swallow the accusations that bubbled in her throat.

"If I hadn't won a scholarship to Parsons, you never would have allowed me to dabble with something so self-indulgent as art," Avery went on. "You didn't approve when I took a job in graphic design instead of academia. You hated the way I decorated my apartment in Chicago. You detested every guy I dated. *Especially Mike!*"

Miriam didn't even bother to deny it. "I was only trying to see that you lived up to your father's and my expectations."

Avery never doubted her father's feelings, doubted his love for her. He'd encouraged her, doted on her, made time for her.

He'd been gone twelve years and she still missed him.

Avery stepped back from the steam table, spoon in hand. "It was never Daddy's expectations I had trouble meeting," she accused. "It was yours!"

Her mother lifted her chin in that way she had, glared at her daughter as if it were she, not Miriam, who was in the wrong.

Avery felt the flush of fresh anger singe right up into her hair, and knew she had to get out of there. She needed to get away from the steamy smell of turnips, stewed apples, and pumpkin pie. She needed to get away from all those slack-jawed women who'd be talking for months about what Avery Montgomery had said to her mother while they were dishing up Thanksgiving dinner.

Avery needed to get away from her mother, who had neither denied her accusations nor apologized. *But then, Miriam never apologized.*

Avery looked down at the dripping spoonful of sweet potato casserole in her hand, then noticed the toes of her mother's favorite shoes peeking out from beneath the hem of the long, canvas apron all the women wore.

Before she could think, before common sense could get the best of her, Avery slung that gooey orange glob of sweet potato casserole right onto her mother's favorite gray suede gillies.

With shaking hands, Avery tore off her own big apron. In a quivering voice she apologized to the whole of the Women's Fellowship for her outburst. On wobbly knees she left the church kitchen and stumbled up the stairs.

✻

Avery cried all the way home. She hadn't meant to confront her mother in a kitchen full of the ladies of the Women's Fellowship, people both of them had known for years. She hadn't meant to dredge up every criticism her mother had ever voiced of her, or reveal all the soft, sore places inside her.

She hadn't meant to deliberately dump sweet potato casserole on her mother's shoes.

Avery let herself into the house and cried some more. It was Thanksgiving, a time when families should be together, yet her house was silent and empty.

Any other year, she and Ted's wife Nancy would have had the stuffing made by now and had the turkey in the oven. They'd be having a second cup of coffee to fortify themselves for peeling the mound of potatoes and cutting up the squash and green beans. Any other time, Fee would have been in the dining room humming a little to herself as she lay the table with Avery's best china and silver. Any other time, Mike would be bringing the extra chairs and serving table up from the basement.

Avery missed all that familiar activity with a deep, resonant ache that had nothing to do with the fact that Mike was spending Thanksgiving at his sister's in Kansas City.

She missed the enormous basket of cinnamon rolls Mike's mother Myra always baked for them. She missed the spicy smell of Janice's mincemeat pies. She missed Ted and Nancy's daughters sneaking upstairs to play with Fee's old dolls, missed the *click* of Myra's knitting needles, and the deep-voiced commentary from the living room as Mike, Janice's husband Rich, and Ted immersed themselves in whatever football game was on TV.

She wanted to sneak out on the front porch after dinner for one illicit cigarette with Janice. She wanted to stuff the children into their coats and herd them down the street to the park to play on the swings. She wanted her house alive with people and warmth and the inevitable bickering that went with any holiday get-together.

Avery wanted her own little family back together—but as the days went by, she became less and less sure that was possible.

She spent a good long while prowling from room to room, then finally settled on the window seat in the dining room and let the drowsy warmth of the November sun dry her tears. As she sat, she reached out and stroked the smooth, paddle-shaped leaves on the Christmas cactus she'd potted weeks before to give to Fee. She smiled to herself when she saw how many small ruffled leaves had sprouted at the ends of the cactus's graceful branches. She touched a few knotty bumps where buds had begun to form. They were the buds that would ripen and unfurl into spectacular multitiered blossoms in time for Christmas.

Come Christmas, she meant to present Fiona with this cutting from Great-Grandma Letty's cactus. It was her way of expressing the love and approval that had been passed from Letty to Ada, from Ada to Miriam, from Miriam to her over a span of better than a hundred years.

By tradition, the cactuses had always been presented at Christmas, full and ablaze with flowers. Except for Avery's, of course. Thinking back on how she'd received her own Christmas cactus, Avery saw it underscored every single word she'd said to Miriam this morning.

❋

AUGUST 1985

A baby. Oh, God! Her baby—hers and Mike's.

A delicate little darling with a ruddy fluff of hair, perfect pink hands, and a mouth pursed as if she were about to inquire just exactly what she was doing here when she'd been perfectly warm and happy where she was. As if she were about to ask why these two strange people staring down at her were crying and laughing and hugging each other.

At least that's what Avery *thought* the baby must be thinking.

She smiled at Mike, standing by the side of her hospital bed, haggard, unshaven, the scrubs they'd given him to wear into the delivery room sweat-stained and molded to his body. Still, he was grinning like he owned the world.

Both of them had looked forward to this moment for most of their married life, and now Avery was holding their perfect baby daughter in her arms. For the moment, at least, she felt calm and confident, and so full and happy she could not stop smiling.

"I love you, Mike," she whispered, fresh tears rising in her eyes. "Thank you for being there to breathe with me and push with me and hold my hand. Thank you for giving me this precious little girl."

Mike flushed, more pleased and proud and sure of himself than Avery had ever seen him.

"I love you, too, Avery," Mike answered, stroking his daughter's silky cheek. "I promise, I'm going to be the best daddy any girl ever had."

"I know you will," she assured him.

Just then, Myra and Janice burst in. They'd spent all night pacing the waiting room and were abuzz with caffeine and delight that everyone was fine.

Not long after, Avery's dad arrived, tall, nattily dressed as always, and clearly on his way to work at the university. "You did well," he told Avery as he looked down at the pink dab of child everyone was standing around admiring.

"You did well, too, son," Jonathan Parrish said and reached across and shook Mike's hand. It was a moment of approval Avery could tell meant a lot to her husband. "So what are you going to name our little girl?"

Avery looked to Mike, indicating that he should be the one to tell everyone. "What we agreed on is Fiona Parrish Montgomery."

"Fiona after my mother," Myra sniffled.

"And Parrish to connect the baby to our family," Avery told her dad.

"She's a beautiful little girl," Jonathan Parrish said, beaming at all of them with a grandfather's pride. "I couldn't be more proud of my daughter and son-in-law than I am today."

Miriam breezed in when her classes were over late that afternoon. "Your father tells me we have a granddaughter," she said from the doorway. "I stopped at the nursery to see her, but they said she was in here."

Avery had just finished feeding Fiona and drew back the blanket so her mother could see her. The baby blinked, yawned, and rubbed at her nose with her tiny fists. Avery had never seen anything more endearing.

"She has big ears, don't you think?" Miriam observed.

Avery looked up, shocked by her mother's unwarranted criticism. She drew Fiona protectively against her, outrage hot in her throat. "I imagine she'll grow into them."

"Well, your father's certainly taken a shine to her," Miriam offered with a shrug. "You'd think he never saw a baby before."

"Maybe it's because she's his *granddaughter* that he's taken such a shine to her," Avery pointed out and glanced toward the arrangement of sunflowers her father had had delivered an hour ago. They sat beside the lovely little bouquet of deep-pink sweetheart roses Mike had dropped off on his way to work.

"Dad seemed to think Mike and I have done all right for

ourselves." In truth, her father thought they'd done a good deal more than all right. Once Myra and Janice left, and Mike had gone home to shower and shave, her father sat with her awhile. He'd held her hand and reminisced about the morning she was born, how beautiful she'd been, how proud he was of her. How proud he was of her now.

That was the gift that her father had always given her: the certainty that she was loved and appreciated and treasured. It was a gift, Avery thought looking down at her daughter, she meant to give her darling little girl every day of her life.

Miriam pulled up a chair to the side of the bed and settled in it with a sigh. "Your father tells me you've named the child *Fiona*."

"It's Mike's grandmother's name," Avery said, ignoring her mother's dubious tone. "It means fair, Mother. Pure. Beautiful."

"I know what Fiona means."

Avery couldn't help hoping for some sign that her mother approved of the name, of the baby, of the fact that Avery had become a mother herself.

"Fiona's a name with character," Miriam sniffed. "We can only hope that once she's grown into it, it will suit her."

Avery was still trying to think how to respond when Miriam bent and rummaged in the narrow, flat-bottomed tote she'd brought in with her.

"I thought it was time I gave you this," she said and set a cutting from Great-Grandma Letty's Christmas cactus on the edge of Avery's nightstand.

Usually a mother gave her daughter this special family gift at Christmas when the plant was gloriously abloom with fuchsia blossoms. It was August now, and Avery could see the cutting was fresh, not even rooted yet. But even knowing the cactus was an afterthought didn't spoil the graceful arc of the leaves that draped over the edge of the pretty cut-glass vase her mother had put it in. It didn't spoil the acknowledgment that came with the snippet of plant.

Did this finally mean, Avery wondered, that after graduating magna cum laude from Parsons, that after her package designs had shown up in stores all over the country and won awards, that after nearly three years of marriage to a man who loved her with all his heart—Miriam finally approved of her? Finally approved of what she'd done and how she'd chosen to live her life?

In spite of her questions about her mother's intent, Avery's eyes teared; she was moved by Miriam's token of respect and regard.

In the weeks and months that followed, Avery nurtured both her daughter and the cutting from the Christmas cactus. By Christmas, when Fiona was a jabbering, happy baby who smiled at everyone, the cutting her mother had given her was potted and ablaze with flowers. And Avery knew the plant would continue to grow and flourish until it was time—many years from now when her daughter was grown—to pass a cutting from the Christmas cactus on to her Fiona.

✴

Later that Thanksgiving afternoon, all four generations of the Parrish and Montgomery women gathered to have dinner together. Because Fiona had insisted that the meal be her treat, they'd decided to meet at Denny's and had done their best to enjoy themselves.

That wasn't easy. Samantha was cutting teeth and yowled as much as she was quiet. Fiona had a terrible cold and sounded like she ought to be home in bed. After Avery's outburst in the church basement that morning, Miriam and Avery barely had a word to say to each other, though both of them were excruciatingly polite.

Though the gravy wasn't lumpy or the turkey dry, Avery knew none of them wanted this Thanksgiving to start a new family tradition. Finally they boxed up their pumpkin pie for later, hugged good-bye in the parking lot, and went their separate ways.

"Please don't let Christmas be like this," Avery found herself whispering over and over as she drove back to the house on Prospect Street. "Please, can we have Christmas together as a family, like we always have?"

But if that was going to happen, it was up to her to get her family back together. Avery didn't have any idea how she was going to do that, and she was running out of time.

Chapter 15

✳

S ome days even the good news was bad.

Fee picked at the raveling sleeve of her favorite purple sweater and tried to block out what her faculty advisor was telling her. That was pretty much impossible, since she was telling Fee exactly what she'd always wanted to hear.

"You're a wonderful young astronomer, Fiona, and this is a once-in-a-lifetime opportunity to work with some of the best people in the field!" Margaret Gunderson exhorted her. "You've got to accept!"

Dr. Gunderson had buttonholed Fee outside the lecture hall after organic chem, preventing her from going someplace quiet to scan the pages Professor Weinblat had assigned.

As if Dr. Gunderson hadn't screwed her already.

"Tell me again exactly how I qualified as a summer assistant at the Kitt Peak Observatory?" Fee asked.

"I submitted the application packet in your name for early admissions." Dr. Gunderson beamed, both at her own initiative—and her success. "Professor Bingham and Dr. McDowell both wrote glowing recommendations. Then I asked Chairman Faretti to have a word with the director of the observatory on your behalf. They're old friends; it's why Director Olsen at Kitt Peak has agreed to hold this position open for you until the first of the year."

The very idea of being offered a chance to work with the staff at Kitt Peak, and some of the finest astronomy equipment in the nation, sent gooseflesh scurrying down Fiona's ribs.

"You have an aptitude, Fiona," Dr. Gunderson went on. "I suspected it the first time you raised your hand in intro to astronomy. You confirmed it when I saw the way you handled a telescope."

Yeah, well, she ought to have an "aptitude." She'd been mesmerized by the planets and constellations since she was little. Just thinking about the nights she and her dad had stayed up late exploring the splendor of the night sky, made a knot rise in Fee's throat. Especially after the things they'd said to each other last Sunday. If she could handle a telescope and find her way around a star map, it was because of him.

God knows, this position at Kitt Peak sounded wonderful. If he knew, her dad would be so excited that she'd been offered an internship that would give her a chance to assist first-class astronomers with their observations. Maybe she'd even be able to do some seeing on her own.

"You have the kind of ability that should be nurtured," the older woman went on. "Accepting this position would be a first important step on the road to becoming a professional astronomer."

This was a chance to learn, to do work she loved, to meet people who held the keys to the wonders of space—and any career she might ever hope to have in astronomy.

It was a fabulous opportunity—but one Fee was going to have to refuse.

Knowing she needed not the expanse of the cosmos but the security of an education degree, made Fee feel like the walls of Dr. Gunderson's office were closing in around her. The air went dusty and stale with the smell of books. A hint of formaldehyde drifted down the hall from the dissection lab.

For a moment the orange juice Fee had gulped down at Casey's house this morning backed up in her throat.

"You know that I'm a single mother, don't you, Dr. Gunderson?" Fee asked quietly.

The older woman nodded, but Fee could see she didn't get it. Word around the science department was that Dr. Gunderson had turned down the chance for marriage and a family in pursuit of her PhD. She'd worked on scientific teams on three continents before she came to teach at Larkin. What did Margaret Gunderson know about raising a child and the responsibilities that came with it?

"I have a daughter who's less than a year old," Fiona went on, doing her best to explain. "In spite of having a scholarship and grants, I still have to work to feed and clothe her. I have to come up with money for lab fees and books, for rent and gas—and Samantha's day care."

"You're not thinking about turning this internship down, are you, Fiona?" the older woman asked, incredulous and clearly dismayed.

Fee took a shaky breath. "I don't see how I can accept it."

The instant she read the description of the program Dr. Gunderson had given her, Fee realized how many hours she'd be expected to work at the observatory and how hard each of the interns would be pressed in the ten weeks they'd be at Kitt Peak.

"I need to spend this summer getting a little money ahead, so I can do my student teaching next fall," Fee explained.

"They *are* offering a stipend—" Dr. Gunderson gestured to the brochure describing the position, encouraging Fee to confirm that for herself.

Fee made no move to do that. "That stipend would hardly be enough to pay for a decent place to live in Tucson, much less day care."

The choice she'd made so cavalierly on the road to California dragged at her.

"Surely your parents would be willing to help financially once they realize what a wonderful opportunity—"

"No, they wouldn't."

Nor would Fee ask them to. She was the one who'd screwed up her life, and Fee had too much to prove to go running to the people she'd betrayed just because she needed help.

"Or maybe they'd look after—"

Fiona snorted. "My parents and I aren't on the best of terms right now."

Margaret Gunderson compressed her lips. "Maybe your grandmother—"

"Dr. Gunderson, my grandmother is eighty-four years old. She has a life of her own here at the university, and I'm not about to ask her to wear herself out looking after my kid."

Dear God! She really *was* going to have to turn down the chance to work at Kitt Peak!

Admitting that ate at Fee's insides. Her breathing thickened and her throat prickled with the threat of tears. What Fiona needed to do was thank Dr. Gunderson for her extraordinary and unexpected kindness—then get the hell out of there.

"It isn't that I don't appreciate your interest in me." Fee wished her voice didn't sound quite so wobbly and uncertain as she spoke. "It means the world to me, Dr. Gunderson, that you all have such faith in my abilities. But I'm just not in a position to take advantage of this program." Fee pushed to her feet. "I hope you understand."

"You have until the first of the year to let them know if you're going to accept the internship, Fiona," Margaret Gunderson pointed out.

Like having until the first of the year was going to make a difference in her answer.

If Fee had learned anything in the last seven months, it was that she didn't have it in her to abandon her little girl—or ignore the responsibilities that came with her.

"Don't refuse this out of hand," the older woman warned her.

"I'll give it some more consideration before I write to them," Fee promised, because she owed Dr. Gunderson that much.

At last, she escaped into the hallway. She turned instinctively to the left, not sure where she was going but needing to get there fast. The halls were pretty much deserted at this time of day, and she stalked toward the light at the end of the hall. She needed a place to collect herself almost more than she needed air to breathe.

She had nearly reached the big double doors that led out to the loading dock when someone burst out of the stairwell and all but ran her down.

It was David Lowery.

She saw his mouth widen in what she supposed would have grown into a grin of greeting, but then he must have recognized the dejection in her face. Without a word, he wrapped an arm around her shoulders and swept her out into the gray November day.

He didn't ask her what was wrong. He didn't say so much as a word to her. He just tugged her into a protected niche between the side of the science building and the door, and wrapped her up in his arms.

Fee pressed her forehead, nose, and chin into the center of David's chest and stood there panting into the folds of his dark green sweater. But she didn't cry.

She stood there breathing the scent of him, ginger and wool and something faintly chemical. She let herself take refuge in his warmth and shifted her burdens to someone else for the first time in a very long while.

David just stood and held her. Other students came and went. A FedEx truck pulled up to deliver packages. The clock in the tower of the ad building struck two.

Fee was missing child psychology, and she didn't care.

It felt too good being with David, solid and sure and comfortable. Fee slid her arms around his waist and pressed in closer.

"It'll be all right," he whispered against her hair.

He didn't even know what had happened. He didn't have any idea what was wrong. Still, as ridiculous as it seemed, Fee felt better.

※

Ted had been gone not quite three weeks when Mike decided he ought to stop on his way into the farm to check the box for mail. It was nearly dark when he pulled his Silverado to the edge of the road and climbed out of the cab. As he did, the wind whipsawed through him, bitter and sharp-edged, making the muscles in his shoulders constrict against the cold.

Ted's mailbox was like everything else on the farm, so worn and battered it took three or four good pulls to get the damn thing open. When Mike finally managed it, he could see that whoever was driving rural delivery had piled, then stuffed, and finally crammed Ted's mail inside.

Mumbling under his breath, Mike gathered the mess up in his arms and carried it back to the Silverado's warm, dim cab. In the glow of the map light, he sorted what Ted had received into piles: advertisements, charity solicitations, and catalogs. He'd gotten a sample of Irish Spring, a girly magazine Mike stopped ogling in high school, a postcard inviting him to the pancake supper at the Masonic Temple, and a stack of bills. He quickly plucked out four that were overdue, set aside letters decorated with stickers and crayoned hearts from Ted's three girls, and finally unearthed an envelope addressed to himself.

Cold slimy dread congealed in his belly when he recognized the "Hope House" logo in the corner. It was the place he'd taken Ted for rehab.

He sat looking down at the cream-colored envelope wondering if this was a bill for their services, some paperwork he needed to attend to, or maybe a report on his brother's progress.

He doubted it was something he wanted to read, but the curse that came with being the older brother was having to step up and take responsibility.

With a sigh, Mike tore off the end of the envelope. There

was a handwritten letter inside, two full pages of Ted's broad, disorganized script.

The chill in his stomach crept deeper as he sat imagining what Ted had to say to him. Mike had forced Ted into rehab. He'd browbeaten him and shamed him. He'd told his brother his children would hate him if he didn't get help.

This was probably Ted's retaliation. Mike's hands were shaking as he tilted the pages of the letter toward the map light and started to read.

November 23—

Dear Mike,

Things here are going okay. This isn't a place I'd book for a dream vacation, but the food's not bad and I'm learning things. Stuff about the twelve steps and how to use them to stay clean and sober. On the whole, they sound pretty sensible. But after all these years I've spent drinking, I'm afraid they won't be all that easy to follow. Still, since I really want to change the way I've been living, I guess I'm going to have to figure out how to work through them one day at a time.

It's steps eight and nine I'm writing you about. Those steps have to do with making amends to the people I wronged while I was drinking. They recommend we do that face-to-face, and I do mean to talk directly to Nancy, Mom, and Janice about it as soon as I leave Hope House. I've got a full page list of other folks I need to look up and apologize to when I get back to Larkin. Just looking at who I'm going to have to confront scares me a little, but it also makes me realize how long drinking has been screwing up my life.

I had to ask for special permission so I could write to

you, though, because a lot of what I have to say just can't wait. Being here has given me a lot of time to think, mostly about myself, but also about Dad and Mom and how things were when we were growing up. I've been thinking a lot about you, Mike, and how I've been taking advantage of you for as long as I can remember.

There's never been a time when you haven't looked out for me. The first time I can think of was the day I wanted to go swimming in the creek. I couldn't have been more than four or five, and considering how fast the water was running, I probably would have drowned if you hadn't jumped right in and pulled me out.

The thing I didn't remember until the other day is how Ma used the switch on you when you brought me home. She said you should have known better to take me wading, and you never said a word in your own defense. You never told her that you'd probably saved my life, and I didn't have the gumption to tell her, either.

Looking back, I can see how you were always looking out for me. You'd do my chores when I forgot. You punched out Ben Bristol the time at school when he picked me up and hung me on the fence by those rainbow suspenders I wore so much when I was in first grade. You always saw I did my homework, and somehow you got me through Mr. Keckler's algebra class. You were always getting me jobs, lending me money, hauling me out of whatever scrape I managed to get myself into.

You helped me up every single time I fell down, and I never once thanked you.

I'm sorry for all the times I've turned your kindness and your generosity against you to get what I wanted. I'm sorry for taking advantage of how responsible you've always felt toward Janice and me. I'm sorry I never even thought to tell you I appreciated what you were doing.

I'm sorry I pissed on the wheel of your Silverado.

For a long time now, I've been a drunk and a screwup. But I want to change. So I thank you for dragging my sorry ass all the way here to Olathe so I can learn how to do that. So I can be a better dad to my kids than our dad was to us. So I can learn what I have to do to make a fresh start.

Writing you this letter is part of doing that. I can't promise that I won't ever screw up again, but I can tell you I haven't had a drink in fifteen days. I can tell you I'm not going to have one today. I'm going to do this one day at a time, like they tell us we have to do. I'm going to let tomorrow take care of tomorrow.

So I'll buy you a cup of coffee when I get back to Larkin. I'm learning to drink it strong and black.

Your grateful, hopeful brother,
Ted

Mike read the letter twice with tears in his eyes, then he crossed his arms on the steering wheel and buried his face in his forearms. He sat there for a very long while as gusts of wind battered the truck and the season's first flakes of snow swirled in the beam of the headlights.

He sat there as Ted's words penetrated his mind and heart. He breathed a little easier as the fist of fear that had been clenched tight inside him since he was a boy slowly relaxed. He sat there as the snow dusted the ruts in the road and let go of years of lonely responsibility, released the tangled knots of anger and bitter resentment. He sat there and gave up the burden of being Ted's keeper, realizing all at once that he could hang on to his love for his brother without having to answer for the choices he made.

So this is what it's like to forgive someone, he found himself thinking. As that thought expanded in his mind, Mike knew it was an important lesson—one he needed to learn well and remember.

❊

Sometimes life sees fit to give you object lessons. Sometimes it makes you realize that no matter how angry and pissed off you are, you have it pretty damn good.

It was nearly midnight and Fee had just gotten out of the shower when someone came tapping on the door to her apartment.

"Another stupid frat boy," she muttered as she knotted the belt of her robe around her waist and padded down the hall, "too drunk to find his way back to his own damn apartment."

She peered out the peephole to make sure, but the light in the hallway was out again. All she could see was some guy's looming silhouette, someone she didn't recognize and didn't want to hassle with.

"Go away!" she barked, leaning close to the door. "We don't want any."

She'd already turned away when a soft voice stopped her.

"Fee, it's Dave. I saw your lights were on. Can you let me in?"

Though it was way too late to be entertaining visitors, Fee caught something she couldn't quite identify in Dave's voice, something that made her snap the dead bolt and tug open the door.

He stood in the hall outside hunched and immobile, as if he'd come this far and couldn't take another step. She reached out and clasped his hand, drawing him into the apartment.

"Oh, David. What's happened?"

He swallowed hard, and even in the dimness she could see his eyes were swollen and red. "It's my mom," he said, his voice low and raspy. "She died."

"Oh, David," Fee pushed up on her tiptoes and wrapped her arms around him. "I'm so, so sorry."

He hugged her back, hanging on tight, leaning into her as if he needed her to hold him up.

"She went in for her chemo this afternoon," he whispered, resting his cheek against her damp hair, "but something went wrong. She had some kind of reaction and her heart stopped."

"Oh, Davey."

"They got her back," he went on miserably, "but she wasn't really there, you know. All they really did was give Dad and Melissa and me a chance to get there. To say good-bye. And then—" As close as she was holding him, Fiona felt the shiver of grief run through him. "—she just stopped—stopped breathing."

Fee didn't know what else to say to him except that she was sorry. She murmured his name and rubbed that broad sinewy back. She stroked the thick, faintly bristly hair that had grown long and a little too shaggy on his nape. Standing there in the hall, she rocked him gently, shifted from foot to foot like she did when she was comforting Samantha. They stepped right and left and right again so they were almost, but not quite, dancing.

They held on to each other for a good, long while, David

bending over her, Fee's face turned into the whiskery curve of his throat. Fee hadn't had much experience with someone she loved dying, except her grandfather when she was a kid. But she did understand the penetrating sadness of having to say good-bye to someone you loved. She understood the bone-deep regret of all the things you'd never have a chance to say to someone who'd loved you unconditionally once, but who was lost to you now and forever.

Fee pulled David even closer, crooning words of understanding and comfort against his throat. And when Dave finally raised his head, Fee could tell by how wide and vacant his eyes were, that he barely knew where he was. He didn't have any idea why he'd come here or what to do with himself next.

Fee knew instinctively and tightened her fingers around his big hand. She closed and locked the door, then drew him gently into the kitchen.

"I'm going to make some tea," she said, putting the kettle on. "My grandma says tea always makes things better."

Dave nodded like a sleepwalker.

"I didn't know your mom very well," Fee put water in the teakettle. "So why don't you tell me about her."

"Besides the fact that she only just turned fifty-one?"

She heard the bitterness in David's voice, the outrage that his mom had been taken from him. That she hadn't lived out the span of years he thought she'd ought to have been allotted.

"I think every time we lose someone we love—" she said, measuring tea into the tea ball. She'd chosen chamomile because she wanted something soothing. "—we feel like they left our lives way too soon. I don't think it matters a bit how old they are."

David shook his head, his face dark, his eyes stormy. "She shouldn't have gotten cancer; it wasn't fair. She took care of herself. She ate right and exercised. She didn't smoke."

Fee put the tea ball in the pot and waited for the water in the kettle to boil. "I guess none of us gets a guarantee that we'll live to a ripe old age."

David braced back against the counter and hunched his shoulders. "She and Dad had all these plans, you know? Once Dad retired, they wanted to travel.

"They were sort of hippies when they were young and hitchhiked all over. They spent a whole year bumming around Europe before they settled down and had Melissa and me. They wanted to go back and visit some of those places now that they could afford to sleep in real hotels and didn't have to live on bread and cheese."

He swiped at a tear with the back of his hand. "Mom wanted to visit Australia and see kangaroos in the wild. She always had a thing for kangaroos; I don't know why. And Dad was trying to talk her in to hiking a piece of the Appalachian Trail."

Fee reached across and squeezed David's forearm by way of comfort and held on until he looked at her, until he accepted the understanding she was offering. Once he had, she let him go and turned away to wet the tea, put the pot and cups and a plate of Samantha's graham crackers on the tray she carried into the living room.

As she poured tea for David, Fiona couldn't help wondering if there were things her parents had planned to do together and places they wanted to go she'd never known about. Before she left she never really considered that her parents had lives beyond their work, their family, and her. Now that she had her own life and her own responsibilities, *now that she'd grown up,* she saw and had begun to understand her parents' feelings and motives, their decisions, and their disappointments.

It was as if she'd been stargazing, studying only the biggest and most brilliant stars. Then a cloud had rolled away, revealing the complex network of sky that had been obscured by her youth, her selfishness, and her myopia.

Now that she'd developed the maturity to see beyond herself, she wondered if because her leaving had turned her parents against each other, they were going to miss spending the rest of their lives together. That doubt, that weight came to rest on Fee's bony shoulders, giving her something else to feel guilty about.

She handed David his tea and watched as he receded into the corner of the lumpy, chenille-covered couch.

"Are there things you wish you'd said to your mother while you had the chance?" Fee asked softly, thinking of all she ought to say to her own. "Or were there things you wish you hadn't said?"

The last time she'd seen her dad, she'd shoved at him and called him an asshole. What if that was the last conversation they ever had?

"You know—" David said, resting his head on the back of the couch "—when Mom got cancer we started having these really good talks. Not Mom and little Davey, but like adults. We said a lot of things to each other. We looked at pictures. She told me about stuff that happened when I was little." His eyes teared up. "We said how much we loved each other. I had the chance to tell her what a great mom she'd been when Melissa and I were growing up."

Fee's throat burned, glad that Dave had no regrets when it came to his parents. Wishing she didn't have so many.

She set her cup aside and reached for David again. He curled one long arm around her shoulders and gathered her in, but for a moment, Fee wasn't sure who was comforting whom.

They sank deeper into the couch, shifting a little at a time until they were lying side by side. Fee wrapped her arms around his back. Dave pressed his cheek into her hair, and she thought he might be crying. She held him tighter until they were tangled up together, chest to chest and thigh to thigh. It was close and intimate, but not a sexual kind of holding. It was the warm and comforting contact of two dear friends coming together.

"Thanks for letting me come in tonight, Fee," he murmured after a while. "I'd been driving around for hours until I saw your lights."

"It's okay, David," she whispered back. "You're always welcome. I'm glad I was here for you to come to."

She thought he might have brushed his lips against her temple by way of thanks. "I don't know what I'd have done without you."

His voice faded on the last word, faded with what might have been grief or despair or exhaustion. So she held him tighter. She let her hands move over him, smoothing his hair, patting him, and stroking his back. She crooned to him, whatever words of comfort came to her as they lay wound together. Something she'd done must have worked, or maybe David was just plain depleted by grief, because soon Fee felt his ribs rise against her as his breathing deepened. She felt his body gradually go slack as he drifted to sleep.

It felt right to hold him as he slept, to feel so protective and tender toward someone who wasn't your responsibility. To draw satisfaction for yourself from this wonderful closeness. Fee stayed right where she was for a very long time.

Then slowly, so she wouldn't disturb him, she peeled herself away. She stood for a moment looking down at him. Even in sleep, that strong, unexpectedly compelling face seemed marked with grief. In spite of how big he was, how rangy and fit he looked sprawled there on her couch, he seemed raw, exhausted, worn out by his grief.

Somehow Fee couldn't bear to wake him and send him home, so she draped the worn chenille bedspread over him. As she did, a sweet, expansive tenderness spread outward from her breastbone. She didn't know what quirk of fate had brought David Lowery back into her life, but whatever it was, she was glad.

Fee turned off the lights and took her cell phone into the bedroom. She didn't hesitate to make the call, even though it was nearly two in the morning.

A man answered on the second ring. "David?"

"No, Mr. Lowery. It's Fiona Montgomery."

"Fiona!" David's father said her name as if he knew just who she was. As if Dave had been talking to his family about her.

"I called to tell you," she went hastily on, "that David's here with me. He's asleep on my couch right now."

"Is he all right?"

She could hear the tautness in Luke Lowery's voice. His wife had just died and his son had been missing for what was probably hours and hours.

"I think he's as right as he can be right now," she answered. "I'm so sorry to hear that Mrs. Lowery died."

David's father took a long, uneven breath. "Thank you,

Fiona," he said. "I appreciate your condolences—and for looking after David tonight. You want to wake him up and send him home?"

Fee hesitated, thinking about how hollow and drained David seemed. It made her feel like she was helping somehow by watching over him, by giving him time to regain a bit of his strength.

"I was thinking he might just as well stay until morning, Mr. Lowery," she offered, "unless you want him there with you."

His father hesitated and then sighed again. "We've got some rough days ahead of us," he conceded. "Let David sleep while he can."

"I'll look after him," Fee promised. "He'll be fine here with me. I just wanted to be sure you knew where he was."

"Thank you, Fiona," he said, his voice deepening. "You're a good friend to our David."

"Your David has been a good friend to me, Mr. Lowery. Good night."

She broke the connection and sat staring down at the phone. Luke Lowery had said she was a good friend to David. Somehow hearing that settled at least a bit of the turmoil that had been churning in her.

Now if only she could find a way to be a better daughter.

※

Miriam

✳

"Fiona," Gran's voice drifted up the stairs to where Fee was headed for the attic to put away the boxes that only two hours before had been filled with Christmas tree ornaments. "Would you bring down the tree skirt your great-grandma Ada made? I keep it on the top shelf of my closet wrapped in a sheet."

"Sure," Fee shouted back.

She and Gran and Samantha had spent the day picking out Gran's Christmas tree, a stately balsam that now stood almost completely decorated in Gran's front room. It was a wonderful tree, tall and straight, filling the house with that wonderful it's-almost-Christmas smell.

Samantha seemed to like it, too, because she jabbered and clapped her hands every time they plugged in the lights.

Once Fee had stowed the boxes, she entered her grandmother's bedroom. It had always been her favorite room in the house, with its tall four-poster bed and the needlepoint window seat that overlooked the garden. It smelled like her grandma, too, of attar of roses, Ben-Gay, and Sweetheart soap.

The tree skirt was easy enough to find; it was right where

Gran said it was. But as she turned, Fee's gaze fell on the wood-framed photograph on the corner of her grandmother's writing desk. It was Jonathan Parrish, the husband her grandmother had woven her life around, the father her mother talked about with tears in her eyes. He'd died when Fee was eight, so her memories of him weren't really all that clear.

Fee paused and picked up the photograph. Because people spoke of her grandfather with such affection and respect, she was curious about him. He didn't look any more extraordinary than she remembered, with a long, narrow face, high brow, and slicked-back hair. But she could see the warmth and intelligence in his eyes behind the gold-rimmed glasses, and in the photograph he had a pleasant quirk to his mouth as if he were amused and ready to smile.

It must have been who he was, not what he looked like that made him so special, Fee thought.

She could see a lot of this man in her mother, and more than a bit of him in her own face. As Samantha's features changed and she lost that babyish roundness, would Fee find hints of Jonathan Parrish in her, too?

Maybe it was being a mother herself, Fee reflected, that made the family connections so fascinating. Or maybe it was because Christmas was almost here, and it was a time when whole families got together to celebrate. Of course, she knew that wasn't going to happen with *her* family *this* year, and she knew that she was the reason.

Fee frowned and set the picture of her grandfather back on the desk. Beside it sat one of Gran's Christmas cactuses. She had them strategically placed around the house, all of them bristling with buds and ready to bloom.

As she reached out to touch one of the tiny bright-pink

knots that would burst into flower one day soon, Fee noticed the old-fashioned black-and-white composition book that lay open in the center of her grandmother's desktop. Gran's spidery script filled the page, and Fee realized suddenly that Gran kept a journal. Judging by the size of the pile of notebooks on the corner of the desk, she'd been keeping journals for a very long time.

Shamelessly intrigued, Fee picked up the open notebook and began to read.

⁂

DECEMBER 12TH

Today I'm going with Fiona and Samantha to pick out a Christmas tree for the house. I've always loved doing that— buying the tree, getting out Great-Grandma Mary McIntire's German ornaments and Mama's embroidered tree skirt—because each of those things connects me to my past and to people I've loved and lost.

Of course, going out to get a Christmas tree always reminds me of you, my darling Jonathan.

Do you remember what a hard year 1937 was for all of us? It was at the height of the Depression. You were struggling to stay in school. There weren't jobs to be had for masons; my fathers and brothers hadn't worked in months. We wouldn't have had any money coming to the household at all if it hadn't been for my job at the telephone company.

Though I'd been eyeing the Christmas tree lot where you were working all week, I deliberately waited until Christmas Eve to go in and look. I thought you might be selling the trees for less by then, and I could afford at least a small one.

It was snowy and cold and getting on toward dark, but the

lights strung around the tree lot at the corner of the square were bright and cheery. I was just considering a likely-looking specimen a head taller than I was when you appeared out of that miniature forest.

You were bundled up to within an inch of your life, wearing the ugliest knitted cap I'd ever seen pulled down over your ears and an equally unsightly muffler wrapped over your nose and mouth. (How was I to know your baby sister had knitted them for you?)

What I saw between those rows of ragged stitches were the warmest, friendliest eyes I'd ever looked into. You stood there for a moment without saying a word, just looking at me in a way that made my cheeks get rosy—and not just from cold.

"I'm closing in about ten minutes, miss," you finally said. "If you want a tree, you'll have to make your mind up soon."

"I like this one," I told you, "but I'm a little short of cash right now."

You laughed. "Isn't everybody?"

"I'll just go have a look at those smaller trees before you close," I said.

You turned and frowned at the few scraggly pines leaning against the side of the makeshift shed. "That was our most popular size, and I'm afraid there's not much left."

I'd turned to go and take a closer look, when you caught my sleeve. "I'll tell you what, miss," you offered. "Why don't you just take the tree you want, and I'll charge you what I would for one of the smaller trees."

"I couldn't expect you to do that," I protested.

"Once I lock up, miss, it'll be Christmas Eve," you said with a shrug. "These trees will go for firewood day after tomorrow."

As it turned out, I was your last customer. Once you'd

turned off the lights and locked the shed, you carried my tree as far as the sidewalk.

"Thank you," I said as I took hold of the tree, surprised at how heavy and awkward it was. "You go on home now and have a nice Christmas with your family."

You wagged your head. "I'm just headed back to the dorm, miss. I couldn't pay my fees for next semester and buy a train ticket, too, so I decided to stay here and work at the tree lot."

You sounded a little lonely, but resigned.

"So what are you studying at the university?" I asked, though I knew Mama would be wondering where I was.

"Mathematics," you said. "I want to teach it in college. And what do you do?"

The wind was blowing down Payne Street in a gale, swirling snow around us. I shivered, but I couldn't bring myself to leave.

"I work as a telephone operator," I managed to say though my teeth had begun to chatter.

You must have seen how cold I was, because you stepped away. "I hope you and your family enjoy the tree."

"It's going to be beautiful!"

As you turned to go, something seized up inside me. "Wait!" I called out. "Mr.—"

You turned back. "Parrish," you said. "My name's Jonathan Parrish."

"Mr. Parrish, I'm Miriam Avery. Would you care to come home with me for dinner? It won't be anything fancy, but no one should be alone at Christmas."

"That's very nice of you, Miss Avery," you demurred, "but I wouldn't want to be any trouble to you and your family."

Even then you hated being beholden.

"*It's no trouble to set another place. With so many of us around the table, we'll hardly know you're there.*"

"*Well…*"

"*Please, Mr. Parrish. You were so kind about letting me have the tree I wanted. Mama loves Christmas and will be so pleased to have such a beautiful tree—thanks to your generosity.*"

I remember standing there with my heart beating in my throat waiting for you to accept the invitation, wanting for reasons I didn't understand back then, for you to come home with me.

"*Well, then,*" *you said in capitulation.* "*If I'm going home with you, the very least I can do is carry that tree.*"

We chatted all the way back to the house, and when you emerged from your knitted cap and scarf, I saw how very handsome you were.

After Mama's excellent dinner and a bit of Papa's home-made wine, we put up and decorated the tree. Once the lights were twinkling and the ornaments and tinsel were in place, everyone in the family brought out the little gifts we had for one another.

I remember being embarrassed that you had no gift to open, but it didn't seem to matter. You laughed as hard as the rest of us when my brother Tommy gave Mama an IOU saying he'd do the ironing the whole month of January, and Bud presented Papa with a tin of his favorite pipe tobacco. I gave Mama an apron I'd made for her from one of the dresses I'd outgrown. And when Raymond opened the sheet music Kenneth had given him, he sat right down at the piano. While he played, Mama and Papa and you and I waltzed around the living room.

Then Mama brought out one last gift.

"*Everyone here, except of course Mr. Parrish,*" Mama began, "*knows the story of how Gill McIntire gave my mother Letty a Christmas cactus the Christmas before he was lost on the USS* Maine *in Havana Harbor. The year I turned nineteen, my mother presented me with a cutting from that Christmas cactus to indicate that she approved of the man I'd chosen for my husband.*"

She smiled at Papa before she went on.

"*Over the years, the gift of a cutting from Letty's Christmas cactus has come to be a gift of love from mother to daughter. It's come to acknowledge that a daughter has stepped up to take on her family responsibilities. It's come to represent our approval and acceptance of her as the next generation of McIntire women.*

"*That's why this year I have chosen to give a piece of Letty's Christmas cactus to my daughter Miriam. She is the one who has kept our family together this past year. If it weren't for her position at the telephone company, there's many a night we'd have gone to bed hungry. We might not still have a roof over our heads, or still all be together if it hadn't been for her. I'm so proud of Miriam for working so hard and for being so generous.*"

Do you remember, Jonathan, how she brought that Christmas cactus to me? How she put that gloriously blooming plant in my hands and kissed me?

Do your remember what you said? "Any young woman who would do what you have done for your family will make some lucky man a wonderful wife."

Did you know right then that you and I were meant to be together, my darling Jonathan? Did you start to love me that night as I started loving you?

That was so long ago, seventy years give or take a few, and

I still remember that evening as if it were etched in glass. I re-
member the bitter cold and the smell of the pines. I remember
your generosity in giving me the tree I wanted. I remember
how proud I was to be walking home with a college boy, and
how pleased I was to introduce you to my parents.

I remember how handsome you were, how it felt to
waltz with your arms around me that first time, and the
warmth in your eyes when Mama gave me that Christmas
cactus.

That I remember it all so clearly makes me miss you more
than ever. I know I will dream of you tonight, my darling
Jonathan, and at least in my dreams we will be together.

Fiona blinked back tears as she carefully placed the open
journal on her grandmother's desk where it belonged. Yet
even as she did, her fingertips lingered over those lovely,
lonely words.

How much her grandmother must have loved her grandfather.

How much all the McIntire women had loved the men
they married: Letty and Gill, Ada and Thomas, Miriam and
her Jonathan. Even Fiona's mother and father—for all that
they were living apart—had shared the kind of love that
could bind a couple for the rest of their lives.

Would Fee ever find that kind of love herself, the kind of
love that would last a lifetime? She'd loved Jared—and
would always care for him because he was her daughter's father—but that love had been transient, immature. Would
she ever share a life with a man she cared for enough that
she'd still be writing him love letters years after he had died?

Considering that every other woman in the McIntire
family had found love and deep contentment with men

who adored and honored them, Fee hoped that one day—when she was ready—she might find that kind of love, find that kind of man for herself.

But for now, what she wished for even more was a Christmas when her family could truly come together. When she'd look and see her daughter playing with her new toys beneath the tree, see her grandmother still robust and healthy, laughing at little Samantha's antics. See her father settled on the couch with his arm around her mother amid a jumble of boxes and wrapping paper at their feet.

She wished that sometime in the future—in spite of the mistakes she'd made—she'd prove herself worthy of a Christmas cactus of her own from Great-Great-Grandmother Letty's plant. And the chance to pass it on to her own daughter.

"Fiona?" Gran's voice spiraled up the stairwell. "What's taking so long? Are you having trouble finding the tree skirt?"

Fee flushed and gathered Great-Grandma Ada's handiwork more closely against her chest. "Just found it," she called back.

With one final glance at the journal, she left the room, knowing now, in a tangible way, what to hope for herself—at Christmas, or any other time.

Chapter 16

✳

Sometimes Fee wondered if her mother had a clue. Hadn't she told her mom she had three papers due right after the holidays? Hadn't she *told* her she'd be spending every spare minute she had doing research? And didn't her mom call her at the library anyway, then practically insist they meet for lunch?

"You have to eat," her mother coaxed when Fee tried to beg off.

Fee conceded that she did, especially if someone else was paying the check. She arrived at the Sunny Spot just before noon, cold and windblown from her walk down University Hill. "I have a lab at one," she warned when she reached her mother's table. "What's so important?"

In spite of Fee's tone, her mother glanced up and beamed at her. Having someone's face light up at the sight of you did a lot to improve your mood.

"I'm so glad you could make it, honey." Avery rose and gave her a quick, hard hug. "I know how busy you are these days."

Fiona had settled down beside her mother before she

noticed the table was laid for three. "Is Gran joining us?" she asked.

"No."

Fee saw her mother's smile wobble just a little. Apprehension pressed up beneath her ribs like an inflating balloon.

"Dad isn't coming, is he?" Fee asked, horrified. "You didn't set this up to bring Dad and me together, did you? Because, Mom, he and I—"

Her mother rose to greet someone who'd come up behind where Fee was sitting.

"Hello, Margaret," she said. "I'm so pleased you could join us on such short notice."

Fiona craned around and her mouth fell open when she saw Dr. Gunderson standing over her. How in the world did her mother know Margaret Gunderson?

"Avery," Dr. Gunderson greeted them crisply as she sat down. "Fiona."

Dr. Gunderson wasn't in her professional, I'm-a-woman-scientist mode today. Instead of a lab coat, she had on a fuzzy pink sweater. Her sleek gray bob looked full and soft beneath her knitted hat.

"The crepes here are very good," Avery commented, and the way she said it seemed to indicate she was buying Margaret Gunderson's lunch.

Something about the exchange made Fee go all weightless inside, and her agitation grew as the waitress took their orders.

"Fiona," her mother began once the menus had been whisked away. "Margaret called this morning and mentioned you'd been offered a summer internship at the Kitt Peak Observatory. She says that's quite an honor."

Fee whipped around to stare at her advisor. The idea that the two of them had been discussing both Kitt Peak and her made Fee even more impatient and itchy. What was Dr. Gunderson thinking, getting her mother involved in this?

"Did Dr. Gunderson also tell you," Fiona said pointedly, "that I decided not to take the internship?"

"And why would you decide that?" her mother asked in a tone that reminded Fee a shade too much of Gran.

"You must know perfectly well, Mom, why I turned it down," she said as reasonably as she could. "I can't just go gallivanting off to study black holes or something when I have Samantha to consider."

"But you *do* still want to be an astronomer, don't you, Fiona?"

Of course she wanted to be an astronomer. She'd wanted to be an astronomer since she was in grade school. Going off for a year and a half to play at being a rock star hadn't changed that, but it had pretty much quashed her chances of ever actually doing it. Accepting that was the hard part.

"What I want," she insisted, trying to sound resolute, "is to get my education degree and teach science in a high school." Though she made a point of smiling and nodding, Fee could see her mother wasn't buying that.

"While Dr. Gunderson and I both think you'd be a fine teacher, Fiona," she went on just like Fee knew she would, "we know your real gift is for astronomy."

Fiona scowled at one woman and then the other. Hadn't either of them figured out how hard it had been for her to turn down this internship? Any astronomy major with a pulse would jump at a chance like this.

"When I left L.A.," she said levelly, though her throat was starting to burn, "I accepted that I was going to be raising

Samantha by myself. In order to do that, I knew I was going to have to make some tough choices. Changing my major was one; refusing this internship is another."

Her mother gave another of those pleasant nods that meant she wasn't finished arguing.

"Margaret and I have talked about this, and we think we can arrange things so you *can* accept the internship and spend the summer at Kitt Peak."

Margaret Gunderson braced her forearms on the table and leaned toward Fee. "I just talked to a professor I know in Tucson about you house-sitting his place over the summer."

Fee could hardly believe one of her profs had gone so far out of her way to make this happen. Her chest filled up with gratitude—and sudden panic.

"That's very good of you, Dr. Gunderson," Fee said and meant it. "But you know there's more involved in me accepting the position at Kitt Peak than having a place to stay."

"I know you're concerned about money," her mother put in. "But if you decide to accept the internship, I'll cover your tuition and books next fall."

Fee sat back, shocked. She knew to the penny how much that was. "What will Dad say?" Fee wanted to know, more than a little embarrassed to be discussing family matters in front of Margaret Gunderson.

"It doesn't matter what he says." High color pinked her mother's cheeks. "Your father won't admit it, but he knows this is what we ought to do."

Fee wasn't the least bit sure her father would feel that way, especially after she'd stormed into the observatory and called him an asshole. But even more important than fall tuition or a place to stay in Tucson, was how she would take care of Samantha if she accepted the position.

"Most internships require you to work pretty long hours," Fee argued. "At an observatory, I expect that will include lots of nights. There's no way I can look after Samantha and meet Kitt Peak's requirements."

Samantha's welfare was her responsibility, one she'd taken on willingly. But in this case, it was the insurmountable problem Fee knew she couldn't resolve.

"Well—" her mother hesitated as if she wasn't sure how Fee would react to what she had to say "—I thought maybe you'd let Samantha stay with me while you were in Arizona."

The offer sucked the air right out of Fiona's lungs, her reaction a combination of surprise, gratitude, and resistance. She fumbled for a reason to refuse. "But—but how could you do that? You work every day. You have the Holding Company to run."

"Since Casey's been providing day care while you're in class," her mother said, as if she'd already thought this through, "I expect she'd be willing to keep Samantha for me, as well."

Fee drew in breath to argue, but her mother continued determinedly. "Look, Fiona, this is something I want to do. I haven't had much time with Samantha, and looking after her while you're in Tucson would give me a chance to get to know my granddaughter."

Her mom made it sound like Fee would be doing her a favor by agreeing to this. But when she thought about what leaving Samantha really meant—no hugging and cuddling her daughter, no standing over her as she slept to remind herself why she was working so hard—a cold hollow ache opened up inside her.

"But if I accepted the internship, I wouldn't see Samantha for ten whole weeks!"

Her mom's eyes warmed as if Fee's reluctance to be away from her daughter was something she recognized and understood.

"Don't you think I know how hard it is to go away on business when your kids are little? Don't you think I understand exactly how much you'll miss her. If the reason you're refusing the internship is that you don't want to be away from your daughter, that's all right. But if you're turning it down because you're afraid of the challenge, or because you think you don't deserve this chance—that's something else entirely."

"Oh, Mom," Fee said miserably. "I really screwed things up for myself, didn't I?"

Though this was neither the time nor place for such a private discussion, Fee couldn't seem to hold back the words. "I'm so sorry for taking off the way I did. I'm sorry for stealing your necklace, even though I knew how much it meant to you. It never occurred to me how much what I was doing would hurt you and Dad. I was stupid and thoughtless—and, Mom, I'm so, so sorry."

Fee had been midway through her junior year at the university, still as fascinated with astronomy as she'd always been, but restless. Her mother watched over her like a hen with one chick, and her father's hopes for her future were a burden that grew heavier every day. She'd been ready to spread her wings and Starburst's offer had come like a call to high adventure.

She'd answered it with openhearted confidence, excited

about the band's prospects and thrilled to her toes to be on the road with Jared and her friends. Only later when reality set in and Fee discovered what it was like to live night and day with four guys, after she realized she was pregnant, had her expectations dissolved into disillusionment. Only after Samantha was born did Fee look back and see all she had given up.

"I adore Samantha and I can't imagine my world without her," Fiona confessed, not quite able to meet her mother's eyes, "but I know having her before I was ready to care for her and support her was a mistake."

"We all make mistakes, Fiona," her mother consoled her, her own voice catching in her throat. "I wish I'd tracked you down when we first lost touch. I shouldn't have let your father convince me the reason you'd gone silent was that you didn't want anything to do with us."

Fee saw the fresh lines of worry in her mother's face, recognized the sadness still lingering in her eyes, and realized just how much what she'd done had cost her mom.

She saw how much her mother must love her, to forgive her for all the mistakes she'd made and all the pain she'd caused.

Even though Dr. Gunderson was watching, Fee clasped her mother's hand and apologized. "I'm sorry for the things I said and the way I left. I'm so sorry for all the ways I hurt you."

"I know you are, Fiona." Her mother's fingers flexed, holding Fee's hand even tighter. "But you mustn't spend your life looking back. You shouldn't deny yourself this opportunity because you don't think it's something you deserve. Let me help you make the most of the chance Dr. Gunderson has secured for you. Accept the internship at Kitt Peak."

"It'll give you a real taste of what it's like to be an astronomer," Dr. Gunderson encouraged her.

"But what if I go ahead, take the position this summer," Fee asked, "then find out I can't be an astronomer without shortchanging Samantha?"

"Making sacrifices for the people you love, Fee"—her mother nodded sagely—"isn't the same as denying your ambitions. I started the Holding Company when you were just a little girl. But even though I was working, I tried not to let that interfere with being a good mom to you. Did you feel like you got less of my attention because I was too caught up in work?"

Fee remembered how her mom had made a point to be at parents' night, every piano recital and Girl Scout meeting. She'd been there to hold her head when she was sick and mopped up afterward. She'd been a shoulder to cry on when friends were mean or the world disappointed her.

Fee shook her head. "I never felt that, Mom. Not even once. But you had Dad to help. I'm raising Samantha by myself."

"And it looks to me, Fee, like you're doing a very good job of it."

Fee flushed, realizing how much she needed those words, how much she needed her mother to tell her she was doing all right.

"Fiona," her mother began, looking right into her eyes. "If this position at Kitt Peak is something you want, then it's something the people who care about you want for you. Margaret has already found you a place to stay. I'd love a chance to take care of Samantha while you're gone. Casey will support you in whatever you decide. We'll work together to figure out the details. But you need to write and accept that internship before it's too late."

Fee's throat went tight. "You really think I should?"

"Neither one of us would be here, Fee," her mother assured her, "if we weren't sure."

Fee looked at the two women at the table, first her mom and then Margaret Gunderson. She didn't even try to hide the tears in her eyes. "I don't know how to thank you."

It was Margaret who offered the exact criteria. "You can thank us, Fiona, by becoming a damn fine astronomer."

※

What on earth is going on? Avery wondered as she pulled into the Holding Company's parking lot. Four UPS trucks were lined up at the loading dock. Big cardboard boxes were stacked head-high in the bay, and when she got upstairs, she found towers of cartons piled shoulder to shoulder along the walls and in the aisles of office area.

"Cleo!" she shouted, barely able to see from one side of the room to the other. "Cleo, what the hell's going on?"

Cleo waved at her from behind a wall of cardboard boxes. "Yes, I see," she was saying, the phone to her ear. "Uh-huh. Uh-huh. So this wasn't a mistake. Can you give me the name of someone else at the company I can talk to?"

She jotted a name on a memo pad and hung up.

"Well," she said, facing Avery, her Raspberry Rainbow mouth pursed tight in a frown. "You remember the distributor we contracted with to box up and ship our lambs to the Elite stores?"

"Yes."

"He closed up shop."

"What?" Avery asked incredulously. "Without notifying us?"

Cleo nodded. "Apparently he sold the contract to someone else who took delivery when the containers arrived in

Los Angeles from China. But since those folks aren't distributors, they signed for the lambs and forwarded the boxes to us COD."

"You mean, all these cartons are filled with our lambs?"

"And according to UPS, there are more coming. Five hundred and thirty-four cartons of lambs, to be exact."

Avery stared at the boxes that already occupied every spare inch of floor space for as far as she could see. Then, with a sinking feeling in her stomach, she realized exactly what all these cartons meant.

"But if all our lambs are coming here," she exclaimed, "no one is delivering them to Elite's stores."

"Un-huh," Cleo confirmed.

"That means it's up to *us* to count them, repack them, and get them delivered to the stores by the first of the year!"

"I'm afraid that's exactly what it means," Cleo said grimly.

"And if we can't get them into the stores by that deadline—"

"We don't get paid."

And if they didn't get paid... Avery couldn't think right now about what would happen if they didn't get paid.

"You think you could call Elite and ask for a little more time?" Cleo suggested.

Avery shook her head. "Mr. Marshall was dubious about doing business with us to begin with, and when we signed the contracts, he made it exceedingly clear he wasn't going to cut us any slack."

Cleo's carefully plucked eyebrows knitted over the bridge of her nose. "So we either get Sheepish shipped out on time . . ."

"Or we go bankrupt," Avery finished simply.

The two of them stood in the very heart of the Holding Company, listening to the hum of machinery and the chime of voices. Feeling the industry, the warmth and camaraderie among the women who worked here, they couldn't let the company fall apart.

Avery reached across and squeezed Cleo's hand. Cleo nodded and squeezed back. Then Cleo sat down at her computer terminal, began pulling up the addresses of the Elite Card stores, and printing labels. Avery ordered shipping supplies, then called the post office.

She hadn't expected to hear Ted's voice at the other end of the line. Mike hadn't mentioned his brother was out of rehab, much less back at work. Avery explained the problem as succinctly as she could.

"Sure, Avery," Ted reassured her when she was done. "I can bring a postage meter right over or you can print out the postage you'll need online. We'll have a truck swing by the Holding Company a couple times a day to pick things up. How soon do you think you're going to be needing it?"

"Tomorrow?" she guessed. Tomorrow was Saturday. None of them were supposed to be working the Saturday before Christmas.

"I'll come by myself about noon," Ted offered, sounding steady and efficient, "and see how many boxes you have ready to go."

She'd barely hung up the phone when the firestorm of fear and responsibility caught up with her, searing her belly and burning at the back of her throat. If they lost the Holding Company it would be her fault. It would be because she'd tried too hard, reached too far. If they had to close the doors and all of these women lost their jobs, it would be because she'd gambled far more than she had a right to. And how would she ever live with herself?

With an effort she pushed the thought away, straightened, and went back to work.

By three o'clock, when everyone assembled in the coffee room, it was the only island of calm in an ocean of chaos, and Avery's nerves were humming like high-tension wires. It was up to her to bring her ladies up to speed.

"I probably don't have to tell you that we're having an infestation of stuffed lambs," she began, managing to elicit a titter of laughter. "And I want to thank each and every one of you for pitching in to get them off the trucks and stowed away. But it looks like we've got a pretty big challenge ahead of us."

Avery settled back on her heels and laid things out. "The reason the lambs are here instead of on their way to the Elite Card stores like they're supposed to be, is that our distributor reneged on his contract. We'll deal with that through legal channels, but the fact remains that the Holding Company is now responsible for getting the lambs shipped off to the Elite stores so we meet our deadline. That means we need to turn all these lambs around and ship them out by Tuesday."

"But Tuesday is Christmas Eve," Nora O'Malley complained from the back or the room.

"Yes, I know." Avery acknowledged Nora's concerns with a nod. "Which is why I'm so sorry I have to ask you this. I know this close to Christmas you've all got trees to trim, gifts to wrap, and baking to do. But we're going to need your help to meet that deadline."

She stepped closer to the tables where the women were gathered. "I know how hard it is to give up time with your family at Christmas." she said. "But we ll try to make it worth your while. We'll pay time and a half for overtime to anyone who comes in to work. I'll make sure we have people to supervise if you need to bring your kids in with you. If you need transportation, I'll come and pick you up myself."

She drew a long, slow breath and looked into the faces of the women; women who'd worked so hard today. Women she was asking to work even harder tomorrow.

"I know I'm asking a lot of all of you," she went on with a lift of her chin, "especially because some of you had reservations about this project and the decisions I made. But it's come to the point where the future of the Holding Company quite literally depends on the next few days, on getting Sheepish counted and boxed and shipped out so he'll be in the Elite Card stores by the first of the year."

The room rustled with whispers, speculation—and probably dread.

Avery tried to sound positive and energetic as she went on. "Cleo and I are going to stay tonight to organize the shipping procedure so we can start first thing in the morning. If you're available to help us do that, please stay. If you can come by tomorrow, I'll be unlocking the door at seven A.M. If all you have to give is a few hours, come by anyway. If you can, bring your friends, your relatives, the people down the street. We need every pair of hands we can muster to get these lambs shipped out."

"You really think we can get all those lambs in the mail by Christmas Eve?" June Federson asked, speaking, Avery suspected, for all of them.

Avery pasted a big, bright grin on her face. "Of course we can, if all of us work together."

She kept that smile firmly in place to reassure her ladies

as they filed past her out of the coffee room. Avery just wished she was as sure of success as she was pretending to be.

⁂

Avery sent Cleo home about four A.M. They'd done all they could do, prepared everything they could prepare. The sprint to the deadline started tomorrow.

They had five days to open all these cartons and count out all fifty-three thousand four hundred sheep. Five days to pack those lambs into one thousand sixty-eight cardboard boxes, seal them up, label them, load them into the post office trucks, and send them on their way.

Once Cleo had gone, Avery ambled through the fluorescent-lit silence of the Holding Company turning off lights. Her footsteps echoed on the linoleum as she went from one section of the operation to the other. She trailed her fingers over the sewing machines and cutting tables, rubbed the fuzzy plush against her cheek and sniffed the sizing.

She'd built every bit of this business with her talent and her determination—and her own two hands. She'd built it for herself, but she'd also built it for Marta and Phyllis and Jean and Nora. She'd built it on the things she believed in: safe toys, fair wages, the importance of home and family, and that working toward a common goal made everyone stronger.

She'd wanted so much to have the chance to expand on that and on what all of them had accomplished together. She'd wanted that chance so much she'd gambled with things she shouldn't have risked: the jobs and welfare of women whose loyalty to her company couldn't be measured in dollars and cents. She'd risked the company itself, this entity that meant so much to her. It had give her fifteen years of creativity and accomplishment, provided work for women who'd shared the joys and sorrows of her life, just as she'd shared theirs.

She'd put every penny she and Mike had saved in jeopardy, the house they'd worked so hard to make into a home —and maybe even their marriage. She ached with regret when she thought of Mike, but she knew she needed to focus on the task at hand.

It had come down to the simple things. Would they make their deadline or would they fail? Would they save the Holding Company or would it go bankrupt?

Avery vowed to do everything in her power to tip the balance, but it wasn't really up to her anymore. She couldn't do this by herself. She wasn't entirely sure she could do it even if everyone who worked at the Holding Company helped. But by God, she knew they had to try.

Not long after six o'clock, Avery awoke to the sound of someone pounding on the door downstairs. She stumbled out of her office in her stockinged feet to see what the ruckus was.

Forty people stood shivering in the parking lot. June Federson had her teenage daughter and three friends in tow. Marta Petrovich showed up with her husband Gregor and their college-age son. Nora O'Malley had dragged her three sisters in with her, all of them grouchy and grumbling but ready to work. Mary Dorn, who'd been recently widowed, introduced William Razzoli as her "new beau." Three of Phyllis Nordstrom's neighbors had come because Phyllis wanted to be here but couldn't leave her son alone. Half a dozen young people from Cleo's church showed up.

By the time Miriam and Fiona arrived just after eight o'clock, production was in full swing. Someone set Fee to taping boxes and June Federson put Miriam in charge of the checklist of parcels that were ready to ship.

Ted came by just before noon for the first load of the packages. He looked better than he had in months. He'd gained a few pounds at the rehab center and didn't seem so gaunt and hangdog. There was color in his face and his eyes were clear. With surprising efficiency, Ted organized some of the men to help him and the driver to load up the mail truck, gave Cleo a receipt for the packages, and headed back to the post office.

Not half an hour later, Mike arrived, a huge stack of pizza boxes in his arms.

Avery caught her breath at the sight of him. Tall and handsome, he strode in like a knight in shining armor come to rescue her not with a broadsword, but with lunch for the growing multitudes. She loved that he'd come without being asked, loved the genial way he greeted everyone as he made his way to the coffee room. She loved the way his gaze sought hers across what seemed like half an acre of boxes and lambs, and the pure sizzle of energy that ran down her backbone when her eyes met his.

He dropped off the pizzas and went to unload the rest of the truck. Trust Mike to know just what they needed: cases of soda, a couple cartons of toilet paper, garbage bags, rolls of packing tape, and extra mat knives.

While everyone else was finding places to eat, Mike fixed plates for the two of them and steered Avery into her office. Though the head-high cartons blocked both the windows into the manufacturing area and most of the sun, Avery didn't bother turning on the lights. She just dropped down on the couch and put her head in her hands.

Mike nudged the door closed behind him and settled

beside her. "Looks like you're off to a pretty good start," he observed quietly and tried to hand her one of the plates.

"What we finished this morning is hardly a drop in the bucket!" Avery moaned, scrubbing at her face with her hands. "How are we ever going to get all these lambs counted and shipped? How are we going get them off to where they belong in just four days?"

"It's going to be all right, sweetheart," he promised and nudged her with the plate again. "Come on now. Have some pizza. Pizza fixes everything."

"Does it?" she asked and smiled in spite of herself.

Sometimes pizza *had* fixed a day of Fee's tantrums. It helped the time Mike fell out of the tree trying to rescue the cat and sprained his ankle. It made the afternoon she'd decided to put red rinse in her hair seem at least a bit less gruesome.

"Yeah," he said as if he were remembering, too. "It fixes everything. Eat."

They ate, and the gooeyness and the tomato and the spice did make Avery feel better. But she'd barely swallowed the last bite when she pushed to her feet.

"I've got to go," she said.

Mike reached up from where he was sitting and caught her hand. "Not just yet, boss," he said and tugged her back down onto the couch with him, "I've got a question that really needs answering."

Avery eyed the door, then shifted her focus to him. "All right."

"So how come I had to find out what was going on at the Holding Company *from my brother*?"

Avery glanced at him and then away. "Did that hurt your feelings?"

"Yeah," he admitted. "Haven't I always been your go-to guy when you were in trouble? Why didn't you think I'd help you this time?" He linked his fingers with hers and his voice went quiet. "Don't I have a stake in this, too?"

She understood far too well what Mike was risking for the sake of Sheepish and her hopes for the Holding Company. It was why she hadn't called him.

"Sheepish is my concern, I didn't want you having to worry about this."

"Worry about what? Worry about Sheepish or the money—or you?"

Regret fired up the live coals simmering in the pit of her belly. Tears stung the back of her eyes. "I know precisely how much you have at stake, and I understand how much it would hurt you to lose the things I've risked to get this project financed. Especially the house."

She looked down at the way their fingers laced together. "I saw the care you took with every window you stripped and reinstalled, with every spindle you turned for the porch. I loved how carefully you prepared the soil for every rosebush you planted. I remember how hard you worked to pay off the mortgage ahead of time, and how proud you were when you did."

They'd drunk a six-pack of Michelob and burned the mortgage in the garden.

"But what I don't think I realized until I was living there by myself is how full those rooms are of memories." When Mike nodded, she turned her hand in his and clasped it tighter. "But what I also came to see was that our house means more to you than that. It's not just our home, is it, Mike? It's the only place you've ever felt like you belonged."

Mike gave a gusty sigh. "After the way I grew up, Avery, I was looking for someplace where I knew I could make a nest, someplace I knew I'd be safe. I wanted peace and security, a rock I could build my life on. And that's what we had."

"And you let me gamble with all that?" she asked, her voice starting to fracture.

"I made my choices, too, sweetheart. I signed the papers at the bank," he said as he drew her to him. "I knew what I was doing. This isn't entirely your responsibility.

"What scares me more," he admitted, "is losing you the way I've lost touch with lots of other things that really matter."

He meant Fiona. That he'd come even this close to admitting he regretted losing contact with their daughter made Avery's throat close up. But as much as this concession meant to her, it was a long way from getting their family back together.

She started to cry.

"We'll get through this, sweetheart," Mike said, hugging her tighter. "Whatever's happened in the past, we've gotten through it together."

But they hadn't "gotten through" these last three months unscathed. Mike was living out at the farm. Fee was running her life on nerve and pride. The Holding Company was two steps away from going broke. And right or wrong, Avery felt responsible for all of it.

"It'll be all right," Mike murmured and drew her closer. She nuzzled into the wide, sweatshirt-covered haven of her husband's chest. It was such warm, familiar territory: the fresh-cut-lumber smell that was so much a part of him, the tender nook between his shoulder and throat, the bulwark of his strong arms linked around her. Her tears came harder, but Avery knew she was safe, safer with Mike than she'd ever been anywhere.

Mike hugged her and let her cry. Then, in a single, smooth movement, he stretched out on the couch and pulled her over him. "It's all right, Avery," he kept murmuring as he stroked her hair.

Avery sighed and nestled deeper, wanting so much to believe him.

It was dark when Avery awoke—and Mike was gone.

She pushed off the blanket he must have draped around her shoulders and sat up, dizzy and disoriented. What was going on? How long had she been sleeping?

Ten minutes was too long for someone who had tens of thousands of sheep to count and box and send on their way. She scrubbed her face with her hands, jammed her feet into her shoes, and wobbled to the door.

The moment she opened it, she was enveloped in a hum of activity. Cartons from China might still be piled to the rafters, but folks were working hard to empty them, repack the sheep, and ship them off to their new homes. As she took a closer look, she saw the people doing that weren't just the ladies from the Holding Company. They were civilians, people she knew from her life around town, from church or civic groups or the university.

Margaret Gunderson and three or four people Avery recognized from Larkin's science department were counting lambs. Loretta McGee and half the checkers from the Food-4-Less were ferrying cartons of counted lambs into the shipping area.

Avery grabbed a box, followed them, and found owners from many of the shops along Main Street checking invoices. David Lowery and his dad were sealing boxes, and Larkin's mayor and three members from the Board of aldermen were affixing labels and postage.

"Mr. Mayor," Avery said, approaching them. "What on earth are you all doing here?"

Billy Williams set down his stack of address labels. "When we heard you needed help, my Georgia said to me, 'If you expect any of the ladies to vote for you in the next election, Billy, you'd best get down to the Holding Company and lend a hand. Don't you know what Avery Montgomery's done for the women here in Larkin?'"

"So here we are," Sal Martino chimed in, grinning beneath his fuzzy mustache. "We couldn't let anything happen to the Holding Company. You pay lots of *taxes!*"

Avery reached out and clasped each of their hands. "Thank you for coming," she whispered through a clot of threatening tears. "And thank you for your help."

While the men got back to work, Avery wandered back toward the coffee room, where she discovered the ladies of the Lutheran Women's Fellowship had catered supper. Fee was there working her way through a plate of food that would have done credit to a lumberjack.

"You still here?" Avery asked, sitting down beside her daughter.

"I left to take Gran home, caught a nap, and thought I'd come back for a little while since Casey has Samantha."

"I appreciate you pitching in," she said.

"Oh, hey. Whatever."

"You see your father while he was here?" Avery ventured, sure she was treading on thin ice by asking that.

Fiona answered with a shrug.

"Did you talk to him?"

"He asked me how Samantha was," Fiona said, helping herself to a second helping of potato salad. "Mostly we scowled and danced around each other."

The spark of hope she'd harbored since Mike admitted how much he'd hated losing contact with Fee abruptly dimmed. Christmas was only five days away, she had the Sheepish problem to contend with, and Fee and Mike weren't speaking.

So maybe she ought to give up the idea of getting everyone together for Christmas.

As if she had read Avery's mind, Fiona sniffed. "And don't get your heart set on some big, fuzzy Christmas reconciliation, because that's not going to happen."

Cleo's arrival in the coffee room saved Avery from having to respond. Cleo looked well rested and well groomed. Avery looked down at herself and thought by now she probably smelled.

Cleo fixed her a plate, then one for herself.

"Did you see all the people arriving, hon?" Cleo asked her, grinning a Watermelon Sorbet–colored smile. "Four of my girlfriends from high school are out there packing boxes. Some of the guys Mike knows from the lumber company just came in. Vi and her whole Sunday school class will stop by after church tomorrow. It looks to me like we might make this deadline after all."

Avery looked out at the people taking off their coats and pitching in. She couldn't believe so many of the people in town were showing up out of the blue to help. After putting everyone at the Holding Company in jeopardy, she didn't deserve this kind of support. But here they were, people from all over coming together to help her when she needed them.

It wasn't quite the Christmas miracle she'd had in mind, but it was really pretty wonderful.

✻

"My God!" Avery breathed as she sagged against the side of the mail truck. "We did it!"

It was nearly three o'clock in the afternoon on December twenty-fourth, and she and Ted had just loaded the very last box of Sheepish the Lamb.

"Yeah"—her brother-in-law lowered the back of the truck with a *thump*—"we did. I've never seen so many people so willing to come and help. It seemed like every man, woman, and child in Larkin stopped by the Holding Company at one time or another in the last five days to drop off cookies or lend a hand."

"Yes," Avery agreed and her throat went gummy with tears again.

What Ted said was very nearly true. People Avery hadn't seen since high school, friends of her mother's and Fee's, members of both Cleo's and Avery's churches, guys Mike worked with, and even the waitresses from the Sunny Spot all showed up to print labels, pack boxes, or make sandwiches and coffee for the people who did.

Her Holding Company ladies had been marvelous, working long hours and keeping everybody organized. Avery had made sure their Christmas bonuses reflected that.

In the end the whole Sheepish affair had taken on the atmosphere of a barn raising, neighbors helping neighbors accomplish something they couldn't have done on their own.

Thinking how much Ted had taken on himself, Avery

reached across and gave her brother-in-law a great big hug. "We couldn't have managed this without you, either, Ted."

"I'm nothing more than a humble postman doing my job," he said, but she could tell he was pleased with the compliment. "This is the biggest shipment our poor little post office has ever processed—*and* we managed to do it during the Christmas rush!"

Sobriety agreed with her brother-in-law. He looked good and even sounded better, more settled and hopeful. Avery knew the first weeks after rehab were crucial for a recovering alcoholic, but Ted seemed to be handling them pretty well. Having Mike out there at the farm probably helped. So did having something to focus on besides himself.

"I suppose I ought to let you and Allen get on the road," she said, stepping back from the truck. She glanced toward where Allen Warren, who'd be driving the mail truck to the distribution center in Kansas City, was sweet-talking Julia Stevens.

"Hey, Allen," Ted shouted. "Can we get the show on the road? I'd like to get to KC in time to see my kids hang up their stockings for Santa."

Ted was bumming a ride to Kansas City so he could spend the holidays with Nancy and his daughters. "This'll be the first time I've seen the girls," he confided as they waited for Allen to say his good-byes, "since I signed in to rehab."

Avery sensed the tension in him and knew Ted had a lot more riding on the next two days than he was willing to admit. She curled a hand around his shoulder and squeezed it gently.

"Even if you and Nancy haven't seen eye-to-eye for a

while, you're still Daddy to those little girls. They're not going to be thinking about anything except how happy they are to see you."

"That," he said, a wry twist to his mouth, "and what Santa's going to bring them."

Avery glanced away, trying not to ask about Mike's plans, but she couldn't seem to help herself. "Do you—" She paused and swallowed hard. "Do you know where Mike is spending Christmas?"

She could sense a kind of concern in Ted she hadn't known he was capable of feeling. "I think he's means to spend Christmas out at the farm."

"All by himself?"

"Mike says that since he'd be horning in wherever he went, he'd rather be by himself."

Ted might as well have lobbed a grenade into the center of Avery's chest. Guilt and searing heat curled outward from her breastbone.

"Not that I'm in a position to be giving anyone advice," he went on staring down at the toes of his postman shoes, "but have you ever thought about how hard this whole separation thing has been on Mike?"

"Yes, I have."

"Then you know what Mike wants for Christmas more than anything is to get his life back together."

It was what Avery most wanted to give him. "Do you think he's willing to make peace with Fiona?"

Ted raised his eyebrows. "And her with him, huh?"

Avery's hopes of a Christmas reconciliation had fallen to ashes as she watched the complicated dance Mike and Fee had been doing to avoid each other.

"You know, I did a lot of thinking about Mike while I

was in rehab," Ted went on. "It made me realize how much
he's done for me. He protected me lots of times when Dad
was drunk. He made sure I finished high school, bailed me
out of one jam after another, and"—he flashed Avery another wry glance—"lent me money. I never appreciated any
of that when he was doing it, and I never once thanked
him." Ted's gaze held hers. "I never once asked myself why
he did it, either   at least not until recently."

"He did it because he cares about you," she assured him.
"Because Mike would give anyone he loves the shirt off his
back."

"Yeah," Ted nodded. "But *why* would he?"

Avery frowned; she couldn't understand what Ted was
getting at. "Because he's such a good guy?"

"My brother *is* a good guy," Ted acknowledged. "But I
think the reason Mike does what he does is because he
thinks it's the only way people will care about him. Because
he's always wanted to be the most important person in
someone's life."

"Mike is the most important person in my life!" she declared hotly, offended that Ted could question how much
she loved her husband.

"Is he?" Ted's eyebrows lifted with skepticism. "And if
he's so important, Avery, how come you've made being with
him conditional on him patching things up with Fiona?
Isn't the real reason he's going to be sitting out there alone
all day tomorrow because he hasn't been able to do that?"

Heat flared up in her; she stepped angrily away from her
brother-in-law. Yet deep at the core she knew what Ted
meant. If she was honest with herself, she'd have to admit
that she'd been gradually withdrawing from Mike ever
since Fiona left. That it was that withdrawal, that loss of

confidence in their relationship as much as the conditions she'd placed on him, that separated them.

But could Mike really doubt she loved him? Could the distance she'd put between them really make Mike think he wasn't important to her?

"You know," Ted said, "it took me sitting in therapy a couple of hours a day to figure out that because Pa hated himself so much, he didn't have any love to give to his wife and kids. Mom never made any bones about loving Janice best. Mike tried hard, but never got what he needed from me. I was way too busy resenting him to give anything back."

Ted looked straight at her, his eyes the same dark blue as Mike's. His gaze was penetrating, newly perceptive, as if the world around him had come suddenly into focus.

"So, Avery," he went on, "do you really understand how much Mike loves you? How much he's done for you? How much he's risked for you? You say he's the most important person in your life, but do you love him as much as he loves you? Do you love him enough to give him what he's been looking for all his life?"

Avery should have been angry at the questions, but instead she stood there in the thin December twilight suddenly cold down to her bones. Something in Ted's words, in his new objectivity and the things he was asking, resonated inside her and opened a yawning well of doubt.

As if he knew what he'd done, Ted turned and shouted to Allen Warren. "Hey, you think we can get this rig on the road sometime before midnight?"

Allen gave Jean a quick peck on the cheek and jogged back to the truck.

Ted started around toward the passenger's side, but Avery caught his arm. For an instant she just stood there, new respect for Ted dawning in her. She knew she ought to tell Ted how she felt, how much she appreciated the insight he'd given her. Instead she gave him another long, hard hug, then kissed his cheek.

"Merry Christmas, Ted," she whispered.

"Yeah, Avery," he said, and she realized he understood all the things she wasn't in a position to say to him right now. "You make it a Merry Christmas, too."

As Allen cranked the engine, Ted hustled around and climbed into the truck's high cab. Avery stepped back and stood with Jean to wave good-bye. Once the truck was out of sight, Avery turned and headed back into the Holding Company.

She was halfway up the stairs to the office when she ran out of energy. She sat with a *plop* and listened to the silence. Everyone had gone home to their families. There were no voices trading gossip, giving directions, or singing Christmas carols. All the machinery was off and the air was still. Every last Sheepish was on his way to where he belonged. It was Christmas Eve and never in her life had Avery been so exhausted.

She rested her head in her hands and closed her eyes, but as tired as she was, she couldn't put Ted's questions out of her mind.

How could Mike doubt that she loved him? Didn't he remember how she'd thrown her arms around him in the lobby of the Palmer House Hotel and laughed for joy the day he'd asked her to marry him? Could he possibly have forgotten how they made love right on the hardwood floor in the living room the afternoon they'd closed on their house? Was it possible he could question her feelings after the way she'd settled Fiona in his arms the day they'd brought her home from the hospital, giving him the gift she'd grown inside her just for him?

Did he really believe he wasn't the most important person in her life? That she'd put their daughter ahead of him? But then, wasn't that what she'd been telling him all these months? Hadn't she been making her love conditional on his reconciliation with their daughter?

Or was it Mike himself who didn't think he was deserving? Was it Mike who feared that even the most beautiful moments with his wife and daughter were hollow underneath? Had Mike been afraid that if he reached out to grab the laughter and the joy, it would be snatched away? Had he believed that no matter how hard he tried to make a strong and safe life for himself and her, he'd lose everything eventually because he wasn't worthy?

But how could he possibly think that after the twenty-three years they'd had together?

It was as if he'd internalized all the terrible, taunting things his father had said to him, taken his mother's preference for his sister as evidence of some flaw. It was as if he'd absorbed Miriam's criticism as if it were poison.

Avery could see that as hard as he worked, as much as he gave of himself, Mike never thought he'd done enough. That he needed to be reassured that she loved him every single day of their lives. Why hadn't she known that? Why hadn't she understood this man she'd lived with and loved for twenty-three years?

As devastating as Fiona's leaving had been for her, it must have been worse for Mike. Considering how much time they'd spent together and how close they were, Fee's leaving was the kind of intimate rejection that confirmed the doubts Mike harbored about himself: that he didn't deserve happiness, that he wasn't worthy of love.

Avery rummaged in the pocket of her sweater for a tissue and wiped away the flood of tears.

After Fee was gone, hadn't Avery chosen their daughter over him, made her love conditional by demanding he forgive Fiona? And by doing that, she'd offered Mike the proof he'd been afraid all his life of discovering: that he wasn't worthy of her, that he just wasn't good enough. That the person he loved most in the world loved someone else better.

"Oh, Mike," she whispered, her heart crumbling. She adored her daughter and her granddaughter because they were hers, forever a part of her. But what she felt for Mike transcended that. He was her husband, her lover, her soul mate, the person she wanted to be with and care for the rest of her days. And it was time she told Mike in no uncertain terms how she felt.

Avery reached resolutely for the cell phone in her pocket. It was Christmas Eve and Mike needed to know that he belonged somewhere. That he belonged with *her.*

But the cell phone chirped before she had a chance to dial his number.

"Mike?" she answered eagerly, not bothering to look at the display.

"No, Mom, it's me." It was Fee and she was crying.

Avery jumped to her feet. "Where are you, Fee? What's wrong?"

"It's Samantha, Mom. She's having trouble breathing. I don't know what to do!"

"Hang up. Call 911!" Avery said as calmly as she could. "I'll meet you at the hospital."

She bolted up the stairs to get her coat.

Chapter 17

✳

Sometimes a girl just needed her mother. Especially when her baby couldn't breathe. Especially when they arrived at the hospital in an ambulance with sirens blaring.

Fee gathered Samantha out of the crib the moment the ER doctor finished examining her and paced the floor, terrified that there was more wrong with her baby girl than they were telling her. Terrified of the frantic *beep* of medical monitors, of someone calling for "Jesus" a few rooms away, and the constant bawl of children crying.

Even over the cacophony, Fee could hear her baby's raspy breathing and feel Samantha's ribs bellow beneath her hands. Why weren't the doctors doing something? *Didn't they see her baby was turning blue?*

Just when Fee was ready to come apart, her mom came bustling into the treatment room.

"Oh, Mom!" she moaned, her knees nearly buckling with relief.

Her mother tested the heat of Samantha's forehead with the back of her hand, listened to the baby breathe, then wrapped an arm around Fee's shoulders. "Samantha's going to be fine, sweetheart."

Fee nodded, desperate to believe her. "She—she was coughing a little last night, and I thought she'd picked up Derek's cold. Then this morning she seemed..."

"Better," her mother prompted, nodding. "Yes, I know."

"But tonight..." Fee's voice shook so hard she could hardly say the words. *"Oh, Mom! Tonight..."*

"You did the right thing, Fiona, getting Samantha to the hospital." Her mom sounded so sure and calm and matter of fact. "Did the doctor say anything about her having croup?"

"Yes, croup." As rattled as Fiona had been during the examination, she remembered that. "He gave the nurse a list of instructions."

"Then she'll be in any time now to start treatment."

"When?" Fee all but pleaded. "When? Don't they know how sick Samantha is?"

"I doubt you're going to believe me, honey," her mom told her gently, "but Samantha's going to be right as rain by morning."

Fee huffed in disbelief and strode away, cradling her wailing daughter closer. She'd just managed to get Samantha quiet, when her cell phone chirped and set her off again.

She motioned for her mom to dig the phone out of her knapsack and take the call. Avery cupped her hand over the mouthpiece. "You phoned your grandmother?"

Fee shrugged as she paced back and forth.

"Yes, Mother," Avery said into the phone. "We're at the hospital now. They say it's croup...Uh-huh. Uh-huh... Samantha's going to be fine...Yes, that *is* her coughing. I know she sounds like a seal...No, don't you come down here, Mom. You know how you hate hospitals . . . I'll call you if we need you . . . Okay. Okay. Okay, good night."

"Oh, Fee," her mother said as she folded the phone away. "Don't *ever* call your grandmother for something like this. She's hopeless in a crisis."

"She is?" Fee asked, surprised.

Before she could question her mom about Gran, a roly-poly nurse with graying hair and a name tag that said "Molly" bustled into the room. She was carrying a bag of saline and what looked like half a mile of plastic tubing.

"You Grandma?" Molly asked the moment she clapped eyes on Avery. "Why don't you take young Mom here out in the hall while I start this IV."

"Will Samantha be all right without me?" Fee asked, her voice wavering.

Molly took the baby in her arms and gave Fee a reassuring smile. "This is only going to take me a minute, hon. Go on outside with your mother."

Fee couldn't quite bring herself to leave, but Avery wrapped an arm around her shoulders and ushered her into the glare of the fluorescent-lit hallway. To Fee's immense mortification, the instant the door to the treatment room whooshed shut behind them, she burst into chokey, chest-heaving tears.

Her mom wrapped her up and hugged her tight.

"Samantha started running a temperature yesterday," Fee confessed in a gulpy whisper. "I gave her Tylenol, and I thought she was doing okay. Then this afternoon she started screaming and coughing so hard. And when she breathed . . . Oh, Mom, her chest sucked in and out in a way I've never seen. And I thought . . ."

"I know exactly what you thought," Avery murmured.

It felt so good to have her mother here beside her, felt so good to have her stroke her hair like she used to when Fee was little. It was okay to be scared now that her mom was here, now that she didn't have to shoulder all the responsibility. She burrowed a little deeper into the crook of her mother's neck, and breathed the sharp, clear scent of her Diorissimo perfume.

"It's all right, Fee," her mom began shifting from foot to foot, rocking her the same way Fee sometimes comforted her own daughter. "You got Samantha the help she needed. And, thank God, she doesn't have anything serious. She's going to be fine; I promise you."

Fee wanted so much to believe that.

"It's the change in the weather that brings croup on," her mother murmured instructively. "There must be half a dozen kids in here tonight with what Samantha's got. Just listen."

Fee raised her head and she could hear children barking that same wracking cough all up and down the corridor. "How did you know that?"

Her mother rubbed her palm up and down Fee's back. "You used to get croup on a pretty regular basis when you were little. Don't you remember the nights we'd sit in the bathroom together with the shower running?"

On some level, Fee must have remembered that. She'd done the very same thing with Samantha last night.

"But it was easier for me when you got sick," Avery went on quietly, "because your dad was always so calm and patient."

Fee nodded, regret pinching her heart when she thought about her father.

Just then, Samantha screamed so loudly both of them jumped.

"What are they *doing* to her?" Fee wheeled toward the treatment room, but her mother caught her arm.

"Probably starting the IV," Avery answered gently. "Now blow your nose and take a breath. If you're upset when you go back, Samantha will know and be upset, too."

When they stepped back into the treatment room, Molly had the baby half submerged in a sink full of water, and Samantha wasn't happy. Fiona said as much.

"You wouldn't be happy if you had a fever and we dunked you in a tepid bath, either," Molly said and stared her down. "Now, can you bathe this baby, Mom, or should I have Grandma do it?"

Fiona bristled. "I'll do it."

"And Grandma?" Molly went on giving orders.

"Yes, ma'am!"

Molly seemed to bite back a smile at Avery's tone. "I just got the IV going in our sweet girl's ankle. Can you hold her foot out of the water so it doesn't get wet?"

The doctor looked in on them a short while later. "Samantha has a simple case of croup," he told them, "but just as a precaution we're going to keep her overnight here at the hospital. Are you going to stay with her, Ms. Montgomery?"

Fiona stiffened. "Of course I'm staying! What kind of a mother do you think I am?"

The doctor's eyes crinkled just a little at the corners. "I think you're a good mother, ma'am. You brought your daughter in so we could take care of her. Now don't you worry anymore; she's going to be fine in the morning."

Fiona nodded, mollified. "That's what my mother said."

"Well, you know." He grinned outright this time. "As I get older, I discover that mothers are right about a lot of things."

When the respiratory therapist arrived to set up the crinkly plastic croup tent and nebulizer, Samantha's temperature was already down and she was breathing easier. As Molly and the therapist began to drape the tent, Fee climbed right up onto the gurney to lay beside her daughter and hold her in her arms.

When the orderly came to wheel the two of them away to a room, Fiona slid her fingers under the plastic draping and gave her mom's hand a long grateful squeeze. "Thank you," she whispered.

Her mom nodded and smiled and squeezed right back.

Never, until tonight, had Fiona fully grasped what it took to be a mother—and never in her life had she appreciated her own mom more.

※

When Avery left the hospital just after ten P.M. on Christmas Eve, she discovered it had started to snow. Big theatrical flakes, the kind that kept pelting Jimmy Stewart in *It's a Wonderful Life,* tumbled past the lights in the parking lot, swirling thick and feathery as goose down.

"Christmas is off to a heck of a start *this* year," she muttered as she trudged up the hill through the accumulating snow. She stopped in her tracks when she saw Mike braced against the fender of her Forester. Her heart lifted at the sight of him. Warmth spread through her as weariness and tension drained away.

"Been here awhile?" she guessed as she approached. Judging by the snow caught in his hair and piled up on the shoulders of his jacket, the answer was yes.

"I came over right after I picked up your message."

She'd been so caught up with Fee and Samantha, Avery almost forgot she'd called him. "You should have come in."

Mike gave his head a quick, decisive shake. "How is everybody?"

"Everybody's fine. Samantha has croup."

"Croup!" Mike exclaimed on a stutter of laughter. "Serves Fee right after all the times we had to bundle her up at midnight and bring her here."

Avery stepped up close beside him. Even in the middle of a snowstorm she could feel his heat, feel the heat of their shared memories drawing her closer.

"We were always good together in a crisis," she said, re-membering.

When Fee started with that barking cough Avery would scoop her up, take her into the bathroom, and turn on the shower. If sitting in the steam didn't loosen the constriction in her chest, Mike would have everything gathered up and the truck running in the driveway.

"They're keeping Samantha overnight just in case," Avery filled him in. "Fiona's staying with her."

He nodded; he knew the drill as well as Avery did.

"I bet this scared the hell out of her," he said. "It always did me."

"Me, too," Avery admitted, shivering a little at the memory.

"Too bad new parents have to learn this stuff the hard way," he observed, his mouth pursed a little as if he remem-bered learning that way, too.

"We certainly never had anyone to ask," Avery agreed. "Your mom was living in Kansas City by the time we had Fee."

"And Miriam was never very good in emergencies."

In those long, terrifying, croupy nights, in the hundred

other childhood crises, Avery had always leaned on Mike. And he on her. Having each other to count on had gotten her through a lot of things. Things that were bigger and scarier and a whole lot more devastating than croup.

Avery leaned close enough that their shoulders brushed. She clasped her icy fingers around his wrist brushing the warm, pulsing band of skin between the bottom of his sleeve and the top of his glove. She stroked that sensitive flesh by way of thanks.

"I'm glad you came," she whispered.

He shrugged and looked past her into the swirling snow. "Samantha's my granddaughter, too."

Something about the quiet intensity in those four words stirred things up inside her again. Her throat went thick with the threat of tears as a stubborn, totally irresponsible ripple of hope rose through her.

"Why don't you follow me back to the house?" she proposed, wanting to keep him talking, wanting to keep him close. Not wanting to go home alone—especially tonight when she had things she needed to say to him.

"You sure?" he asked, watching her intently.

Avery expanded the invitation. "I can make coffee and sandwiches."

"It *has* been a hell of a way to spend Christmas Eve," he said and turned toward his truck.

✳

To Avery, it felt like old times having Mike here at the house. It felt like old times to have him sitting at the kitchen table with her, the glow of the pendant lamp lining the contours of his wonderful face. It felt like old times seeing his hands wrapped around his favorite ironstone mug; hearing the deep, warm ripple of his voice lap over her; smelling the sweetness of fresh-cut wood on his clothes and in his hair.

They'd sat like this a thousand times, cupped here at the core of the house they loved. It felt like settling into an old and very particular kind of contentment.

It felt like old times—and yet everything was different now.

It was different because Mike was different, because she was different. They were both older in ways that suddenly mattered, more world-weary, less impervious and sure of themselves.

Far less sure of each other.

"I'm glad you're here," she said for the second time tonight and, needing to touch him, stroked the back of his hand with her fingertips.

"I am, too."

She saw the way his gaze drifted over the cabinets and the sink, the windows and the tile, as if he was making sure that in spite of having risked this house to finance Sheepish, everything was still intact. She could see how much he belonged to this place; he'd left his mark in every molding he'd cut and every stroke of his paintbrush. He'd poured the best of himself into restoring this house and making it their home. He'd poured the best of himself into binding the three of them into a family, too.

"You know, for all that I grew up out there at the farm," he ventured, glancing down into his cup as if looking at her would make the admission too difficult, "it just doesn't feel like home to me."

"That's because all your best memories are here, Mike," she told him softly. "And I want you to know that every single one of those memories is safe with me."

He didn't ask her what she meant. He just raised his head, slipped her a smile that warmed his eyes—then changed the subject.

"So, did you get all our little fuzzy buddies off in the mail?"

"Every last one," she confirmed. "Ted and Allen Warren chauffeured them into Kansas City this afternoon."

"Good," he said on a gusty sigh. "Good."

"Ted organized everything and made sure we had what we needed." She wanted Mike to know how well his brother had done. "He's like someone I barely recognize."

Someone who'd come back from rehab not only with the tools and the determination to change his life, but with insights about his brother that surprised even her.

"I couldn't be prouder of what he's accomplished," Mike admitted, "but he's still got a lot to work out."

Avery shifted her shoulders a little. "I guess we all do."

"Yeah," Mike agreed. "Like things with Fiona."

Avery looked across at him, astonished. Until now, he'd staunchly refused to discuss Fiona with her.

Then, as if he realized he'd said more than he intended, Mike pushed to his feet. "You want more coffee?"

Avery watched him cross the kitchen to the coffeemaker, trying discern what he was thinking. Why had he showed up at the hospital? Was he really willing to talk about Fiona, to work things out with Fiona?

Avery waited until he returned to the table with the coffeepot before she spoke. "Now that Fee's settled back in Larkin, I intend to have a normal relationship with her. I want to be part of Samantha's life." Avery dipped her head and smiled. "I want to be a doting grandmother."

She was determined to be honest with Mike, even if lying

might make a reconciliation with him less difficult. She refused to compromise on things that were—and really always had been—nonnegotiable.

"I see now that I was wrong when I insisted you stay
away from her." Mike admitted, his focus on pouring coffee,
not on her. "I was wrong to think you could."

"I felt like you were making me choose between you."

"I thought..." His voice dropped so low she could barely
hear. "I thought you'd already chosen."

The things Ted had said this afternoon came back to her.
She looked up at Mike. "Why would you think that? Haven't
I always had love enough in my heart for both of you?"

He stood over her, lines scored deep between his eyes. "I
always thought you did, Avery. But when Fiona ran away, it
felt like she eclipsed everything else in your life."

Including me. He didn't say the words, but she heard the
accusation.

"All you ever talked about was Fee," he said, looking
down at her, "where she was and how she was and what she
was doing. And didn't I miss her? What I missed, Avery, was
you. What I missed was having you look at me as if you actually saw me, what I missed was you trying to understand
at least a little of what I was feeling."

"But, Mike, we'd already lost one child!" she protested.
"We lost little Jonathan before I even had the chance to hold
him, and I walked around for months after that happened
like there was a hole in me. I filled that hole with raising Fee
and starting the Holding Company—and loving you.

"When Fiona left," Avery said, holding his gaze with her
own, "I knew I couldn't lose my only baby. I couldn't lose
her, no matter what."

Mike nodded. "In a way I understood that. But when she

left, I felt like I'd lost not just her, but you. Not just you, but my place in the world."

She heard the echo of his childhood in those words, the fear that no matter what he did or how hard he tried to take care of his family, he'd never truly belonged. She thought they'd settled that years ago by belonging to each other, by forging their own family.

"It nearly killed me," he went on, "when she threw away everything she said she wanted, and turned her back on the things we'd worked so hard to give her. I was so ashamed that she could steal from us. And seeing the way she hurt you . . ."

Avery rose from her chair and slid her arm around his waist. "She hurt you, too."

"What I hated most—" he said, drawing a breath that shivered with emotion "—was the way she tore this family apart. It made me feel as if I'd failed—again."

"'Failed,' Mike?" she asked him. "How?"

His eyes had gone dark with shame, and she wondered how long he'd kept this bottled up. Or had he tried to explain after Fiona left, and she'd been too preoccupied to listen?

He let out a gusty sigh. "You know how things were out at the farm when I was growing up." Avery squeezed his waist by way of affirmation. "I know your family wasn't everything you wanted it to be, either. When we got married, I thought we made a family that was better and stronger than the families we'd come from. One where we loved each other and did things together—and we were *happy*."

He looked down at her, his heart in his eyes. "We were happy, Avery, weren't we?"

"Of course we were happy."

"And I thought that made us the perfect family."

They used to laugh about that sometimes, but now she recognized a dark vein of longing beneath Mike's laughter. He'd tried to create a perfect family to replace his imperfect one. No wonder his disillusionment had run so deep.

"Oh, Mike," she whispered, reaching up to touch his cheek. "Our family was never perfect, but we loved one another. I think the three of us *still* love one another way down deep."

"Is that what you think, Avery?"

She looked up into those blue, blue eyes and saw the depth of his doubt. More than anything she wanted to erase that, let him know that was exactly what she felt, exactly what she wanted.

"I'll tell you what I *know*, Mike," she said, taking her courage in her hands. "What I know is that I'm tired of being without you. I want you to come home. I want your truck in the driveway when I pull in. I want to make dinner with you and talk to you about everything, like we used to do. I want to snuggle on the couch with you and watch TV. I want to roll over in bed and feel you beside me.

"What I *know* is that I want to feel married to you again. I want you to stay with me, Mike, tonight and always." She looked up into his face and asked him what might well be the most important question of their married life. "So, Mike, will you stay? Will you stay with me tonight?"

He tangled his fingers in her hair and tipped her face to his. "Oh, Avery, sweetheart, I want so much to stay, but there's so much we haven't settled."

"We've settled us, haven't we?"

"Yes."

"And if we've settled us, we'll find a way to settle every-thing else," she said, and willed him to believe her.

"But what about Fee?" he asked softly.

She sensed his need for an answer to the question that had lain unresolved between them for months. The ques-tion that had driven them apart.

"She's part of our family, Mike," she spoke, praying for the words that would convince him that they could work things through, that they would be all right at the end of this. "Fiona's part of our lives. As long as you and I are com-mitted to being together, we'll find a way to let her in again."

For a long moment she waited, then felt the tension in him drain away. "Then let's try," he whispered.

Avery rose on tiptoe and pressed her lips to his. Mike kissed her back intently, as if they were sealing some vow between them. As they stood there in the middle of the kitchen, they leaned closer, held tighter. They immersed themselves in the balm of tenderness after too much time and too much loneliness.

When at length they broke off the kiss, Avery smiled up into his eyes. "I love you, Michael Simon Montgomery."

"I love you, too, Avery Ada Parrish Montgomery."

"I want to be your wife tonight," she whispered. "So can we make this our new beginning?"

Mike didn't answer. He just put his hand in hers and let her lead him up the stairs.

※

Mike felt like a ghost returning to a place he'd always loved. As Avery led him through the house, he saw the fa-miliar gauzy light of the moon filtering through the bank of dining-room windows. He heard the creak of the stair he always swore he'd fix. He smelled the scent of Avery's perfume as they crossed the landing to their bedroom.

He paused just inside the door to savor his first real taste of homecoming. The light reflected off the snow was faint and blue, and he could see the shape of the room, the angle of the eaves that embraced their bed and the wide span of the windows beside it. He looked long and hard at the tall four-poster where he and Avery had made love so many times.

Avery tightened her grip as if she thought he might vanish if she released him. But he was never going to leave—neither this place nor her.

This old house had been both his haven and Avery's dream, something he'd claimed for both of them board by board and nail by nail. The life they'd made here, the child they'd raised came as close as he was every going to come to creating something perfect.

Something special and unbearably precious.

Something he'd very nearly lost forever.

Tonight he was going to take his chance to claim it all again, to lie with Avery, to please her and hold her—and make her his wife again in every way.

So he let her draw him toward her side of the bed and, when she asked, placed both his hands in hers. "I love you, Mike," she said, looking up with a glow in her eyes. "I want you to stay with me forever."

"I love you, Avery," he whispered. "And now I know how much."

They'd come together in this room and on this bed more times than Mike could remember. Sometimes they'd wrestled and laughed and pummeled each other with pillows. Sometimes they'd arrived fired with passion or drugged with desire. Sometimes they shared themselves in a quick, efficient joining. Sometimes they wound themselves together in a slow, languid dance, opening to each other in a sinuous flow of kisses and caresses.

Tonight when Mike made love to her, it would be a reunion, a declaration of what he felt for her. What they felt for each other. It would be a healing, a confirmation of how much they loved each other, that they couldn't live their lives apart.

Still clasping his hands in hers, Avery stepped closer, creating an embrace by guiding his hands around her. As she did, Mike felt the warmth of her pressed intimately against his chest and belly. His erection rose against the front of his jeans, throbbing in response to her.

For an instant he was tempted to push Avery down on that wondrous shimmery quilt and take her, knowing full well how she would respond to him. But he wanted tonight to be perfect, wanted to convey with something far more intimate than words how much he loved her.

With an effort he quelled his impatience and bent his head to kiss her. He gently brushed her lips with his, reacquainting himself with the shape and texture of her mouth, the taste and sweetness of her response.

As if he could have forgotten.

She rose up on her tiptoes and kissed him back. Still clasping their linked hands, he pressed them against the hollow at her waist, snugging her against him. As he did, Avery arched her back, pressed the fullness of her breasts into his chest, then leaned her hips against him.

He laughed deep in his throat and kissed her back, kissed her with the expertise of a man who knew his wife and exactly what she wanted. He kissed her until both of them were flushed and bothered and wanting.

Avery eased back in his embrace and slid her hands between them. With practiced ease she opened the buttons on his woolen shirt and skimmed it down his arms. She jerked the thermal jersey he'd worn beneath it from the waistband of his jeans, tugged up the hem, and removed that too.

The air of the bedroom was cool against his skin in contrast to the heat of her palms gliding over him. That touch was every bit as compelling as he remembered, delicate yet with a slow, trailing stroke that made his breathing catch in his throat.

As her hands drifted over him, he reached for her, opened the zipper down the front of her short woolen jumper and let it slide to the floor. He peeled away her blouse and dispensed with the rest of her clothes in turn.

He had forgotten how deliciously womanly she was— and how uncommonly beautiful. She stood pale and elemental in the moonlight, her reddish hair dark against her shoulders. She had full, deep breasts and the hips and belly of a woman. It was a body that had been tenderly and well used, a body he had turned to in the night's deepest dark and found fulfillment. One that had given him infinite pleasure and two precious children.

It was the body of the woman he'd adore until the end of time.

As Avery folded back the shimmering bed quilt, he stripped off the rest of his clothes, then turned to her. She lay on the far side of the bed watching him, then slowly she raised the covers, opening them in invitation.

They came together length to length, smooth skin gliding against rough, hard muscle firm against softer flesh, heat seeking heat beneath the chilly bedclothes. They moved slowly, tangling together, fitting their hollows and curves together in old familiar ways, ways their very cells remembered.

"Oh, Mike," she whispered, as if she was as overwhelmed by the deep familiarity as he.

He cupped his hand to her cheek and kissed her. In the space of a breath, the space of a heartbeat, the sweet, inexplicable magic was upon them. They reached and touched and flowed together in ways that were second nature to both of them. Their hands found and stroked the most sensitive angles and curves. Their mouths lingered, savored, and explored. Their bodies brushed intimately, heightening desire in ways that were both breathtaking and wondrously familiar.

They came together with the same anticipation, with the same sense of rightness they'd always felt. Avery opened and encompassed him. Mike pressed inside, filling her fully and completely.

"Oh, God!" he whispered as he lay over her. "It's so good to be home."

He could see the tears glittering in her eyes as she wrapped him close against her heart, but she didn't say a word. She didn't say that being together was right or real or necessary. They'd been apart and now they were together again. It was surely the way the two of them were meant to be.

Joined loin to loin and heart to heart, the pleasure came to take them. It swelled through them as they moved, a slowly mounting heat, a growing sensitivity, a trembling quake of desire echoing between them.

As the erotic turmoil flooded their senses and engulfed

them, they clutched each other and cried out in recognition of the bond that could never be broken. They clung together in the shivery aftermath, murmuring and petting each other.

There were no words for the significance of this joining, but each of them knew that they were together again, together in a way that seemed stronger, sweeter, and more enduring for the time apart.

In the hazy softness that would soon give way to Christmas morning, they spooned together and slept replete.

Chapter 18

✺

Avery's phone rang at seven-thirty on Christmas morning. Mike planted a damp, shivery kiss at the top of her spine, then rolled over in bed with a rustle of sheets. He answered, listened for a moment, then handed the phone to Avery without saying a word.

"Was that Mike?" her mother demanded, sounding shocked and incredulous on the other end of the line.

"Santa doesn't sleep over, Mother."

"Are you two getting back together?"

Mike had gone into the bathroom and when Avery heard him turn on the shower, she shifted on her pillows and pulled the covers up to her nose. She was feeling languorous and content this morning.

"Maybe," she answered.

Miriam was silent for as long as it took for her to reorder her priorities. "Well, then," she asked, every bit the perfect hostess, "shall I set another place for Christmas dinner?"

Avery scowled at her mother's suggestion. She hadn't thought that far. She didn't want to have to think that far. What she wanted was time alone with Mike. Time to settle in, time for things to feel comfortable and habitual, not tentative and fragile. Not like they were still feeling their way along.

"I don't know."

Miriam sniffed with what was clearly disapproval.

Whether that sniff expressed her opinion about Mike, his moving home, or Avery's inability to give her an answer about dinner, it sent Avery shooting straight up in bed. "Now, don't you go sniffing, Mother," she warned her in a furious undertone. "There will be absolutely no more sniffing where Mike is concerned. Do you understand me?"

For a moment Avery thought Miriam intended to ask her what she meant or argue that she'd never "sniffed." Instead she acquiesced.

"Oh, fine!" she snapped and changed the subject. "Fee called from the hospital just after six o'clock to say Samantha is fine this morning and being discharged."

"I told Fee she would be all right." Still, Avery breathed a little easier knowing she'd been right when she'd predicted Samantha's speedy recovery.

"So as soon as I got the turkey in the oven," her mother went on, "I went over and picked them up."

"You picked them up from the hospital?" Avery asked, feeling excluded. "Why didn't Fiona call me?"

"She knows I'm up at the crack of dawn anyway," Miriam defended her granddaughter. "And after the week you've had, I think Fiona intended to let you sleep.

"I dropped them off at the apartment. Fee said she was going to try to catch a nap herself before they come over for dinner. I told her we'd eat about three o'clock. Is that all right?"

The good news was that Samantha was fine, and that she

and Fee were home again. The bad news was that now—oh, God—now Avery had to do her part toward Christmas dinner.

"I haven't made a single pie," Avery hastily apologized, wondering if there were apples in the crisper and whether she had shortening enough to make the crusts.

"I baked pies last night," her mother informed her. "Since you and Fiona wouldn't hear of me coming down to the hospital, I had to do *something useful.*"

Miriam put both a kindness and a reproach in the same sentence, Avery reflected. How like her mother.

"Thanks for making the pies, Mom," she offered, still shaking her head. "Would you like me to come over early to give you a hand getting everything pulled together?"

"That would be nice," her mother answered. "And you *will* let me know about setting that other place, won't you, Avery, dear?"

Avery was just hanging up when Mike ambled out of the bathroom, a towel draped low around his hips. He smelled incongruously of Irish Spring and Avery's floral shampoo. When he sat down beside her on the edge of the bed, she reached out and ruffled the hair on his chest possessively.

Mike put his hand over hers and held it against him. "So what did your mother have to say?"

"She called to tell me Samantha was discharged from the hospital this morning."

"Well, that's good news!" He sighed with relief, just the way she had a few minutes earlier.

"Mom also wants to know if you're coming to Christmas dinner."

Mike hopped up like he'd sat on a griddle and paced

toward the windows. "Is she inviting me, Avery? Or making sure I'm not coming?"

Avery sat up in bed, bunching the covers over her breasts. "If this is going to be our new beginning, I think you ought to decide how you're going to handle my mother—and then just do it."

"Like you handle her?" he snorted.

"Like I handled her at Thanksgiving," she informed him with a lift of her chin. "After I'd had quite enough of Mother's guff."

"So you admit your mother has guff?" he asked, sitting down beside her again and doing his best to hide a grin.

"Yes, I do."

"So what happened?"

"Well, we were dishing up Thanksgiving dinner for the shut-ins in the kitchen at church," she told him, "when I just had my fill of her *guff.* So I told her off, right there in front of every single one of the ladies in the Lutheran Women's Fellowship."

"You did not!"

Avery nodded in confirmation. "Then I decorated her shoes with a spoonful of sweet potato casserole."

"Oh, sweetheart!" Mike hooted and fell back on the bed laughing. "I'm proud of you, but it's way past time!"

Avery stretched out beside him and nuzzled his whiskery throat. He slid his palm the length of her bare back and pulled her closer.

She lay against him, basking in his warmth for a while before she spoke. "I do wish you'd think about coming to Christmas dinner."

He went absolutely still beside her, so still she could hear his heart beating. "Will Fiona be there?"

Avery should have known he'd ask that and just how he'd respond if she told him the truth. Still, she couldn't lie to him—no matter how much she wanted her family back together, no matter how many times she'd imagined them sitting down side by side for Christmas dinner.

"Samantha will be there too," she coaxed.

In a single sleek movement, he disentangled himself from her and rolled off the bed. "I'm sorry, sweetheart, but I just can't go to your mother's if Fee and Samantha are going to be there."

But it's Christmas, she almost pleaded. *It's Christmas, and what I want most of all is for our family to be together.*

"I thought we were going to work through things together," she said instead.

"We are," he said, rummaging in his dresser for underwear. "But it's too soon. I'm just not ready to face Fiona, especially on Christmas Day. And I'm most *certainly* not going to sit down with my daughter for the first time in nearly two years, at your mother's table."

Avery inclined her head. Mike had every reason in the world for refusing. She'd just so hoped...Gathering the sheet around her, she rose from the bed. "Instead of arguing with you, I'm going in to shower."

Mike crossed the room to where she stood draped like a Grecian statue and ran his hand down the smooth, ivory slope of her arm. "I'm sorry, Avery. I know you're disappointed."

"No, Mike, it's all right." She leaned in close to him again. "We'll work through things when the time is right."

Mike had always been a genius at improvising breakfast. By the time she got downstairs, he'd found eggs and half a pound of bacon and turned out two perfect omelets, stringy with cheese. His coffee, as always, was strong and hot.

The two of them lingered at the table. A lot of life had happened in the last two months, and they gradually caught each other up.

Probably the best and most startling revelation for Mike was that Fiona had been offered an internship at the Kitt Peak Observatory. His eyes widened with surprise when Avery told him about it.

"That's the real thing," he said, not even trying to hide the pride in his voice.

"Fee's advisor at the college arranged it," Avery told him. "Dr. Gunderson was outraged when Fee changed her major, so she set out to make it impossible for Fee to leave astronomy."

"We owe that woman a lot," Mike said, still beaming and shaking his head. "It knocks me out that Fee's going to be working this summer at Kitt Peak!"

"Um, well," Avery put down her fork and looked at him directly. "There's probably one other thing you ought to know about Fee's internship."

Mike lifted his eyebrows.

"I agreed to take care of Samantha for the ten weeks Fee will be in Tucson."

For a long, agonizing minute Mike didn't say a word, and Avery's heartbeat boomed in her ears with every second that passed. Mike wouldn't refuse to let Samantha stay with them, would he?

Finally he shrugged. "Like you said...we'll work things out as we go along. Whatever happens, we can't let Fee miss out on this."

Avery could see how hard it was for him to believe that

things could change between his daughter and him. To accept that they could find a way to make their family work again. She leaned across and bussed his cheek by way of encouragement. "I love you, Mike."

"Yeah, well," he said with a scowl. "You love me best when I'm doing what you want."

They sat and talked for a good long time, but as the clock crept on toward eleven, Avery started stacking the breakfast dishes. "Since Mother's ended up making the whole of our Christmas dinner, I really do need to get over there and—"

Mike caught her wrist. "Your mother can wait another minute," he said and set a small package wrapped in bright gold paper in front of her.

Avery looked down at the package and up at him.

"Hell, Avery!" he said. "It's Christmas, and no matter what's gone on between us, I couldn't let it pass without getting you a present."

Avery had something upstairs for Mike—which proved that in spite of everything, they'd been thinking about each other.

"This looks like a jewelry box to me," she ventured.

He shifted closer, sliding his arm along the back of her chair. "I visited Irv."

Her hands were shaking as she untied the deep green bow and tugged the paper away with the crinkle of foil. Inside the velvet box on a bed of amber satin lay a large, luminous black pearl strung on a twisted gold chain. The piece was simple, elegant, and felt far more like who Avery was than her precious string of pearls had.

The necklace was perfect, and for a moment she couldn't speak. She just turned to her husband and touched his face. She stroked the sprinkling of gray in his dark hair, traced the smile on his lips, and flushed at the glow in his eyes.

"Somehow it didn't seem right to replace the pearls," Mike said quietly. "Not that I could have afforded to, anyway. So I told Irv I was looking for something very special. I wanted something that didn't have a thing to do with anyone but the two of us."

Mike was right; this perfect pearl was like the two of them, simple and elemental. It marked a new beginning, marked them falling in love all over again.

She smiled and kissed him. "Thank you, Mike. I can't think of a more perfect gift. Will you help me put it around my neck?"

His fingers were warm against her skin as he draped the pearl around her neck and fastened the clasp. Avery touched where it hung cool and heavy in the hollow of her throat. As she did, she could sense the colors deep inside the luminous black, like the wondrous things she knew about the man she married, the mysterious things she had left to learn. Like the many shadings of her love for him—and his for her.

"This necklace is wonderful"—Avery leaned across and bussed his cheek—"but it's having you here with me on Christmas morning that's by far the finer gift."

She rose and went to retrieve his package from the closet. Mike tore at the paper like the kid he'd never really had the chance to be. Avery fidgeted as he opened the box and lifted off the layers of Styrofoam packing. When he saw the enormous pair of binoculars that lay inside, he looked up at her, delight in his face.

"Oh, Avery! Wow! These are great! I've been wanting a pair of astral binoculars forever." He picked them up gingerly, and paused with the glasses halfway to his eyes. "Did you know there are some things you can see better with binoculars than with a telescope? Things like the phases of Venus."

Avery was only vaguely aware that Venus *had* phases, but it tickled her that Mike was so delighted. "Fee said you'd need a tripod too."

"Yeah." He braced his elbows on the table, raised the nearly foot-long binoculars to his eyes, and turned them toward their neighbor's window.

"I can read Mrs. Franklin's mince pie recipe all the way from here."

Avery laughed, gathered up their dishes, and put them in the dishwasher.

Mike sat fiddling with the binocular's focus until Avery came and stood over him. "Are you sure, Mike, that you won't reconsider coming to Mother's with me? I'm sure Fee would love to see your binoculars."

In truth, she had no idea how Fiona would respond if he was at Miriam's house when she and Samantha arrived. All she could hope for was if he agreed, Mike and Fee would have the kind of Christmas reconciliation she'd been imagining.

He looked up at her, and she could see the possibility skim the surface of his eyes. Then he shook his head. "I can't, Avery. I'm sorry."

"But it's Christmas," she whispered. "How can I go off and leave you here? How can I let you spend Christmas by yourself?"

"It's my choice, Avery," he said and clasped her hands in his. "But I'll be here waiting when you get back."

She did her best to hide her disappointment. "You're sure you'll be here?"

"Yeah," he assured her with a wide Christmas grin. "I promise."

Resigned, Avery stepped away and bustled around gathering up the packages to take to her mother's. Once she'd zipped her boots and slipped into her coat, she scooped the gloriously blooming Christmas cactus from its perch on the window seat and headed outside.

Mike had already cleared the Forester's windshield and put the packages in the car. "So you're giving Fiona her Christmas cactus this year, are you?"

"Hasn't she earned it?" she asked him as she settled the plant in the back and closed the hatch. "Hasn't she made some of the hardest choices anyone ever has to make, then gone ahead and lived up to them? It makes me proud to be her mother, Mike, and I'm so pleased one of my family's traditions gives me a way to show her how I feel about what she's done."

"Yeah," Mike admitted. "I can see that."

It was time for her to go. She raised one gloved hand and patted his cheek. "I love you, Mike. Merry Christmas."

"I love you, too, Avery. I'll be right here when you get back."

"It's so good to have you home again," she whispered and got into the car.

※

Mike stood in the snowy driveway and watched as Avery drove out of sight. He had so damned much to be thankful for. He was home; Avery was part of his life again. And they were going to make the rest of this work out—*somehow.* The knot of gratitude that lay at the base of his throat felt as big as a cannonball.

Christmas this year was turning out so much better than he'd expected.

Mike headed back into the house, pausing to stomp the snow off his boots and hang his coat on one of the pegs in the back hall. He poured more coffee and ambled slowly through those familiar rooms, reacquainting himself with every nook and closet and squeaky stair. He stood in the center of the living room and let the sense of belonging roll over him, this welcoming space with its cool plaster walls and wide oak floorboards; the way the light streamed through the windows in the morning; the particular feel and smell of home.

His home.

Dear God, how he'd missed it. How he'd missed being here with Avery. How glad he was that he'd been able to wake up here on Christmas Day. Of course, there was no tree, not a speck of decoration. With Sheepish the Lamb arriving in a hoard on the very doorstep of Christmas, Avery hadn't the time, or maybe even the inclination, to deck the halls. He wasn't sure when she'd found time to get the packages wrapped.

Since she hadn't had a chance to do it, maybe he should dig out a few decorations or put the electric candles in the windows, at least.

It didn't take him long to get a fire going, put on a Christmas CD, and make another pot of coffee. He started with the candles, then hung wreaths against the mirrors in the living room and dining room. Humming along with Bing Crosby, he fastened the big Styrofoam candy cane to their front door. He stomped outside into the chill wintery sunshine, strung a few lights along the roof of the porch, and draped garland from the railing.

He stepped back to admire his handiwork. Things looked good, festive, *back to normal.* He bet Avery would be surprised when she came home.

He went back into the house, drank more coffee, sat down to bask in the glow of the fire, and opened one of the battered cardboard cartons marked, "Mantel." Avery's treasured Victorian village was inside, all those intricately painted houses and miniature sleighs, all those tiny people skating and caroling and bustling home with packages under their arms. Avery had been collecting the figurines for a decade, and she was still scouring eBay for the few elusive pieces she needed to complete the set.

Mike set his coffee cup aside and ripped back the packing tape of another carton. He flipped open the top of the box—and felt his heartbeat lumber.

There, carefully folded beneath a hazy film of bubble wrap, lay Fiona's Christmas stocking. Avery had made that stocking for Fee's first Christmas. Their daughter had been barely four months old, but Avery had insisted Fiona needed a stocking of her own. So she'd cut and stitched and embroidered for hours, sewing together shimmery bits of cloth and lace and ribbon. She'd stayed up late that first Christmas Eve to finish it, to make something so wondrous and ornate that Santa probably would have thought he was filling the stocking of a princess and not just plain old Fiona Montgomery.

Even though he knew it was a mistake, Mike pushed back the plastic and took the stocking up in his two hands. The fabric was soft beneath his fingertips and warm from being in the box facing the fireplace. This stocking was embroidered with Avery's delicate stitches—and hundreds of memories of his daughter.

How her eyes would glow as she took down her stocking

on Christmas morning. How she'd dump everything out, exclaiming over a harmonica or a box of crayons, over pencils with her name printed on them, over glue sticks or paint. As she got older it had been bottles of perfume and nail polish that set her gasping with delight. She'd always come and hug him afterward, as if she knew long before he and Avery actually told her, that it wasn't Santa who'd brought those special gifts.

The memories of those Christmases with their daughter were as clear as if he'd preserved them under glass—though a couple of years had been pretty disastrous. Once Fee had the flu and threw up all over the Cabbage Patch Kid Avery had driven all the way to Kansas City to get for her. When she was ten, it snowed so hard they couldn't get out of the house, much less out of the driveway to get to Grandma Parrish's. So they'd stayed home, played with Fee's new games and puzzles, and ate meatloaf for Christmas dinner.

Odd as it seemed, he cherished those Christmas memories every bit as much as the years when their holidays had been like something conjured up by Elite Cards. He realized now that he'd been wrong to expect his holidays to be perfect, wrong to expect Avery and Fee to mend the disappointments of his childhood. He saw now that even if the holidays weren't all he'd hoped, it wasn't because he'd failed as a husband and father.

What was harder for him to accept was that he didn't need to create a perfect family in order to make up for the past, or to prove he was a better man than his father had been.

Sitting here with Fiona's Christmas stocking in his hands, he felt the truth of that settle over him. He accepted the notion that it was all right for his family to be less than

perfect, for his marriage to be less than perfect. For Fee—
and him—to be less than perfect.

Admitting that freed him somehow, loosened the knot
of tension snarled beneath his ribs, dissipated the pressure
that had driven him all his life.

He stared down at Fiona's stocking knowing that he had
to talk to her, that he had to tell her that no matter what
she'd done, no matter what he'd claimed that day at the observatory, he'd forgiven her. He had to look into his daughter's face and explain how much he wanted to make things
right between them.

He knew he'd be courting rejection by barging into
Miriam's house on Christmas Day, by admitting in front of
both his mother-in-law and his wife that he still loved his
daughter, that he wanted her—wanted himself—to be part
of the family again. Doing that would take a kind of bravery
Mike wasn't sure he had, so he worked the stocking between
his hands trying to draw strength from the love Avery had
put into it. Sitting there in the firelight, he fancied he could
feel Avery reaching out to both Fee and him, welcoming
them home.

With a single movement, he pushed to his feet. Jamming
the stocking into the pocket of his jeans, he closed the fireplace's glass doors and grabbed up his jacket.

He had to get to Miriam's now, before he lost his conviction.

Or his courage.

✳

Her mother's house smelled like Christmas.

The moment Avery stomped the snow off her boots and
stepped into the hall, she was enveloped in the spirit of the

season. She breathed the sharp, clear tang of balsam and bayberry candles, of freshly baked pies and roasting turkey. Miriam's house looked like Christmas, too, from the pine garland twined around the newel post and balusters, to the glittering ornaments that adorned the hall's brass chandelier, to the tree aglow with lights in the parlor.

Miriam bussed Avery's cheek in an uncharacteristically warm greeting, then ferried the bags of gifts Avery brought into the living room.

Avery set the potted Christmas cactus on the narrow console table in the hall and skimmed out of her coat. By the time she'd hung it up in the closet, Miriam had returned.

"Are you presenting Fiona with her Christmas cactus this year?" her mother asked, eyeing the Christmas cactus Avery had brought into the house.

When she didn't detect the approval she'd hoped to hear in Miriam's tone, Avery turned on her mother. "I think Fee's earned it, don't you?"

"She has had quite a time of it, our Fiona."

It irritated Avery that her mother would second-guess her on this. She ought to be able to present her daughter with her cutting from Letty's Christmas cactus anytime she liked.

"Fee saw that the choices she'd made were wrong for her—and wrong for Samantha," Avery insisted. "She's sacrificed to make a new life for herself and that little girl. I think she's showed remarkable maturity for someone who's barely twenty-one, and I'm proud of my daughter for doing it."

With that declaration, Avery snatched up the cactus and strode down the hall toward the bank of windows and

French doors that overlooked her mother's snowy backyard.

Miriam bustled after her. "I didn't mean to imply that
Fee doesn't deserve a cactus—"

"Good!" Avery bent and set Fiona's cactus on one of the
wrought iron tables her mother, or maybe Fee herself, had
brought in from the patio. "Good, because the decision
about giving Fee her Christmas cactus isn't in the least bit
up to you."

Satisfied that she'd put her mother in her place for a second time today, Avery stepped back to admire the draping
green branches and fiery fuchsia blossoms on the plant she
was giving Fee.

"While you're admiring," Miriam gestured with one
still-graceful hand, "you might want to take a look at the
cactus with the bow on the pot."

"It's beautiful," Avery admitted begrudgingly. She'd always wished she had her mother's way with flowers. "Are
you giving it to someone special?"

Miriam stepped closer. "I'm giving it to you."

Avery turned and stared at her mother. "To me?" Avery
asked. "You gave me a cutting from Great-Grandma
Letty's Christmas cactus when Fee was born. Don't you
remember?"

The idea that Miriam might not recall something so in-
grained in family lore made Avery go cold all over. Fee had
said that Gran was slowing down, but Avery had never
imagined that her mother—

"Of course I remember," Miriam snapped with more
than a little asperity. "But I've done a lot of thinking about
what you said at Thanksgiving."

"What I said?" Avery had said a lot of things that day at the church.

"What you said just before you decorated my favorite shoes with sweet potato casserole," her mother reminded her.

Avery felt the color creep into her cheeks, but she refused to take anything back.

"To be honest, Avery," her mother said, fumbling with the strand of pearls at her throat, "a lot of what you said was true, and I'm more than a little ashamed of myself."

Since it wasn't in Miriam Parrish's DNA to admit that she was wrong—much less apologize—Avery just stood and gaped at her.

"I won't try to excuse the things I've done," she went on primly. "I put your father first in my life because that's what I wanted to do. If you felt you got short shrift when it came to my time and attention, Avery, then I truly am sorry."

Avery's first impulse was to pat her mother's arm and say it was all right, say that she was a woman now and had outgrown the pain of being second best. But no one ever outgrew that by themselves. You needed someone who loved you enough to put you first.

Like she had Mike; like Mike had her.

Before Avery could open her mouth, her mother continued. "And while I'm saying things I don't *ever* intend to say again, I have a thing or two I want to say about Mike."

"'Mike'?" Avery bristled.

"I've always thought you could have found a more *appropriate* man to marry, and I have probably already said a good deal more about that subject than I should have."

"Yes, you have!"

Her mother waved her to silence. "What I want to say

before you start to berate me again is that I believe Mike Montgomery is a good man. I think he's been a very good husband to you, Avery. And while Fee was growing up, he was an exemplary father. All anyone ever had to do to tell how much he adored you and Fiona was to watch him watching the two of you.

"Besides," Miriam amended with a sniff, "your father liked him."

Avery decided to overlook her mother's sniff—this time.

"So," Miriam said and stepped past Avery to pick up the beautiful beribboned cactus. "I want you to have this cutting from your great-grandmother Letty's Christmas cactus. I'm a little ashamed of myself that the one I gave you when Fiona was born was more or less an afterthought. But no daughter has deserved to receive the full bloom of her mother's love and approval more than you, Avery. Nor have any of the McIntire women waited longer than you to be properly acknowledged."

"Oh, Mom!" Avery took the cactus into her hands and blinked back tears. "Thank you. It's beautiful."

She balanced the cactus against her and slipped her arm around her mother. Miriam wrapped her arm around Avery's waist and they stood together remembering the connections that bound them to the women who'd come before, to Ada and Letty. Thinking about the connections yet to come, to all those born and unborn daughters.

Avery hugged her mother closer, aware again of how slender she seemed, how suddenly fragile. And for all that Miriam Parrish was a termagant, how incredibly precious.

"I love you, Mom," Avery said impulsively.

"I love you, too, Avery," Miriam whispered back.

"I know you don't much like admitting that you were wrong—"

"Your father always claimed that was my biggest failing."

Avery bit her lip to hide her smile. "—but it means a lot to me for you to apologize. If Mike were here, he'd say that too."

Miriam leaned closer. "I'm glad you and Mike have gotten things settled."

"If we had everything settled," Avery conceded on a sigh, "Mike would be with me today. But I know now that we can work together to get things figured out."

"I'm glad for you, Avery. Really, I am."

Then, because sentiment always came hard for her, Miriam wriggled out of Avery's embrace. "Now, then," she said with a sniff, "I need to go baste the turkey." Just then the doorbell pealed and Miriam redirected her footsteps toward the front of the house. Setting her new Christmas cactus aside, Avery hurried after her mother.

Fee and Samantha had arrived. The baby was pink and jabbering, and clearly recovered from the croup. Fee looked gray and exhausted; a condition Avery remembered suffering from when Fiona was having bouts of croup herself.

While Miriam took Samantha off into the living room to extricate the baby from her snowsuit, Avery wrapped her arms around her daughter. Fee leaned in close as if her very bones had turned to Jell-O.

"Oh, Mom," she moaned.

Avery didn't have to ask what she meant. She just enveloped Fee and held on tight. "You did well last night, Fiona," she whispered. "You did everything a more seasoned mother would have done."

"Did I, Mom?" Fee's voice was quivery and small. "I can't

remember ever being so scared in my life. When Samantha started turning blue, I thought—" A shudder ran through her.

"I know what you thought," Avery murmured, holding her own baby closer.

"I felt so helpless." Fee burrowed against Avery's shoulder and started to cry. "Even after we got to the hospital, even after they started giving Samantha her medicine I wasn't sure—"

"Oh, honey, I know exactly what you were feeling," Avery offered, remembering. "Nothing's scarier than when your baby is sick or when she's hurt or when something puts her in jeopardy."

"I never want to go through that again," Fee confessed, earnest and wet-eyed.

Avery stroked her daughter's shaggy hair. "I'm sorry to tell you this, Fiona, but you're going to go through it again. You'll go through things that are even worse than this."

"I don't want to imagine anything worse," Fee whispered. "How do you keep going if something so scary happens?"

It was a question mothers and fathers had been asking themselves for aeons.

"Well, you do the best you know how. You comfort your child and put her welfare ahead of your own." Avery hugged her daughter harder, liking the warm, sweet weight of having Fiona pressed close. "Then you hope and you pray that everything will be all right."

Though there hadn't been a hint of rebuke in her answer, Fiona seemed to read a good deal more into what she'd said than Avery intended.

"Dad told me that when I took off with the band, it was—was really hard for you."

Avery nodded against Fiona's hair. Now that she was holding her daughter in her arms, those perilous days seemed far away. She didn't want to burden Fee with how devastated she'd been. She didn't want to admit how much harder that time had been because she hadn't had Mike to lean on.

"Well, I lost sleep and I worried and I prayed a lot," she finally admitted.

"Oh, Mom!" Fee murmured miserably and threw her arms around her mother. "I'm so, so sorry."

Avery hugged her even tighter. A child could never have understood what that time had been like for her, but Fee was a mother now—and she was beginning to see.

"Well, it's turned out all right, hasn't it?" Avery murmured against her daughter's ear. "You've come back and you've brought me—brought all of us—the wonderful gift of Samantha."

Fee stepped back, wiping tears from her cheeks with her fingers. "I'm so glad that's the way you think of her."

"She's yours, Fiona," Avery whispered. "So of course we love her."

Just then Miriam came back out into the hall with her great-granddaughter bundled in her arms. "Samantha thinks it's time to start opening presents."

The baby laughed and waved her arms, as if she were in perfect accord with her great-grandmother.

It wasn't long before the living room was awash in unraveling bows and crumpled wrapping paper, in topless boxes and tumbled toys. Fee crawled around snapping pictures with her new digital camera: one of Samantha crinkling tissue paper in her hands and laughing, another of Miriam posing with a ribbon in her hair and a silly smile.

While three generations of Parrish and Montgomery women were busy, Avery, who had one more gift to give, crept out into the sunroom to collect it. On her way back, she paused in the doorway of the living room. The gathering inside warmed her heart. Here were the people she loved, the people with whom she wanted to share the joy of Christmas—all except one.

Next Christmas, she promised herself. *Next Christmas Mike will be here with us.*

She swallowed hard, then crossed to where Fiona was sitting cross-legged on the floor beside Samantha. Avery sat down on her heels beside her daughter and carefully set the Christmas cactus just out of the baby's reach.

"For four generations," she began softly, focusing on her daughter, "the women in our family have passed down cuttings from your great-great-grandmother Letty's Christmas cactus. They've been passed down from mother to daughter to show love and acceptance and approval."

Avery glanced up to where Miriam had picked up Samantha, to where her mother sat with tears in her eyes, hugging Fee's beautiful baby in her arms.

"The cactuses are given," Avery went on, "at a time when the daughters have stepped up to accept new responsibilities or times when they have proved themselves. And, Fee, the strength and the courage you've shown in this past year has made me"—she hesitated and glanced at Miriam again—"has made your grandmother and me very, very proud of you."

Avery blinked back tears of her own before she continued. "So from Gill to Letty, from Letty to Ada, from Ada to

Miriam, from Miriam to me—and finally from me to you,"
Avery paused for an instant to look into her own daughter's
pale, sharply angled face. "I present you with a cutting from
your great-great-grandmother Letty's Christmas cactus.
May it bloom in beauty all the Christmases of your long,
long life, and may you follow our tradition and pass a piece
of this cactus along to your wonderful Samantha when she
achieves the same maturity and grace that you have, Fiona."

Avery reached across and put the potted cactus in Fee's
hands. "I love you, Fee, and I'm so proud of the woman
you've become."

As Fee accepted her final Christmas gift, the branches on
the cactus seemed particularly graceful, the blossoms, each
glorious fuchsia tier, more lush and exotic.

"I don't know how to thank you, Mom, for giving me
this Christmas cactus," Fee began with a croak in her voice.
"It means the world to me that after the mistakes I've made,
that you've taken me back into the family. I intend to do my
very best to live up to what you and Gran and Ada and Letty
expect of me, and to raise my own little girl to be a woman
all of us can be proud of."

Fee started to cry. Avery started to cry. Miriam started to
cry, and not to be left out, Samantha squalled in a very loud
voice. Which set all of them to laughing.

They were just blowing their noses and wiping the last of
the tears away when the doorbell chimed.

"I wonder, whoever could that be?" Miriam said as she
handed Samantha off to Fiona and scuffled through the de-
bris to go answer the door. A moment later a draft of cold
air eddied through the room making branches of the balsam bob and the candles flicker.

"My goodness!" Avery heard her mother exclaim. "How good of you to come. Merry Christmas!"

"Merry Christmas to you, Miriam."

At the sound of Mike's voice, Avery jumped to her feet and scrambled for the foyer. As she did, she caught the expression of uncertainty in her daughter's face and paused to give Fee's shoulder a reassuring squeeze.

As she stepped out into the entry hall, Avery saw Mike standing over Miriam and her heart skipped a beat.

Knowing how much courage it had taken to show up at her mother's unannounced, Avery took his hand and drew him all the way into the house. "I'm so glad you came," she said and bussed his cheek.

"I couldn't seem to stay away," he answered gravely.

At those words a wild flutter of hope soared through her.

Once Miriam had closed the door behind him, Avery helped Mike out of his jacket and slung it over the newel post. Then she led him into the living room, led him right to where Fee was sitting on the floor holding Samantha. She knelt beside her daughter and granddaughter, then pulled Mike down onto his knees beside her.

From the doorway, Miriam watched them, boggle-eyed.

"Merry Christmas, Dad," Fiona ventured uncertainly.

"Merry Christmas, Fiona," Mike answered solemnly, his gaze riveted on his daughter.

Fee had to swallow hard before she continued. "Since I don't think you've had a chance to see her up close, I'd like you to meet my daughter Samantha."

"Samantha," he said as if the word were new to him and astonishingly precious. He held out one big hand to his granddaughter. "Hello, Samantha."

Samantha looked first at his hand, then up at him. Her

eyes were round and bright, as if she were taking his measure. Then she grabbed two of his fingers and jammed them in her mouth.

Avery saw Mike's eyes sheen with tears.

"Oh, Fee, she's beautiful," he whispered, his voice tinged with awe. "She looks a lot like you did when you were little."

"I think she looks a little bit like all of us," Fee answered quietly. "She has Gran's long fingers and Mom's green eyes. And I think she has your dimple in her cheek."

The dimple that was plainly visible as Samantha sucked Mike's fingers.

"It's—it's good to meet my granddaughter after all this time," he said a little gruffly, though he never took his eyes from the baby. "I'm glad the two of you are back in Larkin."

"Are you, Dad?" she asked him. "Are you really glad I'm back?"

Mike shifted his gaze from the baby to her. "The truth is, Fiona, I've missed you."

"I've missed you, too," Fee admitted and her eyes welled up. "I'm—I'm sorry for pulling away from you that day in the park, and I didn't mean the things I called you that day at the observatory."

"No, Fee," he apologized gravely. "You were right. I really was being an asshole. I'm sorry I told you I couldn't forgive you—because that isn't true. At least, it's not true anymore."

Avery fought the sob pressing hard at the back of her throat. This was what she wanted more than anything, what she'd prayed for for months and months.

"You mean, if I told you again how wrong I was to leave the way I did," Fee asked him, "and told you how sorry I am for all the trouble I've caused between you and Mom, that you'd forgive me?"

Mike nodded. "Yeah, I would."

"If I apologized to Mom for taking her pearls, do you think she'd forgive me, too?"

Avery answered without hesitation. "I've already forgiven you, Fiona. I understood why you took the pearls, and I didn't worry quite so much because I knew you'd sell them if things got desperate."

"I'm sorry anyway," Fee admitted, her voice shaking. "I'm sorry for everything I did to hurt you both."

Mike slipped an arm around his daughter's shoulders and drew her and Samantha closer. "You'll always be our little girl, Fiona. No matter what I thought or what I said, I never stopped loving you. *We* never stopped loving you."

Fiona's face crumpled. "Oh, Daddy!" she sobbed and threw her arms around her father's neck. "I love you, too."

Avery laid her hands on both their shoulders, weeping because she loved her husband and daughter so much, because her family was back together.

Even Miriam, standing in the doorway, was swiping her eyes with her pristine linen handkerchief.

"I'm so proud of you," Mike told Fee, "for winning the internship at Kitt Peak. You'll be learning from some of the country's best astronomers when you're working there."

"It's the kind of chance I've dreamed of all my life!" Fee said and hugged him harder. But Samantha wasn't happy being squashed between her mother and grandfather, and wailed her protest.

Laughing through her own tears, Avery leaned forward, took the baby from Fiona's lap, and gathered her up in her arms. Fiona squirmed out of Mike's embrace and mopped up her tears with the back of her hand.

As she did, Mike braced back against the couch and worked something out of the pocket of his jeans. "I thought that since it was Christmas you might be wanting this," he said and held the bit of glittery fabric and embroidery out to her.

"You brought me my Christmas stocking?" Fee asked in disbelief. "My stocking from when I was little?"

"I found it this morning"—he glanced up at Avery in a way that warmed her heart—"while I was putting up a few Christmas decorations for your mother."

Fee took the stocking in her two hands, gently unfolded it, ironing out the creases against the knee of her corduroys. The stocking's fabric crinkled a little as she did.

"I think there's something inside," she ventured, looking up at her dad.

"I guess maybe there is," Mike answered quietly.

Avery recognized the uncertainty in her husband's face, the way he curled his shoulders defensively as if he were waiting for Fiona's reaction. What could Mike possibly have put in Fiona's Christmas stocking that would make him so nervous?

From inside the stocking, Fee drew out a creased manila envelope. By craning her neck, Avery could see it looked like something official, some document that had been certified and signed for.

Fee looked up at her father when she saw the return address. "You got a letter from the Harvard-Smithsonian Astrophysical Observatory?"

"Yeah," Mike answered, shifting uncomfortably. "I guess I did."

Why hadn't Mike told her about this? What secret had he been keeping from her? Avery shifted a little closer so she could see.

Fee slid several even more official-looking papers from the envelope, began to read, then looked up from the papers in astonishment. "You found an asteroid no one had ever identified?"

Mike shrugged and bobbed his head.

"Wow, Dad!" Fiona squeaked and gave him a quick hard hug. "How cool is that!"

"Pretty cool," he acknowledged, flushing just a little.

But Avery could see how proud of himself Mike was, how important this discovery was to him. It had given him validation in the field he loved, a field where Mike never felt like he truly belonged.

Fee leaned back in his embrace. "So how did you find the asteroid?"

"Well—" Mike cleared his throat. "I was imaging the ecliptic in Pisces with the CCD camera and spotted it more or less by chance."

"Did you know right away what you found?" Fee grilled him.

"I thought I knew," Mike answered quietly. "But I watched it for a good long while before I reported it."

"Wow, I wish I'd been there to see it with you!" Fee enthused.

"I wish you'd been there, too, sweetheart." Mike reached out and tucked a strand of her shaggy hair behind her ear. "It has been pretty lonely in the observatory all these months. You'll have to start coming again, to get ready to go to Kitt Peak this summer."

"That'd be great, Dad."

"Now, why don't you read down to the next part," he suggested. "The part where it talks about the asteroid's designation?"

Avery could sense there was something else in the document Mike wanted Fiona to see. He chewed his mouth nervously as she turned her attention back to the papers.

"Is that where it is?" Fee asked, rattling off a series of co-ordinates.

"Look at the name, Fiona," he prompted her impatiently. "Look at the name."

She glanced down at the page again, then lifted her gaze to her father. There were fresh tears in her eyes. "You named your asteroid 'Fiona Montgomery'?"

Mike just nodded.

"But why?" Fee sat back on her heels and stared at him. "Why did you name your first discovery after *me*?"

Mike reached across and took Fee's hand, her slender fingers all but disappearing into his big hand—so much like they had when she was little.

"I'd never have seen an asteroid, Fiona, if it hadn't been for you. I'd never have turned a telescope to Alpha Centauri or the moons of Jupiter. I'd never have thought to look in Orion for the Great Nebula, though I probably wouldn't have known there was one, either. I'd never have seen half the things I've seen or gone half the places we went together to look at the stars.

"Because you loved the sky, Fiona, I learned to love it too. So why shouldn't I have named my first discovery after the person who started me on this grand adventure? How else could I thank you for all the nights we spent together studying the stars?" He squeezed his daughter's hand. "How else could I tell you, Fiona, that I still love you?"

Fee threw her arms around her father's neck. "Thank you, Daddy. I still love you, too."

Avery recognized the joy in Mike's face as he held his daughter in his arms. She saw in the way he bent his head to hers and in the way he tightened his arms around those bony shoulders, that he would never let anything in the world come between them again. She saw the way Fee hugged him back.

Avery reached out to both of them, laying her hands on Mike and Fiona as if she were able to bind the three of them together forever. Her prayers and wishes and determination had brought her broken family back together again—and just in time for Christmas dinner.

Acknowledgments

I want to acknowledge the women who inspired this story: my great-grandmother Elizabeth, my grandmother Ida, and my mother Betty, who passed down cuttings from our family's Christmas cactus to me. Thank you all for that and a lifetime of love, wonderful memories, and the idea for this story.

Readers please note: **None** of the vignettes I concocted in the process of writing *A Simple Gift* **in any way reflect** the lives or personalities of my nana, grandma, and mom.

Only the Christmas cactus remains the same.

I also want to thank Joyce Schiller, who has been fairygodmother to a number of my projects, including this one. Her wand-waving involved introducing me to the wonderful Folkmanis Puppets—which in turn led me to the Folkmanis Web Site and Elaine Kollias, who was kind enough to answer my initial questions about the toy business. Elaine was also good enough to pass me along to the remarkable Judy Folkmanis, who really did found her toy business on her dining room table.

I would also like to acknowledge Marjorie Versprille of

Imagine Toys in St. Louis for the insights she gave me into her part of the toy industry.

I could never have written the sections of this book that deal with astronomy without the information and inspiration I drew from Timothy Ferris's terrific book, *Seeing in The Dark: How Backyard Stargazers Are Probing Deep Space and Guarding the Earth from Interplanetary Peril*. I deeply appreciate Rich Heuermann of Washington University in St. Louis for speculating about what equipment Mike might have had in his observatory. I also want to thank Ron and Linda Madl for blue penciling those sections of the novel that deal with the stars. Any mistakes in astronomy as it is portrayed in this book are purely my own.

I am also grateful to Sally Hawkes and Elizabeth Danley of the Arkansas State Library for turning up all sorts of elusive facts on my behalf.

In addition, I'd like to thank David Safran, Katie Bautch, and Kevin Dreyer for their input on various phases of the music business. Rick Dreyer deserves a big hug for his insights about doing business in China. Madeline Hunter and Shirl Henke, who offered me a peek into academia, have also earned my deep appreciation. As did the people on the MORWA loop who shared their stroller stories.

Big thanks to the Tuesday, Wednesday, or Thursday Night Group for sharing the ups and downs of the writing life. Love to the Divas for being the sisters I never had. And a very special mention for Eileen Dryer, who is undoubtedly the world's best critique partner, for easing my step into the unknown.

To Micahlyn Whitt at Bantam and Meg Ruley at the Jane Rotrosen Agency, my warmest appreciation for your enthu siasm for this novel and for shepherding it into new and untried realms.

And as always, my love to Tom, for mailing my mail, buying my groceries, running my errands—and for sticking with me in spite of menopause and deadlines. God only knows which is worse.

About the Author

✳

KARYN WITMER saw her first poem published in the fourth grade and by fifteen had written an historical novel. College, marriage and a career intervened but, after a rewarding stint as an art teacher, she returned to writing and published eleven historical novels under the names Elizabeth Kary and Elizabeth Grayson. For these books, Karyn has received a Waldenbook Award, numerous Romantic Times Awards, and a Romance Writers of America RITA Award nomination. A SIMPLE GIFT is her first foray into contemporary fiction. She lives in the St. Louis area with her husband and cat.